Ann Xmas

The
Garden on
Sparrow
Street

BOOKS BY TILLY TENNANT

An Unforgettable Christmas series
A Very Vintage Christmas
A Cosy Candlelit Christmas

From Italy with Love series
Rome is Where the Heart Is
A Wedding in Italy

Honeybourne series
The Little Village Bakery
Christmas at the Little Village Bakery

Mishaps in Millrise series
Little Acts of Love
Just Like Rebecca
The Parent Trap
And Baby Makes Four

Once Upon a Winter series
The Accidental Guest
I'm Not in Love
Ways to Say Goodbye
One Starry Night

Hopelessly Devoted to Holden Finn
The Man Who Can't Be Moved
Mishaps and Mistletoe
The Summer of Secrets
The Summer Getaway
The Christmas Wish
The Mill on Magnolia Lane
Hattie's Home for Broken Hearts

TILLY TENNANT

The Garden on Sparrow Street

Bookouture

Published by Bookouture in 2019

An imprint of StoryFire Ltd.
Carmelite House
50 Victoria Embankment
London EC4Y 0DZ

www.bookouture.com

ISBN: 978-1-83888-146-7
eBook ISBN: 978-1-83888-145-0

This book is a work of fiction. Names, characters, businesses,
organizations, places and events other than those clearly in the
public domain, are either the product of the author's imagination
or are used fictitiously. Any resemblance to actual persons, living or
dead, events or locales is entirely coincidental.

For Nana Riley, thank you for all the wonderful memories.

Chapter One

It was early November. Snow had been forecast, though it had yet to materialise. Instead, the low clouds were buffeted by a bitter wind that sent loose tin cans hurtling along the pavements of the little town of Wrenwick and tore carrier bags from the grasps of shoppers. It was hardly a magical sight.

Nina's gaze was on the miserable weather beyond the windows as she folded a coat into a carrier bag and smiled at the old lady standing on the other side of the counter. It had buttons missing and a tear at the pocket, but the old lady didn't seem to mind, even when Nina pointed it out to her, just to be certain.

'It'll mend,' she said sagely. 'That's the trouble with young people today – they don't have the make-do-and-mend mentality that my generation has.'

At thirty-five, Nina hardly considered herself a young person, but she smiled and said nothing.

'The best bargains need a little work,' the lady continued. 'I mean, that coat will be lovely and warm when I've sewn new buttons on. I have a whole tin of buttons, you know.'

'Really?' Nina asked vaguely.

'Oh yes. When something is really worn out and I can't repair it any more I take all the buttons off and keep them. So when something needs buttons I have lots to choose from.'

'Wow,' Nina said. 'I wouldn't even think of that.'

'Exactly,' the lady replied with a triumphant nod.

Nina folded more items into the bag with the coat – a cotton blouse with a mad sixties floral pattern, a heavy skirt in green wool with patch pockets and a pair of fur-lined boots with heels worn more on the outside than in. 'You've done well today,' she said, handing the bag over.

'Well, there's so much on sale today. It's even cheaper than usual. I suppose it's because you're closing down?'

'Yes,' Nina said.

'What's coming in its place?'

'A restaurant chain wants to buy the building as far as I know.'

'So it won't be a charity shop any more?'

'I doubt it.'

'Oh… where will I shop now?'

'There are lots of others in Wrenwick.'

'Not like this one,' the lady said. 'This one's the best.'

'Well, it's a shame more people don't think that and then maybe we wouldn't be closing.'

'Where will you be going when the shop closes?' the lady asked, dropping the change Nina had just given her into a purse.

'I have no idea.' Nina forced a smile. She was as unhappy about the shop closing as her customer was, though she was trying to maintain a cheery welcome for everyone – even today when she felt like crying. 'I expect there'll be other volunteering opportunities in Wrenwick.'

'I expect so,' the lady agreed with another sage nod. 'Then again,' she continued, 'perhaps you'll be able to get a proper job, eh?'

Nina's smile faltered, but she pushed it back across her face again. She was used to people thinking that the only reason she worked in the

Sacred Heart Hospice Shop was that she couldn't get anything else, so why let the latest in a long line of thoughtless comments bother her?

'Good luck anyway!' the old lady added cheerfully. She waddled out of the shop, letting the door slam behind her with a violent slap of the old bell.

'*Proper job?*'

Robyn's voice came from the back room behind the till. Nina turned to find her with two mugs of tea. She offered one.

'Daft old trout,' she said as Nina took the cup from her. 'She's the one who comes in here week in, week out, buying her old tat. What does she think we do in here all day if it doesn't constitute a job? She wouldn't have been happy having to serve herself, would she?'

'I don't suppose she means anything by it,' Nina said. 'I suppose she's talking about paid work.'

'I'd like to know when the last time she did paid work was,' Robyn huffed. 'About 1945, I expect.'

'I must admit, I have thought about getting a paid job.' Nina took a sip of her tea. It was strong and sweet – just the way she liked it. She'd miss Robyn's tea when the shop closed. She'd miss a lot of things about her shifts with Robyn – they had so much in common and got on so well. Robyn, who understood like no one else what Nina was going through, had been a rock after Gray's death. In fact, she'd been more than a rock – she'd been a real part of the healing process. At forty-five, she was ten years older than Nina, but Nina often thought she looked almost the same age, if not younger. She certainly didn't look forty-five anyway. She had a young, carefree attitude too, and always knew how to inject a bit of devil-may-care humour into any situation. 'I probably ought to have made more of an effort when all the seasonal work was being advertised.'

'It's not too late to get Christmas work – there are a few weeks to go yet.'

'I would imagine most shops who want extra help for Christmas will have taken it on by now. It's my own fault for procrastinating, I suppose.'

'I wouldn't be too hard on yourself. It's more difficult than people realise to get back into the job market when you've been missing from it for a long time,' Robyn said, sipping her own tea. 'And it's not like it used to be – shops close down around here almost every week now. I've struggled to get a sniff of an interview too. Thank God I've got Eric's death-in-service pension to fall back on. Sometimes I curse him but at least he always made sure to take care of things like that.'

'I'll probably be OK too – I have enough money from Gray's will to last a good while, if I'm careful, and of course the mortgage was settled in full when he died. Every time I think about that I thank God we took that policy out when we first moved in. I suppose now I'm getting back on my feet emotionally it would be good to have a bit extra for a few little luxuries, though. It'd be nice to have a little job somewhere just for that.'

'I'm sure Gray wouldn't have wanted you going without,' Robyn said, nodding agreement. 'It's all very well getting first dibs on the donations coming through here but a girl wants something more than second-hand underpants sometimes.'

Nina laughed. 'I'm not saying we don't get some good stuff. Though I'm glad I haven't sunk to second-hand underpants just yet. More generally I was thinking about the odd holiday, a slap-up meal or a weekend away where I didn't have to worry about how much it was going to set me back.'

Robyn shot her a sideways look. 'You're saying my caravan in Abergele isn't your idea of a holiday?'

'It's lovely, but I was thinking of somewhere with guaranteed sun.'

Robyn looked unconvinced. The last time they'd been up to her caravan for a sneaky weekend away it had rained and the wind had howled and the roof had started to leak. That was the previous July when it was supposed to be warm and sunny, not the kind of temperature that an Inuit would complain about. They'd ended up huddled under a duvet on the sofa watching television together for most of the weekend. Still, Nina had enjoyed the time away, even if it had meant looking out of the window at the churning sea rather than dipping her toes in it.

'Ah. In that case,' Robyn said wryly, 'I'll take my offence back then. You certainly aren't going to get any of that today.'

'We didn't get any of that last time we were there either.'

'True. I don't know why I keep the bloody thing if I'm honest – more trouble than it's worth.'

'I suppose, in the end, my predicament is all my fault for not ever having any ambition before I met Gray. All I've ever done is shop work and I'm not fit for anything else now.'

Nina's gaze went to the windows. Someone had lost their hat in the wind and was chasing it down the street. But then her eyes ran over the interior of the Sacred Heart Hospice charity shop where she and Robyn were safe and warm. It had once been a swanky estate agent office, but the company had fallen on hard times and had long since gone. But the art deco windows and period detail remained, and although it was a faded grandeur now, half-obscured by racks of old dresses, shelves of vinyl records by artists that nobody remembered and boxes of toys, there was a sort of melancholy beauty to the building.

Perhaps that was why the restaurant chain due to take ownership had been so taken by it. Nina had no doubt it would look wonderful restored to its former glory, and be a real boon to the town, but she'd miss it. Sacred Heart had been her lifeline when she was nursing Gray in his final months. While he was still able to stay at home they'd sent her help that she wouldn't have been able to get otherwise, and later, when his motor neurone disease became too much for either of them to cope with, they'd provided the best comfort and round-the-clock care in their bright and welcoming hospice.

When Gray had finally lost the battle and Nina found herself alone, having long since given up work to nurse him, she hadn't known how to fill her days and the aching void of loss that Gray's death had brought. Sacred Heart had been there for her again, offering her support and something to occupy her mind in the form of her voluntary job at the shop. Without that, she was quite sure she would never have set foot outside the house again, choosing to wither away quietly curled up on the sofa. Without Sacred Heart's help and support, she'd have never met Robyn either, the kind of sweet, loyal friend she'd always longed for. Sacred Heart had been there for Robyn too after her husband had died, in just the same way it had been for Nina, and perhaps bringing Robyn into her life had been the single biggest blessing the organisation could have bestowed on her, even if it had been inadvertent.

But all that was about to change. The local authority had put up the shop rent and it just wasn't viable any more. Many suspected dodgy dealings instigated by interest from the restaurant chain in the first place, but the town council had always denied it. Nobody but the people involved would know for sure, and Nina certainly wasn't privy to that sort of information. Neither had she been invited to the board meeting that had been chaired and populated by people who'd never used the charity, who – unlike many of the staff – were paid a real salary, ran it like a business and had decided the fate of a band of people they'd never met without a single consultation. In their opinion, more efficient fundraising opportunities lay elsewhere, in more corporate settings, and there was no room or need for people like Nina and Robyn in the organisation. The only voluntary posts now were in the hospice itself, and the memories of Gray's final months in there were simply too raw and painful for Nina to cope with such powerful reminders of his suffering everywhere she looked every day.

'Still want to sign up for the Wrenwick 10K?' Robyn asked absently. 'The deadline for applications is this weekend.'

Nina raised her eyebrows. 'It wasn't me who said she wanted to sign up for that. I'll happily cheer you from the sidelines but that's my limit.'

'Awww, come on. I thought you said you'd do it.'

'I think you dreamt that.'

'I'm pretty sure I didn't.'

'Seriously? Have you seen me run? And when I say "run", I'm using the term very loosely here. I look like a wounded ostrich.'

Robyn laughed, but she had a look on her face that Nina knew only too well – she wasn't taking no for an answer.

'We can train after Christmas,' she said. 'The weather will be warming up then and it'll get us out. You won't be the only wounded ostrich; I'm a shit runner too. Anyway, Tracy says loads of people walk the course so we don't need to be the world's best runners.' Robyn nudged her. 'Come on… It's for a good cause.'

'What cause?' Nina asked. 'Sacred Heart?'

'For anything you like. We could run it for Sacred Heart but we could run it for any charity. It'll be a laugh.'

'It would be for the spectators when I come steaming towards them looking like I need a poo.'

'That's the spirit!' Robyn said, now deciding that she'd take Nina's lack of an outright refusal as her agreement. 'I'll put us both down then. We have to pay twenty quid to enter but we could easily cover that from the sponsorship.'

Nina shook her head. 'If I must do it then I'll pay my entrance fee. I can't ask someone else to fund my ultimate demise – think of the guilt they'd be saddled with for the rest of their lives.'

'Goody two-shoes,' Robyn said with a smirk. 'Honestly, you make me sick.'

Nina grinned. But then it faded into a sad smile. 'What am I going to do without you?'

'Who says you'll be without me? Just because we won't be working together doesn't mean we can't still see each other from time to time. I mean, we'll be training for the run for a start.'

'I know…' Nina put her cup down and leant on the counter, chin resting on her fists. 'But it won't be the same, will it? I mean, socialising sometimes will be lovely but you'll get busy doing other things, and eventually I expect I'll get busy too, and before we know it we've hardly got any time to see each other at all.'

'Then we'll just have to make the time no matter what else happens. You might be a lazy cow when it comes to keeping your friends but I'm not.'

Nina smiled up at her now and, despite her misgivings, her smile was brighter.

'Here…' Robyn moved towards her with a look of great concentration. 'You've got a big blob of fluff in your hair…' She teased it from Nina's dark curls.

'I bet you'd find all sorts in there if you looked hard enough,' Nina said, taking the fluff from Robyn's stubby fingers. 'Pens, crisps… the occasional sofa…'

'It *is* thick,' Robyn said.

'Like my head.' Nina raised her eyebrows and Robyn laughed.

'Nothing's that thick.'

'Oi!' Nina squeaked. 'Cheeky!'

The bell on the shop door tinkled and a middle-aged man lugged a large plastic bag in.

'Is that a donation?' Robyn called over. 'Only we're not taking any, sorry.'

'What?' The man frowned, looking sorely put out. 'But I've dragged this lot all the way from the car park on Price Street! Are you sure you can't take it?'

'Cancer Research will,' Robyn said patiently, though Nina knew that her friend was dying to let loose some razor-sharp sarcasm. 'It's not that much further along.'

The man wiped a sleeve across his sweaty forehead. 'So you don't want it?'

'It's not that we don't want it or that we wouldn't ordinarily take it,' Nina said. 'It's just that we can't.'

'Why not? You're a charity shop, aren't you?'

Robyn was unable to hold in the sigh of exasperation this time. 'A soon-to-be-closed charity shop if you read the signs in the window. We can't sell that stuff if we're closed.'

'Though we do appreciate you thinking of us,' Nina added. 'And I'm sure the Cancer Research shop would be very grateful for it.'

'That's bloody miles away!' the man muttered. He looked as if he might launch another complaint, but then seemed to think better of it. He dragged his bag out instead, the door slamming behind him.

'Miles away…' Robyn said with a huff. 'It's two doors down!' She drained her cup of the last drops of tea. 'I'll bet that bag was full of shit anyway – he looked the type. Some people think we're just here to dispose of what the municipal tip won't take.'

'Well, Cancer Research will get the pleasure of rooting through it now,' Nina said, finishing her tea too and handing the cup to Robyn, who was edging towards the doorway to the staff kitchen. 'I suppose we'd better get the rest of this stock boxed up for when the van comes to get it.'

Robyn nodded. 'I'll just wash these and I'll be with you.'

Nina watched her go. And then she turned her attention to a rack of children's clothes with a sigh. Packing up this shop felt like finally packing up her last solid connection to Gray and she didn't want to do it. But some choices in life were never yours to make and some things were taken from you before you were ready. Nina knew that by now, better than anyone. She could rage all she wanted but it wouldn't change a thing, and she knew that well enough too. She'd learned over the last couple of years that if she could turn all her rage and grief into a force for good, it hurt a lot less than if she let it grow into thorns around her heart. So while her last day at the Sacred Heart Hospice Shop had been heavy and hectic, at least heavy and hectic had kept her mind off the fact that it *was* the last day.

With that thought, she began to pull the clothes from the rails and fold them into neat piles.

A manager they'd never met before arrived during the last hour of trading with instructions for the removal of the stock they hadn't been able to sell, and had left with a vapid handshake and a half-hearted thanks for Nina and Robyn's hard work before taking the keys from Robyn and locking the door for the final time. Nina and Robyn had stood outside on the pavement and watched him drive off, then they'd headed to the nearest Wetherspoons for chips and a beer. The last supper, Robyn had called it, but really neither of them could quite believe that it was all over. Neither could they quite bring themselves to let go; chips and beer was just another way of prolonging the goodbye, stretching it just that bit further.

But, as the skies darkened beyond the windows of the pub and the lights went on in the sleepy northern town of Wrenwick, Nina's thoughtful gaze went to the windows. The yellow streetlights illuminated the municipal buildings of grey stone and reflected off wet roof slates; they shone onto the old Victorian swimming baths where the date of its opening stood proudly etched into the brickwork over the entrance, and they gave a yellow glow to the mix of Edwardian and art deco shops that made up the high street – some restored to their former glory, others crying out for a little tender loving care to make them beautiful again. Wrenwick was a town that had seen a rollercoaster of fortunes over the years, a fact reflected in its eclectic town centre, but one thing was always constant – the friendliness and community spirit of its residents.

And then their supper had been cut short by the arrival of Robyn's teenage son, Toby, looking for his bus fare home.

'God knows what he does with all the bus money I give him at the start of every week,' Robyn had said, ignoring a scowling Toby as she scrabbled in her purse to find very little spare change in there.

Robyn had ended up leaving early to drive Toby home instead, so that even their extended goodbye had been taken away from Nina in the end.

Nina had headed back to her own little terraced house on Sparrow Street. The houses here had once been pokey worker's cottages, back in the days when there had been a booming textile industry in these parts, belonging to a factory that looked down from a hill where the landscape almost all belonged to the owner. The old factory was now a museum, and the houses of Sparrow Street were all double-glazed with loft conversions, extensions and conservatories, satellite dishes and hanging baskets adorning the fronts, the grime of Wrenwick's industrial past sandblasted from their red-brick façades.

Beyond the town boundaries there were moors of green and black that Nina could see from her bedroom window. On a clear day she'd watch kestrels hover high above them and on stormy days she'd see grey clouds settle on the highest points. Once she'd looked at them with Gray, loving the perfect spot they'd managed to find for their first house. After his death, though the memories pained her, she hadn't wanted to give up this perfect spot and looking up at the moors was a bittersweet pleasure.

They'd decorated the house together and every panelled door, every patterned wall, every rug reminded Nina of the choices they had made, back when he'd been well enough. Every room was decked in warm, muted tones that, together with the narrow windows and low ceilings gave the place a cosy, cocooning sort of feel, a place where you could shut the world out at the end of a busy day and feel as if you were burrowing into a warm nest like a little mouse. The master bedroom still had the patchwork quilt on the bed that they'd bought together, the colourful rag rug Nina's aunt and uncle had got them for a moving-in present and the tall anglepoise lamp overlooking the bedside table that Gray had chosen for himself to read by at night before he went to sleep.

At home and safely inside, Nina locked the front door. Then she put the radio on and ran a hot bath, where she stayed until the water had gone cold. It gave her time to think about the things that she hadn't wanted to think about before, the things that now she had no choice but to consider. The biggest of these things was: what the hell was she supposed to do with her life now?

In the bedroom she got into fluffy pyjamas. Gray smiled down at her from the wedding photo hanging on the wall. By the time of their wedding, he'd already been consigned to his wheelchair. People had never said it, but Nina knew that plenty thought she was mad to be marrying him, given his prognosis. Sometimes the idea of their disapproval made her sad and sometimes it made her angry, but mostly she thought that if that was their attitude, then they must never have felt real love and she was sorry for them. She loved Gray so much that she'd have married him no matter what. She wouldn't have changed a thing about their time together, only that if the universe had been a bit kinder and miracles possible, Nina could have had him for just a little longer.

As it often did, her mind went back to the first time she'd laid eyes on him. She'd left her umbrella on the bus home from her job at a now closed shoe shop and he'd leapt off miles before his own stop to get it back to her. He was handsome, good-humoured, totally at ease with himself, and the attraction had been instant for both of them. The following night they'd met up in a local pub for their first date. He was five years older than her very young nineteen, but his gregarious and fun-loving nature more than made up for her shyness and inexperience. Whenever she was with him it was like she'd been only half-alive before he'd come into her life, like she was able, finally, to live life to the full through him. He was so confident, so kind and patient, so sure of himself, so capable of opening the world up to her, that it hadn't taken her long to fall in love, heart and soul, with him and everything he believed in.

Within a year they were living together in a little flat above a florist, and barely a day went by when he didn't come up the stairs without a

bunch of something pretty he'd picked up from the shop on his way
through. He'd cook her favourite meals on days when she had to work
late and have them waiting on the table for her with wine and a smile
and she'd always forget how tired she was. Sundays would see them
stay late in bed, sometimes making love, sometimes just talking, until
the morning was old and he'd get up to make her coffee.

She worked hard in the shop and he spent his weeks as an insur-
ance underwriter and, while their existence was dull and uneventful
in most people's eyes, they were happy. They saved and made plans
for the places they would visit, the house they would one day buy,
the wedding they'd have and the children that would follow, but there
had never seemed to be any rush for any of those things because in the
meantime they had each other. Their love was quiet and constant, and
sometimes it was so right and natural, so unburdened by the problems
that other couples seemed to have that it felt like a fairy tale, too good
to be true. Sometimes Nina was almost scared that she was having it
so good that the universe would come and demand its payment for
too much happiness.

And then, not long after they'd taken the leap and bought their own
little house on Sparrow Street, it happened. It started with a strange
twitch in his hands, then the unexplained and sudden episodes of weak-
ness, the dropping things for no reason, and finally, Nina had persuaded
him to go to the doctors. There were tests, a few weeks of anxiety, of
hope, of sometimes optimism but more often crushing pessimism, and
then his disease was diagnosed and reality came crashing in. Nina's
worst fears were realised – she'd had it too good and the universe had
come to collect on her debt after all.

It was Nina who'd proposed to Gray in the end. At first he'd refused
her, not wanting her to burden herself with that kind of tie to a man

who was deteriorating fast, but then she'd reasoned that she was staying with him until the end regardless, so what difference did it make? It was unlikely they'd see any of the places they'd dreamt of or have the children they'd wanted, but the wedding was one thing they could make happen, and eventually he'd agreed. And, despite everything, it had been the most wonderful day of her life.

Leaving the Sacred Heart shop, or rather, Sacred Heart leaving her, brought back memories of Gray more forcefully and painfully than she'd had for a while. If she lay on the bed in the stillness of her room now and closed her eyes, she knew she'd hear his breaths next to her, feel the warmth of his body, sense the touch of a hand resting on her belly as he slept beside her. If she tried hard enough, she could almost believe he was still alive.

But then her eyes would open and the pretence would fade and life would return – her life without Gray – lonely and methodical. Two years after his death there was a contentment of sorts, an acceptance of what was and couldn't be changed, but there was no magic. Not that she'd sought any; she'd simply been doing her best to get by, to move on and build something she could work with, to fill the void Gray had left with something… anything. In time, the mourning had begun to feel like a memory, a ritual to be observed; her life had simply seemed duller and colder without Gray in it. She still missed him every day but she didn't cry every day any more; she only tried her best to find colour where she could, and working at the Sacred Heart shop had done that. Robyn had done that, and all her wonderful neighbours on Sparrow Street who'd all tried their best to take care of her had done that.

Nina went to the dresser drawer and took out a DVD in a blank case. She opened it up and read the scrawled label, then took it downstairs to put it in the player.

Chapter Two

The screen showed Nina in a lace-sleeved wedding gown. Her dark, unruly curls were piled onto her head, a delicate tiara nestled in amongst them. Her hair had always been and continued to be a constant source of frustration – often difficult to control and impossible to style – but she'd been so happy that day that it had looked better than it ever had or would do again. Her dress had a deep V that teased at the creamy skin of her cleavage, and beneath the generous folds of her skirt her feet were clad in her battered old Doc Marten boots. Nina's aunt had been horrified to learn that Nina had no intentions of wearing more traditional wedding footwear, but that had only made Nina more determined to stick stubbornly with her old faithfuls. One half of the happy couple was already in a wheelchair, Gray had joked in Nina's defence, so it seemed only prudent that she should wear shoes that guaranteed she wouldn't end up flat on her face with a broken ankle. Typical Gray. If Nina was happy, he was happy. If she'd wanted to get married in a refuse sack he'd have readily agreed. He cared for convention even less than she did, but either way he'd have gone with what she wanted.

The camera panned to him now. Nina was reminded of how well he'd looked that day. She'd always supposed that it had been the happiness of the occasion that had lent him strength. He'd certainly paid for it in the days and weeks afterwards, Nina having to nurse him at home in lieu of the honeymoon other couples had to look forward to.

In an attempt to keep costs down, Nina's uncle, rather than a professional, had been filming, and she smiled now as the camera wandered momentarily from the bridal couple onto the congregation, settling on Nina's aunt Faith. Nina recalled now with a fond smile how she'd noticed her uncle get distracted, and how she'd caught a little wave from him to his wife. Perhaps they'd both been reminded of their own wedding day. In the next second he'd seemingly remembered that this wasn't his wedding at all and he'd quickly shot back to follow the ceremony again. As the camera had whipped back, it caught a fleeting shot of Nina's dad, doing his best to look as if he wasn't crying, though everyone knew he was.

The DVD continued to play. Nina fluffed her lines, and Gray tripped over her middle name twice before he managed to say it. He looked so handsome as he blushed amidst the polite and affectionate laughter of their very closest family and friends that the Nina of now, watching from her sofa, almost let out a sigh of longing. She carried on watching as the vicar announced them husband and wife and they kissed, and even though she didn't cry all that much these days, tonight she knew she would.

If she were here now, Robyn would have asked Nina why she would put herself through such an ordeal when it was bound to upset her, and Nina wouldn't really be able to explain. But then, Robyn had handled the death of her husband Eric very differently. Eric's motor neurone disease had seen him fade far more slowly and painfully than Gray, and though Eric and Robyn had been together a lot longer, Robyn freely admitted that by the time Eric's disease had been diagnosed they hadn't been in love for years. They were simply one of those couples who worked well together as a team, who shared the care of their son and ran the house together and secretly thought that one day perhaps they'd have the courage to set out and see what the world had to offer instead of the life they'd settled into.

But Robyn had nursed Eric to the end anyway, out of a sense of duty and affection for the love they'd once had. Once he'd had his diagnosis there was no way she'd have left him, and really, she'd admitted frankly to Nina, what would have been the point when the inevitable conclusion would part them eventually anyway?

When the end came, though it had been painful for their young son, Toby, as it was in many ways for Robyn too, it had also been a relief, a guilt-ridden lifting of a burden. Robyn had talked about it to Nina, of course, and they'd shared their experiences and thoughts, but it wasn't the same at all. Robyn simply wanted to put that part of her life behind her and concentrate her energies on raising Toby as a single mother.

On the TV screen, Nina bent to kiss Gray. He mouthed *I love you*. The Nina of now, sitting curled on her sofa with tears tracking her cheeks, watched herself say it back. Till death do us part, they'd promised, and there had been no choice but to be true to their word because they'd both known it was coming anyway.

Nina jumped now, dragged from the past by a loud rap at her front door. She glanced up at the clock with a frown. For a moment, slightly irked by the lateness of the hour and the imposition on her private time, she considered ignoring it. But then the idea that one of her older neighbours might need help pulled her from the nest of cushions on the sofa and she made her way to the door.

After a brief glance through the spy hole Nina relaxed. It was Ada and Martha from number seventeen. Twin sisters in their eighties, they went everywhere together. There was some speculation amongst the other residents of Sparrow Street that they might just go to the toilet together too, but Nina left that notion to the less charitable members of their community to ruminate on. They were standing outside in matching coats. Nina just knew that beneath those coats they'd have the same long cotton nightdresses and identical pairs of boots poking out from beneath. They even had the same pink curlers rolled into the front of their hair. In fact, they were so identical that Nina knew which was which only because Ada wore glasses and Martha didn't, though Nina was often vaguely surprised that Martha didn't just buy a pair anyway so she could continue to confuse the street.

Pulling her dressing gown tighter, Nina opened the door.

'Ada… Martha… what brings you out at this time of night?'

'We're so sorry,' Ada began.

'But the bulb in our kitchen has gone out,' Martha finished.

'We went to get Nasser,' Ada said.

'But he wasn't in,' Martha said.

'And Yasmin said she couldn't do it because of her vertigo.'

'Then we tried Ron.'

'But he was out too.'

'We would have called on Kelly.'

'But you know she doesn't like to be disturbed after nine.'

'Not that you'd get an answer once she's had her sleeping tablets.'

'And she does like a drink…'

'You want to see how many bottles go out with the recycling,' Martha put in darkly.

'I haven't and I have no idea how much she drinks…' Nina said, cutting her off. She had, but she wasn't in the mood to gossip about it now.

'So we wondered…' Ada said.

Nina held up a hand to stem the flow. 'I'll come. Do you have a replacement bulb?'

'Oh,' Ada said.

Martha frowned. 'We didn't think of that.'

Ada gave an apologetic look. 'How silly of us.'

'It's just a regular bulb?' Nina asked. 'Nothing fancy?'

'Well, it switches on and off like all the other bulbs,' Ada said.

'Yes, it switches on and off just the same,' Martha confirmed.

The information that it switched on and off just the same as all their other bulbs wasn't quite as useful as Ada and Martha seemed to imagine, but Nina nodded. 'I might have a spare,' she said. 'Come in for a minute while I have a look.'

Ada and Martha stepped in and huddled together in the hallway like newborn kittens, thanking Nina with every other word as she rummaged in her understairs cupboard. It took a few minutes, but eventually she found a bulb that she thought might do the trick.

Without bothering to get dressed, she followed Ada and Martha out of the house, putting her front door on the latch to leave it open.

Ada and Martha's hall smelt of fried fish and it didn't take much guessing to figure out what they'd eaten for supper that evening. The walls were lined with posters of puppies posing in various receptacles – puppies in Wellington boots, puppies in plant pots, in buckets and baskets. For two ladies apparently so enamoured with dogs, Nina had often thought it strange that they'd never actually owned one – at least not in all the ten years she'd lived on Sparrow Street.

'Kitchen, you said?' Nina asked.

'Yes,' Ada said.

'The kitchen,' Martha confirmed.

Nina nodded. 'Do you have some stepladders?'

'Oh no,' Ada said.

'Oh no,' Martha repeated. 'They broke and we never bought any new ones.'

'Right,' Nina said doubtfully.

'We have a chair,' Ada said.

'It's quite big,' Martha added.

'I'll have to make it manage,' Nina said.

In the kitchen, Martha dragged a chair out from beneath the table for Nina to stand on. Luckily, she was reasonably tall and could reach. Martha shone a torch at the fitting and, in another minute, Nina had managed to screw the bulb in and the kitchen was flooded with light again.

Ada clapped her hands together in delight. 'Oh, thank you!'

'Yes, thank you!' Martha said.

'It's really very kind of you,' Ada said.

'Very kind,' Martha said.

'It's nothing.' Nina smiled. 'It's lucky I hadn't already gone to bed.'

'Will you stay for a cup of tea?' Ada asked.

'And cake?' Martha added.

'It's a bit late really,' Nina said. It was a bit late in the day for tea and cake and, besides, she'd been a victim of their baking before and was wiser than to accept an offer of cake these days. It was hard to shake the memory of a fruit cake so dense it had its own gravitational pull. 'But thank you,' she added. 'Maybe another time?'

'Oh, well I expect you'll have some cake after the residents' meeting,' Ada said.

'You are going, aren't you?' Martha asked.

'What residents' meeting?' Nina looked from one to the other. Usually she knew about the monthly residents' meeting in plenty of time but as far as she was aware there wasn't one scheduled for another two weeks.

'Emergency,' Ada said sagely, as if she was the keeper of some great secret.

'About the garden,' Martha added.

Nina frowned. 'What garden?'

'Exactly!' Ada said triumphantly.

'It's such a mess nobody even knows it's supposed to be a garden,' Martha said.

'But somebody wants to build on it.'

'But it's our community garden.'

'And we can't have that.'

'So we're going to ask the council to let us make it nice again.'

'And then nobody will be able to build on it.'

'That's right.'

Nina's frown deepened. 'I don't want to be the one to pour water on the fire here, but I don't see the council giving up the land just like that if they have a buyer for it, not just so the residents can plant petunias in there. And what on earth could we do with it anyway?'

'I don't know,' Ada said.

'It's all Nasser's idea,' Martha said.

'He'll have something up his sleeve,' Ada said firmly.

'Oh, he will,' Martha agreed with a confident smile. 'He's very clever.'

'So you're coming?' Ada asked.

'You must,' Martha said. 'You're ever so good in meetings.'

Nina shoved her hands deep into the pockets of her dressing gown. 'When is it?'

'Friday,' Ada said.

'At seven o'clock,' Martha finished for her.

Nina didn't see a lot of point in any of this but she was a part of this community and liked to contribute where she could, so she nodded.

'Of course I will,' she said.

It wasn't like she had anything better to do anyway.

Chapter Three

The community centre always smelt of damp, sun or rain, winter or summer. It was a new building, less than ten years old, but everyone in the town of Wrenwick agreed that it had been thrown up in rather a hurry and on a tight budget by a contractor who'd simply been out for maximum profits and wasn't all that concerned about how well the structure lasted once they'd done their bit. Already there were gaps between the window frames and the walls, cracks in the ceiling and loose flags on the path outside. Today the wind whistled into the main hall and set everyone shivering with every chilled gust, despite the heating being at full capacity. But since the council had sold off their eighteenth-century beauty – a former merchant's house that had been in use as a meeting room and community centre for many years – to a hotel chain, the residents didn't have a lot of choice but to use this draughty old box.

Wrenwick was a pretty town, but Nina often felt that the prettiness of Wrenwick might also be its undoing. Its elegant old buildings were in demand from the retail and leisure chains sweeping through the rest of the country, swallowing places that had been blessed with their own distinct identities before the chains had arrived and turned them all into clones of the last place they'd overrun. Nina hated that. Gray had hated it too – it was one of the many things they'd agreed on. They both hated to visit a new place and find that it contained just the same things they had in their own town. Nina loved independent, quirky shops and cafés; she loved to be surprised when she walked into a store, to find things she couldn't find anywhere else. They still had some in Wrenwick, but with every passing year they got harder to find.

Nina sat next to Robyn now, who had taken her coat off but still had a thick woollen scarf wound snugly around her neck.

'I can't believe you talked me into this,' she hissed in Nina's ear. 'You do know there are more exciting Friday nights to be had, don't you?'

'You mean like watching the soaps?' Nina whispered back with raised eyebrows. 'Your brain will rot if you watch too many of those.'

'My brain will rot here,' Robyn shot back. 'At least I'd be entertained in front of the telly.'

'Give it a chance,' Nina said. 'You love a good fight and I've got a feeling that a good fight is what we're going to get here when it all kicks off.'

Robyn grinned. 'Fisticuffs? Why didn't you say so in the first place; I wouldn't have complained about coming.'

It was Nina's turn to grin now. But then their attention was drawn to a rickety lectern situated at the front of the room where a short, balding man was clearing his throat as his gaze swept over the people seated in front of him.

'Aye, aye,' Robyn said in a low voice. 'It's about to go off.'

'Thank you all for coming,' the man announced as the chatter in the room died down. 'My name is Nasser—'

'We know!' someone in the crowd shouted. 'We move your bins from our driveway every Wednesday!'

There was a ripple of laughter around the room, and when it died down, Nasser began again.

'Quite,' he said with a smile. 'I just thought I'd introduce myself for anyone I hadn't had the pleasure of meeting before. But as most of you seem to know me, you'll probably also know why I've called this meeting.'

'Because he loves the sound of his own voice,' someone behind Nina said in a carrying whisper. Nina threw a quick glance over her shoulder but couldn't see who it might have been. She looked at Robyn, who'd clearly heard the quip too and returned Nina's look with one filled with mischief. Nina knew her well, and she knew that heated discussions were her favourite type. In fact, Robyn didn't consider a meeting to have been a proper meeting at all until someone had been insulted or shouted down.

Nasser had moved to Sparrow Street a few years before. Nina knew he was a refugee but she didn't know where from and he didn't often talk about what he'd been through before he'd arrived in Wrenwick. She thought that, perhaps, whatever he'd experienced was so horrible he didn't want to talk about it and so she'd never asked. She'd heard he'd been a doctor or a lawyer or something very important in his home country, but nobody was really sure about that either.

He could be a tad officious and it was true that if ever there was a crisis on the street – real or otherwise – it was a pretty safe bet that he'd be getting involved somehow. He thought of himself as the street's unelected representative in all things civic, but while some people found him irritating because of that, Nina had no issues with him at all. As far as she was concerned, it was good that someone cared enough to take action, even if some ridiculed him for it – and perhaps even despite the fact that he was probably aware of the ridicule. He'd always been very kind to Nina too, and she had no doubt that he had a good heart and what drove him was the community's best interests. Certainly, she was more than happy for him to take charge now.

'As many of you will be aware,' he began again, 'we have information of a plan by the council to sell our community garden.'

This announcement wasn't greeted with much of a reaction at all. People liked their outdoor space, but perhaps a lot of them were worried that they were just about to be asked to do something that would involve giving up their own time and money.

'It *does* look like a tip,' someone said.

'That's because nobody has ever taken responsibility for it,' Nasser said sternly. 'It doesn't have to look that way if we do something about it.'

'It's winter,' someone else said. 'What are we supposed to do about it now? It's nearly Christmas. Gardens are for summer.'

'So gardens disappear during the winter?' Robyn turned to the speaker. 'What a load of crap. You can still make them tidy and plant for the summer months.'

'Actually,' Nasser put in, 'that brings me to my second point, and I have only just come to discover this for myself. Due to budget cuts, there will be no Christmas decorations in Wrenwick this year.'

This time there was a collective gasp of horror. Take away the spare ground that was mostly home to the odd Twix wrapper and people were mildly annoyed because they thought they ought to be, but take away their Christmas street decorations and they were genuinely incensed. Not that the decorations in Wrenwick had ever been anything spectacular. Like the town itself, they'd been pretty but fairly unassuming – a string of lights from this lamppost to that, some silvery snowflakes hanging from the odd tree, a giant 'Merry Christmas' motif at the entrance to the town hall. It didn't seem plausible that they'd be too expensive to put up again this year, but if Nasser's report was right, the decision had been made for some reason that nobody outside the council understood.

'They can't do that!' someone cried.

'They *are* doing that,' Nasser replied steadily. 'Along with the closure of the mobile library and the playgroup on Chaffinch Road.'

'Disgusting!' someone shouted.

'So you see,' Nasser continued, 'the upkeep of our little community garden is probably very low on their list of priorities. But I, for one, think it would be a great shame to lose this space. Before we know it some private investor will be building shops or flats on it and then we've lost it forever.'

'So there *isn't* a buyer for it?' Nina asked, thinking about what Ada and Martha had told her.

'Not yet,' Nasser said. 'I've heard that somebody might be interested but there's nothing concrete yet.'

'Who's told you that?' Robyn asked.

'I can't say,' Nasser replied with a tap to the side of his nose. 'I will say that if it continues to stand there covered in weeds and rubbish the council will decide it's a liability worth getting rid of.'

'I won't miss it!' someone at the back of the room shouted. 'I've got enough to do with my own garden!'

'Lucky it's not all about what you want!' Ada cried.

'Yes, lucky!' Martha agreed.

'Never mind the garden,' someone else said, 'what about Christmas?'

'Well,' Nasser said. 'I did take the liberty of making a few phone calls to the council offices. Unfortunately, because of health and safety reasons, they won't allow us to put up street decorations ourselves. We can put lights and other festive things up on our own properties, but they say there's a risk to town infrastructure if we put things up on the street.'

'What the hell does that mean?' Nina turned to see that Ron, one of her closer neighbours, had spoken. He was a bullish-looking man with grey bristles for hair.

'I suppose it means that we might damage phone lines and things,' Nina said with a shrug.

'We can fix the garden!' Ada said, her small voice quivering as she struggled to make it heard.

'Yes, we could do that,' Martha agreed.

'Nobody cares about the garden,' Ron said.

'You mean you don't,' Robyn retorted. 'What, have you taken a poll or something?'

'What's it got to do with you?' Ron said. 'You don't even live here!'

'She lives close enough,' Nina replied.

'Close enough isn't here on this street.'

Nina chose to ignore Ron's retort and turned to Nasser, though she addressed the room as a whole. 'If we can't put decorations up on the street and we have a piece of spare ground doing nothing except gathering rubbish, couldn't we utilise that ground to put up Christmas decorations?'

A slow smile spread across Nasser's face. 'We'd have to clear the ground to use it for our decorations so it would then be ready to plant if we wanted to prepare a garden for the summer,' he said. 'That's a very good idea. But we'd have to get permission from the council to do that. I've put the question of a garden to them and they are going to get back to me on that, but I didn't ask about decorating it for Christmas.'

'I don't see what the difference is,' Nina said.

'I'm sure the council would be able to find one,' Nasser said with a wry smile.

A young woman on the row in front of Nina put up her hand. Nina recognised her as Kelly, the neighbour that Ada and Martha had tried their best to gossip about the night they'd come for help with their light bulb.

'Yes, Kelly?' Nasser said.

'Surely,' Kelly began slowly, 'the council ought to be glad to dump the responsibility of all this on us, especially if they can't afford to do it. I don't see why it would be an issue if it shuts us all up and gets another problem off their desks.'

'Because,' Nasser said patiently, 'town councils are notoriously counterintuitive when it comes to common sense.'

Kelly frowned. 'I don't follow.'

'It means they're thick and stubborn,' Robyn cut in and everyone laughed, the tension immediately draining from the room.

'Thank you…'

'Robyn,' she replied with a brisk nod at Nasser.

'Not quite how I'd have phrased it,' he continued, 'but in a nutshell, it's safe to say they don't always take the most rational approach to a problem. So if everyone here is happy to allow me, I propose to take a petition signed by you all to put forward our case.'

'To do what?' Ron asked with an unmistakable scowl. If the rest of the room was coming round to the idea of saving their garden, it didn't look as if he was.

'To tidy the garden and decorate it for Christmas.'

'Waste of time,' Ron said. 'It'll just be a mess again in the new year.'

'Not if we look after it,' Nina said. She turned to Nasser. 'Should we approach them about keeping the garden beyond Christmas? Like, for good?'

'And how much is all this going to cost?' Ron cut across Nina's question.

'I don't know,' Nasser said steadily. 'I'd done some rough calculations for the street decorations before I'd been told that we couldn't have them and I'd worked out somewhere in the region of five thousand—'

'Pounds!' Ron spluttered, veins popping in his forehead now. 'We haven't got that sort of money!'

'We'd have to do new calculations based on the new idea,' Nasser said, sending a pleading look for patience to the rest of the room as a new mutter of dissatisfaction spread through it. 'But I'm sure whatever we need we could raise between us.'

'I haven't got time to muck about with that,' Ron said.

'I'd help with that,' Nina said. 'I have time on my hands and I'd be glad to do what I can.'

Nasser smiled. 'Thank you. It's good to know we can count on your support.'

'We'd help too!' Martha cried.

'Oh we would!' Ada added, because it was utterly against the known laws of the universe for one of them to speak without the sentence being book-ended by agreement from the other. Nina couldn't help but wonder how much help the sisters would be. If their gardening was anything like their baking, not very much. She couldn't see their little back yard from hers and she'd never been out there, but Nasser's wife, Yasmin, had told her that it was mostly filled with plastic gnomes and gnarled-up plants that the ladies refused to accept were actually dead.

'I still don't think you can garden at this time of the year,' someone said. Nasser looked at him.

'Nina has already explained it, Tully. We can clear the garden anyway for Christmas, and while we do that there's no harm in planting bulbs for the spring.'

'That's assuming that the council tells us we can keep it,' Tully said.

'Well, yes,' Nasser conceded.

'We could put hardy shrubs in too,' Nina said.

'Yes,' Nasser said. 'There's plenty we could put in that would be green all year round.'

'I still don't see the point,' Ron insisted. 'It's a lot of money for nothing if you ask me.'

'Oh, you're a mean one, Ron Furnival!' Ada scolded.

'Rotten humbug to the core,' Martha agreed.

'There *is* no point.'

'Only to make everyone smile.'

'But we all know that's an impossible task with you.'

'Never seen you crack a smile in all my fifty years on this street,' Martha concluded, folding her arms across her chest with an emphatic nod, which her sister mirrored.

'I'll smile when you two pop your clogs and give us all some peace,' Ron said savagely, which sent another hiss of disapproval around the room, this time aimed at him rather than at any plans Nasser might have proposed.

'There's no need for that,' Nasser said, looking faintly appalled. 'We're a community, aren't we? What's happened to community spirit?'

'You can all enjoy your community spirit,' Ron said. 'And I'll enjoy keeping my money for more important things than a Christmas tree.'

Robyn pursed her lips. 'Then why *are* you here?' she asked, turning to face him again with a glare that would have smelted iron.

Ron looked furious, but he also looked like someone who didn't have an answer. The previous year Ron and his wife had left Sparrow Street for the sunshine of the Costa del Sol to retire. He'd come home three months later without her, thankful for the house that they hadn't managed to sell while they'd been in Spain, and he'd resettled back in England. His wife hadn't returned. Nina wasn't sure whether they were planning to get divorced, but it certainly didn't look as if they were a couple any longer. Ron didn't seem particularly upset by it and neither was his wife, Yvette (so those in contact with her said), and you didn't part without good reason, particularly when you'd gone to the trouble of moving your entire life to a new country. However, neither had divulged the reason for the split, though plenty of people on Sparrow Street agreed that if they'd been married to Ron, they'd have moved to Spain to get away from him too. The fact was, though, that no matter what had caused Ron to come home, getting used to life in England without Yvette couldn't have been easy, and Nina wondered whether he came to these community meetings simply because he had nothing better to do. He certainly never seemed to enjoy them and she often wished he'd make life a little more pleasant for them all and just stay away.

'I suggest,' Robyn cut in before Ron had time to find a reply, 'that if you've got nothing useful that you want to contribute, you can bugger off back to your telly at home – a place, judging by the size of you, you're very often sitting in front of.'

Ron folded his arms and glowered at Robyn but he didn't make a move to leave. Then Nina heard someone ask if Robyn lived on Sparrow Street, and someone else replied that they didn't believe so, which was more the pity because Sparrow Street could have done with more people with the balls to stand up to Ron Furnival. Despite this, Nina only hoped that Robyn hadn't ruffled too many feathers because she loved Robyn's kind heart and dry humour, and the way she called a spade a spade, and she wanted her neighbours to do that too. They wouldn't if they couldn't get past her outspoken first introduction.

Perhaps Robyn was suddenly sensitive to Nina's concerns, because when she spoke again now her tone was more conciliatory.

'Look, I know I don't live on the street but I do live in Wrenwick. It pisses me off to see how the council are gradually ripping the soul out of our lovely town. All they care about is money and development. Like the Sacred Heart shop that Nina and I used to work at. You know it's been sold to a restaurant chain – I don't know, probably going to be another burger bar or something, and of course we need another bloody burger bar. So I'm up for helping you lot if you'll have me. A win here is another win against the erosion of our community values – right? We win here and it's another two-fingered salute to the council leaders in their big houses on the hill who don't have to live with what's going on in the ordinary streets of their town.'

Ada and Martha stood up simultaneously and began to applaud. Whether they really knew what they were applauding for was another matter entirely.

'Thank you,' Nasser said, making a small gesture for Ada and Martha to take their seats again. 'I'm sure everyone here appreciates your kind offer.'

'If the people at the council thought we were doing something really useful with the space, they might be happier to let us have it?' Tully suggested.

'A lovely Christmas garden *is* good,' Ada said.

'Oh yes,' Martha agreed. 'It *is* good.'

'But not terribly useful,' Nina put in, and she glanced at Tully, who nodded. 'I see Tully's point,' she continued. She looked at Robyn now. 'I think we may have some ideas, right?'

Robyn looked confused. 'We do?'

'Well,' Nina said patiently, 'both our husbands were nursed by the Sacred Heart Hospice. And I'm sure countless others have been nursed there over the years, many dear to people gathered here. In fact, I bet everyone here has lost someone over the years in tragic circumstances. So what if, instead of spending all that money on street decorations we made it a garden of memories? We could… I don't know, plant trees or shrubs for people we've lost? Or we could put out lanterns for them, light candles or something? People could come and see, and they could add their own if they wanted to and maybe make donations to various local charities?'

'Like pay to have someone remembered?' Nasser asked.

Nina turned to him and nodded. 'Surely the council couldn't veto that if we approached them with a proper plan?'

Nasser nodded thoughtfully. 'You may be on to something there, although I'm not sure of the long-term potential.'

'We could work on that too,' Nina said. 'Make some longer-term plans and present them when we present this.'

'If we could get hold of someone at the council who's been in the same situation they might be more sympathetic,' Robyn said. 'In fact, I might know someone.'

Nina gave Robyn a sharp look. If the someone she might know was who Nina thought it was, then she couldn't imagine how that conversation would go. Still, Robyn was a grown woman and Nina could hardly stop her.

Her friend didn't seem to notice Nina's questioning gaze. Perhaps she wouldn't be as bothered as Nina supposed she might be. All Nina knew was that she wouldn't be approaching an ex-boyfriend for a favour if they'd parted in the way Robyn had parted from hers.

Nasser's gaze ran over the small crowd seated before him. 'Does anyone else have any thoughts on this?'

'I like it,' Kelly said. 'I'd light a lantern for my gran. I don't know about planting trees, though. We might run out of room quite early on and it would end up looking like a very weird tiny forest.'

'That's true,' Tully agreed. 'Exactly what I was thinking. And after Christmas a little patch of trees is just begging for trouble. Kids hiding in it, causing mischief. Especially that gang of lads from Bluebird Street – little shits…'

There was some murmur of agreement before Tully continued. For the past two or three years there had been antisocial incidents and petty crimes and everyone knew who the perpetrators were, even if they couldn't prove it. It had been pointless anyone trying to talk to the boys' parents too, previous complaints having fallen on deaf ears.

'With a proper open garden we can see what's going on in there.'

'What about the money?' Ron spoke again for the first time since Robyn's rebuke. 'Do we still have to shell out for this lot?'

'Nobody has to *shell out* for anything,' Nasser said, doing his best to smooth a sour look into something more neutral. Ron was clearly getting on everyone's nerves with his constant complaining. Robyn was right about that: if all this pained him as much as it seemed to, it was difficult to see why he'd bothered to come to the meeting at all.

'There must be a way of doing it all between us on the cheap,' Kelly said. 'My brother works at a builders' yard – I can ask him if he can help.'

'Good plan,' Nasser said. 'Though perhaps just hold that thought until we get an absolute go-ahead from the council, and that will mean going to them with concrete proposals first. Nina… as it was your initial idea, would you like to take on the garden of memories and elaborate on a plan, see what you can come up with?'

'I'd be happy to,' Nina said and smiled. As she did, she felt Robyn's hand close over hers and squeeze tight. They were in this together, always, and Nina's heart swelled with the knowledge that despite the tragedies that had dogged both their lives, it was tragedy that had bound them as friends too, a friendship that was solid and real and, for Nina at least, heaven sent.

'I'll take a look at that with you if you like,' Robyn said.

'Thanks,' Nina said.

'So I think we'll need teams to take charge of different aspects of the planning – we can't expect Nina to do it all,' Nasser said. He looked at Kelly. 'If you're talking to your brother at some point anyway, would you be happy to look at garden design?'

'Of course,' Kelly said, flushing and smiling proudly. Delicate and nervy, she was someone with an artistic flair but little confidence in it, as evidenced by the beautiful pottery made by her own hand that lined the shelves of her home, but which produced a self-conscious blush every time it was praised by a visitor. There had been rumours that she'd come to Sparrow Street seeking refuge from an abusive boyfriend, though nobody had ever seen him, and if this was true, it would explain a lot about the low profile she always tried to keep. According to Ada and Martha, there were rumours of a drink problem too, and if that was true then it was hardly surprising given the hardships she must have had to overcome. Whatever the truth, it was only over the last six months that she'd started to gain enough confidence to play a more active role in the community, and she'd started to look happier too. It was nice to see her so obviously thrilled with Nasser's proposal.

'Who's going to go to the council for permission?' someone at the back asked. 'Are you?'

'I'm happy to do that if everyone is happy to hand that responsibility to me,' Nasser replied. He looked at Robyn with a grin. 'And I think I have just the person to come with me. Didn't you say you might have a contact?'

'Possibly,' Robyn said cautiously. 'No promises, though.'

'More importantly,' Nasser added, giving a short nod that acknowledged Robyn's caveat, 'would you be up for the challenge?'

Nina had to grin too. She'd never known Robyn not to be up for a challenge – it was the main reason she'd tried so hard to persuade her friend to come to the meeting. She'd known if there was anything to be done, Robyn would want to get involved.

'Contacts might not be cut and dried,' Robyn said with a smile, 'but challenges I can absolutely do!'

Chapter Four

Robyn had been excited when the meeting was over. They'd spent some time chatting with the residents who'd stayed behind for a cup of tea so that she could get to know the people she might end up working with a bit better. Nasser's wife, Yasmin, had turned up with their three children in tow – all under the age of ten and not exactly suited to sitting through a meeting – and Robyn had made such a fuss of them all that they'd left feeling as if they'd gained a new auntie. Then they'd all been thrown out of the meeting room by an over-eighties keep-fit class that was waiting for the hall and had gone back to their own homes – apart from Robyn, who'd gone back to Nina's for more tea and because they were both so full of enthusiasm for the project and itching to get started.

On the way it had started to rain in heavy, icy sheets, and they'd both been soaked to the bone and frozen stiff. So Nina had got the fire going and fetched fleecy blankets for them to wrap around themselves, and they were now both curled up on opposite ends of Nina's sofa cradling mugs of hot tea while the fire burned with a satisfying roar in the grate.

'I think Kelly's right about the trees,' Nina said. 'I mean, it would be nice to have some more greenery, but it's going to be hard to allocate one to each person we want to remember and it might just be more trouble than it's worth.'

'Well, if we're putting up a Christmas tree anyway, then candles might be the way forward.'

'Lanterns,' Nina said. 'Candles are too dangerous and they wouldn't last two seconds in bad weather.'

'Lanterns then. Suits me… Are you writing this down?'

Nina reached for the pad and pencil that had been set down on the floor beside the sofa. 'Yes, Miss. You know, I'm almost certain there are already holly bushes there, now that I come to think about it.'

'That might be useful. If we run out of tree, or if the tree just isn't practical, we could perhaps hang lanterns from the bushes. Are they big?'

'I'm not sure – we'd have to go and have a look.'

'We ought to make a list of beneficiaries too,' Robyn said thoughtfully. 'Charities we can donate to with the money people pay for their dedication. Put them to people at the next meeting. It's possible not everyone will agree with our list so we ought to let them see it before we go any further with it.'

'I can't see there being a big fuss about that but you're probably right. There's always someone who will unexpectedly disagree with something that seems perfectly reasonable to everyone else.'

'Like that Ron character?' Robyn raised her eyebrows. 'Was he born with an altruism malfunction or has he just worked hard to cultivate it?'

'He's OK really,' Nina said.

'All he thinks about is money.'

'I think he struggles a bit financially since the split with Yvette. I wonder if they put a lot of money into their move to Spain which, obviously, would have left him short.'

'And she's not coming back to England?' Robyn asked.

'It doesn't look like it.'

'Right...' Robyn took a sip of her tea. 'I can't say I blame her. I wouldn't come back to that great miserable lump either.'

'That's what everyone says. I don't know, he can't be that bad. I think he might be quite nice beneath it all.'

'What's he ever done to make you think that?'

Nina gave a vague shrug. 'After Gray died he came round all the time to see if I needed anything. I mean, everyone did but still... I don't suppose he had to.'

'And did you need anything?'

'Not usually but it was nice of him to ask, wasn't it?'

Robyn offered a withering look. 'If it was me, I'd rather he didn't. I don't know why he bothered going to the meeting when all he did was complain.'

'I know. Everyone wishes he wouldn't turn up to them but he always does, and we sort of have to ask even though we don't want to. I think he's lonely to be honest.'

'I'm not surprised – who'd want to talk to that miserable git?'

'He is a bit miserable,' Nina agreed.

'A *bit*? Even his wife's run away to Spain to avoid talking to him!'

'Alright, a lot, but we're stuck with him. I suppose at least he might be handy to have around if there's any heavy hauling to be done in the garden.'

'I think you're confusing fat with muscle there.'

Nina giggled. 'Poor Ron. He's going to get short shrift from you, isn't he?' She turned her attention to the list they'd been writing. Chewing on the end of her pencil, she read down it. 'Do you think that's everything?'

'I'm sure we'll think of lots more in the days to come but it'll do for now.' Robyn glanced at her watch. 'Comfy as I am here on your sofa, I really ought to be getting back to make sure Toby hasn't blown up the house in my absence.'

'You could have brought him along tonight, you know.'

'Oh, he'd have loved that,' Robyn said dryly. 'In fact, I wish I'd known before because he was begging to come and sit in a room full of geriatrics to talk about gardens.'

Nina laughed again. 'I suppose not. I don't really know what kids are into but I suppose even I know it's not that.'

'It's absolutely anything but that. Anyway, surely your own teenage years aren't that far behind you that you can't remember the days when all you thought about was stealing fags from your dad and ways to lose your virginity?'

'My dad didn't smoke and I don't think I knew what my virginity was until I met Gray.'

Robyn's eyes widened. 'Are you kidding me? Gray was your first?'

'First and last,' Nina said with a rueful smile.

'How the hell did you manage that?'

'A helpful combination of ugliness and crippling shyness.'

'Ugliness? But you're lovely!'

'I'm not, but thank you. Let's just say that if I look OK now, the years since I was a teenager have been a bit kinder to me. This hair didn't help for a start, and I had shocking acne.'

Robyn almost sighed with longing as her eyes went to Nina's head. 'I'd kill for your hair.'

'You wouldn't have done back then; it was totally uncontrollable. It's not much better now to be honest.'

'At least it doesn't look like someone gave you hair as an afterthought,' Robyn said.

'I like your hair,' Nina replied warmly. 'It's nice and shiny.'

'My hairdresser says it's fine,' Robyn said. 'Which means there's hardly any point to it at all. If only my waistline could be as fine.'

Nina giggled. 'Your waistline *is* fine.'

'It's just cracking if you're a walrus,' Robyn said. 'I suppose there's nobody to blame but myself for that – I'm just too fond of the cakes to do anything about it now.'

'I think you're perfect as you are. Life's too short to diet.'

'Says the size-ten woman. Anyway,' Robyn added impishly, 'I said I was a bit on the porky side, but I never said I wasn't perfect.'

Nina snorted. 'OK,' she said, trying to get her laughter under control now, 'we'd better finish up or you'll never get home to Toby. Oh, who's this person at the council you're going to target for help?'

'Nina, you know who it is.'

'Well, I did wonder if it was Peter, but… are you sure that's a good idea?'

'We're both adults, aren't we?'

'But… well, won't it be a bit awkward to approach him?'

'We parted on fairly good terms.'

Nina raised a sceptical eyebrow.

'OK, so it was a bit difficult, but there's no blame with me and I figure he owes me the favour.'

'And you won't be tempted to get involved with him again and get your heart broken again?'

'My heart wasn't broken.'

'You raged for weeks.'

'That wasn't heartbreak, that was just anger.'

'And you're all better now?'

'It's been six months – plenty of time to get over that git. It'll be strictly professional.'

'And if you find out that his wife has gone this time…?' Nina asked, raising her eyebrows again.

'Wouldn't change a thing,' Robyn said firmly. 'One chance with me and that's it.'

'Right.' Nina smiled. 'So what makes you think he'd be willing to help?'

'Despite the mess he made of everything, he's a decent bloke and I know his dad had Alzheimer's so I think the charity thing will appeal to him.'

'You don't think having this much contact will make you regret your decision to end things with him?'

Robyn shook her head.

'I know you better than that,' Nina said.

'I don't know. I can't get anything past you, can I? I suppose I can't deny there's still something there. Maybe it wouldn't be so bad if it led to other things… I'm not getting any younger… Toby's growing up too quickly and soon he won't need me… I don't want to end up alone…' Robyn sighed. 'Take your pick from those and many other reasons.'

'And you think Peter will be the answer to all that?'

'Maybe not. I think he would help with the garden, though, and that's what we're really interested in here.'

'I don't know. It all sounds like a big ask to me.'

'You don't think he'd help?'

'I don't think you should be putting your feelings on the line for our garden.'

'I won't be. It's not like I want to marry him or anything.'

'I just hope it doesn't backfire on you, that's all.'

'Of course it won't. You worry too much.'

'I know. I can't help it.'

Robyn drained her cup and handed it to Nina. 'I'll call him tomorrow; it'll be fine, you'll see. In the meantime, I'd better get back to Toby. Reckon my shoes will have dried out by now?'

Nina glanced towards the trainers that were sitting next to the fire. The steam that had been wreathing away from them for the last hour seemed to have stopped now. 'Probably,' she said.

'If they have or haven't, I suppose I'd better get them on anyway,' Robyn said. 'Thanks for the tea.'

'Thank you for coming to the meeting. Your help means a lot to us... to me.'

'Like you said,' Robyn said with a grin, 'I'm always up for a challenge, and this seems like one hell of a challenge to me. How could I resist?'

Chapter Five

When Nina went to drag her bins out for collection the next morning, Ron was out too. His garden was half the length of the street away from Nina's, but he came over to speak to her anyway. After his behaviour at the meeting, Nina couldn't imagine why, but perhaps there was more truth in what she'd said to Robyn about him being lonely than she'd realised.

'Need some help with that?' he asked, looking at the bin Nina had just deposited at the kerbside.

'Thank you, but I've already done it,' she replied. It was quite obvious to anyone that the task had been accomplished.

Ron shoved his hands in his pockets and jingled some loose change, looking apologetic. 'Oh… right. Just thought I'd ask. They're heavier than they look, aren't they?'

'Yes.' Nina gave him an awkward smile. 'But the wheels help.'

'Of course… they do.'

They lapsed into silence. Ron looked at the worn old slippers on his feet while Nina glanced up and down the street, as if to find help or inspiration from one of her neighbours. But they were alone, and when she looked back at Ron, he was regarding her now with an expression that suggested some kind of internal struggle.

'I expect you're busy today,' he said finally.

'Well…' Nina began.

'Of course,' he continued. 'A lot to do when you're on your own, isn't there? Nobody to help with the chores is there?'

'No,' Nina agreed. 'But you get used to it.'

'Do you?' Ron asked.

Nina gave a half-smile. It looked as if Ron was struggling with the separation from his wife more than he let on.

'Eventually,' she said. 'You've not heard from Yvette, then?'

'Hmmm? Oh yes, she phones all the time. Wants to know if I'm alright, you know...'

Nina wondered if that was true, but Ron was hardly going to say so if it wasn't. She felt sorry for him but there wasn't much she could do – there wasn't much anyone else could do about the situation between Ron and his wife except Ron and his wife.

'I'd better...' she began, indicating her house, 'you know... lots to do.'

Ron gave a solemn nod. 'Of course. So you'll let me know if you need anything? Anytime. I'm always just down the road after all.'

'Thank you,' Nina said. 'That's kind.'

Ron looked down at his feet again.

'How's the job hunting going?' she asked, her natural empathy undoing her once again as he looked up. Instantly she regretted the impulse to show an interest. She had plenty to do inside, including her own job hunting, but now she'd handed him the perfect opportunity to hold her up. He shook his head and gave a theatrical sigh.

'Terrible. Nobody wants a man pushing sixty. I wish I'd never given up my old job to go to Spain – worst thing I ever did. I had it cushy in the post office.'

'You could go back? They'd have you, wouldn't they?'

'It's not the same now. When I joined back in the day it was a job for life with a good pension and reasonable working hours. Now it's all zero-hours contracts and working till you drop. As for a pension, none of those young lads starting work now will have a penny put aside when they get to my age. You have to feel sorry for them.'

'You do,' Nina agreed, though she didn't really know anything about any of that. 'But you weren't to know how things would turn out for you when you decided to go to Spain.'

Ron gave that grave shake of his head again, as if he was a world leader just about to declare war. 'I should have done. I shouldn't have let Yvette talk me into it. And now look – she's living it up in the sun and I'm here alone with no job.'

And then it began to rain, and Ron looked up at the heavens as if in melancholic appreciation of some divine irony.

'Biggest mistake I ever made,' he muttered, looking back at Nina. 'Should never have listened to her.'

Nina's heart went out to him. For all the awkwardness, she hated to see him so down. It half-crossed her mind to talk to Robyn about whether they could engineer some sort of match for him with another single woman they might know, but then she checked herself. In the real world, not the world of Jane Austen novels, that sort of meddling usually ended in trouble. It was probably better to let fate take this one – when the right woman for Ron came along, Nina could only hope that fate would bring them together.

'You've got good neighbours and friends here,' she said. 'Even if the weather isn't quite as good as it is in Spain. At least you have that.'

'Hmm,' he said, sounding unconvinced.

'Well, maybe getting involved in the garden project will help you feel more positive then. It'll certainly keep us all occupied for a few weeks and it will bring everyone together.'

'Oh, I haven't got time for that,' Ron said bitterly.

Nina stared at him. 'What?'

'I haven't got time.'

'But you… surely you've got *a little* time to spare!'

If any of them had time to spare, she'd have thought it was Ron. She couldn't help but feel that his refusal was a bit mean in the circumstances, and she half-wished she hadn't defended him to Robyn the previous day. She could also have pointed out that if he was lonely and fed up with his wife living in Spain, then there was a cure for that and it was called making friends with his neighbours.

'Nasser wants to stop getting ideas above his station,' Ron continued. 'He's no better than any of us but he doesn't half think he's someone.'

'I think he genuinely wants to improve things for the community,' Nina said sharply.

'He's a jumped-up little captain.'

'Steady on! Don't you think that's a bit unfair?'

'Well…' Ron said, sounding like a chastised child now.

The rain was getting heavier and colder and Nina could feel it beginning to soak through her jumper.

'I really ought to get in,' she said, glancing up at the rapidly darkening sky. She didn't want to lose her temper with Ron, but she could feel the frustration building at his attitude.

'Right,' Ron said, sinking his hands deeper into his pockets. If the weather was bothering him he wasn't showing much sign of it. Nina had the impression he'd quite like to keep her out a little longer, but she was very aware of how wet she was getting now and catching pneumonia wasn't exactly at the top of her to-do list.

'Well, I'll see you later then, Ron,' she said.

He nodded and, without another word, turned and began to walk back to his house, leaving Nina to hurry inside herself. You could only have so much sympathy for someone's situation, and Ron didn't exactly make himself easy to sympathise with. It wasn't something she had time to worry about right now, though, because she'd plenty enough worries of her own.

It had taken Nina most of the morning to make her CV look at least semi-appealing and sign up to an employment-agency website. Although she'd eventually managed to register without too much of a hitch, she wasn't altogether convinced that her CV was going to have potential employers lining up outside her door. She certainly wouldn't employ herself on the basis of what experience and work record she had to offer, that much she was sure of. In the end, it had all been a bit depressing and, after trying and failing to get Robyn on the phone for a chat to get it off her chest, she glanced up at the clock and remembered that she'd arranged to go and have lunch with her dad anyway. She didn't think he'd mind if she arrived early and so she headed out.

The morning's downpour had stopped and a weak sun was pushing through the clouds, which meant that she could do the walk across town instead of taking the bus. The air and exercise would do her good and give her an opportunity to blow the cobwebs of misery from her mind.

Twenty minutes later she was standing outside her dad's pristine bungalow. At least, the house itself was pristine, though the garden was usually anything but. At any given time there might be three or four different cars on the tarmac driveway in various states of disrepair. She could see his feet now, sticking out from beneath an orange Ford Cortina that looked as if it belonged in a seventies cop show. There were bits of the engine spread out around the car, and bits of what might well be engines from other cars, along with half an old Astra. Nina smiled as her dad's feet tapped in time to a tape player which sat beside his workspace, blasting out rock music. Led Zeppelin, if Nina's memory served her correctly. She'd certainly heard enough of it growing up that she ought to remember it, even if it had never been her favourite music in the world. If he'd been playing it at its current volume in Sparrow Street there would almost certainly have been complaints, but everyone here knew Winston Alder was a little deaf in one ear and they forgave him the odd loud session.

Nina let herself in at the gate and bent to switch the tape player off. Her dad rolled out from under the car, his frown crinkling into a smile as he saw who had interrupted his music.

'Oh, hello, love! I wasn't expecting it to be you just yet!'

He got up and Nina reached to kiss a cheek whiskered with hair as white as hers was black. The hair on his head had thinned considerably over the years but it was still a decent thatch for a man in his seventies – at least he always insisted it was – even if that was as white as flour too. He was still quick and wiry, and kept lively by his hobby of rebuilding old cars which he sold on to provide a little income. The evidence of his hobby littered the driveway now, and Nina had had to tread carefully as she'd navigated the path.

'I know,' she said. 'But I was feeling a bit fed up and I didn't think you'd mind.'

'Fed up?' he asked, his smile fading into a look of concern. 'Everything alright?'

'Oh, it's nothing serious,' she said, forcing a cheery smile. 'Just a bit of this and that… you know how it is.'

He reached for a rag from his waistband and wiped the oil from his hands. 'Want to tell me about it anyway?'

'Maybe over a cup of tea? I could put the kettle on while you finish here.'

'Oh, I reckon I've just about done enough for today,' he said, glancing at the detritus of his morning's work.

'How about I start in the kitchen while you clear it all up then?'

'Lovely,' he said. 'What do you want for lunch?'

'I'll have a look in the freezer,' Nina said, knowing full well that she wasn't going to find anything fresh in the house. Winston had coped admirably since the death of Nina's mum but that had never stretched to healthy eating. Still, what he had in the freezer and store cupboards provided a reasonably balanced diet, even if none of it was fresh, and so Nina had decided long ago not to worry about it; he certainly wouldn't have thanked her for nagging him over it.

She made her way up the drive, leaving him to collect his tools and put away his radio.

'There's a nice bit of cod if you fancy that,' he called after her.

She turned and nodded before letting herself into the unlocked house. In the hall hung an old wedding photo of her parents – her dad in a sharp suit with a mop of thick hair, her mum looking radiant and adorable in a calf-length wedding dress of white lace and white silk shoes, her hair swept up into a voluminous bun, wearing false eyelashes that could have knocked passing cyclists off their bikes.

'Hello, Mum,' Nina said, blowing a kiss at the photo. 'You look lovely as always.'

Nina's mum smiled on as Nina carried on down the hall.

They'd lost her ten years earlier. Nina had been twenty-five when she died and it had changed everything. Nina and her dad got by now, but they'd both had some hard years. Having Gray had helped when Nina's mum had first died, but then shortly afterwards came his own terrible diagnosis and Nina had felt for a while that life was too cruel to make it even worth bothering. But she'd pulled herself together because Gray had needed her and, no matter what else was happening, she'd had to think of that.

Nina's dad, Winston, had barely changed the house since his wife's death. Right down to the fake plastic roses, the colour leached from the outer petals by the sun as they gathered dust in a crystal vase on the windowsill, the reminders of Miriam Alder were everywhere. The prints she'd hung, the sofa she'd chosen, the wallpaper she'd spent a frustrating Sunday putting up, complaining all the while that Winston would rather piece together a rusting old Volvo than help her, the rug they'd brought back from a holiday in Turkey, the china rescued from an elderly aunt's house… Nina imagined that her dad took comfort in the thought that a little of his wife remained, captured in all the things she'd once owned and loved, that she was still in every room, because Nina herself felt the same way about the things she'd kept after Gray's death.

She headed to the kitchen, eyeing the dishes in the sink. It looked like more than one day's washing up, but that was no surprise. Winston had told Nina on more than one occasion that he didn't see the point in filling a bowl with hot water until he'd produced enough dirty crockery to justify it, and living on his own as he did on mostly frozen food, that took quite a while to do. Now that she was here, however, Nina decided that she'd quickly do them before they had lunch to get them out of the way, as she always did. Her dad would watch dolefully like a chastised little boy, refusing to help on principle but feeling as if he ought to just the same.

Nina was gratified to see a healthy stock of food in the freezer – oven-bake fries, sausages, breaded fish, beef burgers and bake-at-home pies. It was the sort of inventory one might find in a student's freezer, but Nina was used to pulling a decent meal together out of what he had in. She'd brought fresh vegetables to go with it, and a Victoria sponge as a treat for afterwards.

She'd just turned the oven on to warm it when her dad came in. He'd changed out of his overalls and now sported worn old combat trousers and a faded Thin Lizzy T-shirt.

'Aren't you cold in that?' Nina asked mildly.

'It's a bit parky but I've put the heating on so it'll warm up in a minute.'

'Don't you want to put a jumper on?'

'No, you're alright, love.' Winston sat down at the table and Nina resisted the impulse to roll her eyes.

'Do I have to go searching for one?' she asked. 'Or shall I let you freeze to death?'

'You can search all you like but I doubt you'll find a clean one – I haven't done any washing this week.'

'Why not?'

'There wasn't enough to make a full load so I thought I'd save it for next week.'

'So you're planning on wearing T-shirts all week even though it's November?'

'It's warm enough in the house,' he said with a frown. 'Don't nag me.'

'I'm not nagging. If I do it's only because I worry about you. I don't do much else for you so at least let me do that.'

'You do enough, love,' he said with a frown that smoothed instantly to a smile. 'I'm lucky to have you.'

'Well then, it's a good job you adopted me all those years ago, isn't it?' Nina said briskly, going to fetch mugs as the kettle clicked off. 'A kindness gets a kindness, just like Mum used to say.'

'I'll make the tea,' Winston said, getting up to take them from her. 'What are we having for lunch?'

Nina relinquished the tea duties and went to check the temperature of the oven. 'I don't know – what do you want? Did you want the fish?'

'If you do.'

'I'm easy either way.'

'Right, fish it is.'

'I've brought some veg.'

'No mushy peas? I think there's a tin in.'

'Veg, Dad. Never mind five a day – it's five a year for you. It'd be five never if I didn't come round.'

'Mushy peas count, don't they?'

'I'm pretty sure they don't. If you like I'll put them on too, but you're having some fresh with them.'

'Alright then,' Winston said sulkily. 'What's for afters?'

'Victoria sponge.'

'From that cake shop?'

Nina smiled. *That cake shop* could have been anywhere, but as far as her dad was concerned there was only one cake shop in Wrenwick worth patronising and she wouldn't dream of getting him one from anywhere else. It was the cake shop her mum had always gone to, a business now run by the third generation of the same family using only fresh and natural ingredients.

'Yes,' she said.

'Lovely!' Winston rubbed his hands together like a character from a fifties comic strip and Nina had to laugh. She loved his funny ways. She loved *him*, loved spending time with him, loved looking after him and nagging him to stay well, loved that she was lucky enough to be the child who'd been chosen by him and Miriam out of all the children they could have chosen instead. She'd never felt sad or incomplete from the knowledge of her adoption; she'd only ever felt incredibly lucky and grateful that such a beautiful couple had given her the chance of a happy, secure life that many others never got. She loved him all the more knowing he'd saved her and she'd never been troubled by the identity of the biological parents who'd given her up, because they *had* given her up and, thus, had removed themselves from her life and her future. There was no bitterness in her about any of it – that was just the way things were.

An hour later they'd mopped up the last blobs of fresh cream from their plates of cake and a second pot of tea was brewing.

'So what do you think?' Nina asked.

Winston folded his arms and regarded her shrewdly from across the table. 'I think it's a cracking idea. If you want help let me know.'

'I think we've got it covered for now,' Nina said. 'At least for the moment, unless Nasser decides to make the project even bigger than it is now.'

'Still, I'd like to help,' Winston said. 'I might be old but I've still got a bit of go in me – could do a bit of digging, fetching and carrying, that sort of thing.'

Nina smiled. 'In that case I bet you'd be welcomed. Maybe you should come to the next meeting with me.'

'Let me know when it is and I'll ask my secretary if I have a gap in my schedule.'

Nina laughed. 'I thought I was your secretary!'

'You're my everything, love,' he said with a grin. 'So have you decided who's getting the donations?'

'I thought we'd give to the Sacred Heart, obviously. And Cancer Research in memory of Mum. I'm sure plenty would be up for supporting that anyway.' She paused. 'Who else do you reckon?'

'Something for the kiddies?' he asked.

'That's not a bad idea. We'll ask for suggestions of children's charities at the next meeting. Basically, if it's close to someone's heart then we'll probably find a way to support it.'

'I'm sure there'll be no shortage of suggestions,' Winston replied approvingly. 'So what about your job? I know you're looking but will you have time to do one with all this lot?'

'I'd have to make time if I got a job offer, I suppose. I don't think anyone on Sparrow Street would expect me to give up the chance of paid work, and I think they're just glad of any time anyone can spare.'

'Have you seen anything that might suit you?'

'Not yet. But I'm not going to start panicking about it just yet. I don't think I need to worry too much until after Christmas.'

'I think Dave might need someone at the pub,' Winston said. 'I could ask him for you.'

'I haven't had any bar experience, though. Does he know that?'

'I don't expect he'll care,' Winston said. 'He always liked you and I think that would be enough.'

'I'm not so sure.'

'It's not exactly a swanky cocktail bar, is it? It's only the Feathers – a little pub like that full of local folks won't be expecting anything special. It wouldn't take you an hour to learn how to pull a decent pint and then you'd be away.'

Nina nodded. 'In that case I don't mind giving it a try if he's still got the opening and he's willing to take someone who doesn't have bar experience. Thanks, Dad.'

'I'll let you know what he says when I've had a chance to ask him.'

Nina got up to clear the table while her dad poured the tea. It was then that she heard the faint ringing coming from the handbag she'd stowed beneath the table. Pulling out her phone, she noted Robyn's number on the display.

'Hello!' Nina said brightly. 'I tried to call you earlier.'

'Oh, I know,' Robyn said. 'I'm sorry I couldn't pick it up. I'm at the council offices… in Peter's office, actually. At least, I was; I've just left him.'

'I thought you and Nasser were going to get an appointment at the council and go together?'

'We were, but then I thought about it and I thought, strike while the iron's hot and all that. I still had Peter's number from before so I thought, why not give him a call? What's the worst that can happen?'

'So how did it go?'

Robyn laughed. 'He was like putty.'

'Really?' Nina asked, raising her eyebrows. She suspected that the conversation had been a lot more awkward than Robyn was making out, given her history with Peter. 'Didn't he wonder what on earth you were doing just turning up out of the blue?'

'I suppose he did seem a bit surprised.'

'Surprised? I should think it was more than that.'

'Not when I explained to him what we wanted. And I did remind him that he owed me big time.'

'I'm sure he really enjoyed being reminded of how he screwed up and you dumped him.'

'He deserved to be dumped,' Robyn shot back. 'That wasn't my fault!'

'I know that, but it doesn't change the fact that he probably wasn't pleased about you walking back into his life again after all these months he's spent getting over you.'

'He could have said no when I phoned, but he didn't. He asked me to go to his office.'

'Probably thought you were going to take him back.'

'Even Peter's not that stupid,' Robyn said.

'Booty call then? Sex with an ex?'

'Not even funny!'

'OK, OK… so tell me what happened.'

'He said he was glad that I'd felt able to go to him for help.'

'He did?'

'Yes. And he says he knows who to talk to and they like him so they'll probably be receptive to his suggestions.'

'Which means…?'

'Which means get your charity list drawn up, because I think we're on!'

Chapter Six

Ada and Martha had turned up to the meeting (which was presently adjourned for a refreshment break) with tubs of cake. The cake currently sat on a table surrounded by teacups and an urn. Nobody was quite sure what sort of cake it was and the other meeting attendees could be forgiven for eyeing it with some suspicion. They'd all made the mistake of trying Ada and Martha's cakes before and most had been left traumatised by the experience. Only Ron tucked happily in, but then Ron would eat anything if it was free and it was going down so fast he probably couldn't taste it anyway. Nina watched him now and couldn't understand why he'd even bothered to turn up again after the last meeting.

Ron had behaved so far, however, and the meeting had gone well. People had been happy with many of Nina's suggestions, including the list of charities that she and Robyn were proposing to give memory-tree donations to, and had made some agreeable ones of their own. Robyn had brought Peter along and the poor council rep – who insisted he wasn't as big a noise as people might have supposed – had been inundated with queries and questions, which he'd answered as best he could and with surprising cheeriness. Whatever the situation between him and Robyn now, whether the past they'd shared had been discussed or not, they seemed to be getting along and behaving like grown-ups and Peter was proving as good as his word when he'd offered to help.

The first thing the meeting had agreed on was that the spare ground needed some serious tidying up before they could do anything else. A task force had been put together comprised of the more able residents, ones who could also spare the time. They'd make a start as soon as possible, pruning back the wilderness of weeds and clearing the rubbish that currently choked it. The meeting had also agreed that not only should they have the memory tree for Christmas, but that the garden should function as a garden of remembrance all year, a little oasis of calm to sit and contemplate and reflect on the people they'd lost, or maybe just on whatever else life might be throwing at them. To that end, they'd plant bulbs ready for the spring to brighten the space, and people would tend it on a rota through the year to make sure it stayed tidy and green. It also needed fencing, some landscaping and some kind of irrigation system to ensure it didn't dry out if they had a hot summer.

As Nina helped her dad and Kelly pour out tea to hand to the meeting attendees, she glanced to the far side of the room to see Robyn and Peter deep in conversation. Every so often Robyn would laugh loudly at something he'd said or flick her hair with a coy look. For someone who was only supposed to be talking to Peter again to make the most of his council connections, she was doing a remarkable impression of someone who actually still had deep feelings for him. Nina couldn't deny that the thought worried her. Robyn had been hurt by the way things had ended with Peter more than she'd ever admitted – it had been so obvious it hadn't needed saying. Going back there now, even if Robyn had no intentions of starting anything up with him again, promised to be emotionally perilous at the very least.

'It's a nice cup of tea…'

Nina turned to see Ron offering up his empty cup. She blinked, her eyes watering, suddenly overwhelmed by the aftershave that was radiating off him in potent waves. It was a wonder Kelly's asthma hadn't been triggered, though Nina noted from the corner of her eye that she was backing away out of range, probably just in case.

'I wouldn't mind another if there's one going,' he continued.

Nina refilled his cup. 'I didn't make the tea; I'm only helping to serve it.'

'Oh. Well it's good anyway.'

'I'll tell my dad – he'll be glad to hear it.'

'Hear what?'

It was Winston's turn to pay attention to the conversation.

'The tea,' Nina said. 'Ron likes it.'

'You're Nina's dad?' Ron asked, looking suddenly uncomfortable. He offered his hand in greeting but he looked as if he'd now rather be heading off towards the exit than drinking Winston's tea, however good and free it might be.

'Winston Alder.' Nina's dad nodded with a grim smile as he shook Ron's hand.

'Alder… but I thought Nina's name was Munro…'

'Married name,' Winston said patiently, though Nina couldn't help an internal smile because she knew what her dad was probably thinking. It seemed that Ron suddenly realised how silly he'd sounded too.

'Of course…' he mumbled.

'So you live on Sparrow Street?' Winston asked.

'Yes.'

'Ron was very kind to me after… Well, you know,' Nina said.

Winston fixed Ron with a frank gaze. 'Thank you for that,' he said.

'It was really nothing,' Ron said.

Winston nodded. 'Ron...' he said thoughtfully. 'Are you the fella who spent time living in Spain?'

Nina coughed loudly, trying to warn her dad that he was heading into a conversation he really didn't want to have, but Ron saved any further embarrassment by cutting it short himself.

'I think I'm needed...' he said before rushing off.

'Dad!' Nina scolded.

'What?'

'Why did you bring that up?'

'I didn't think it was a secret,' he said mildly. 'I was just going to ask him whether he liked it there.'

'Well, it wasn't a secret exactly but it's a bit... awkward. You know, because his wife didn't come back with him...'

'Oh!' Winston said. 'I'd forgotten about that bit.'

She gave an exasperated shake of her head. If her dad was going to drop her in it whenever he met any of the people she'd been gossiping about, maybe she needed to stop feeding him so much gossip about what went on in Sparrow Street. However, any further thoughts on that subject were cut short by the arrival of Nasser.

'Oh, hello,' Nina said brightly. 'Haven't you managed to get a cup of tea yet?'

'No, and I'd love one,' he replied.

Nina poured some out while Nasser extended a hand in greeting to Winston. 'You must be Nina's dad.'

'That's me.'

'We do appreciate your help,' Nasser said warmly as they shook.

'Always happy to help.' Winston smiled. 'Though I'm not sure how useful any of my skills will be to you.'

Nina handed Nasser his tea. 'Don't worry, Dad,' she said, 'I'm sure we can find something you'll be good at.'

'The most important thing is that you're here,' Nasser said. 'Man-power and commitment, that's what we need more than anything else. We're not looking for experts, just willing hands.'

'I can certainly offer those,' Winston replied cheerfully. 'So when do we start work?'

'I'm hoping we'll be able to begin just as soon as we get the official go-ahead from the council. Peter's waiting for confirmation from his boss and he's going to let us know just as soon as that comes through.'

'Well, I'm sure he'll be in close contact throughout the process,' Winston said with a sly grin at Nina, who glanced across to see that Peter and Robyn now had their heads close together in earnest conversation. It looked as if everyone else in the room had been forgotten. While anyone not in full possession of the facts might have found it amusing, Nina wasn't quite so sure.

'It's good to have him on our side,' Nasser said. 'It certainly makes things more straightforward if all we've got to worry about is doing the work and not a battle to get the land in the first place.'

'But it's never going to be *our* land,' Nina reminded him.

'Of course. What I mean is that at least we'll be fairly safe to invest time and effort into making it nice without fear that someone will come two weeks later to bulldoze everything to the ground again.'

Let's hope so, Nina thought. There were no guarantees of anything in life. She hated the cynic in her and she wished she could stop thinking like that all the time, but she couldn't help it. While she tried hard to be optimistic and to see the best in everyone and every situation, sometimes the scars of her past made it harder than she'd like. But she didn't say so now, because what would be the point in infecting everyone else with her own doubts? Maybe this time would be the time that proved her wrong?

'I have to say it's been a very productive meeting,' Nasser continued. 'It just goes to show what can be achieved when the community pulls together. It's most gratifying. Even Ron came back and I didn't think he would after last time.'

'I suppose he must have had a change of heart,' Nina said.

'Good for him,' Nasser said. 'We can always do with an extra body.'

'Well, you've got mine for as long as you need it,' Winston said.

Nina smiled at him. 'Thanks, Dad.'

'We're very grateful.' Nasser nodded in agreement. Then his gaze ran over the assembled crowd, pockets of people chatting in different parts of the room, some drinking tea – only Ron stuffing cake into his mouth as if it might suddenly be outlawed – all together, here for one joint purpose, and he smiled. He looked like a man satisfied he'd already done a good job, no matter the outcome from here on in. Perhaps he had, Nina thought, because people had busy lives and were often wrapped so firmly in them that they were disinterested in anything that didn't directly affect them. It was good, if a little surprising, to see so many here today. In fact, she was certain there were more here today than there had been at the first meeting and that could only be a very good thing – it meant people had been enthused enough by the proposals to get their friends and family involved too.

Then Nasser clapped his hands together once, and the sound rang with a great sense of purpose.

'Right,' he announced, 'it's time we drew up some final plans to make all this talk a reality!'

There was a frustrating two weeks before work could start. The right people at the council had to be approached and persuaded that the project would benefit the community and wouldn't give anyone at the town hall a headache. Eventually, they got the go-ahead, but it had been a nail-biting and fraught couple of weeks while they waited on the decision.

Nina used the time to make plans for her remembrance lanterns and to help get the word out about their garden. She and Robyn put posters up at the local shops, doctors and dentists, playgroups and nurseries and local places of worship. Robyn tried the local newspaper too; they were only vaguely interested and didn't bother sending a reporter to cover the story, but they did allow them some free space to post a notice asking for support. Nasser had a contact at the community radio station and, though he asked her if she wanted to go on and talk about her remembrance project, Nina felt that he was far more eloquent and confident than her and he'd be better doing that himself. Nasser didn't necessarily agree, but they did agree to put the debate on hold until they'd had some kind of confirmation from the radio station that one of their presenters was interested enough to come and talk to any of them, regardless who ended up with the job. Robyn even sent a cheeky email to the regional television station. She was disappointed, though not entirely surprised, to get no reply. Nina was more philosophical than Robyn and Nasser when it came to that kind of indifference – she supposed that their little street project was pretty unimportant in the grand scheme of things, and very few people outside Sparrow Street, let alone Wrenwick, would be interested.

There had been some lively discussion over what the donation amount for dedicating a lantern ought to be too. Nina had said that she thought one pound was affordable to anyone and would encourage wider participation, whereas Robyn argued that a measly pound was ludicrous and they'd barely collect anything for their charities with that kind of donation. She'd wanted to ask for five pounds per dedication, and after some to-ing and fro-ing, they'd settled on a compromise of three.

Then they'd had to source the lanterns themselves. Nina and Robyn had scoured furniture and home improvement shops, but it wasn't as easy as they'd first supposed. The lanterns either weren't right, were too expensive, or the stock wasn't guaranteed. Eventually they'd found an online supplier where they could order batches as and when. The sample order had arrived – a delicate little storm lantern just big enough to hold a single candle – and both Nina and Robyn knew instantly they'd found the right ones.

So it was on a bright winter's morning that around a third of Sparrow Street's residents, along with a few of their friends, family and people from the neighbouring streets, gathered on the spare ground that would become their community space and garden of memories.

Nina yawned as she and her dad stood together waiting for everyone to arrive. When her alarm had gone off that morning she'd been very tempted to switch it off, turn over and go back to sleep. There was no way Robyn would have let her get away with that, though, and even Nina, tired as she was, wouldn't have been able to sleep through Robyn hammering at her front door to wake her up. So she'd got up and dressed, tipped a strong coffee down her throat and headed out. The morning was dull and grey and a brisk wind rattled down the street. It didn't feel like morning at all; it felt like night had refused to be shown the door.

'Keeping you up, are we?' Winston asked, cocking an eyebrow as Nina let out another yawn.

'Do you think anyone would miss me if I headed back home for another hour in bed?'

'Well I'm not covering for you, so on your own head be it if you get caught.'

Nina laughed. 'Thanks for nothing,'

'I have to say, I'm quite looking forward to getting started,' Winston said.

It was Nina's turn to cock a disbelieving eyebrow at him. 'Really?'

'Well, it makes a change from messing around with cars all day, doesn't it?'

'I thought you liked messing around with cars.'

'I do. I like chocolate too, but that doesn't mean I want to eat it morning, noon and night.'

'I could,' Nina said. 'I could eat chocolate in my sleep too. I could be in bed right now, dreaming about chocolate with a drip feeding chocolate directly into my arm.'

'It was your idea for us to do this,' Winston said.

'A girl can change her mind.'

'Not this girl or this time,' Winston said in a mock scolding tone.

Nina looked round to see a new arrival. 'Oh, Ron's here then.'

'You said he wouldn't come.'

'I thought he might not,' Nina said in a low voice. 'To be honest I thought it might do us a favour if he didn't. All he'll do is eat all the food and complain about everything. That's what he usually does anyway.'

'He's a charmer then?' Winston asked with a wry smile.

'Oh, absolutely,' Nina said with one of her own.

Their appraisal of Ron's usefulness or otherwise was interrupted by Robyn's voice. She'd arrived with Toby a few minutes earlier, both of them looking stony-faced and barely on speaking terms. Nina knew he'd got a day off college due to a broken boiler because Robyn had told her so on the phone the previous evening, and she'd also told Nina that she was going to bring him along to help rather than leave him in the house doing nothing all day. However, judging by the look of distaste on his face as he viewed the tangle of damp, mouldering weeds covering the spare ground, he'd almost certainly decided that sitting in a freezing cold classroom would have been preferable to this.

Nina could well imagine the conversation he and Robyn had had the previous evening and she supposed, knowing Robyn as she did, it would have been hard for Toby to say no when she'd asked him to come. They were speaking now, but neither of them seemed happy about it as Nina caught snatches of the low conversation.

'Stop moaning,' Robyn said tersely. 'It's a few weeds; anyone would think I'd asked you to go down a sewer or something.'

'It's going to take hours,' Toby whined. 'I've got stuff to do.'

'Like what?'

'Revision.'

'Don't make me laugh! You've never willingly revised for anything in your life! Besides, your mocks are weeks away; it won't kill you to take a morning off your hectic revision schedule.'

'Everyone here is really old,' Toby grumbled, at least having the decency to lower his voice as he uttered the insult.

'Don't be ridiculous. What, you think people over thirty speak Swahili or something? You can still talk to people who don't know what an emoji is; you won't explode or anything.'

'Can I just do the morning then?'

'So you can go and waste the rest of the day with that bunch of losers you call friends?'

'There's nothing wrong with them.'

'Maybe not to you there isn't. I can see plenty and I don't think you should spend so much time with them.'

'I don't. I'm always doing stuff like this with you.'

'This is the first time in years I've asked you to go somewhere with me!' Robyn gave him a pleading look now. 'Surely you can spare one day? For me? For something that's important to me and Nina? It's in memory of your dad too.'

At this, Toby looked suitably shamefaced. 'My jeans will be wrecked,' he said, clinging onto the argument, though Nina knew and, by the look on her face, so did Robyn, that he'd given in. Toby adored his dad and had been devastated when they'd lost him. Nina knew that one mention of him would have Toby bending to his mum's will whether he wanted to or not.

Robyn gave him a hug, which he returned stiffly and with a look of utter embarrassment.

'Just look at it as something character-building,' she said. 'And you'll be able to put it on your CV when you start applying for apprentice-ships or jobs.'

'What, I can say I managed to clear a load of shit from a scrap of ground?'

'Trust me, it's the sort of thing prospective employers will lap up. They'll think you're all public-spirited.'

Toby opened his mouth – probably to argue again – but everyone's attention was diverted to Nasser, who called the gathering to order.

'Can I just have a minute with you all?'

The crowd turned to face him and listened as he thanked them for coming and began to delegate tasks.

'Nina, Robyn and…'

'Toby,' Robyn supplied.

'Ah,' Nasser replied with a warm smile. 'Always happy to see new faces. Thank you for coming to help, Toby. Would you three be able to prune? The perimeter shrubs and bushes especially are very rangy and overgrown. You might want to pick up some thick gloves from the box by the gates over there.'

Nina and Robyn nodded, while Toby just looked at his cutting-edge trainers with some regret.

'Winston… it would be great if you could join forces with Kelly and do some painting. The shed for a start is showing quite a lot of exposed wood.'

'The shed might need a good clean first,' Winston said, looking across at the grubby building with some doubt.

'You could be right,' Kelly put in. 'No point in trying to paint over the grime.'

Nasser nodded. 'It's your project so do whatever you see fit. If you want to clear it out and clean it down, that's fine by me.'

'So we might not get to paint it today because it will need to dry out first,' Kelly said.

'Let's not worry about that now,' Nasser said. 'Rome wasn't built in a day and I'm sure we'll all be coming back again to do more on here anyway.'

There was a loud groan. Nina saw that it had come from Ron's direction. 'We're not building Rome.'

'It's a saying,' Robyn snapped. 'Surely even you've heard it before.'

'Ron and Mitch…' Nasser turned to the two men now, holding up a conciliatory hand to smooth any budding animosity between Ron and Robyn, who seemed to raise each other's hackles on sight. 'Could you work together?'

Ron looked at Mitch, and Mitch – a man in his sixties who lived at the very end of Sparrow Street and whom Nina didn't know all that well – looked at Ron. They both wore the expressions of two men who would rather do anything than work together. But they were both stocky and well-built and it was no surprise when Nasser went on to ask them to ferry the wheelbarrows of rubbish and garden waste to a waiting skip.

Nasser then went on to delegate further tasks to various groups of people. Most were fairly happy to let him do this, although some tried to interfere or assert their own authority, and some just downright complained. But he was a tenacious and firm leader, and eventually everyone fell into line.

There was a lot of chat and excitement as they began, but it didn't take long for the mood to sober as the reality of the work hit them. It was backbreaking and often boring, and it was only a sense of camaraderie and optimism for the nicer bits of the transformation that would follow that kept everyone going. Toby did as little as it was possible to get away with, gingerly lifting the odd solitary branch here and there and snipping it delicately before taking a leisurely walk to the nearest wheelbarrow and tossing it in. Robyn didn't chastise him, though; she only snorted with laughter every now and again, throwing Nina an amused look.

'He's here,' she said as he took his third stick to the rubbish pile. 'I don't suppose I can expect more than that.'

'I can't say I blame him if I'm honest,' Nina replied with a wry smile. 'I sort of feel that way about it myself. Promising to do this stuff is one thing but doing it is quite another.'

'Yeah, I can't say I wouldn't rather be having a spa day. Still, it'll be good when it's finished.'

'I hope so,' Nina said. 'But next time I go to a community meeting full of bright ideas about doing up a garden, please feel free to slap some sense into me.'

Robyn laughed. 'It would be my pleasure.'

By the time everyone had agreed to stop for a lunch break roughly half the area had been cleared. It now lay waiting, soil turned to expose debris that needed to be sifted from the surface, already beginning to look like an exciting blank canvas. Nasser had ordered new topsoil and that was due to arrive at the end of the week, giving them a clear deadline to work to, and which had been paid for by way of what Robyn referred to as a '*quick whip-round*'. They had plants to follow that had been paid for in the same way and everyone had given generously. Although Nina had expected people to get behind the project, she'd been seriously taken aback by the amount of their own money people were happy to put in.

Lunch had been organised in much the same way as the work they'd gathered to undertake. Every day throughout the duration of the project, it had been agreed that different neighbours would take it in turns to provide bits of the meal that everyone who was working that day would share. Today, Martha and Ada had made more of their generally inedible cake, labouring under the misapprehension that people's polite comments about their baking meant they actually liked it. Judging by the decoration, it was some kind of almond sponge, though it was anyone's guess really. It lay suspiciously untouched for the most part – as it often did – though, just as always, the sisters hardly seemed to register that this might say more about the cake than people's well-meant white lies did. Kelly had baked sausage rolls and mini vegetable pies that were going down rather better, and Nasser's wife Yasmin had provided flasks of divinely spiced vegetable soup. Nina and her dad had got up early and made piles of sandwiches together – perhaps the laziest option – but people seemed happy to eat them anyway.

Everyone sat together now on walls, upturned crates, folding chairs, boxes, car bonnets… wherever they could get comfy to share the meal. Despite all his complaints, even Ron had managed to break a sweat and sat heavily now, panting as he twisted open a flask of soup and poured himself a mug. Many had expressed quiet surprise to see him there at all.

Nina felt good and happy as she ate, sitting in between Winston and Robyn while Toby had taken himself off to the nearest fast-food restaurant to spend an hour with some friends. Robyn had warned him that he had to come back for the afternoon session, though even she had conceded now that it wouldn't surprise her all that much if he didn't.

'This soup is amazing!' she said, taking a sip. 'I wonder if Nasser's wife can give me the recipe.'

'I've got a feeling she probably makes it up as she goes along,' Nina said. 'She's that sort of cook, you know? Just knows how to put things together and make them taste wonderful.'

'I'll ask her for some pointers anyway,' Robyn said. 'Honestly, Toby doesn't know what he's missing.'

'There's probably too high a risk of vegetables in there for him to risk it,' Nina said.

Winston and Robyn both chuckled.

'I'm sure he'll enjoy his cheeseburger,' Winston said.

'He'd enjoy this soup if he gave it a chance,' Robyn said.

'Probably, but it would be too uncool to admit it,' Winston replied cheerily. 'I was a young man once and I remember that pressure to look for peer approval well.'

'Did they have cheeseburgers in the Middle Ages then, Dad?' Nina asked.

Winston laughed. 'Cheeky madam!'

Nina turned to Robyn, munching on a tuna sandwich. 'I'm amazed you got Toby to come.'

'He didn't have much choice; it's part of his punishment,' Robyn replied with a dark look.

'Punishment?'

Robyn let out a heavy sigh. 'I don't know what's got into him lately. The slightest thing seems to set him off. Apparently, he lost it over a seat in the college canteen last week and tried to beat the crap out of another lad. I imagine the other lad was just as bad – both determined to square up to each other and then neither wanting to lose face – but... well, that's just not Toby; at least it didn't used to be. I have to wonder... when Eric died I thought at first we'd get through it together and it seemed like we were. Toby was just... well, he didn't seem to be that affected, apart from missing his dad like crazy. There must have been something going on in his head, though, something he wasn't letting anyone see. Now, as he gets older, I'm beginning to wonder if the lack of a father figure is becoming a problem for him. And I think maybe he's always carried issues relating to Eric's death, more than anyone realised.'

'You think maybe it's just taken a little while for this to start showing itself?' Nina asked. She hadn't had anyone else to think about when Gray died. It was just her and her grief that she'd had to deal with. Of course, his family had her support, but they had lots of other support too and it didn't really matter whether the quality of what she was able to offer was good enough or not.

But Robyn had Toby and Toby only had Robyn. Would Nina have managed any better in the same situation? Would she have been able to deal with the extra burden? It had been tough enough to deal with her own grief, let alone that of a child who was relying on her, a child who looked to the one parent he had left to show him the way, to make life better for him again. She and Gray had always imagined they had plenty of time for children, but then his diagnosis came and all that had changed. They'd talked about trying for a family before he got too ill, and the doctors had gone through alternatives with them like freezing sperm, but in the end, Nina had wanted to focus on him. She hadn't wanted another thing to worry about, to be disappointed about if it didn't work, to make Gray feel like a failure if she didn't get pregnant. And, if she was honest, she'd been selfish. She had wanted it to be just her and him, until the end; she hadn't wanted another human demanding their attention, getting in the way. Often, she regretted that decision now, because at least if they'd had a child she'd have had some part of him with her, but it was too late for regrets, no matter how keenly she might feel them.

Robyn nodded. 'I just don't know what to do about it. He's a good boy but I feel as if that good boy is slipping away and I don't know how to stop it from happening.'

As Robyn shared her concerns, Winston chewed thoughtfully on a sausage roll. He hardly looked to be listening, his gaze on a bank of heavy cloud rolling across the rooftops. But then he spoke.

'Does he have a job yet?'

'He doesn't have a lot of time with his college work,' Robyn said, sounding a bit confused by the question. 'I know a lot of his friends have part-time work as well but…'

'Do you think he'd want one?' Winston asked.

'I expect he'd appreciate the extra money,' Robyn said. 'There's not much around, though, is there? And what there is pays terribly for lads of his age. I don't think he ought to worry about it just now – he needs to concentrate on his college work.'

'It doesn't sound as if he's really doing that at the moment,' Nina said gently.

'Well, no, but... as soon as we get over this hump he'll be OK, I'm sure.'

'What does he want to do after college?' Winston asked.

'I don't think he really knows.' Robyn reached for a sandwich from Nina's plate.

'Maybe if he worked, he might start to discover what he likes and what he doesn't,' Winston said. 'It might focus his mind a bit too.'

Robyn bit into her sandwich. 'I suppose it might. At least, I expect it couldn't make things any worse, and it might do him good to mix with people other than the gang he hangs out with at college. I mean, they're OK but they're not exactly future prime ministers or anything. I think Toby is bright and he can do better but he's not going to while he's keeping that company. I suppose it might help him grow up a bit to work.'

Winston nodded slowly, his gaze still on the looming cloud. 'How does he feel about cars?'

'Cars?' Robyn repeated blankly. 'He can't drive yet – couldn't afford the lessons for a start...'

'But would it be an area of interest?'

'I suppose he's as interested as the next boy,' Robyn said. 'Why do you ask?'

'I was just thinking I could do with some help,' Winston said. 'If he's interested, that is. It wouldn't pay much and it would be on a very casual basis, but I'd give him a good education and those sorts of skills are always handy to have.'

'They certainly are, if only to save money on future garage bills,' Robyn said with a smile. 'I suppose I could ask him, see what he thinks.'

Nina looked at her dad with a small smile of her own. He didn't really need help renovating his cars and he certainly didn't have a lot of spare cash to pay an assistant. She recognised one of his finest qualities at play now. Nina's dad saw a young life in peril, a future hanging in the balance, and he wanted to help steer it the right way, to help save it if he could.

'Thank you,' Robyn said. 'I can't promise he'll say yes, but I think it's a brilliant idea and I'll certainly work on him.'

'There's no pressure, of course,' Winston said. 'If he's interested I'd be glad to have him, but if it's not for him I completely understand.'

'As far as I'm concerned any lifeline is gratefully accepted,' Robyn said firmly. 'I really appreciate the offer whether he takes it or not – though if he says no we'll be having words…'

'It's pointless making him do what he's not interested in,' Winston said. 'See how the land lies. The offer's always open even if he says no and then changes his mind later.'

'Well…' Robyn looked at her watch. 'He ought to be back in the next ten minutes so if we get a quiet moment I'll ask him about it.'

Winston nodded his agreement. Nina smiled at him, her heart bursting with pride. The world was full of unsung heroes and, right now, there was no bigger one in her eyes than Winston Alder.

Chapter Seven

It was mid-afternoon when the sky turned leaden and the rain began to lash down. The volunteers rushed to collect up equipment and belongings that might get damaged in the downpour and then dashed for shelter in the nearest open house where they could chat and wait for the weather to improve. Even though their own homes were only feet away, it seemed almost everyone was enjoying the novelty of working closely with people they didn't see all that often too much to give it up just yet. That house happened to belong to Ada and Martha. For their part, they were thrilled to suddenly find themselves so important and useful.

'Come in,' Ada beckoned, 'come through to the kitchen.'

'Yes,' Martha chimed in. 'Come to the kitchen. We can have a cup of tea.'

'Tea will get us warmed up,' Ada said.

'Yes,' Martha agreed, 'tea would warm us up.'

There was a silent, collective sigh of relief. Tea everyone could handle, just as long as they weren't forced to eat some of the sisters' dreadful cake.

Ada and Martha didn't get a lot in the way of visitors and so they only had four chairs in a compact kitchen that, like elsewhere in the house, sported an alarming collection of puppy posters. These ones, however, were stuck on the walls with Blu Tack, some curled at the corners from cooking steam, some faded from the sunlight coming in the south-facing window. Nina suspected that if any of them were taken down there would be a perfectly stencilled rectangle of darker wall behind them.

There were a lot more than four people in that kitchen now, so almost everyone stood around while the sisters dashed about trying to find enough cups. They didn't have enough of those either in the end, so Kelly went to collect some from her house to make up the shortfall. Some people said they'd prefer coffee, which sent poor Ada and Martha into a tizzy because they didn't buy it, and so Kelly went back to her house to pick up a jar of that too.

While she was gone, Nina and Robyn took drink orders. Nina glanced across the kitchen to see Toby hoisting himself up onto a worktop to sit, legs dangling forlornly and looking very much like a fish out of water. Working alongside a bunch of adults he didn't know was one thing, but having tea with them in a tiny, slightly unnerving kitchen was quite another. He looked as if he'd have preferred to take his chances out in the rain, though it was testament to the effort he was making that he'd come back from his lunch at the burger bar at all.

Nina couldn't help but reflect, as she watched him look around the room, just how like his dad he was. The same chestnut hair, same deep brown eyes, the same freckles shading his nose. Every time she saw Toby he looked more like Eric, and Nina mused that the same thoughts must have occurred to Robyn.

Given what she knew about their complicated marriage, Nina wondered how Robyn handled that. It must have been a source of conflict to have such a strong, physical reminder of Eric in her house every day, to love him so much when her love for his father had been so much more uncertain and complicated. But whereas Eric had been rock solid, a man who knew exactly who he was and what he wanted, Toby was like a lost soul – it was plain to see for anyone who cared to look long enough.

It was hardly surprising, though, when you considered what a tough childhood he must have had. Nina nursing Gray as his wife had been hard enough; she couldn't imagine how it must have been to be a young boy growing up in a house filled with Eric's illness, where every decision and every thought had to be for him before anything else, where the constant fear of the inevitable must have been utterly overwhelming for his young brain.

She went back to her order list, and when she looked again she saw that her dad had struck up a conversation with him. At least, it was a conversation of sorts because there was definitely more effort on Winston's part than there was on Toby's, who simply pulled his cap down firmly onto his head, looking as if he would rather be anywhere else than this crowded kitchen.

'I have to admit to being a bit worried that he'll be too much for your dad.'

Nina turned to see that Robyn was now following Winston and Toby's awkward interaction too.

'He wouldn't have made the offer if he didn't think he could handle it,' Nina said. 'He wants to help and he thinks he can see a way to do that.'

'I know. I think he could help too, but the risk of it all backfiring worries me. I'd hate to think of Toby upsetting or hurting your lovely dad.'

'Dad'll be alright. You can bet he'll be ready for any scenario – he knows how to handle more than you might think.'

Robyn nodded thoughtfully, her gaze still trained on her son across the room, who was now staring at his feet as Winston chatted. 'If your dad says to you at any point that Toby's visits are too much, or that he's finding it hard work to communicate with him, you must tell me. I'd hate to think of him struggling.'

'I will; you don't have to worry about that. So you think Toby will say yes to Dad's offer?'

'I'm not going to give him a choice. I've decided anything that gives him less time to hang around with that gang of wasters he calls friends is OK with me. Not only that but he'll be learning new skills and making a bit of money too. It's a no-brainer really, isn't it?'

'You never know, it might be the money that sways him in the end,' Nina said. 'I bet he'd like to have a bit of his own so he doesn't have to keep coming to you.'

'That's true.' Robyn looked at her now, and in her eyes, Nina saw hope mixed with a pervading, lingering despair that made her heart ache for her friend. Robyn had already lost her husband – was she afraid now that she might lose her son too? Was she afraid that no matter what she did – what anyone did – she'd lose him anyway? 'He needs a good male role model,' she continued. 'I do my best with him but he needs what Eric would have been able to give him.'

'You do a fantastic job,' Nina said. 'Nobody could argue with that.'

'Oh, I can take care of his everyday needs. But sometimes I think he needs a man to talk to, someone to tell things that he doesn't feel he can tell me.'

'I think my dad might know that.'

'He's a smart bloke.'

'He is. I think he and Toby will get along. Although Toby might not be so keen on his music choices,' Nina added with a smile.

'Good!' Robyn said. 'Anyone who can turn him off that awful rap onto something with a tune should receive a knighthood as far as I'm concerned.'

'Even if it's naff old rock music?'

Robyn grinned. 'There's nothing wrong with a bit of Black Sabbath. If Toby comes in wanting to bite the head off a bat, I'll consider his musical education a job well done.'

Nasser came over to them then, phone in hand. He turned it to show Nina a weather forecast on the screen.

'I think we might have to call it a day. It's annoying but it looks as if this rain is here to stay.'

'People will be disappointed not to have made more progress,' Nina replied, frowning at the phone. 'Plus a lot of people can't make it again tomorrow – many took time off work especially.'

'I realise that, but it's not really practical to carry on working in such heavy rain – all we're doing is creating a mud bath.'

Nina looked at Robyn.

'He's right,' she said flatly.

Nina gave a reluctant nod. 'I don't suppose anyone would thank us for ruining their shoes and clothes.'

'Or for pneumonia,' Robyn added.

'Perhaps we can use the time to do other things?' Nasser suggested. 'As we're all here together anyway.'

'Like what?'

'Like help you design the campaign for the charity lanterns? The more input the better, I'd have thought.'

'Yes, I suppose we could do that,' Nina agreed, feeling happier already. 'If Ada and Martha are happy to let us use their kitchen for a while longer then anyone who wants to stay to help can, while anyone who'd rather call it a day is free to go home with our thanks.'

'Excellent!' Nasser said. 'I'll go and have a word with them now.'

It had been Nasser's idea to invite the local radio DJ to come and cut the ribbon and declare the garden open. Nobody had really expected Sammy Star – the gravelled voice of Wrenwick Community Radio – to say yes but they'd all agreed that it would be nice to mark the occasion with something memorable after they'd all worked so hard to get it finished in what had been really a very short space of time. People had pitched in for odd hours here and there, when they'd been able to get away from work and family commitments, while Nina (who, having had no luck on the job front, hadn't a lot else to do) had done her best to be there as often as possible as a sort of deputy foreman/coordinator when Nasser hadn't been able to due to commitments of his own. In fact, she'd really quite enjoyed it because it had made her feel more useful than she had in a long time. A part of her was actually sad once the garden was finished.

Sammy Star was there now, cutting the ribbon as Nina and almost all of Sparrow Street looked on. They'd attracted a good crowd from the surrounding area too, perhaps intrigued by the promise of an up-close-and-personal event with a local celebrity.

'He looks nothing like you expect him to, does he?' Robyn whispered in Nina's ear. 'He sounds like sex on a stick when you listen to him on the radio, but in real life he just looks like a stick.'

Nina giggled.

'And the eighties called,' Robyn added. 'They want their mullet back.'

There was a polite ripple of applause as Sammy declared the garden open, and then almost immediately people began to drift away. Nina had to admit that their modest little plot was hardly the most exciting thing to happen to Wrenwick but she'd expected a little more enthusiasm than that. She was proud of what they'd achieved with few resources and even fewer funds, and she was sure that the team of residents, and perhaps others, could at least stop and appreciate that for a minute or two. But it seemed people had better things to do and had lost interest now that Sammy had done his bit.

'Nina!' Nasser waved her over to where he now stood with the DJ. 'Come and meet Sammy – you too, Robyn!'

Nina glanced at Robyn, biting back a grin. It looked as if they were about to get up close and personal with Robyn's favourite stick.

'Nasser tells me you two are the brains behind the charity aspect of the garden,' Sammy said in a rumbling voice that sounded as if it couldn't possibly have come from such a lanky frame. It was like hearing the voice of Pavarotti coming from Mickey Mouse.

'Well, it's not all us…' Nina began. Nasser waved away her modesty.

'Take some credit where it's due,' he said. 'You two have worked hard on it.'

'What made you want to do something like that?' Sammy asked.

'We both lost our husbands to motor neurone disease,' Robyn said. 'Originally, we wanted to raise money for the Sacred Heart Hospice who helped us through it, and that's how it really started. Then we realised that there would be a lot of people who were missing loved ones from all sorts of diseases and tragedies, and we thought perhaps we could help the organisations that they'd turned to as well.'

'There's no master plan,' Nina said. 'Just a simple donation in return for a lantern on the big fir tree dedicated to a lost loved one. All the money we collect will go to a variety of good causes we've approved with our residents' association.'

Sammy nodded sagely. Nina found herself distracted by his hairline. Surely it couldn't be that black and that even on a man of his obviously advanced years?

'Maybe you'd like to come on my show and talk about it?' he asked.

'Really?' Nina looked at Robyn, who grinned.

'We'd love to!' Robyn said, but Nina wasn't so sure. Still, she supposed, if they went on the show together then at least she could feel safe that Robyn – naturally more outgoing than her – would do most of the talking anyway. Perhaps it wouldn't be so bad and it would certainly help get the word out about their fundraising.

'Fantastic,' he said. His gaze wandered to the garden. 'Is there any more to do here or…? I mean, it's very nice.'

'We're pretty much done,' Nina said.

'Oh.' Sammy looked unconvinced and Nina could understand why. They'd managed to tidy the land up and put a few plants in, but even she couldn't deny it had hardly lived up to the ambitious plans they'd started out with. But nobody had banked on going over budget so quickly, and once they'd used the money from their own pockets they had found it tough to raise more from anywhere else. It was close to Christmas and people had enough to worry about, so the collective decision had been taken to do the best they could with what they had and to leave it at that until they could look at raising more sometime in the new year. Which had meant no landscaping, no ornamental fountain and no fencing. But Nina still thought it looked pretty with its neat flower beds and borders, and even though it was perhaps a bit barren now, it would be filled with colour once the bulbs they'd planted came out in the spring. There were overhanging trees and secret corners, bird boxes and feeders, little insect hotels put in for the children to wonder at during the summer and colourful wooden benches for their parents to sit and watch. Smooth paths ran through it and beneath one of the larger trees was a rope swing. It wasn't going to win any prizes for garden design, but it was theirs – a little oasis of peace created by the community she loved, a little bit of heaven for them to share.

'So when do you want us to come down to the station?' Robyn asked.

'How about Wednesday?' Sammy said. 'I've got a slot around ten – the head of Wrenwick Primary was supposed to bring his Year Six choir in to sing for us but the whole ruddy lot of them have gone down with chicken pox.'

'Oooh, that's great!' Robyn said. 'Not about the chicken pox,' she added hastily, 'my Toby had that when he was three... he was a miserable little sod with it.'

She looked at Nina for approval. Nina nodded. With no sign of a job interview despite the dozen or so CVs she'd sent off, it wasn't like she'd anything better to do.

'I'll see you then,' Sammy said, beaming at them.

'You will,' Robyn said, grinning back at him. 'Thanks so much!'

Sammy bid goodbye to them with a last megawatt smile and went back to talk to Nasser. He was having a word with Peter, who'd taken some time out from the office to be there. When Nina looked at Robyn, she caught a wistful look as she watched Sammy greet them.

'You really like him, don't you?'

'What?' Robyn turned to her. 'Sammy?'

'No.' Nina laughed. '*Peter*. So what's going on with you two?'

'I like him but it's not that simple.' Robyn's shoulders seemed to slump. 'He told me his wife is still living at his house.'

Nina stared at her. 'Still? But I thought... Wasn't that the issue when you broke up last time?'

'Yes – the only one really. If not for that...'

'Hasn't it occurred to him that he really ought to do something about it then? They've definitely split up?'

'Ages ago – well before I went out with him.'

'Has he divorced her?'

'Not yet.'

'You think he doesn't want to?'

'No. I know he does – at least he says so.'

'It's a strange way to go about things.'

'He says they're definitely separated even though they live in the same house. He says the only reason they're both still there is because neither of them has enough money to get somewhere else. I get it, but it's just too weird for me to think of them living together, even if what he says is true and they're not in the same bed at night. I think he was hoping we'd…'

'And I think maybe you were too.'

Robyn nodded. 'But I couldn't get my head around his living arrangements last time and I'm no better at it this time.'

'You should have told me. I can't believe you've been bottling this up when you could have talked to me.'

Robyn shrugged. 'I suppose I felt stupid.'

'God, of course you're not!'

'Well,' Robyn said ruefully, 'you did try to warn me where this might go if I got in touch with him again.'

'And I also know that you did it with the best intentions. So, what now?'

'We're off again. I've told him that's it this time unless his domestic situation changes.'

'I'm sorry,' Nina said. 'And you don't want to give it a go at all?'

'What's the point? A relationship that starts off on this footing is hardly going places, is it? So this is me, back to being single and ready to mingle again. Not that my mingling pool is very big these days.'

Nina glanced across at the three men, chatting amiably, and she caught Peter look their way with an expression full of thinly veiled regret, almost as wistful as the one Robyn had sent in his direction.

It was clear they liked each other, but Nina didn't know what anyone could do about it now. Robyn had made her decision and, in the circumstances, perhaps it was for the best that it had come from her head and not her heart.

'Still,' Nina said. 'At least he's helped with all this. I mean, he stuck his neck on the line at that finance meeting to put a stop to plans to sell the land and we ought to be grateful for that. And he's taken the task of finding other ways to cut costs and balance the books and he didn't have to make more work for himself like that. He did that for us....' Nina paused. 'I daresay he did it for *you*...'

'He did,' Robyn said. 'I want to believe he's a good bloke and he's being straight with me, but it's hard, you know?'

'For what it's worth, he seems honest enough to me. And don't forget' – Nina nudged Robyn playfully, hoping to lift the mood a little – 'your intentions weren't completely honourable at the start.'

'They were very honourable,' Robyn said with a little laugh that showed Nina was getting somewhere. 'They were for a very good cause.'

'Charity.' Nina nodded.

'Well, yes. And for a chance to stick it to the man!'

Peter looked across again with a small, sad smile. Robyn didn't flinch and she tucked away whatever emotions she might have been feeling so that she looked perfectly calm and carefree. It made Nina sad to see. She'd honestly always thought Robyn and Peter looked like a good match and it was a shame to see that things would never work out for them. But she could also see why his home situation might make Robyn nervous, particularly as, for whatever reasons, he hadn't been straight with her from the start about it.

Sammy bid Nasser and Peter goodbye and walked back to the Mercedes he'd parked at the kerb. Peter said something to Nasser and then turned, as if he might come and talk to Robyn and Nina. But Robyn didn't give him the chance. She simply walked away. Poor Peter, already on the way over, had no choice but to come to Nina anyway and make awkward small talk.

He was a slight man, not much taller than Robyn, who was no giantess. He carried a little extra weight too, but his dark eyes were kind and sincere and they crinkled into a nervous smile as Nina greeted him. If he'd wanted to run after Robyn, it seemed he had enough of a sense of decorum not to.

'It's been a long day,' Nina said, indicating that she was talking about Robyn by a little flick of her head in the direction her friend had just taken. 'Emotional – you know?'

'For both of you, I would imagine,' he replied earnestly. 'Robyn told me you lost your husband too – this must mean a lot to you.'

'Yes.'

Peter shoved his hands in his pockets and looked to the garden. 'It's a nice thing to do in his memory.'

'Well, it's not just about that, but, yes… We're both very grateful for your help. Everyone is.'

Peter waved away the thanks. And then he looked to Robyn's retreating figure, perhaps wondering if she might come back to join them if he waited a while. But after a few moments, during which she showed no indication that she was going to return, he looked at Nina.

'Good luck with the fundraising,' he said.

'Thanks.'

He nodded, and then left her to walk back to his own car.

Poor Robyn, Nina thought. Poor Peter too, for that matter. If dating was going to be this complicated for her second time around, Nina was glad she'd decided long ago that she just wasn't going to bother.

Chapter Eight

'Don't you dare tell him that you think five pounds is a lot of money,' Robyn warned. 'We don't make apology for it and we don't make it sound like a rip-off – we say it steadily and proudly and we expect people to give it gladly. It's for a bloody good cause after all.'

'I wasn't going to,' Nina said with a hint of reproach in her voice.

'I know you. It'll come out without you realising it. Five pounds is a perfectly reasonable donation, and folks can cough up if they want to or not if they don't – it's a free choice and you don't need to get a guilt trip over it.'

'I thought we'd agreed on three. You've gone with five all of a sudden and you could have at least run it by me before we got here today.'

'Because I had time to think about it and three is just ridiculous for all the work we've put in. If I'd told you, you'd have tried to argue the toss.'

'I would – it's almost Christmas for a start.'

'What's that got to do with anything?'

'People are short of money for anything but Christmas things.'

'Bollocks! Anyway, isn't Christmas supposed to be about charity?'

'No, it's supposed to be about drinking and eating and getting into debt buying presents you can't afford.'

Robyn grinned. 'They can bloody well cut back and give us the money instead. Their Uncle Alf doesn't need soap on a rope or dodgy aftershave from the market – he's probably got a cupboard full from all the other years he got it and never used it.'

Nina turned back to the window with a faint smile. Outside on the road, the traffic roared past under a grey sky. She and Robyn were sitting in the reception of Wrenwick Community Radio. It was hardly Broadcasting House, but they weren't going to let Sammy and his eager local listeners go without making some money out of them. At least, money for their charities. Nina's stomach still churned, though. She wasn't comfortable with this situation at all, but as long as Robyn took up the slack, she might get away with a few grunts of agreement in the right places. Nobody who knew them both could deny that Robyn was the talker anyway.

'And we're both happy with the twenty-third of December for the grand unveiling?'

'Do you think it's too close to Christmas?' Nina asked vaguely, her gaze still on the window. 'I mean, I know we agreed it but…'

'I think it means people are more likely to be charitable because they'll be full of festive spirit.'

'I suppose so…'

The next time she took her eyes from the window it was to see that Sammy was coming out of a side door to greet them. Nina and Robyn stood up.

He smiled. 'Ladies!'

His hair looked blacker and more solid than ever, as if someone had covered his head with tyre rubber. Nina wished she could stop staring at it and she hoped he wouldn't notice because she really didn't think that she could.

'Thank you for coming,' he continued.

'We should be thanking you for letting us,' Robyn said. 'It'll really help our campaign.'

'Let's hope so, eh?' Sammy said in his rumbling voice. 'If it helps in any small way then I'll be very happy to offer the slot. Come on through to the studio and we'll get set up. Have you ever done anything like this before?'

'Never,' Robyn said.

Sammy looked at Nina.

'I've never even been inside a radio station,' Nina said.

'Well that's good!' Sammy said with a laugh. 'It means you won't notice how bad I am at this stuff!'

'Oh, I'm sure that's not true,' Robyn said, laughing too. 'But, yeah, at least we wouldn't know the difference.'

Despite having no experience of the inside of a radio station, Nina was still surprised by the lack of sophistication in the studio when Sammy led them in. She'd expected swish décor and gleaming equipment, but what she found was headphones held together by sticky tape, swivel chairs with the stuffing spilling out of them, filing cabinets with broken handles and a line of dirty mugs that looked as if they might not have been washed for quite a few shows. There was a distinct smell of damp too, and a bucket at the corner of the room hinted at frequent leaks when there was wet weather.

'If you two would like to park your lovely selves behind that desk there…' Sammy said, directing them to the right place, 'I'll get my bit set up and then we might just have time for a quick coffee before the show starts. Can I offer you one? It's only instant, I'm afraid – we have a kettle at the end of the hall but that's about it.'

Nina's involuntary glance went to the discarded mugs on another desk. She guessed Robyn's had too as they both politely declined the offer.

'No worries,' Sammy said cheerfully, clearly not noticing anything amiss. 'Make yourselves comfortable here. I've got one or two things to check before we start.'

'So we can talk?' Nina asked.

'I was rather hoping that you would,' Sammy said with a laugh.

'I mean while you're doing whatever you're doing,' she replied. 'We won't be out on air or anything if we chat here next to the microphone?'

'Oh – no, of course not! I'll let you know when you're on air but, for now, nobody will be able to hear you outside this room so chat away!'

Sammy went to a bank of computers and a desk covered in buttons and started to tinker. Robyn looked at Nina.

'How are you doing there?' she whispered.

'A bit nervous. You?'

'I'm OK. It'll be fine, you know. There's literally going to be about twenty people listening. And it's not like he's interrogating us, is it?'

'So what's that great big lamp he's pointing at us now?' Nina asked. Robyn grinned.

'See – you can't be that scared if you can still crack jokes.'

'I'm not scared – I can just think of lots of other things I'd rather be doing. Like having teeth drilled… without anaesthetic.'

'Right, ladies!' Sammy clapped his hands together. 'Me and the team are ready for you!'

'Team?' Nina asked, looking around the studio containing just the three of them. Sammy cocked his head at a lucky waving cat, its golden paw steadily beating back and forth.

'Jackie's my right-hand man – gives me plenty of moral support when I need it.'

Robyn laughed. 'Jackie?'

'Jackie Chan… the actor? I got him in Hong Kong so it seemed only fitting for a name.'

Sammy donned a set of headphones and instructed Nina and Robyn to do the same with two sets he'd placed in front of them, then pressed a button to play the opening jingle of his show. Nina's stomach was doing somersaults but she looked across at Robyn, who was rock solid and calm, and she instantly felt better. Robyn had her back, as she always did, and Nina suddenly felt silly for being worried at all.

'Good morning!' Sammy purred as the jingle came to an end. 'You're listening to Sammy Star on Wrenwick Community Radio. With me this morning I have Robyn Brassington and Nina Munro, two lovely ladies who've popped in to tell us about a fundraising project they're involved with. But before we do that we'll have a tune. How about this classic from the eighties – the best decade ever invented – "Money's Too Tight (to Mention)" by the awesome Simply Red…'

'Fitting track,' Robyn said as he turned off the mic and put the record on air.

Sammy was quickly flicking through some notes and he looked up at her. 'Sorry?'

'Money too tight to mention,' she said. 'Fitting when we're talking about raising money.'

'Oh… yes, right…'

Nina and Robyn exchanged a look of confusion. He'd gone from incredibly friendly to incredibly vague. He looked down at his notes. Had one of them said something wrong, something to offend him? Nina could hardly imagine what in the few minutes since they'd gone on air.

'Is there anything we can't say?' Robyn asked.

'What?' Sammy looked up.

'You know, things we have to be careful about because we're on the radio? Things we're not supposed to talk about?'

'No… um… the sponsors… you know…'

Sammy stopped and his gaze went slack for a moment. Nina couldn't pinpoint just what had changed, but whatever it was had been sudden and swift. She glanced across at Robyn and could see that she'd noticed something too.

'Is everything alright?' Robyn asked. Sammy just stared at her. And in front of their eyes he seemed to turn grey. He began to sweat – it ran down his face – and then he clutched at his arm, his eyes bulging.

Nina shot up from her seat. 'Sammy!'

'Holy shit!' Robyn cried. 'Nina – do something!'

'What?'

'I don't know!'

'Sammy…' Nina called, her voice filled with panic now. 'Sammy, what's wrong?'

There was no time to wait for a reply. In the next second he began to slide sideways from his chair. Nina raced around the desk to catch him. He was solid and heavy as a felled tree and he was struggling to breathe.

'Call an ambulance!' Nina cried. 'I think he's having a heart attack!'

Chapter Nine

Nina closed the front door and locked it behind her. She leant against it and looked around her silent hallway with a sigh of relief. It didn't matter who called or knocked on her door or what they wanted, because she wasn't answering tonight. She was exhausted – physically and emotionally – and she needed time to collect her thoughts and restore her energy.

Kicking off her shoes, she let them tumble into a corner of the hallway before shrugging off her coat and hanging it on the balustrade, and then, with a weary sigh, she went to the kitchen to find the half-bottle of brandy that had been stuffed in the back of the cupboard since before Gray had died. It had been that kind of a day and, if she'd thought her life had become boring in the two years since she'd found herself living alone, today had made her realise that perhaps she ought to be careful what she wished for. If the day she'd had counted for excitement then she'd take boring any time. It was the sort of day that, once upon a time, she'd have told Gray all about, and he'd have smiled and told her how amazing she'd been, and they'd have snuggled together on the sofa where she'd have felt safe and cared for in his arms, where she'd have been able to forget all the stresses that had gone before.

The kitchen was cold – the heating had been on for a good hour or so but it didn't seem to have made much of an impact. Perhaps she was just feeling it because she was so tired and drained. She could turn up the thermostat, but a fluffy jumper and enough brandy would probably do the same job eventually.

Locating the bottle and blowing off the dust, she poured a measure into a mug. In the past she'd have mixed it with lemonade but she didn't have any and desperate times, as the saying went, called for desperate measures. She had no doubt that this was just the sort of desperate time the saying was referring to. She knocked it back and then slammed the mug onto the counter before closing her eyes for a moment while the alcohol worked its magic.

As the warmth spread through her she opened them again and took a deep breath before reaching for the bottle and a second helping.

Sammy was in a critical condition, but he was alive and things looked hopeful for his recovery. Nina didn't dare dwell on the idea that it might have turned out so differently but the events of the day had shaken her badly anyway. It was one thing to have nursed a husband, to have watched him slip gradually away, but quite another to witness an event so violent and sudden, one that could have killed Sammy almost instantly and certainly if he'd been there alone. Luckily the ambulance response was quick and it was they – not Nina and Robyn, as the crew had tried to insist – who'd saved him. They'd rushed Sammy off to the hospital and, after a brief discussion, Robyn and Nina had followed in Robyn's car. They had no idea whether a broadcast of any kind had gone out in his absence – there was really only a skeleton staff on duty at the station, which hadn't seemed to include a cover DJ, so they'd had to assume not. But even if the airtime had been filled with silence, Nina was quite sure that the residents of Wrenwick would survive somehow.

Taking the second mug of brandy to the living room, Nina pulled a throw from the corner of the sofa and climbed beneath it. A hard lump reminded her that her phone was still in her trouser pocket and she took it out to see the missed calls from her dad. She'd meant to call him back on more than one occasion that day but for one reason or another just hadn't got around to it. There was also a text, sent when he'd given up trying to speak to her.

Hope you're OK, love. Toby didn't turn up today. Hope everything is OK with you, please call.

Despite what she'd promised herself about peace and solitude she couldn't leave her poor dad worrying. She was about to dial his number when the phone began to ring and Robyn's name showed on the screen.

'I just wanted to check you were OK,' she said when Nina answered.

'I'm probably about as OK as you are,' Nina said heavily.

'Yeah, I expect so. Weird day, huh?'

'I've had less stressful ones,' Nina agreed. 'Why does this stuff always happen to us?'

'I think we might be jinxed… at least one of us must be. Personally, my money's on you but I won't let that stop me from popping round for tea every now and again.'

Nina smiled and sipped at her brandy.

'Listen,' Robyn continued, 'I know you just got back from the hospital but have you managed to speak to your dad yet? Only I know Toby was going up there today and I wondered how they'd got on.'

'What's Toby said?'

'That's just it – he's not here and he's not answering his phone. I thought maybe he's still with your dad?'

'I haven't spoken to Dad yet but I don't think Toby went. That's what he said when he texted.' Nina paused, the line silent. She could imagine the look of disappointment on Robyn's face. 'Sorry,' she added. 'I would have told you earlier but I've only just read his message.'

'It's not your fault. I should have known that little shit would bail. Honestly, I don't know what the hell has got into him these days.'

'I'm sure there's a reasonable explanation.'

'There may well be but if I can't get hold of him I'm not going to hear it, am I? I'm wondering now if he's trying to avoid me because he knows I'm going to be pissed off – I could be waiting all bloody night for him to turn up.'

'Do you think he's OK?'

'He's fine. He'll be ignoring my calls because he knows I'll wipe the floor with him if he answers.'

'Maybe,' Nina said thoughtfully. 'Maybe he genuinely felt nervous about spending the day with my dad. I mean, he barely knows him and it can be a bit daunting.'

'Or maybe he's a lazy, immature little bastard,' Robyn said bitterly. 'Someone offers a genuine lifeline and he throws it back in their face. There's only so many times you can do that before people stop trying to help and I think he's getting through his quota pretty fast right now. Listen… you don't need to hear this after the day we've had. Honestly, I don't need it either. Let me know what your dad says and I'll keep trying to track my son down and we'll touch base tomorrow, OK?'

'If you need me again tonight call me,' Nina said. 'It doesn't matter what time it is.'

'I wouldn't do that, but thank you,' Robyn said.

'Goodnight. I hope you get hold of Toby soon.'

'Me too. You know, he makes me so angry when he does this but he also scares the shit out of me. They don't tell you about all this stuff to come when you have your cute little baby, do they?'

'I can only imagine how worried you are,' Nina said. 'Remember, call me if you need me.'

'I'll speak to you tomorrow. Get some rest.'

'Bye, Robyn.'

'Bye.'

Nina ended the call and then dialled her dad's number. It rang out for a minute and then went to the answering service, so she could only assume that he'd gone to bed or – more likely – fallen asleep in front of the TV. Either way, it looked as if she wasn't going to be able to talk to him tonight. She sent a text to explain briefly why she'd been missing all day and that she'd speak to him tomorrow, downed the last of her brandy and, though it had only just gone 9 p.m., took herself off to bed.

She woke the next morning to hammering on her front door. She shot up in bed, heart thudding, and then she heard Ada calling through the letterbox. She heaved a sigh of relief, not sure whether she ought to be angry at her rude awakening or happy that it wasn't anything more sinister. But almost instantly there was an upswell of panic again. Why on earth would Ada be beating on her front door like that?

Nina swung her legs out of bed, pulled on a dressing gown and rushed downstairs. When she opened up, Ada had Martha with her, so at least that wasn't the problem – apart from looking visibly distressed, Nina was happy to see that they both looked well enough. Her first instinct had been to wonder if Ada's panic was due to some catastrophe befalling her sister.

'Oh, Nina!' Ada cried.

'Thank goodness you're in,' Martha added.

'Oh yes, thank goodness.'

'We thought you might not be.'

Nina couldn't imagine why they'd think that – it wasn't even eight yet and they knew she didn't work, but she let it slide.

'What's the matter?' she asked.

'Something terrible's happened,' Ada said.

'Yes, terrible,' Martha agreed.

'We were walking.'

'Getting our morning exercise.'

'And we went to see the garden.'

'The garden…' Martha added in a tremulous voice. 'Oh, the garden!'

Ada clapped a hand to her chest. 'Oh, Nina… it's completely ruined!'

Chapter Ten

Nina let them wait in her hallway and raced to throw some clothes on. Then she joined them for the short walk down to the garden to take a look. Surely it couldn't be as bad as they'd said?

When they arrived, Nasser and his wife Yasmin were already there. Nasser turned to Nina, and in all the years he'd lived on Sparrow Street she'd never seen him look so angry.

'Why?' he asked, unable to frame any further question. But there was no need, because Nina could see plainly what pained him and it was horrible. The same small question pinged around her own mind, the same single word that encompassed so much, and any kind of answer evaded her too. The plot of land they'd all worked so hard on, poured their own money into, given time and energy and love to, was wrecked. The pretty coloured benches were splattered with black paint and some had been daubed with offensive words and pictures, as had the potting shed. The insect hotel lay in pieces on the path and the rope swing had been cut down. Shrubs and young trees were pulled up by the roots and huge clumps of grass and earth were strewn about, making craters that looked like battlefield scars, and there was smashed beer-bottle glass in every flower bed. Bird boxes had been ripped from their branches and smashed and even the bulbs they'd planted had been dug up and thrown about.

Nina looked at Nasser, Yasmin, Ada and Martha in turn, but she didn't know what to say. Why would anyone do this? What kind of person came by, saw the transformation from tangled patch of weeds to beautiful community space and felt the need to destroy it? Her eyes welled up with tears. Not because she felt beaten, though she felt sorrow for the wasted hours and money, but through bitter disappointment and fury that the world contained such a person. She was filled with angry determination that this would not be allowed to set them back. They weren't going to give up on their garden so easily.

Without a word she turned and began to march back to her house. When she returned a few minutes later she was carrying a sturdy rubbish sack and sweeping brush, and she silently began work on clearing the glass from the paths. The others watched, open-mouthed, but then Yasmin kissed Nasser on the cheek before she went off too, returning shortly in much the same way as Nina had done, equipped to help the impromptu clean-up operation.

'We'll get help,' Ada said.

'Oh yes, we can do that,' Martha agreed, and they scuttled off to begin knocking on doors. Pretty soon, despite the early hour and the fact that many had jobs to get to, half a dozen neighbours were out helping them.

There was a range of reactions to the destruction of all their hard work, but all were in agreement that they'd come this far and they weren't going to let a setback like this ruin everything they'd done.

Everyone worked steadily for the next hour. A gale was blowing in, whipping up dust and soil and lifting sacks and debris into the air, and every so often there would come the threat of rain. It made the task difficult but nobody complained.

'We can tidy it,' Nasser said quietly to Nina as they took a breather, 'but it needs more money to restore what's damaged. We could do with some proper fencing too, something we can lock at night, otherwise this will keep happening. It's a target now the vandals know it's here and that someone cares about it.'

'It's horrible that someone caring about something makes it a target. I'd like to get my hands on whoever did this and give them a good slap.'

'I've got an idea, actually. Obviously we can't prove it.'

'That gang of youths from Bluebird Street?'

Nasser nodded. 'We're on the same wavelength at least. Although I'm not sure what we can do about it with no proof.'

'What about calling the police? We're going to report it, aren't we?'

'I could do that, but I'm not convinced there would be a lot of mileage in that either. You can barely get them out to anything more serious, let alone this.'

'But we should call them – we can't just let this go.'

'We'll see what people want to do. I honestly don't think they'd want to devote much time to such a petty crime, though. We think it's a big deal but I doubt the police will agree.'

'You could be right there,' Nina said wearily. 'Might it be worth a visit to the parents?'

'The parents are as bad as the kids as far as I can see. I doubt they'd thank me for turning up and accusing their children of this. Even if they were convinced there had been wrongdoing, I'm still not sure they'd do a lot to put a stop to any repeat. Let's face it, they haven't exactly been receptive to complaints in the past.'

'I don't know much about them but I've heard enough to know I don't want to mess with them.'

'We'll just have to repair the best we can and hope that they find a new and more interesting thing to target.'

'And if they don't?'

Nasser shrugged. 'One thing at a time.'

'I'll bet there's no money left in the kitty for any of the stuff we need to make repairs either, is there?'

Nasser shook his head. 'I suppose we'll have to try and raise some more, but people have already given so much, and Christmas is coming…'

'I know,' Nina said. 'All we can do is try.' She looked towards the road to see a Mercedes pull up and a blonde, trim woman in her late fifties get out.

'Oh God,' Nina said in a low voice as she recognised Sammy Star's wife. 'What now?'

Nasser followed her gaze. 'Who's that?'

'Long story. To cut it short I spent the day with her at the hospital yesterday. It's Sammy's wife.'

'Sammy Star? You know his wife?'

'I do now. I'll explain it all to you later.'

Nasser was about to speak again when Nina greeted the woman with a tight smile.

'Diana… how is he?'

'Much, much better,' Diana replied, her own smile a lot warmer and easier. Nina allowed herself to relax at the news. At least Diana hadn't come bearing even more bad tidings because she wasn't sure how much more of those she could take. 'He frightened me to death yesterday.'

'Me too,' Nina said.

'Anyway, I thought I'd better come to thank you properly. With all that was going on yesterday I didn't really have time—'

'You did and there's no need. We just happened to be in the right place at the right time, that's all. How did you know where to find me?'

'Sammy told me about the garden so I thought if I headed here you wouldn't be too far away.'

'He's awake then?'

'Yes.' Diana smiled. 'Already fussing about who's going to cover his show while he's in hospital. I told him it's not only hospital he's got to worry about because the doctor said no work for the next few weeks and I intend to make sure he sticks to that rule. If I know him, he's probably badgering the doctors for a phone so he can ring the station as we speak...' Diana looked beyond Nina where everyone else was still working. 'I thought the garden was finished?'

'It was,' Nina said. 'We had some trouble overnight.'

'Oh no...'

'Vandals,' Nasser cut in. 'They destroyed everything.'

'Well, not quite everything but it wasn't for lack of trying,' Nina said tightly.

'Oh no...' Diana repeated. 'How awful. Sammy will be so upset when I tell him. Is there anything we can do to help?'

'Help?' Nina blinked.

'You and your friend saved Sammy's life – it's the least we could do for you.'

'We didn't really—'

'Of course we want to help!' Diana interrupted. 'Name it – what can we do?'

Nina looked at Nasser for input. This had always been his baby more than anyone else's and she didn't want to step on his toes.

'We're short of funds now,' he said, seizing on the offer of support like the true leader he was. 'We spent everything we had the first time round. I realise it's a big ask but...'

'We can certainly put the feelers out in that regard,' Diana said firmly. 'Sammy will know a few people who ought to be able to help. We're far from rich but we'd be happy to make a donation too.'

'What about his listeners?' Nasser asked. 'Perhaps they can help?'

'Of course. Though it will be a few weeks before he's back on the air, I can have a word with whoever stands in for him to see about airing an appeal.'

'If we get enough, maybe we can do some of the things we didn't manage to do the first time?' Nina asked, looking at Nasser. 'That extra security for a start...'

'What sort of security?' Diana asked.

'We need some proper fencing and gates we can lock at night. This garden isn't just for Sparrow Street either,' Nina said. 'It's for everyone in the area to come and enjoy – you can make that known to your listeners too. The more people who use it, the more people will be invested in taking care of it – at least I'd hope so.'

'I've just had an idea about that,' Diana said. She'd looked thoughtful as Nina spoke and Nina was hopeful that her idea was going to be a good one. 'I have a gardener,' Diana continued, 'comes in once a week to tidy ours – weed, mow the lawn... that sort of thing. How about I donate the next few days when he'd usually be in our garden so that he can come to you instead? He's very good; he'd have you fixed up in no time.'

'You'd do that?' Nina asked, beaming.

'It'd be my way of thanking you. I'm sure he wouldn't mind. I don't suppose it makes much difference to him as long as he gets paid.'

'That would be fantastic!' Nina glanced at Nasser, who looked just as pleased as her by the suggestion.

'Great!' Diana said with a broad smile. 'That's settled then. I'll phone and talk to him when I get home and we'll get it fixed up.'

The residents did as much as they could and called it a day when the rain finally began to come down. Diana called Nina shortly afterwards to report on Sammy's continuing astounding recovery (thanks to Nina and Robyn, she insisted again; Nina again brushing it off and feeling embarrassed by all the praise) and to get Robyn's phone number because she wanted to thank her again too. She also wanted to let Nina know that the gardener she'd promised to contact was happy to oblige. She told her that he had free time the following morning so he'd pop over then to take a look at what needed to be done.

Once Diana had hung up, Nina quickly phoned Robyn to update her on what had happened that day. She also let her know that Diana would be phoning her too with undying thanks for helping Sammy when he'd been taken ill, though Robyn was just as convinced as Nina that they'd really done very little to be thanked for.

'I take it Toby came home OK?' Nina asked, though the lack of panic in Robyn was evidence enough of that fact.

'Eventually, at some ridiculous hour that he just knew would make me angry.'

'Where had he been?'

'Out – that's all he'd say.'

'Did he tell you why he didn't go to see my dad?'

'Said he'd forgotten. Lying little toerag – I know he didn't forget because he mentioned it to me yesterday morning and his memory can't be that bad at seventeen.'

'You know, if he doesn't want to go and work for Dad, Dad won't be offended.'

'I want him to at least give it a try, and he knows that. He knows how important it is to me and surely that's enough to make him give it a go?'

'In the end, you can't make him do something he doesn't want to, no matter how hurt you might be by his refusal.'

'Nobody knows that better than me,' Robyn said. 'It's the curse of the teenage boy. The thing is, I know he'd enjoy it if he gave it a chance. Do you think your dad would be willing to give it another go? Could we fix up another day and I'll drive Toby there myself this time to make sure he got there?'

'I can ask him.'

'Actually, maybe it's better if I have a chat with him myself about it. Can you give me his phone number?'

'Of course. Listen, there's something else I need to tell you about. Diana's arranged for her gardener to come and look over our plot tomorrow morning. He's supposed to be helping us get it straight again.'

'That's nice of her.'

'It is. The trouble is, almost everyone's busy tomorrow morning so I'll have to meet him alone.'

'*Everyone's* busy? Even the terrible twins?'

'Ada's got a dentist appointment – root canal or something—'

'She's still got teeth? Blimey!'

Nina couldn't help but laugh. 'Anyway, you know they go everywhere together so Martha is going with her.'

'And there's literally nobody else? What about the big gorilla man… Ron? He seems like a man who likes to feel important – surely he'd love this.'

'We asked him to help with the repairs but he said he's done his bit and it's not his fault the garden needs doing again. He also said he's not breaking his back to see it wrecked a second time.'

'Mean-spirited sod,' Robyn hissed. 'He barely broke his back the first time. All I saw him do was eat a free lunch – one that he didn't contribute one crumb to.'

'Well, we can't force him to help,' Nina said. 'So, would you mind seeing this guy with me?'

'Scared he might be a psychopath?'

'No.' Nina laughed. 'I'm sure Sammy and Diana wouldn't have him working for them if he was. But I've never met him so I'd still feel better with a bit of moral support.'

'Like you said, if he works for Sammy and Diana he can't be a complete monster, but if you really want me to I'll come.'

'Thanks. You know how nervous I get around new people.'

'I don't know why because everyone who meets you ends up loving you.'

Nina smiled. 'I don't think so, but thanks. So he's supposed to be coming at ten – is that OK?'

'It'll have to be.'

'If it's a problem—'

'No, it's not a problem. I'll pop over once I've dropped Toby off at college.'

'It would mean a lot to me.'

'I know; I wouldn't do it for anyone else, you know.'

'I'll see you in the morning then,' Nina said.

'He'd better be good-looking after all this – got to be some perks for driving across town first thing,' Robyn said with a laugh before ending the call.

Chapter Eleven

The next morning, Nina was sipping her first cup of tea of the day. Her phone was charging on the kitchen worktop and she got up to look as it bleeped the arrival of a text. She let out a groan as she read the message. It looked as if she was going to have to deal with this gardener by herself after all.

> *Sorry, honey, burst pipe. Woke up this morning and there's water everywhere – it's like bloody Titanic. Nothing to worry about but I need to wait for the plumber so I can't meet you this morning. If your gardener is hot and single, put in a good word for me.*
> *Rx*

It didn't matter really – Nina was perfectly capable of showing him what needed to be done – but she would have felt a lot better if Robyn, or at least someone else, could have been there with her. She thought about calling her dad to ask him if he could come but, with less than half an hour until she was due to meet her man, it would be a terrible rush for Winston to get there and it was unfair to ask him so she decided against it.

Going to the mirror in the bedroom she did her best to tame her curls with some divine-smelling serum Robyn had bought for her birthday and clipped the sides up. Despite her efforts, her hair still looked like an explosion in a spring factory, but at least it was out of her face. Then she applied a coat of moisturiser and a slick of lip balm to protect her skin from the cold wind and went to look for her wellies.

When she arrived at the garden a white van festooned with transfers depicting graphics of leaves and trees was already parked on the kerb outside. Nina noted the company name – more of a man's name really.

Colm Quinn
Landscape Gardener

She could hear music coming from the cab; it sounded like soul or Motown, not that she was any expert, and she wondered whether to knock on the window. It was only five minutes to ten, though, and maybe knocking on the window would seem impatient. In the end, she simply took herself to stand by the entrance to the garden to wait, hoping that the occupant would notice she was there. But he had his head down, looking at his phone. Nina took the opportunity to get a better look at him without making it too obvious. He was perhaps her own age, or maybe closer to forty with thick, dark hair. He looked muscular (at least his top half did) and quite tall too.

He looked up finally and she tore her gaze away. Then the music stopped and he stepped out of the van. Nina's hunch had been right – he was very tall, at least six feet if not more.

'Nina?' he asked, walking towards her.

'Yes.' She offered a hesitant smile and a hand in greeting. 'You must be…'

'Colm,' he said warmly. 'I work for Diana and Sammy. She said you would be expecting me.'

'Yes,' Nina said again, suddenly struck by the blue of his eyes. They were very blue, the sort of blue that made you catch your breath without even realising. He took her hand in a gentle grip and shook it.

'Pleasure to meet you.'

'You're Irish,' Nina said.

He grinned. 'Is that going to be a problem? I'm not going to install leprechaun houses in your garden or fill it with shamrock or anything.'

Nina flushed. 'Of course… Sorry. I didn't mean… I just meant I like your accent – it's nice.'

'Why, thank you,' he said, hardly missing a beat. 'I'm surprised it's survived all the years I've lived in England.'

Nina smiled, though she couldn't help but feel foolish. What kind of stupid comment had that been for her to make? What did it matter if he was Irish and why point it out? It wasn't like he didn't already know. No wonder he was so ready to tease her about it. But this sturdy man with his sparkling blue eyes and dark hair and musical accent that made it sound as if he was singing everything was having an effect on her the likes of which she hadn't felt in a long time, one she'd never imagined she'd feel again. She couldn't deny there was something exciting about it, but she couldn't help but wonder if it might make her say more very silly things before the day was done.

His gaze went to the plot of land. The residents had done their best to tidy the paths and put the clumps of earth back where they belonged, but it still vaguely resembled a recently cleared battlefield. He shoved his hands in the pockets of his thick combat trousers. 'So you want to tell me about it?'

'We'd finished it to be honest,' she said. 'It wasn't exactly a master-piece but it looked OK. But then we had visitors...'

'Ah. Diana told me about the vandals. I don't know what's wrong with people.'

'Me neither.'

'You've no enemies who might have had it in for you?'

'What do you mean?'

'Someone might have messed up your garden out of spite?'

Nina paused. 'Not that I know of,' she said uncertainly.

He fixed his gaze on Nina. 'And fair play to you for what you did for Sammy. Saved his life, so I heard.'

Nina blushed again, so hard that if someone had thrown cold water over her at that moment it would have turned to steam. 'I didn't do anything except call for an ambulance... and really my friend did that so I didn't do anything at all.'

'That's not how I heard it.'

Nina shook her head, her gaze going to her feet.

'OK,' he said with a warm chuckle. 'Not one for praise, eh? Fair enough. So what can I do to help with your garden?'

'It's probably easier if I show you,' Nina said, trying desperately to focus on the task in hand.

'So you'd only just finished?' he said, ambling after as she led the way.

'Yes. You probably wouldn't have thought it was very good but...' She shrugged. 'We'd all worked hard to make it nice and I can't tell you how upset everyone was.'

'The whole street worked on it? That's something you don't see every day.'

'Not the whole street but quite a few of us. We're a very close community.'

'Sounds like a nice place to live.'

'Mostly it is.'

He cast a critical eye over the space. 'Mind if I walk it – have a proper look?'

'I'll come with you.'

They began to walk the path slowly, Colm's eyes everywhere, taking every detail in.

'Is that your tree?' he asked, nodding to a decent-sized fir that had survived the onslaught, mainly because it had probably looked too big and solid to tackle.

'My tree?'

'Diana said you wanted to fill one of them with lanterns or something. Something about charity?'

'Oh, that! Yes. The memory tree. The lanterns are for lost loved ones. People make a donation for charity and they dedicate a lantern with a message for someone they've lost. We were going to do it as part of the Christmas celebrations, which we'd also planned to have in the garden before all this happened.'

'Lost, eh? *Anyone* who's lost?'

'I suppose so. If someone makes a donation I can hardly dictate who they dedicate their lantern to.'

'Well, if it's for charity then I might take a wee lantern myself when we're done putting everything right again.'

Nina wondered who he might light his lantern for, but he didn't volunteer the information and, as they'd just met, she didn't like to ask.

'It's a beauty,' he said, turning back to the tree. 'Lucky they didn't damage it.'

'I suppose so. It would have been hard to replace.'

'It would with something the same size. What are you wanting here?' He pointed to a patch of bare earth that had been completely cleared.

'That was supposed to be a lawn,' Nina said. 'At least, it was a lawn until yesterday. We were going to have community picnics and things on there in the summer.'

'Right. And you want everything back in like for like?'

'I suppose so. Nobody's actually said.'

'Well, I could make the space work better for you – not that there's anything wrong with it now,' he added hastily.

'Apart from being a bit bare.' Nina smiled. 'Don't worry, I don't think anyone would be offended by the offer of a little professional advice. None of us is exactly Capability Brown.'

He raised his eyebrows and broke into a broad grin. 'So you know your gardeners then?'

'I visited Blenheim Palace once,' she said, trying not to blush again under his interested gaze. 'I thought it was lovely.'

'Ah, that's a beautiful place,' he said. 'I can't promise yours would look like that but there's a lot of potential here.'

'There's plenty of help on hand too,' Nina said. 'If you needed it. I'm sure most of the residents who pitched in last time would be happy to do it again.'

'I'd be glad of it. Would that be including you?'

'For what it's worth. I have enough time on my hands so it would be a bit mean-spirited of me not to. I'm not much good at anything really, though.'

'I'm sure that's not true.' He scratched his head and then took his phone from a side pocket on his trousers, studying the screen as he scrolled through a list of something that Nina couldn't quite make out.

'Diana says she's happy enough to give me up for this week so I've got tomorrow free. I could make a start then for you.'

'The whole day? Diana said you only worked half days for her and we can't pay the extra so—'

'Don't worry about it,' he said. 'A wee flask of tea every now and again would be grand. To be honest, I wouldn't be doing much else so I might as well be doing something useful as watching daytime TV.'

Nina wondered if she ought to consult some of her neighbours – at least Nasser – before she accepted his offer. But it seemed silly to turn it down and she couldn't imagine why anyone would want to object.

'In that case, thank you,' she said.

'No worries. I'm going to need some supplies. Some of it I might already have on the van or in my storage at home, but if I don't—'

'Let me know what you're short of and I'll see if anyone can help. Whatever it is, we'll find a way to get hold of it somehow. Honestly, I can't thank you enough for this.'

He smiled and her stomach did that strange, unwanted flip again. 'I hope you're still saying that when I'm done.'

'Oh, we will. I mean, it can't look any worse than it does now, can it?'

'I think there's a compliment in there somewhere, eh?'

'Oh, I didn't mean…'

'It's OK.' He laughed. 'I know what you meant. So, is there anything else you need to ask me about today?'

Nina shook her head.

'Then I'll see you in the morning,' he said. 'You'll be here, won't you?'

'Yes… yes, of course. I'll see who else can come too.'

'That'll be grand.'

With a nod and a warm smile that nearly sent her into meltdown, he turned and strode back to his van. As the engine started and he left the street, she was seized by a strange mixture of relief and regret. But there was also a healthy dollop of guilt.

'Oh, Gray,' she murmured as she turned back to her own house, 'I'm so sorry…'

She'd had a busy afternoon reporting back to Nasser about Colm and what they'd arranged (which Nasser approved of wholeheartedly), then calling Robyn to see if she was OK (being careful not to give anything away when Robyn had questioned her about what Colm was like), then going to see her dad to talk about the ongoing Toby situation, amongst other things. By the time she'd climbed into bed that night Nina was exhausted and wondering how on earth she'd ever fit a job in if her life was going to be like this all the time. There was no way she was going to be able to stay awake for a minute, and as her head hit the pillow her eyes closed.

But almost as soon as they had, they pinged open again.

All day she'd tried to avoid the question, but now, in the quiet and darkness of her room, there was no getting away from it. She was definitely more than a little attracted to the handsome gardener who'd walked into her life that day and she felt like maybe she could see he was a little attracted to her too. It was hard to know why, after all this time of feeling nothing but indifference when it came to dating, she should suddenly be struck by this man, but the fact remained that he had made a huge impact on her.

And then her mind wandered, as it often did, to what Gray might say had she been able to talk to him. Would he approve if he could see her now? Would he be glad to see her moving on? Would he have said it was finally time? Given that he'd tried to broach the subject of her meeting someone else many times before he died – despite the fact that she'd constantly rebuffed him, finding the notion too difficult to contemplate, let alone talk about – Nina thought the answer to these questions might be yes. So why did it still feel like she was betraying him?

Flipping onto her side, she tried again to close her eyes. It was ridiculous and pointless to dwell on any of this. For a start, she didn't even know if Colm was single, let alone interested in her. She felt he might be interested, but then again, perhaps that was just his way. Perhaps he was just that charming and attentive with everyone. But her eyes opened again and that look replayed in her head, the broad, warm smile as he re-evaluated her and seemed to see something he liked. She wanted him to look at her that way again tomorrow, and she wanted to believe that Gray would have been OK with that.

Chapter Twelve

The day started dry but grey. Colm was waiting at the garden when Nina arrived, just as he'd promised. He gave her a cheery wave as she approached the van. They exchanged pleasantries, discussed the weather prospects, took time for everyone who'd gathered to help to introduce themselves to him, and then they took stock of the garden. It hardly looked better than it had the day before, but somehow the mess didn't look so daunting now that they had Colm on their team. Certainly, his optimism and confidence that they'd have everything put back in no time was infectious.

Before they began he delegated tasks as Nasser would but, unlike Nasser, he couldn't help getting involved with all the tasks that he'd given to everyone else. He was like some kind of superman – no sooner had he started the thing he himself was meant to be doing than he'd finished it and was assisting someone else with their task. He whizzed round the garden like a cheerful dynamo, sometimes whistling, sometimes singing to himself, always charming.

'Here… let me help,' he said, coming to take the handles of the wheelbarrow Nina was pushing to the rubbish dump.

'I can manage,' she said, laughing and trying to take them back. 'You're making us all look bad doing everything!'

'I'm not, I'm just more used to this work than you. You're all doing a grand job.'

Nina relinquished her grip and let him take the wheelbarrow. He gave her a smile and she couldn't decide whether the now familiar flutter at the sight of it was welcome or not. Why couldn't she stop doing that every time he looked at her? It wasn't right – she wasn't ready for this, not yet. That's what she'd been telling herself for the last two years, so why was she so desperately attracted to him?

Then she heard Nasser's voice – a welcome distraction. He'd promised to come when he could to see how they were getting on. He stood now at the entrance to the garden in his work suit. Nina made her way over to save him getting his leather brogues muddy. She was working there today with Ada, Martha and Kelly under Colm's capable direction. Not exactly an army but the only people willing or able to take the time out of their usual daily routine to help. They'd all started the day with profuse apologies to Colm that he'd got a bunch of weedy women as labourers, and he'd replied cheerily that they'd probably be a lot more reliable than many of the labourers and apprentices he'd had in the past – male or female.

'How's it going?' Nasser asked.

'Good,' Nina said. 'Colm's absolutely brilliant – honestly, I think it's going to look better than ever.'

'It's just a shame about the extra costs,' Nasser said.

'Yes, that bit we could have done without. But Colm's services come free of charge, remember. That's something at least – and so far he's been very generous with spare bits and pieces from his own shed.'

'That's kind of him – I must have a word with him.'

'I could call him over—'

Nasser shook his head. 'Sadly, it will have to wait – I have to get back to work. I only popped out to see if you were OK but my lunch break is nearly over.'

'Oh, well that's OK. It's a shame you can't stay longer, though.'

'I'm as frustrated as anyone about it. Thank you for taking charge, Nina.'

Nina dismissed the thanks with a soft laugh. 'I'm hardly doing that; if anyone's in charge right now it's Colm.' She glanced back to where he was returning from a skip with the now empty wheelbarrow. He put his hand up in a cheery wave to acknowledge Nasser, instinctively seeming to understand that they'd been talking about him and not seeming to mind too much. Instead, he turned and said something to Ada and Martha, who both squealed with delight and began to giggle like dizzy schoolgirls.

'I'd better go,' Nasser said. 'I'm really sorry I can't help out today.'

'Seriously, you don't need to worry. I know you'd be here if you could.'

'I'll talk to you later if that's OK?'

'Of course.'

'In fact… I wonder whether it might be a good idea to call another meeting in the next few days.'

'I think it would be. We can at least gauge where we're at and find out who still wants to be involved in the project. It's pointless and really just annoying to be pestering people who've had enough.'

'My thoughts too,' Nasser said, though his tone told her that he didn't approve of the notion that any of their previous supporters might want to desert the project now. Not when they were needed more than ever – for morale if nothing else – and not when they'd probably benefit from the finished garden as much as everyone else would.

'OK, well, I'll see you later perhaps?'

'I'm sure you will,' Nasser said. 'Actually, Yasmin is cooking lamb tagine – perhaps you'd like to come and eat with us?'

Nina smiled. 'That would be lovely but I have my friend visiting tonight – you know, Robyn?'

'Ah, yes! You'd both be welcome to come if I just let Yasmin know to make more.'

'Oh no, don't make more work for Yasmin on our account.' Nina smiled. 'We've got plans to cook and I already have the ingredients in. Another time when we can give her a bit more warning would be lovely.'

Nasser inclined his head in a little bow. 'Of course; I'll look forward to it.'

Nina watched him walk back to his car for a moment before turning back to her own work.

'Everything alright?' Colm asked as she took up a rake and began to clear some thinned-out branches from the path.

'Oh, yes,' Nina said. 'Nasser was just saying that he wished he could help but he has to be at work today.'

'Ah, we'll be just fine without him. It's only a wee place and I'm sure me and my girls can handle it.'

Nina raised her eyebrows and he grinned.

'You say that…'

'You're doing a grand job so far—' he began but was cut short by a squeal from nearby. They both turned to see Martha flat on her back in a patch of mud. Colm raced over, Nina close at his heels.

'Martha!' Nina cried.

But when they got close, they could see that she was laughing so hard she was almost crying and that was partly the reason she was struggling to get up. Ada put out a hand to drag her up and a second later she was in the mud too, laughing almost as hard as Martha. This made Colm laugh, and then Nina started.

After a minute or so they managed to control themselves and Colm gave both ladies a hand to get up.

'You're not injured, are you?' Nina asked. She didn't think it was likely given their good humour but it didn't hurt to check.

'Oh no,' Ada said.

'Not a bit,' Martha put in.

'But we are covered in mud.' Ada looked down at herself.

'Quite covered,' Martha agreed. 'We look like farm pigs.'

'Oh, we do,' Ada said and started to laugh again.

'I think you look grand,' Colm said, 'like proper labourers now. No foreman trusts a worker who's too clean.'

'What about you?' Ada said with a wicked grin. 'You look quite clean to me.'

'Oh, not dirty at all,' Martha snorted, picking up on the banter.

'Oh… I'm as dirty as the next one,' Colm said with a mischievous glint, sending both Ada and Martha into new fits of giggles.

'Oh you!' Ada cried, slapping him playfully on the arm.

'Naughty!' Martha joined in.

Nina smiled as they continued in this way, Colm winding them up more and more with every witty riposte. He looked her way and she felt her legs almost give way as he threw her an impish grin. Though she tried to deny it, she was more attracted to Colm than ever. What on earth was she going to do?

The light was failing when Colm finally called time on their day's work. Nina found it frustrating to have to stop when they were making such good progress but she understood why. She said goodbye to Kelly, Ada and Martha and then went to Colm's van to thank him as he packed his things.

'Are you free tomorrow?' he asked as he fastened the tapes around some digging equipment to secure it in the back of his van.

'To work on the garden?'

'Yes.'

'But… well, haven't we already taken up enough of your valuable time?'

'I was just thinking I've got a couple of hours free first thing if you want me.'

'Won't you have clients to get to?' Nina asked, certain that Diana had told her Colm only worked for her and Sammy once a week.

'It's the morning I'd normally take off,' he said with a warm smile that set her pulse racing again. 'I won't be doing much else with it.'

'Oh… well, in that case I expect I could be here. I'm job hunting right now but I don't have anything as yet so I'm free quite a lot.'

'That must be tough.'

Nina shrugged. 'It's OK; there's a few irons in the fire, as they say – my dad's got a friend who owns a pub and they can't say yes yet but they promised as soon as they have an opening they'll let me know. And I've got a little money to keep me going so I'm not too worried yet; I'm sure something will come up.'

'I'm sure it will,' he agreed. 'So if I come at nine you can be here?'

'Yes. Do you want me to see if I can round up anyone else to come?'

'That'd be grand if you could. So I'll see you tomorrow.'

Nina nodded and watched as he climbed into the driver's seat and started the engine. Then the van turned the corner of the street and was out of sight. She already missed him. What was more, she'd barely given Gray a thought all afternoon and she couldn't quite decide how she felt about that.

Chapter Thirteen

Robyn turned up twenty minutes late for their tea date and dumped a carrier bag onto Nina's dining table. Nina wasn't worried about the lateness, but she felt certain that it had something to do with ongoing worries about Toby. She'd ask later when they'd eaten.

'I got supplies,' Robyn said.

'I told you I had plenty in.' Nina went to look while Robyn hung her coat over the back of a chair. 'You didn't have to get all this.'

'I know, but I was passing the shop anyway and you know I hate to turn up empty-handed. What are we eating anyway?'

'Curry.'

'I thought so – the poppadoms were a lucky guess then, weren't they?'

'Weren't they just?' Nina emptied the bag and placed the extra bits out of the way on the worktop. Then she went to the fridge to get out the ingredients for their meal.

'I'm sorry I couldn't make it this morning,' Robyn said, taking the onion Nina had just handed to her and a knife from the block. 'How did it go? Is Sammy's gardener hot? I'll bet he was; I'll bet it was like *Lady Chatterley's Lover...*' Robyn laughed. 'Did you put in a good word for me?'

Nina was silent as she worked out how to respond. Could she tell Robyn about how attracted she was to Colm? She didn't even know how she felt about it herself, torn between wanting something to happen and feeling guilty about the possibility. What would Robyn think of it? Her friend had been ready to date for some time now, and, indeed, she had dated a lot since Eric's death. But her relationship with Eric had been very different to the one Nina had shared with Gray and Robyn would be the first to admit that.

'He seems nice,' she said eventually.

Robyn turned to her with a vague frown. 'That's it? That's all you've got for me? What's he look like?'

'I don't know... kind of tall. Dark hair, blue eyes...' Nina's description tailed off as she thought about those eyes. She shook herself. 'Quite good-looking, I suppose.'

'Oooh! Sounds promising!'

'He's coming back tomorrow.'

'Is he? I think I might have to get involved tomorrow then.'

'You'd be welcome,' Nina said, slicing up two chicken breasts. 'You know that.'

'Do you know if he's spoken for?'

'I'm not completely sure, but I don't think so.'

'In that case I'm definitely coming over tomorrow. I might even have to crack open that new mascara I got the other day – let's face it, I need all the help I can get these days.'

'Don't be daft, you look lovely. Any man would be mad not to fancy you.' Nina added the chicken to the onions and garlic Robyn was already cooking. 'What's happening with Peter, then? Is that definitely over?'

Robyn's whole body seemed to somehow deflate to half its usual size. She had arrived full of banter, as always, but Nina got the impression she was still sad about what might have been with Peter.

'I don't want to think about him,' she said tersely.

Nina nodded. She was dying to know more, but she had to respect Robyn's request and so she dropped the subject. She went over to the cupboard for a jar of sauce. Sometimes she'd make her own, but tonight she was tired and it was easier to take the lazy option.

'How's Toby?' she asked instead and immediately realised she'd leapt from the frying pan into the fire as Robyn's expression darkened.

'There was another "*altercation*" at college,' she said, using her fingers to make speech marks to indicate that the word '*altercation*' wasn't her word at all. 'I had to go in again and see the head of year. Then I got Toby home and we had a massive bust-up because I told him he wasn't to spend any more time with that gang of boys. That's what made me run late for you.'

'I bet that went down well.'

'You'd be right. I don't recall having a brain transplant, but it must have happened at some point because I should have remembered from being a teenager myself that if your parents tell you not to do something then it makes you want to do it all the more. And don't even get me started on undesirable friends…'

'Hmm.' Nina wrenched the lid from the jar. It came away with a pop. 'What's so bad about them?'

'Let's just say if there's a fight you can guarantee they've either started it or are happily wading in. Then there's the antisocial behaviour, the hanging around on street corners and harassing people…'

'Oh,' Nina said. 'I see why you might be a bit worried about him then. So he was straight out with them again?'

Robyn nodded. 'Little shit.'

'Well… have you tried talking to their parents?'

'I would if I knew who they were. Toby won't give me any details and neither will the college so it's a bit difficult. Though,' she added, 'if the parents are anything like the kids, I don't suppose talking to them is going to get me very far. It'd probably get my windows smashed.'

'They're that bad?'

Robyn shrugged. 'What I've seen. I don't know, maybe they're not. I only know that Toby has changed since he started to spend time with them and I don't like the road they're taking him down at all. I suppose it could be a phase. Maybe in a year's time I'll look back on this and laugh at how I overreacted.'

'Oh, Robyn… I don't know what to say.'

'I just have to hope he grows out of it. Part of me wonders if he's scared of these other boys too and that's why he daren't walk away from them now – you know, he's got in too deep with them and he's worried about repercussions if he tries to distance himself. Plus, it would mean him having to find other friends and that's not always easy part way through the college term when friendships are already forged. He's not as tough as he pretends to be and this behaviour I'm seeing right now is just not him – I feel like something's got to give; I just hope it doesn't end in tears when it does.'

Nina handed Robyn the opened jar of sauce; she tipped it into the pan with the onions and chicken while Nina went to rinse some rice.

'Where is he tonight? Is he still out with his friends? I suppose it's a silly thing to ask whether you might have brought him here for his tea?'

Robyn gave a wan smile. 'He's supposed to stay with Eric's parents tonight and they've promised to pick him up so he's supposed to be back at the house waiting for them by now. Honestly, if he'd refused to go I'd have thought twice about coming for tea tonight and, yes, you're right – he wouldn't have come with me. He kicked up enough of a stink about going to his grandparents and yet he's always loved spending time with them, especially after Eric died. It was only after

I threatened to take him out of college and send him back to his old school's sixth form that he backed down.'

'You'd do that? Didn't he absolutely hate his school?'

'I think he hates the memories. Don't forget that he was a pupil there when we lost Eric so he associates it with that horrible time.'

'I suppose he must. What about my dad? Do you still think Toby would want to spend time with him?'

Robyn shook her head as she stirred the curry. 'Even if he'd agree to go I don't think I could send him there while he's behaving so badly – it doesn't seem fair.'

'If anyone could distract him from all this bad stuff, I think my dad could.'

Robyn was thoughtful for a moment. 'Maybe,' she said finally. 'I'm not completely dismissing the idea but I think we ought to wait.'

'What if waiting just leads to more trouble? Didn't you say not so long ago you were going to drive him over yourself and make sure he went in?'

Robyn shrugged. 'I know I did, but now I'm not so sure. I suppose I'll only have myself to blame for calling it wrong if this all backfires on me but honestly, I just don't know what to do for the best. God – at times like these I really wish we still had Eric. He'd have known what to do and he'd have handled it better than me.'

'I don't suppose you'd have been in this situation if he hadn't died.'

Robyn looked at Nina. They didn't keep secrets – never had and never would. 'You know we would have been divorced by now if he hadn't got ill, so who's to say really?'

Nina nodded. She'd always appreciated Robyn's refreshing frankness. Robyn wasn't ashamed for what she thought were human emotions beyond her control and she never hid anything she felt from Nina.

'I suppose you might not have been together, but you would still have been able to share the parenting. The support would still have been there.'

Robyn licked a blob of sauce from her fingers. 'That's true. If nothing else, Eric was reliable and he would have seen Toby right. I don't suppose we'd have been in this situation at all if we still had Eric. All water under the bridge now. We don't have Eric and it's pointless wishing we did.'

'Do you ever think… well… do you ever think if you got with another man that he might be a good influence on Toby?'

'Are you talking about Peter here?'

'Not specifically.' Nina looked up from the rice. 'Are you?'

'Not happening,' Robyn said. 'Toby couldn't stand him the first time I dated him anyway. Come to think of it, Toby hasn't been all that keen on any of them.'

'Maybe he feels like you're trying to replace Eric.'

'Well… when you think about it, that's exactly what I'm trying to do.'

'Not exactly,' Nina said, going hot as the idea occurred to her. If Robyn really thought that dating someone new was an attempt to replace Eric, did that make her attraction to Colm an attempt to replace Gray? She would never have seen it that way, but perhaps, in the cold light of day, that was exactly what she was doing. 'Eric will always be a part of your life, won't he, even if you end up remarried?'

'Of course he will. I'm just saying that it is sort of like replacing them when you really think about it.' She looked up at Nina and stopped stirring for a moment. 'Replacing someone doesn't mean they never existed though, if that's what you're worried about.'

'Me…' Nina gave a self-conscious laugh. 'Why would I be worried?'

'You're always worried about something,' Robyn said, stirring the pan again.

'I'm not.'

'Yes, you are. I know you. The man of your dreams could walk in that door right now and all you'd think about was how you'd be letting Gray down if you so much as looked twice. For all I know you could have already turned down the man of your dreams – you could be doing it twenty times a day, worrying about if that means you've somehow betrayed Gray. The way I see it, Eric isn't here so I'll never know what he thinks and neither is Gray. We can't ask them, so all we can do is carry on living for ourselves and not worry about it.'

Nina went to get some plates from the cupboard. Coming from Robyn it sounded so simple. Maybe it was for her, but for Nina, nothing had felt simple since Gray's death and she couldn't imagine that anything ever would again.

The next morning was dry and bright, darts of crisp sunshine skimming the rooftops of Sparrow Street. When Nina arrived at the gates of the garden with Winston and Robyn, who'd met her at home and walked along with her, Colm's van was already parked at the kerb and he stood chatting with Ada and Martha. Seeing their approach, Ada and Martha greeted Nina's party enthusiastically, while Colm just gave her a warm nod of acknowledgement.

Her stomach dropped, however, as a new complication arose. As she'd feared, Robyn perked right up at the sight of him and went into full charm offensive mode. It was hard to deny that a lot of women would find Colm attractive and clearly it was too much to ask that Robyn not be one of them. But Nina also realised that she only had herself to blame because if she'd been more open with Robyn about the fact that she did like Colm, her friend would be keeping a respectful distance right now, mindful of Nina's feelings. As it was, poor Robyn didn't have a clue, and Nina couldn't really complain.

'Pleased to meet you,' Colm said as Nina introduced her dad and best friend. 'You're here to help today?'

'Yes!' Robyn said, and Nina knew exactly what that bounce was in her step because she knew exactly what made her friend tick. Not only had Robyn quickly come to appreciate Colm's good looks, but she'd also appreciate that he had an accent that could sing birds from the trees.

'That's grand,' Colm said, sounding more Irish than ever and sending a palpable frisson of excitement through the assembled women. As he went on to explain the plan for their morning's work, Robyn shot Nina a grin full of meaning.

'*Oh. My. God!*' she mouthed.

Nina returned a weak smile, the best she could do. It was going to be a long morning.

Once they'd wrapped up for the morning, Colm having a paying customer to get to after lunch, he told them that he wasn't sure when he could come back again, but he promised to let them know through Diana as soon as possible. He could have offered his phone number (and certainly Robyn had tried hard enough to get it) but he didn't, which left Nina wondering why – the most obvious and easiest way for him to keep in touch would be to give one of them his phone number. But then she spotted Robyn standing at the side of his van, copying the phone number listed along with his name. Here was a woman who wasn't troubled by the notion that he might have refrained from offering his phone number for a reason.

The second time around, the manic appetite to get the garden finished had definitely tailed off. Many of the army of helpers they'd had at the start just weren't there, and those who always did turn up – Kelly, Ada and Martha – were tired. Canvassed by Nina for support to repair the damage, many had told her that they didn't see the point in doing it all over again just for it to get vandalised as soon as it was finished. While Nina could see what they meant, it saddened her. As she'd worked today, she'd resolved to talk to Nasser about it. But for now, with Colm gone, the others decided to pack up too. Ada and Martha went home for lunch while Robyn went to pick Toby up from a half-day at college so he couldn't go out with the friends who were causing so much trouble and Kelly had a hair appointment – all of which just left Winston and Nina.

'You know what I fancy?' Winston said once Robyn had left. 'Pizza.'

'I can do pizza for you; I'm sure I have a pepperoni in the freezer—'

'Is that pizza place still open on Wrenwick plaza?'

'Roberto's? I think so.'

'That's the one. Your mum used to love it there. Just for treats, you know, but she always chose it for her birthday.'

'I know.' Nina smiled. 'I remember.'

'I have a sudden hankering for it,' Winston said. 'Care to join me?'

'I'd love to.'

Winston had driven over in an old Ford Anglia – one of the handful of cars that he'd refurbished over the years and hadn't been able to part with. It was a gorgeous sage green, lovingly waxed and polished so that it gleamed, the interior upholstered in soft cream leather. Every time Winston took it out he received admiring glances and compliments. Nina had to agree that out of all the cars he'd kept it was her favourite, even if the old engine sounded like that of a Boeing coming in to land. They walked back to Nina's house and it stood waiting for them outside where he'd left it to walk along with her that morning. As they got in, the comforting smell of the beeswax leather treatment he used regularly to keep the seats from cracking welcomed Nina like an old friend.

They chatted about this and that as they drove the mile or so into town – nothing of consequence and all good-natured. Winston listed the cars he'd seen that he might buy, ones that he'd been outbid for at auction, ones that he'd steered clear of once he'd taken a good look at the bodywork, and Nina listened, content to let him ramble as her gaze idled on the town passing by outside the window. She was always glad to hear him enthuse about his cars, because it meant he was occupied and happy. The more camshafts, brake pads, engine fans and bumpers that littered his driveway, the happier Nina was.

At the restaurant they got a table easily because it was a weekday and at the tail end of the lunchtime rush. Nina was assailed by a thousand memories, both pleasurable and painful, of coming here with her mum on special occasions or random treat days, and later with Gray as she'd introduced him to it and he'd loved it as much as her. The most authentic pizza outside Napoli, the sign outside boasted, and the population of Wrenwick seemed to agree because Roberto had been feeding hungry patrons since the early seventies when old man Roberto – who had since retired and handed the restaurant to Roberto junior – had first opened it. In that time the décor had barely changed – perhaps the blinds or the table coverings had been replaced and renewed – but the faded old wall frescos showing scenes of Venice, Florence, Rome, Lake Garda… they still remained, looking now like something that an archaeologist might unearth in an Ancient Roman settlement. Nina was not one to shy away from progress but some things she liked to see stay just as they always were. As the festive season was fast approaching, it was now also festooned by garlands of tinsel, which looked almost as old as the décor they obscured, and a plastic fir tree – trying valiantly to persuade onlookers that it was dusted with Alpine snow – stood next to the restaurant entrance.

After being seated at a small table by the window, they ordered their meals and a jug of water and the waiter left them.

'That's old Roberto's grandson, you know,' Winston said as they watched him go to the kitchens.

'How do you know that?'

'I'll bet you a fiver – you can see the resemblance a mile off.'

'Don't worry – I'll keep my fiver. I believe you.'

He looked at Nina with a smile. 'This is nice, isn't it? We haven't done this in a long time.'

'I'm sorry.'

'It's not your fault – I didn't mean that.'

'I know, but I suppose I've just been wrapped up in a lot of other things. I've still got to find a job – though I had no idea how hard that would be – and the garden is taking more time out of my weeks than I imagined it would. It's not cheap either and I couldn't afford to do it every week.'

'This one's on me.'

'Dad, no—'

'I want to,' Winston said. 'I wish I could do more for you, but at least let me do little things every now and again.'

'Dad, you know I don't ever feel neglected—'

'Still,' he said, his gaze travelling to the young waiter who was returning with a carafe of water for their table.

'Thank you,' Winston said with a little nod as the boy set it down and then walked away again. He couldn't have been older than seventeen or eighteen. Nina's mind went to Toby. She wondered if Robyn was alright. It upset her to see her friend sad and lost, desperate for help and guidance that Nina just wasn't equipped to give. She was just about to say something to her dad about it when he spoke.

'I used to think money was important, that I ought to always have some put aside, but as I get older and I see more and more people start to disappear from my life I start to wonder if there's any point in worrying about money. You can't take it with you, so why bother trying to keep hold of it?'

Nina frowned. 'Dad… Are you trying to tell me something?'

'What… Oh, no!' He laughed and she heaved a silent sigh of thanks. 'Don't worry – it's nothing like that. I'm afraid you're going to have to put up with me for a while yet – at least, if I have any say in it.'

'Well then, don't talk like that because it scares me.'

'I'm sorry, love; I didn't mean to. I should have realised. I just meant that life's too short – and that's one thing we both know well enough.'

'Yes, it is.'

'And sometimes you just have to stop worrying about what's right and proper, what others think, and do what makes you happy.'

'I know that too,' Nina said carefully, wondering where this conversation might be going. 'But sometimes there's more to it than that,' she added. 'Sometimes it's hard to let go of your past and move on.'

'I see you struggle with that every day.' Winston poured a glass of water from the carafe.

'Yes, I don't deny it, but I'm not unhappy, Dad. You don't need to worry about me – when I'm ready, I'll move on.'

'Will you? I'm not sure that's true. Do you disapprove of new relationships? Do you feel Gray would disapprove?'

Nina reached for the carafe and poured water for herself. 'It's not like I can ask him,' she said briskly. She wasn't sure she wanted to have this conversation, certainly not with her dad.

'Of course not, but you must have a gut feeling. You knew him better than anyone; you must be able to guess at how he'd react and what he'd say if he could tell you.'

He'd have been glad, Nina thought. He'd have wanted her to be happy. He would have hated to see her alone, the way she'd been so determined to be alone. He would have said she'd earned her happiness. She had, hadn't she? Hadn't she been a loyal and loving wife until the very end? So why couldn't she accept that?

Their conversation was put on pause once more as the waiter brought complimentary breadsticks and olives to their table. They thanked him and he left again.

'That Colm seems like a nice fella,' Winston said, reaching for a breadstick. 'Shame about his wife.'

Nina paused, her hand halfway to the olive bowl. She looked up at Winston. 'His wife? I didn't know he was married.'

'I don't think he knows if he's married or not either,' Winston said with a wry smile.

Nina frowned. 'What does that mean?'

'She's been living in some hippy community or something for the last five years on some remote Scottish island. Never comes home, hardly calls. I should imagine it's enough to drive a man mad.'

Nina was thoughtful for a moment. 'How long did you say she'd been gone?'

'Five years. Doesn't contact Colm and hardly his poor daughter either – her daughter too, I might add. Your mum would have been horrified if she'd heard a story like that. I should say that's reason enough for him to try and divorce her – I'm surprised he hasn't done it already to be honest.'

'He's got a daughter?' Nina asked, wondering why Colm hadn't mentioned it. But then, perhaps he would have if she'd thought to ask.

'She's fifteen, I think he said.'

'And he told you all this?'

'Today.'

'It's a big deal to tell a complete stranger,' Nina said doubtfully.

Winston gave another faint smile. 'I think I've just got one of those faces. I'll tell you what, I don't know how he stays so cheerful with all that hanging over him, and having to bring up a teenage daughter alone too.'

Nina bit into a breadstick, her mind a jumble of thoughts.

'You never know what life's got in store for you,' Winston continued, shaking his head. 'That's why you have to make the most of the good times.'

'I know.'

'Poor fella must get lonely sometimes.'

'He's got his daughter at least.'

'You were always a comfort to me after we lost your mum, but it's a different kind of lonely…'

'Do you think he misses her?'

'I'm sure he does,' Winston said with a distant look, and Nina realised that he wasn't really talking about Colm any more. He was thinking about how much he missed Nina's mum.

'Oh, Dad…' Nina reached across the table and gave her dad's hand a squeeze.

'Steady on,' he said with a half-laugh, throwing a glance around the restaurant. 'People will think I'm your sugar daddy.'

'Well, if they were minding their own business then they wouldn't be thinking anything, would they?' Nina raised her eyebrows and Winston laughed again.

She took a sip of her water. Colm wasn't exactly single but not exactly spoken for either. And he had a daughter too? Did that change anything for her?

'Anyway…' Winston began before taking a deep but significant breath. Nina paid him her full attention now because she recognised that breath. 'All this has got me thinking,' he continued. 'There's one thing I haven't dared to tell you, though I knew I'd have to soon. Under the circumstances, now seems as good a time as any.'

Nina put her glass down and stared at her dad. What on earth could he have to tell her that he hadn't dared to until today? Why did she have the feeling she wasn't going to like it?

He licked his lips and took a swig of his own water.

'Dad…' Nina prompted. 'You can't start the tale and then keep me hanging.'

'Right… of course. Well, I've been… I've sort of been taking a lady friend out. Pam, her name is. I met her at the car auctions. I like her, Nina. She's not your mum, of course… and she'd never take your mum's place because nobody could ever do that but… I like her very much. And she likes me. And, well…' He paused and took another gulp of his water. 'Nina… I don't mind telling you I'm fed up of being on my own.'

'Well, if you like each other then I don't have any issue with you dating her at all,' Nina said with a relieved smile. 'Is that what you thought? If she makes you happy, why would I mind if you spend the odd afternoon with her?'

'That's just it,' Winston said, eyeing Nina warily. 'I don't want to spend the odd afternoon with her. I'm going to ask her to marry me.'

Chapter Fourteen

What with her dad's revelations and Robyn's flirting with Colm, not to mention all the drama around Sparrow Street garden and Sammy Star's heart attack, Nina wasn't sure how much more she could take. Her quiet existence had suddenly turned into a maelstrom of upheaval, events hitting her one after the other; it seemed her life was destined to be anything but peaceful right now.

She'd managed to get some early-blooming daffodils at the florist, though they'd cost a lot more than they would have if she'd bought them in a couple of months' time. But she'd liked their bright cheeriness and she thought Gray would have too. She bent now to place them at the base of the headstone. As she'd walked through a churchyard that was still damp from early-morning rain, the paths slick and bare branches dripping, she'd noticed other graves had Christmas wreaths on already, though it wasn't even December yet. She wondered whether people had laid them early because they liked being early. Perhaps they might not be able to come back at Christmas, or perhaps it was simply that they didn't want to.

'I know it's been a while,' she said, standing up again and looking at Gray's name, engraved in the marble. 'Sorry about that – things have been a bit hectic. You know me; always getting dragged into any drama that's going, and usually they're nothing to do with me in the first place.'

Around her there was a surprising amount of birdsong. Whenever she visited she'd always spot the odd robin or wagtail hopping along the wall of the churchyard, but there just seemed like a lot today. The sun was out now after the wet start; while not hot enough to dry the ground, it gave out a weak lemony glow that flooded the churchyard. It wasn't exactly raising the temperature, but perhaps just its light was enough to make the birds happy.

'There's plenty to tell you,' she continued. 'You'll never guess – Dad's getting engaged. I don't mind telling you, I never saw that coming. I thought when he was trying to tell me… I thought…'

She'd thought her dad had been going to say something about her and Colm, that he could tell she liked him, that she ought to take a chance on a second chance, that she ought to stop feeling so guilty about living her life without Gray. She pushed the notion from her mind, along with the image of Colm's face.

'Anyway, I think he was a bit scared to tell me but I don't know why. I'm not that scary, am I?' She laughed lightly. 'If he likes her then I'm happy for him. I mean, I haven't met her yet so at least I think I'm happy for him. She might be horrible and then I don't suppose I would be. Is it bad that a bit of me hopes she's horrible so I can tell him so? It's not that I want him to be alone, but I want… well, you know, I don't want him to forget Mum. Like I don't forget you.'

Nina paused. She'd said that but hadn't she been thinking of another man only seconds before? 'But then, I don't suppose it's any of my business who he marries, so even if I don't like her I don't suppose it matters. I suppose what matters is that he likes her – and at least he won't be lonely…'

Nina let out a sigh as she gazed at the stone. She could talk and talk like this for hours. Sometimes it helped, and sometimes not so much, but she'd never been able to equate what stood there with the man she'd loved – not really. It was a symbol, a focal point, something to connect them even after death had parted them, but now as she looked at it, she couldn't feel any of that. She felt only an overwhelming sense of sadness and loss. It wasn't just a symbol, a connection or a focal point; it marked the place where he lay, beneath the ground, all that remained of the man he'd been, the man she'd loved more than she'd had words to express. And the idea of it left her feeling so hopeless, so bereft, so lonely that she could barely draw breath now for the weight it placed on her heart.

'I'm sorry,' she said quietly. 'I'm so sorry, Gray. I just don't want to be like this any more and I don't know if I can keep coming and doing this with you—'

'Nina?'

She spun around, hastily drying her eyes. A slender woman on crutches, hair cut into a severe crop, thick mascara bleeding into the creases around her eyes, stood on the path.

'Connie!'

Nina threw her arms around the woman.

'I haven't seen you in a while,' Connie said as they broke apart. 'I thought… well, I thought perhaps you'd met someone and… you know…'

'Oh no,' Nina said quickly. 'Nothing like that. I've meant to come a lot more often, but I've had so much going on. I'm sorry, I ought to try harder—'

'There's no need to apologise,' Connie said. 'I'm nobody to judge. I just wondered, that's all, because I used to see you almost every time I came.'

'I have been, though – perhaps the timing's just been out.'

Connie nodded. 'That must be it.'

'You've come to see Gray too?'

'I was just passing really and I thought I'd call in and say hello.' She inclined her head at the daffodils Nina had placed on the grave. 'They're lovely – so bright and cheerful. You got them?'

'Yes. It looked a bit bare and everywhere can be so dull at this time of year.'

'That's true enough. Sometimes I think it must be lovely to be able to hibernate like a hedgehog.'

Nina smiled. 'How have you been?'

'Oh, you know… the same as always. Joints are stiff most mornings now but I get going eventually.'

'But you're still managing to get out and about occasionally?'

'I do my best. It's not good to stay in and dwell on things we can't change, is it? And you've been keeping busy?'

'Yes, fairly.'

'Good; I'm glad to hear it.'

'Look, I'm sorry I haven't called for a while. It's unforgivable—'

Connie shook her head. 'I'm not your responsibility. You know I'll always be glad to see you when you have time to visit but I don't expect you to feel any kind of obligation. You worked so hard to care for Gray when I couldn't, and for that I'll always be grateful. When I hated my own failing body for preventing me from doing more for him, I knew at least that he had you.'

'He never complained; he understood. He wouldn't have complained anyway; no matter whether he had anyone to look after him or not – he just wasn't like that.'

'I know, but I'm his mother. The one thing I was put on this earth to do was raise my son. My one job was to care for him and in the end I couldn't even do that.'

Nina opened her mouth to argue but Connie spoke again.

'I suppose that's all water under the bridge now. There's no use in moping about what can't be changed.'

'Are you OK, though? Coping?'

'As well as I always was – as well as anyone does. I really ought to ask that of you… you've been crying.'

Nina rubbed at her eyes, though she was hardly going to be able to rub away the telltale swelling. 'Oh, you know how it is when you come here. I don't think it will ever get any easier.'

'Yes, yes I do.' Connie's gaze drifted to the grave. 'I know only too well. Life can be cruel, can't it? First my Terry and then our boy Gray, both taken from me before their time.'

'But what's the alternative?'

'I ask myself that sometimes. There's my darling Gray, my only boy, lying there, and here am I, still alive, still hobbling around, still useless, an old lady. How is that fair?'

'None of us get to choose. Perhaps it's just as well that we don't because there'd be a lot of lives unlived in a bid to trade places with those we loved. We'd have both traded to save Gray, but I don't think for a second that's what he would have wanted.'

Connie's eyes misted as she shook her head. 'Of course it's not. I can hear him now, telling me not to be so daft. Ignore me, I'm a silly old woman.'

'You're not at all,' Nina said, smiling through new tears. She sniffed them back and looked at her watch. The afternoon was ageing fast and dusk here in the churchyard didn't creep quietly across the land, but rather fell like a heavy blanket dropped onto it, sudden and swift. Nina had been here enough evenings to have experienced it and had almost lost her way trying to find the exit gates when she'd lingered too long. 'Listen, I'm sorry I haven't been around so much lately. But I was thinking… do you have time now? There's a café along the road; we could get a warm drink and catch up?'

Connie smiled, and for a heartbreaking moment Nina saw Gray's smile. Sometimes, though she'd never tell Connie, that was what made spending time with her so hard for Nina.

'I'd like that,' Connie said. 'I'd like that a lot.'

Nobody had done any work on the garden for a couple of days. Colm still hadn't been in touch and Nina guessed that he probably had too much paid work on to do theirs for free. Nina did have some spare time to put in, but she was nervous about doing anything without guidance in case she ruined some new grand plan that she wasn't aware of, so she decided to wait a while in the hope that Colm would be able to return. If it turned out that he couldn't, then they'd just have to figure something out, but until they heard otherwise, it seemed like the best course of action.

Besides, if she was completely honest, she was beginning to feel as if she lived in that garden and was quite glad of the break. She and Robyn had been to see Sammy and Diana instead at their home. Sammy had been discharged from hospital, his doctors thrilled by his rapid progress. He'd had to promise to cut out the cigarettes and alcohol completely, lay off the breakfast fry-ups and family-sized chocolate bars – a promise that Diana would see that he kept, even if he didn't want to. He'd been well – chatty and cheerful despite the banning of all his favourite vices – and they'd both made a huge fuss of Robyn and Nina, treating them to a slap-up lunch (salad for Sammy, which made him look grumpy for the first time that day), steak and chips for everyone else. (Diana responded to his complaint by saying that the reason she was allowed to have steak and chips when he wasn't was that she hadn't eaten steak and chips virtually every day of her adult life and perhaps if he'd had the occasional salad in the past, he wouldn't be in a position where he was forced to eat it now.) They shared a bottle of champagne and Diana did relent and let Sammy have a tiny taste. He looked like a little boy being allowed one sweet out of the bag for good behaviour as he slurped happily. And while all this was going on, Robyn gushed over Colm and his help. Diana smiled knowingly.

'He's single, you know,' she said.

'Is he?' Robyn asked, all innocence and disinterest. 'It hadn't crossed my mind to ask. I'm single too – how about that?'

Diana laughed. 'I'll see what I can do,' she said, tapping the side of her nose, and Nina felt as if she'd just been punched in the gut. Perhaps she ought to tell Robyn that she liked him. But then, what would that achieve? Would it sound petty, like she'd only decided she liked him because Robyn did? Maybe Robyn and Colm wouldn't even happen, and if Nina just waited, she might get her chance? Either way, was he really worth jeopardising a friendship for? Or did this whole situation just make her seem like a ridiculous teenager? It certainly made her feel like one at times.

They'd left Sammy and Diana after lunch and Robyn had offered to drive Nina home. It was just as they'd turned into Sparrow Street that Nina stared out of the car window and cried for Robyn to stop.

Robyn jumped in her seat. 'What the hell…?'

'Stop!' Nina repeated. 'The garden!'

Robyn pulled up and killed the engine while Nina tumbled out of the car. Robyn quickly joined her and they stood together on the pavement, staring at the slick, gleaming iron fencing that now hugged the perimeter of Sparrow Street community gardens.

'When did this go up?' Robyn asked.

'I have no idea; I didn't really look this morning but I'm sure it wasn't there then.'

'I take it from your reaction you didn't know it was coming.'

'Not a clue.' Nina looked at Robyn. 'Perhaps we ought to go and see Nasser.'

'It's hardly vandalism, is it? I would imagine he knows about it already.'

'But surely he would have run a plan like this past everyone else?'

'Perhaps he didn't think he had to. Let's face it; nobody's been all that interested since the place was wrecked.'

Nina was thoughtful as her gaze went back to the fencing. It really was stunning – chic and sturdy and freshly painted in a smart black lacquer. 'Looks expensive. I wonder where the money came from.'

'*There's* a question you might want to ask Nasser,' Robyn said.

'Do you think it might have been Sammy? He *has* been super grateful since his heart attack, even though I still don't know why because we didn't really do anything.'

'Surely he'd have said something while we were there?' Robyn said doubtfully. 'Sammy's generous but I don't think he's the anonymous donor type. I think if he'd paid this type of money for something he'd want some credit for it.'

'But I don't know who else it could have been,' Nina insisted.

'Well, if it is Sammy then that's another thing we have to thank him for because so far he's coming through pretty well for us. There's the radio exposure, sending us that sexy hunk of Irish to look at every day, and now this. If he wants to keep on giving gifts like that I'm not going to complain.'

Nina recalled Diana's promise to put in a word for Robyn with Colm. Was that one of the gifts she was so eager to receive?

'Let's see if Nasser is in,' she said, rallying herself. 'Maybe he can shed some light on it.'

Yasmin invited Robyn and Nina in with a broad smile.

'I'll warn you now,' she said as they followed her along the hallway, 'he's grumpy because he's got some work thing to finish for a colleague who's off sick.'

'Oh,' Nina said, 'I'm sorry – I never thought… Would it be better if we came back? It's not urgent or anything.'

'No, don't worry – you're here now and he'll probably be glad of the distraction if I know him.'

From the upper floor Nina could hear footsteps thudding across the ceiling and squeals of childish laughter.

'Keep it down up there!' Yasmin called as she passed the foot of the stairs. Then she led Nina and Robyn through to the conservatory where Nasser was sitting on a cane sofa, laptop balanced on his knee and a frown sewn into his forehead.

'I can't hear myself think with those kids… Oh!' Nasser looked up to see Nina and Robyn. 'Hello! I never heard the doorbell.'

'You wouldn't with all that racket upstairs,' Yasmin said, arching an eyebrow. 'I don't know where they get their energy from, but I'm quite sure I don't have enough to keep control of them.'

There was another squeal, and this time it was followed by wailing instead of laughter.

'OK,' Yasmin sighed. 'Let's go and see who's punched who today.'

She left them and Nasser shut the lid of his laptop. 'What can I do for you?'

'We're sorry to swoop in on you like this,' Nina said, 'but we just happened to notice the fencing around the garden and we wondered if you knew about it. I mean, that would be a strange kind of vandalism if people were breaking in to make things nicer, but still...'

'Oh, I know all about it.' Nasser beamed. 'It was thanks to our new friend, the gardener.'

'Colm?' Nina asked. 'Who paid him?'

'Nobody. He paid.'

'He paid for the railings?' Nina's eyes widened. 'They must have cost a fortune! And he fitted them without payment too?'

'He said he'd been offered them from a demolition site and they looked very new, so he'd snapped them up because he thought they'd be perfect for us. He said we needed more security at the garden and he came this morning with some friends and put it all up in no time. Doesn't it look marvellous?'

'Lovely,' Nina said vaguely. It was an incredibly generous gesture and, even though she'd thought he'd seemed like a nice man, it was just too generous. 'That's it?' she added. 'He's done at the garden now? He's not coming back?'

'He's coming back,' Nasser said. 'He told me he could come tomorrow and hopefully that would be all he'd need to complete if he could get enough help. Alas, I'm unable to come again because I have so much to do at work.'

'Who *can* come?' Robyn asked.

'Ada and Martha, of course,' Nasser replied serenely. As if Ada and Martha were the answers to everyone's prayers. The sisters were proving to be more hindrance than help, though nobody would ever say so because they meant well and they were too sweet to offend.

'Is that all?' Nina asked, unable to hide her disappointment. What had happened to the huge numbers from the day when they'd first broken soil on the Sparrow Street gardens? What had happened to all the community spirit? Had it dried up that easily, at the first sign of a setback?

'You can count on me,' Robyn said, and the eagerness in her voice was enough to wind Nina up in a way that she'd hate herself for later.

'I'll knock on some doors tonight,' she said, trying to ignore the monster of jealousy that was rearing its head again. 'Somebody must be willing to help. After all, we're almost there now and it would only take one big push from everyone.'

'I'm one step ahead of you there,' Nasser said. 'I've been to see those who helped us in the first instance and they either can't come or don't want to.'

'Then I don't see why we ought to,' Nina said flatly.

Robyn and Nasser both stared at her now, but for once she didn't care. She didn't see why she ought to be slogging her guts out when all the other people who would benefit equally from the project couldn't be bothered. She felt like the chicken in the old fable who worked all year growing a field of wheat to make bread while all the other animals enjoyed themselves and yet, when the winter came, they all wanted the bread she'd made, even though they hadn't helped to make it. Well, just like the chicken, Nina wasn't going to be walked all over and she wasn't giving her bread away.

'You've got to!' Robyn said, still staring at her as if at someone she'd never met before. 'I'm coming and I don't even live on this street!'

'Well,' Nina said, 'we all know why you're coming, don't we?'

Robyn's eyes widened. 'What does that mean?'

Nina threw her hands into the air. 'It means I'm done!' Heat rushed through her body, her thoughts jumbled and chaotic, and it suddenly felt as if she'd lost everything that made her Nina. All she had was anger, and it was like all the calm grace she'd strived to maintain over the last two years, all the hurt and resentment she'd suppressed since Gray's death had finally become too much to keep in. All that had happened to her over the last few weeks had added to the pressure, day by day, and today – this. All control was gone and Nina was ready to blow, and the notion, somewhere in the dark, hidden recesses of her furious mind, was terrifying.

'I'm sorry,' she muttered and ran from the conservatory, out through the front door, for the safety of her own house. Feeling as she did, there was no way of telling what she might say, how much she might hurt others, and she had to make herself safe until it had passed.

But before she'd had the chance to lock her own front door behind her, Robyn pushed it open and stepped in.

'What's going on?'

'Please go,' Nina begged. 'I don't know what's happening to me but I don't want you to see it.'

'Well I'm going nowhere, so tough.'

'Please, Robyn – I just need time alone right now.'

'You have too much time on your own – that's why you're like this now.'

'Leave me alone!'

Robyn frowned. 'No.'

'I mean it. I don't want to talk to you right now.'

'To me? What the hell have I ever done?'

'Not just you – anyone.'

'You can and you will. I can wait. I'll put the kettle on.'

Robyn walked through to the kitchen. Seeing her calm, stoic support made Nina feel more wretched than ever, but it had poured cool water on her rage at least. Poor Robyn. She didn't have a clue what was bothering Nina, and Nina could never tell her because she could barely understand it herself. One thing was certain: none of this was Robyn's fault and it wasn't fair to expect her to take it. None of this was anyone's fault really. Or maybe it was. Maybe it was Gray's fault for dying and leaving her like this. Or maybe it was her fault for not being stronger, for not being able to deal with the aftermath better.

She followed Robyn through to the kitchen and sat at the table. Robyn put two mugs out and rinsed the teapot.

'I'm sorry,' Nina said. 'I don't know what came over me.'

'You've got a lot going on,' Robyn said in a brisk tone that suggested she was willing to listen patiently but Nina was not entirely forgiven for her outburst yet. Nina wouldn't blame her for that, considering that some of it had been very obviously directed at Robyn, and it was this that Robyn shrewdly addressed next. 'So, what you just said about me coming to help tomorrow… what exactly was that about?'

'I don't know—'

'Don't bullshit me, Nina; we've known each other too long for that. Is this about Colm? Is there something I ought to know? You like him? Because if I thought for a minute that you—'

'No, of course not,' Nina said, the lie slipping out so readily it even took her by surprise. 'I could never…'

'You can't keep waiting for a man who's never coming back,' Robyn said firmly.

'I *know* that.'

'Do you?'

'Of course. I'm just not ready to be with anyone else yet.'

'You feel like you never will be?'

'I don't know about that. I might be, but the thought of it just feels so wrong.'

'There's nothing wrong in finding love again. Who are you hurting?'

'I know that, but it just feels like...'

'Gray's not here. You can't be unfaithful to a dead man.' Nina winced at Robyn's blunt analysis. She was right but that didn't make it any less painful to hear. 'I mean, for God's sake, it's been two years. You must have at least thought about being with another man!'

'Of course I have!' Nina snapped. She had, and that was part of the problem.

'Then what are you waiting for?'

'I don't know. I mean, I'm not. It just hasn't happened.'

'You haven't done much to make it happen.'

'My confidence was knocked – alright? I'm scared I'll get close to someone and lose them again. I'm nervous about dating because I've forgotten how to even do it. I feel guilty because I loved Gray and I shouldn't be thinking about another man. All sorts of reasons are stopping me from making it happen.'

'Gray's not here so you can tick that one off your list.'

'It's not his fault he's not here.'

'It's not yours either. Why should you suffer?'

'That's easy for you to say – you didn't love Eric.'

Robyn's expression hardened. 'That's not fair.'

'It might not be fair but it's a fact. You've been through men since he died quicker than I've been through teabags.'

Robyn's mouth dropped open. 'What the hell...' she began coldly. 'How can you be such a bitch about it? If you've been thinking that all along then why didn't you just come out and say so? I clearly need some steering onto the path of righteousness because it's not easy for us all to be as perfect as you.'

Nina's eyes misted. 'Oh, Robyn, I didn't mean…'

She was so ashamed of her behaviour, but she couldn't help it and she didn't know how to apologise for what she'd regretted saying as soon as it had come out. Something had finally broken inside her and she didn't know how to fix it, but she needed to if she was going to get back on an even keel. Robyn was right – it wasn't fair but she'd said it anyway. Maybe this was moving on? Maybe this was finally moving forward, away from her life with Gray, towards something else… though she didn't know what, and if this *was* moving forward, she didn't think she wanted it.

'I'm sorry,' she said heavily. 'I wouldn't blame you if you wanted to go because I know I'm not nice to be around right now.'

'I don't want to unless you want me to. Do you want me to stay away tomorrow? If you want me to, you only have to say and I will.'

'Of course I don't. I didn't mean anything at Nasser's house; I'm just frustrated by how little anyone who actually lives here cares and I took that out on you. I shouldn't have done that and I'm sorry. I want you to come… I *need* you to come. Sparrow Street needs you to come.'

'OK…' Robyn said slowly. 'So that means you're coming tomorrow, even though you just said you wouldn't?'

Nina nodded.

'Good,' Robyn said, pouring boiling water into the teapot. 'So now we're going to have tea and you're going to talk to me until we get to the bottom of this business.'

'I don't mind the tea but perhaps not the other stuff.'

'I told you before; that's tough. I don't care what you *want*; I'm more interested in what I know you need. So whether you like it or not, you'd better start talking.'

Chapter Fifteen

Robyn had stayed late, and Nina had been glad of it in the end. Without her friend's patient ear, Nina might have found herself tipped over the edge into something she didn't understand. As it was, though Nina was still unsure where she stood on Colm and how Robyn might react if she admitted that she was attracted to him too, they discussed plenty of other things, and that had made Nina feel much better. Robyn had called Toby once, around six, to check that he was in from college and feeding himself, though Nina suspected that Robyn also just wanted to check he was keeping away from trouble. Then she'd arranged for her parents to call in, which had made Nina feel a lot less guilty about the fact that she was taking Robyn away from the thing that really mattered in her own life just to deal with Nina's meltdown. Before Robyn left, they'd agreed that all was well again and that they'd both be at the garden bright and early the next morning to see through what they'd started. They'd also decided that they would both give their full attention once again to the fundraising memory tree once the landscaping work was finished.

The next morning was grey and dull, but Nina pulled herself out of bed anyway. Someone had to meet Colm at the garden and it might as well be her. She'd had a phone call early that morning to say that Nasser had been to see Ada and Martha the previous evening and they were both utterly exhausted, so, although they'd offered token complaints, he'd told them to rest, because nobody wanted to see either of them get ill from working so hard. He'd negotiated some time off with his boss to come and pitch in for an hour, which he planned to do once he'd tied up a few loose ends. It seemed that Nina's outburst the afternoon before had sent Nasser out on a mission to make sure he recruited more people and he must have been extra persuasive because Kelly was also due to make an appearance for a couple of hours and, most surprisingly of all, so was Ron.

Nina, Nasser and Robyn were there first, and they stood together at the new gates of Sparrow Street gardens watching as Colm's van slowed to a halt on the kerb outside. He got out, whistling the tune that had just been playing on his radio, and bid them good morning.

'I've got something for you,' he said, striding round to the back of his van and opening it up. He pulled out a large tattered box. 'Just by coincidence, this came my way…' He balanced the box on the floor of his van and opened it up. 'It's from the same demolition site where I got your fencing. I thought I might as well have another snoop around to see if I could rescue anything else from there because it's proving to be a useful little place.'

'They were going to throw it away?' Nasser said incredulously as Colm produced what looked like a CCTV camera from the box. It was scuffed and dusty and had obviously been used for some time, but Colm seemed happy with his find.

'So they were,' Colm said. 'I thought of you straight away. If you can find a good place to mount it and charge it up every so often, it should keep you safe. You might need to get a memory card for it too; it's old, but I bet you'd still be able to get the right ones online. At the very least, the sight of it might act as a good enough deterrent, but if you did get any more trouble then you'd have something to show the police.'

Nasser's smile was broad. 'It was good of you to think of us.' He paused, and his smile transformed into a vague frown. 'Do we have to pay for it?'

'Let's just say that there was some lively haggling and, in the end, I reminded the fella that he owed me a favour or two so I managed to get it for a good price.'

'How much?'

'Free.' Colm smiled broadly. 'That OK for you?'

'You're a handy bloke to know.' Robyn grinned and eyed him almost hungrily. Nina knew that look well. It wouldn't be long before the charm offensive was in full swing again. If it was going to be tough to watch, Nina had only herself to blame because she'd had plenty of opportunities to set the record straight with Robyn and she hadn't taken a single one.

'I'd love to know what sort of favour he owed you,' Robyn added.

Colm put the camera back in the box with a grin of his own. 'Now, that would be telling.' He looked at Nasser. 'So you want it?'

'We do!' Nasser said. 'Does it still have installation instructions with it?'

'This is not the original box so no, it doesn't, but I can help you fix it up – shouldn't be too hard.'

'Again, we're in your debt,' Nasser said, sounding so old-fashioned that Nina smiled at him with a deep fondness. He was a lovely man and she'd often thought his wife Yasmin a very lucky woman.

'Pass me a flask of tea and a wee sandwich and we'll say no more about it,' Colm said cheerfully.

'I can do that!' Robyn said, almost leaping to attention like an over-eager army cadet. 'I could run to the deli and get a bacon sandwich… How about it?'

'I've already had my breakfast so maybe later,' Colm said. 'And I'll gladly eat what you have – there's no need to make a special trip to the deli. I wouldn't say no to a cup of tea, though,' he added.

'I'm sure we can do something about that,' Robyn said. She turned to Nina. 'Give us your keys and I'll put the kettle on.'

'There's no need…' Colm began. 'I can always go to the café—'

'No,' Nina interrupted, forcing a bright smile. 'Of course we wouldn't send you to the café.' She looked at Robyn. 'Why don't you stay here and I'll go and make tea? Does everyone want one?'

'Kelly! Ron!' Robyn shouted over to where Kelly and Ron were deep in conversation by the fir tree. They both looked around. 'You want a brew?'

Both of them nodded, though Robyn barely needed to ask Ron, who had never been known to turn anything down if it was free, regardless of whether he wanted it or not.

Robyn turned to Nina. 'I'd better come with you, give you a hand to carry them all back.'

'OK.' Nina turned to Nasser and Colm. 'We shouldn't be too long.'

'Thank you,' Nasser said.

Nina and Robyn started to walk back to Nina's house. For possibly the first time since they'd met – certainly the only occasion she could remember – Nina felt something like irritation towards Robyn. It wasn't like her outburst yesterday, where the catalyst for her meltdown might have been Robyn's comment but certainly hadn't been *about* her; today it was personal.

'He is *so* attractive,' Robyn whispered as they left Nasser and Colm talking. 'You weren't wrong when you said he was good-looking.'

'Did I say that?' Nina asked, trying to keep her voice even.

'You know you did. You said you weren't attracted to him but—'

'I'm not,' Nina said firmly.

'OK.' Robyn shot her a swift sideways look. 'Good. As long as I know where I stand.'

'What do you mean?'

'I'm going to ask him out.'

Nina's head snapped round.

'Really?'

'Why so surprised? Can't I ask a man out? Women ask blokes out all the time – it's not that weird. Maybe you should try it...'

'I didn't mean that, I meant... well, you've only just met him.'

'Isn't that the case for all the thousands of people who pick up in clubs and pubs and it works out OK for lots of those. Anyway, life's too short to wait for him to do it. I think he likes me...' Robyn turned to Nina and when she spoke again her voice was less certain. 'Do you think he likes me? I mean, does it seem that way to you? Do you think he'd say yes? You'd tell me if I was making a big fat fool of myself, wouldn't you?'

'Of course I would,' Nina said in a voice so irritatingly level it was even beginning to annoy her. She was terrified that what she'd experienced the day before, the way she'd lost it with everyone, was going to happen again – even now she could feel the beginnings of it. What was wrong with her? Why did she feel so angry about everything but so powerless to do anything to make it better? 'I'd always tell you my honest opinion.'

She would, and her honest opinion was that Colm would probably find Robyn attractive and that they'd probably have a good time if they went out on a date. They were both free, both obviously looking for something – love, a good time with no strings… who knew? Robyn was cute, lots of fun, confident, gregarious – all in all a pretty good prospect. If Nina was Colm she'd say yes to Robyn – at least, she couldn't imagine why he'd say no. She pushed thoughts of any alternative conclusion to this situation firmly from her thoughts. Why shouldn't Robyn get the chance? Her bravery at least deserved it.

'I think he'd be mad not to say yes,' Nina said carefully.

'And he's definitely single? I don't want another Peter situation…'

'I'm fairly certain he is; I mean, I told you about the absent wife last night, didn't I?'

'That's not the same at all. Absent wives I can deal with – it's the ones that still live with them I've got problems with…'

'And he has a teenage daughter…'

'Well, that's OK – I have Toby. If anything, that makes us a better match.'

At her front door Nina rifled in the pocket of her parka for her keys and opened up. 'I suppose it does,' she said.

As they went through to the kitchen, once again she tried not to think of a reality in which Robyn was dating Colm. Not that she had any right to mind, and she had to keep reminding herself of that.

'Shall we make it in the pot and let them pour their own?' Robyn asked, her voice cutting into Nina's thoughts.

'Sorry…?'

'Shall we make a pot of tea and let everyone help themselves rather than do lots of mugs?'

'Oh… right. I don't think the teapot will hold enough – at least not for a decent cup.'

'OK, it'll have to be mugs then. I just thought using the pot might save us some teabags.' Robyn turned to her with a shrewd look. 'Are you sure you're OK? If this is anything to do with yesterday…'

'I'm fine.' Nina forced a smile, though it was possibly the hardest thing she'd ever done. 'I feel much better after our chat.'

Robyn shook her head. 'Grief's a funny thing, isn't it? Just when you think you've got the upper hand, it creeps up and gives you another slap round the head.'

Nina nodded, certain now that what she'd told Robyn the night before – half-true anyway – had been enough to satisfy her friend that her outburst had been nothing more than a relapse of her mourning for Gray and frustration that she was unable to move on. That much was true – she missed him more than ever, but she was sick of being stuck in the same rut of missing him, knowing he was never coming back, but still being unable to see past all that. People often told her that time would heal, but it didn't seem to be doing a very good job for Nina.

'I have to say,' Robyn added, 'I don't quite believe you. I don't think you're right this morning.'

'I am, honestly.'

'Want to know what I think?' Robyn continued, ignoring Nina's assurances, 'I think you're lonely. I mean, you said you're lonely sometimes but I think you're *really* lonely.'

'I couldn't possibly be really lonely with so many lovely people around me.'

'I don't mean *that* sort of lonely, and I think you know what sort of lonely I mean.'

'Maybe,' Nina said carefully. 'The trouble is I'm not ready to do anything about it.'

'That's it – maybe you are but you haven't realised it yet.'

Nina shook her head. 'Every time I think about being with someone else I feel so guilty, like I'm thinking of having an affair.'

'Ah,' Robyn said with a satisfied grunt. 'So you *have* thought about it.'

'Well… of course I have,' Nina said. 'I mean, I wouldn't be human if I hadn't, would I?'

'So have you thought about it with anyone in particular?'

'No,' Nina said, hoping the emphatic lie would end the current line of questioning. 'I just don't see anyone that way. Maybe that in itself answers the question really – maybe I'm not ready after all.'

'But you did say Colm was quite good-looking.'

'That's just an observation because you asked me what he was like. It's like saying his hair is black or his eyes are blue.'

'Well I'd club him over the head and drag him directly to my bed right now. Don't tell me you haven't at least thought the same thing.'

'I don't know about the clubbing bit,' Nina said, trying to make light of the conversation, though she really wished now it would take a different turn. 'Do you think we should take some digestive biscuits out?' she asked, going to the cupboard. 'I'm sure I have a pack in here somewhere.'

Robyn clicked her tongue against the roof of her mouth, as if to show impatience with Nina's avoidance tactics, but if she really did think they were avoidance tactics then she didn't say so.

'Sure,' she answered. 'Whatever you think.'

Nina found the biscuits and checked the date on the pack before putting them on the tray to take out with the drinks.

'So,' Robyn asked casually after a moment, 'if I ask Colm out, you're sure you don't have any issues with it?'

'He's very nice; why would I have an issue with it?'

Robyn gave her a doubtful look.

'Honestly,' Nina said, forcing another smile. It seemed to be the only way they'd come out today. 'I don't mind at all. Go snap him up before someone else does because I think he'd make someone a lovely boyfriend and I'd rather it be you than anyone else.'

Robyn grinned. 'Maybe I will,' she said, pouring hot water into the mugs one by one. 'At least I'll see how today plays out and if it seems promising then I'll go for it. That is, if I read it right.'

'You'll read it right,' Nina said, 'you always do. And he'd be crazy to turn you down so I'm sure he'll say yes.'

Robyn picked up the tray. 'Right then, let's go and start phase one… bribery with tea and biscuits.'

Nina pushed aside the regret that lay heavy in her gut and the sadness mixed with envy. She would be happy for her friend, and she would offer support and encouragement, because a woman who was brave enough to take a chance instead of hiding away, terrified of new beginnings, deserved all the support and encouragement Nina could give.

'That's a sight for sore eyes!' Colm grinned as Nina and Robyn returned with their tray of refreshments. 'Biscuits too! I'll be coming here again, so I will.'

'That's very kind,' Nasser said, taking a cup.

'Oooh, lovely!' Kelly said, taking one too. Then Ron grabbed the pack of biscuits before Colm could reach them and took a handful before slapping them back on the tray with enough force to break every remaining biscuit. Robyn opened her mouth, set to give him a piece of her mind, but was stopped by Colm's good-natured laugh.

'Someone's worked up an appetite already,' he said, taking a digestive for himself. It snapped instantly in his hands. Ron glared at him, cradling his haul like Gollum with his Precious and, despite the situation, it was hard not to laugh.

'I'm giving up my time,' Ron said sourly, 'and they're supposed to be for everyone.'

'Yes,' Robyn said. 'They're for *everyone*.'

Nina could have safely bet her house that Robyn was dying to make some additional sarcastic comment about how everyone had given up their time and if biscuit allocation had been based on hours given in good humour then Ron would have to hand all but a lick of chocolate back from his stash.

'I reckon,' Colm began, taking a sip of his tea as he surveyed the garden, 'if we get a good day and push on we could be done here by nightfall.' He looked at everyone with a broad smile, his gaze finally settling on Nina. 'And you could get your campaign back on track.'

'That'd be amazing,' Nina said, and she almost meant it. Of course she wanted to get the memory tree project going again; it was just the bit about the garden being finished that she wasn't so keen on. Once the garden was done there'd be no need for Colm to come back to Sparrow Street and she'd probably never see him again. Then again, the alternative outcome here might be that he ended up dating Robyn, and that might be just as unbearable as not seeing him at all. She was beginning to wish she'd never met the man.

After they'd finished their tea and biscuits, Colm gave directions and instructions on what he thought still needed to be done and the best way to do it and they all began work. Spirits were surprisingly high considering manpower was thin on the ground – even Ron didn't look completely miserable as he raked over the soil in a plot that would be home to a trellis of climbing roses. However, it wasn't long before he was dropping hints that were about as subtle as a sledgehammer that he was thirsty and wondering when the next cup of tea might be available. Kelly volunteered this time, which was lucky, because if Robyn had been forced to go and make a second pot so soon after the first, she might just have tipped it over Ron's head.

So they all stopped again, because it seemed only polite when Kelly had gone to the trouble of popping back home to oblige, and then Ron needed the toilet so he disappeared. It was a good hour before he came back muttering about his *old problem*. It seemed that nobody much liked the ominous way in which he labelled his old problem and so nobody asked about it, and Ron's expression was sourer than ever as he took up the rake again, clearly disappointed that not one of his neighbours found his old problem as fascinating and mysterious as he did.

They'd been back at it for about ten minutes or so when Nina, who was helping Robyn lay (i.e. wrestle hopelessly with) some weed-proof membrane, heard Nasser hail someone in greeting. She and Robyn looked up at the same time to see Peter arrive. Nina glanced at Robyn and noted the way her features tightened. She saw them exchange a brief look of recognition, of perhaps regret too, before Robyn returned to her task without a word.

'Don't you think you ought to go and say hello?' Nina asked.

'What for?'

'I don't know… because it doesn't seem right to ignore him? It seems like he wants to be friends if you can't be anything else.'

'Perhaps he does,' Robyn said shortly, but she made no move to abandon what she was doing.

'Would that be so bad?'

'Maybe not for others but for me… too messy. We're together or we're not – I can't be doing with that in-between limbo stuff.'

'Well then, perhaps you ought to at least put him straight because he doesn't look like someone who's getting that.'

Robyn looked up again, and although Peter was talking to Nasser his gaze kept flicking over to her.

'I'm sure he'll work it out for himself eventually,' Robyn said, returning to her work.

Nina rolled her eyes. 'And you think *I'm* difficult.'

At this, she caught a fleeting grin on Robyn's face. It was encouraging; it showed that she wasn't completely heartbroken over Peter, nor was she completely angry with him. Perhaps she wasn't really as cold and unmoved by his attempts to reach out as she might pretend to be.

'Well,' Nina continued, 'I don't think he's worked it out at all. In fact, he's on his way over…'

Robyn straightened up, and despite the resolute set of her shoulders as she faced him, a hand strayed to her hair to smooth it down. Nina held back a smile. For all Robyn's tough talk, all her flirting with Colm, it was as clear as day that she still had a lot of affection for Peter. Maybe they'd work it out after all. And guilty as that might make Nina feel because her reasons for wanting that outcome weren't entirely pure, she still found herself wanting it.

'Hi,' he said awkwardly.

Nina smiled. 'Hello, Peter.'

'How's the work going?' he asked, though nobody standing there thought for a minute he cared what was happening in that garden.

'Good,' Nina said. 'Um… I've just got to see Nasser about something,' she added, scurrying off, just knowing that Robyn's irritated glare would be following her. She looked back to see Peter begin an earnest conversation and, to her credit, Robyn seemed to be giving him time to speak. It looked promising.

It was then that Nina, her attention still fixed on what was happening behind her, thudded into something large and soft, throwing her off balance.

'Oh!' she cried, immediately feeling arms close around her and looking up into Colm's face. 'Oh! I'm sorry!'

'My fault,' he said with an apologetic smile. 'I should have said something but I didn't see you hurtling towards me until it was too late. Besides,' he added with a look that was somehow impish, 'I'd plenty of time to catch you.'

Nina almost leapt from his arms, her cheeks scarlet. Did that mean he'd wanted to catch her? Had he deliberately let her run into him?

'Totally my fault,' she said. 'I should have been watching where I was going.'

'Let's just share the blame and leave it at that,' Colm said, still looking far more amused by the whole thing than Nina.

'Yes.' Nina straightened her clothes. Not that there was a lot of point: what with the mess from the garden and the fact that she hadn't worn her best anyway, it hardly made a difference to the way she looked. She hadn't wanted to ruin anything good, but she was beginning to wish she'd worn something a little more flattering than her old jeans and a sweatshirt she'd picked up from the Sacred Heart shop before it had closed down.

Colm plunged his hands into his pockets and looked towards Robyn and Peter.

'They're an item?' he asked.

'Oh,' Nina said, unable to deny the lurch of disappointment that he was even asking. Did that mean he was interested in Robyn after all? 'Robyn and Peter? They used to be,' she added. 'I'm not sure where they're at now, to be honest. I only know it needs work.'

'She's a feisty one, isn't she?'

'She is – a force of nature.'

'If I knew him better, would I wish him luck or warn him to wear a tin hat?'

'She's not that bad,' Nina said. 'She's really lovely when you get to know her.'

'I don't doubt that.'

'Very attractive.'

'True.'

'She's going to be a real catch for someone.'

'For some lucky man, to be sure. Perhaps your man Peter there – looks like he's keen.'

Colm turned to Nina with a smile

'About that lantern,' he began after a pause.

'Lantern? You mean on the memory tree?'

Nina recalled now that he'd mentioned taking a lantern before. She'd wondered who it was for – perhaps she was about to find out.

'How would I get in touch with you when I'm ready to buy one?'

'Well, it's not exactly *buying*…'

'What else is it? I give you some money and you put up a lantern for me. Sounds like buying to me.'

'I just prefer to call it donating.'

'Well, how do I donate?'

'I expect we'll have a website. Maybe a number people can call if they don't like using the internet – some don't, especially the pensioners. I haven't really finalised it yet, being so busy here and everything.'

'Would that be *your* phone number?' he asked, a bit too innocently.

Nina's cheeks began to burn again. 'I don't know. Do you think it's a bad idea to use mine?'

'Depends who you're giving it to,' he replied, a definite gleam of mischief in his eyes now.

Nina hauled in a breath, so light-headed that she felt she might faint, every sense, every awareness heightened. His obvious flirting had caught her off guard and she didn't know how to react. She only knew that something was coming, something big, and this time she might be brave enough to take the leap.

'Oh… well, I…'

Words wouldn't come out. Nina had never felt so useless, less capable of responding. She wanted to be able to express herself but she couldn't. She wanted to tell him to go ahead and ask, and that the answer would be yes. But then, her eyes travelled to where Robyn was still talking to Peter. It wasn't just about Gray now, or whether Nina was ready or not, was it? Robyn had made her own intentions towards Colm clear – what would it do to their friendship if Nina did this now?

'It's him you fancy?' Colm asked, cutting into her thoughts. She shook herself and turned to face him, not realising that she must have been staring at Robyn and Peter. The question was so unexpected, so completely and utterly off the mark that Nina began to laugh.

'Peter? No! It's not like that at all!'

'So… what about me? You could maybe fancy me?'

'Oh God yes!' she said, realising instantly that perhaps her admission had been a little too fervent and not cool at all.

He let out a low chuckle. 'So, I was wondering then… you might also fancy a drink with me sometime?'

'Oh… I don't know…'

He frowned slightly. 'I'm sorry, I'm reading this wrong? I thought…'

'Oh, I'd love to, but it's just…' Nina looked across at Robyn again.

'So it's your friend?' Colm said. 'She doesn't approve of me?'

Nina's eyes widened. 'Are you kidding? She's practically been throwing herself at you since the day she met you! Don't say you haven't noticed!'

'Oh.' Colm grinned, and, rather sweetly, he blushed almost as deeply as Nina had earlier. There was something quite gratifying about the fact that it wasn't her this time. But then his grin faded. 'Does that mean you're going to refuse me?'

Nina gave an awkward shrug. Hearing it like that it sounded trite and silly. She and Robyn were grown women who knew by now how love and friendship worked – they simply had to sit down and talk about it, and it was really Nina's fault that they hadn't already. Robyn would have gladly done it and she'd tried, which made Nina feel even sillier. But then, hadn't it been about more than just being attracted to the same man?

'I don't know much,' Colm said, 'but I think your dilemma might sort itself out.'

Nina looked back. Robyn was close to Peter now. She was smiling and so was he – if Nina knew anything about body language it looked as if they'd very much patched up their differences.

'So…' Colm began again, his voice low now and oh so achingly sexy. 'What do you say? You… me…? That drink?'

'I don't…' Nina began a response that was so automatic, so well-programmed that it made her want to slap herself. It was the one she didn't really have to think about, the one that caused the least emotional upheaval, but it was the one that would leave her lonely again while the rest of the world lived and loved without her.

'One drink,' Colm cut in. 'Just friends, no funny business if you don't want it. What harm can it do?'

Nina hesitated, despite all that ran through her mind. What was wrong with her? Why couldn't she say yes? She looked at Robyn and Peter again. They were kissing. Then she turned back to Colm and was trapped in those blue eyes as soon as their gazes met. Shyness and terror, boldness and excitement, and about another million different emotions raced through her, but in the end, she smiled. She could do this. Why not? Other people did it all the time. Other people moved on; were they all wrong to seize a second chance? She had a suspicion that if Gray had to approve another man for Nina, he'd have approved a man like Colm.

She nodded finally, her heart thumping. When words came, it was as if they'd come from someone else's mouth. It was as if life was about to change in ways she couldn't imagine.

'Yes,' she said. 'I'd like that.'

'There's something I should probably tell you before we get that far, though,' he added. Nina looked at him and suddenly he looked troubled. 'I'm married. Separated, but some are still bothered by the fact—'

'I know,' Nina said breathlessly. 'I mean, my dad told me.'

'Ah – of course he did. And I have a daughter too. She's fifteen.'

'I know. Dad told me that too.'

'So you're OK with all that?'

'Of course I'm totally OK with your daughter. I honestly don't know about the other thing. I suppose for now. I mean, I'm guessing that you asking me out means it's properly over?'

'Without a doubt,' he said with a grim nod. 'She's never coming back and I gave up waiting a long time ago.'

'I know how you feel.'

'You lost your husband, so I'm told. How long has it been?'

'Two years.'

'And you haven't…?

Nina shook her head. 'No… it's just never happened. Never quite the right circumstances, I suppose, and perhaps a little my fault too if I'm honest. That doesn't put you off, does it?'

'Of course not,' he said. 'I understand it must have been hard. I can take things as slowly as you like, you know.'

Nina smiled. 'I think I might be a bit sick of taking things slowly. Why don't we just take things as they come instead?'

Chapter Sixteen

Nina was relieved to see that Colm had turned up in a car rather than the work van he'd been coming to Sparrow Street in. With his company name emblazoned across the sides, it was a bit too conspicuous for her liking. It was still hard not to feel guilty, as if she was doing something she shouldn't be (even though she wasn't), and she didn't want to draw attention to who was picking her up. The last thing she needed was to be the focus of gossip on Sparrow Street. Almost as soon as the knock had come at her front door, she was out, hurrying to his car so that they wouldn't be seen lingering on the doorstep.

'You look lovely,' he said as he opened the passenger door for her. She paused for a second and looked down at herself. She was wearing a midnight blue velvet dress that hadn't seen the outside of her wardrobe for a long time now. Gray had loved seeing her in it and she'd tussled for a good hour over whether to wear it tonight. In the end, she'd been unable to find anything else that seemed right for the occasion, and she'd shoved the guilt from her thoughts and put it on. When she'd looked in the mirror, the outfit finally complete with a delicate heart necklace, dramatic eye make-up and her hair piled up loosely with a silver clip, she'd been forced to admit that she'd felt pretty good.

'Thank you,' Nina said shyly, desperate not to dally.

'I thought we might go to the Old Apple Loft,' he added, getting into the driver seat. He turned the key and the engine purred quietly.

'Do you mind if we don't?' Nina asked. 'It's just that…'

His face fell. 'Christ; I should have realised. God, I'm sorry – you went there with your husband?'

She nodded, already aware of so much that she was making taboo when perhaps it didn't need to be. But she couldn't go somewhere that reminded her so strongly of Gray, not now when all this was still so new.

'Sorry. You don't mind, do you?'

'It's me who should be sorry – great lump I am. I should have asked you… Let me think…'

Nina knew a few pubs and bistros around the area but the problem was that she only knew them because Gray had taken her to them during the early days of their relationship when they went out a lot, so suggestions from her were going to be pretty non-existent. She just hoped Colm would think of somewhere new.

'How do you feel about driving out of town?' he asked after a moment of drumming on the steering wheel as he looked pensively along the road.

'That sounds OK. Where were you thinking of?'

'There's a little place sits on the canal. They have a nice menu too. I'm just trying to think what it's called.'

'Is it the Dovecot?'

'That's the one – should I be worried that you know it?'

'No.' Nina smiled. 'I only know it because Robyn mentioned it to me – Peter was going to take her there.'

Colm grinned. 'Ah… how's that going?'

'Robyn and Peter? It's early days and they've hit rocky ground before but she seems really happy that they're giving it another go. I think

they might be in with a chance now that the wife is out of the way…
Oh…' She blushed. Had she said the wrong thing now? Had she put
her foot in it by reminding Colm of his wife? Were things always going
to be this new and awkward? She hoped they'd get to the stage soon
where they wouldn't be.

'That's good,' he said, not seeming too concerned. 'And she hasn't
disowned you because we're going out?'

Nina let out an anxious breath and smiled. 'Oh no; she's happy
for us.'

'I'm sure you're relieved about that.'

'A bit.'

'The Dovecot then?'

'Sounds lovely.'

Colm smiled at her again, that dazzling, breathtaking smile of his,
and then turned to the road as he pulled away from the kerb. The
moment they left Sparrow Street, Nina felt lighter.

'Where's your daughter tonight?' she asked.

'Oh, she's out at a friend's house. She'll be happy enough to stay
the night so there's no rush to get back.'

'That's good. I suppose it must be hard organising your time around her.'

'Not as hard as it once was. She's fifteen now and not so keen for
a bedtime story these days.' He chuckled softly at his own joke. 'But
when her mam left us, my little Polly was the only thing that stopped
me from going mad. Without her… well… she gave me a reason to
keep going. We've had our ups and downs but she's a lovely girl – even
though I may have a biased opinion there – and I'm proud of her.'

'Does she miss her mum?'

'Every day, I'm sure. For the first few years she asked Santa every
Christmas to bring her back, even though she was a bit too old to

believe in Santa. It was a way of expressing her sadness, you know. But as you'll know, you get used to that hole in your life and you end up working around it, don't you?'

'The lantern you wanted to donate for… who's it for?'

He shook his head, and when he answered his voice was strangely gruff. 'Polly had a twin when she was born. For about an hour, anyway.'

Nina took a moment to understand what he'd said, and then she turned to the window, her eyes misting. She'd been so wrapped up in the tragedy of her own past that she'd never imagined something like that in his.

'All water under the bridge now,' he said in that gruff, struggling voice again, and it was clear that it wasn't water under the bridge at all. It was also clear, however, that this was not a conversation he wanted to have right now.

'I suppose Polly misses having a woman about the place?' she asked.

'Oh not really – there've been plenty of those.'

'Oh,' Nina said, going cold now. How many emotions could one person go through in a minute? Lots of women? Had she got him wrong? Was he some kind of serial dater?

'Yes – cousins, aunts, grandma, plenty of friends… She's got plenty of female input.'

'Right, I see,' Nina said, feeling foolish again. She could only hope the rest of the night wasn't going to be as fraught as this because she didn't think she'd be able to take it. 'Are you still friends with your wife's family?'

He threw her a sideways look. 'As much as can be expected. They don't blame me for what happened – at least they say they don't – and they're there when Polly needs them.'

'I suppose it must be awkward, though.'

'They always knew Jane could be difficult. To be honest, when she went off it was no great surprise to anyone, even her family.'

'Is it hard to move on though? Being married to someone who's not there, I mean? Does it feel a bit like limbo?'

'For all intents and purposes we're divorced – I just haven't got round to sorting the formalities yet. To be honest, I never really had a reason either. I suppose I just got used to the situation.'

'Would you have been together now if she hadn't run away?'

'Who knows? Maybe not. Things were often rocky.' He looked at her wryly. 'You're very interested in my domestic arrangements.'

Nina flushed. 'Sorry.'

'Don't be. I'll take it as a good sign you're interested enough in me to… I don't know… maybe look beyond tonight…?'

'Oh no!' Nina said quickly. 'I rarely look beyond tomorrow's breakfast these days.' She gave a self-conscious laugh. 'No point, is there, because you can never tell what's coming.'

'That's for sure,' Colm said. 'How long again is it you've been on your own?'

'Two years.'

'And there's *really* been nobody else in all that time?'

'No. Why do you ask?'

'I just find it hard to believe. A woman like you…'

'A woman like me can be very silly and wrapped up in grief. It took me a long time to work that out. In fact, I think I might still be working that out. Does it worry you? Put you off? That I might come with baggage?'

'We all come with baggage if we've lived long enough and fully enough,' Colm said gently. 'Life has a way of making things interesting in one way or another. But I want you to know that my intentions are as honest as they can be,' he added.

'Maybe they can be *honest* but not completely *honourable*.'

He chuckled. 'I definitely can't promise honourable seeing you look so good in that dress.'

The conversation was quickly becoming more than just finding out about each other – it almost felt like each of them had somehow set out their stall, laid out ground rules that the other could understand and play by accordingly. They'd both suffered different kinds of loss but, in the end, they'd both lost. They'd been hurt in different ways, but they'd both been hurt. They'd both been left alone and they were both looking (whether they knew it or not) for someone to heal them.

The conversation turned to lighter topics, and for the rest of the drive they talked mainly about the garden on Sparrow Street, about the other residents, about Colm's job, Polly's school reports and extra-curricular activities, the state of Sammy and Diana's garden when he'd first been employed by them, about his work schedule and the unpredictable nature of self-employment. By the time they'd reached the old thatched pub overlooking an idyllic spot near a canal lock they were like old friends, so that once they'd been seated at a table in a snug booth there was hardly any first-date awkwardness at all. They had drinks Colm had fetched from the bar and snacks were on their way from the pub kitchen, and Nina finally felt something like settled in his company.

'How come you moved to England?' she asked. 'You must miss Ireland?'

'It's not so hard to get there and we visit a lot,' he said. 'And in case you're wondering, I didn't come here for love. I came here long before I'd met Jane.'

'So what brought you?'

He gave her a sheepish smile. 'Would you believe that foolish young me thought I might find adventure here?'

Nina raised her eyebrows. 'There's no adventure in Dublin?'

He chuckled. 'Plenty to be sure. But a young man can get bored and want to see somewhere new, doing things that his parents wouldn't approve of.'

'So you came here?' Nina asked incredulously. 'To Wrenwick?'

'Not at first.' He smiled. 'I started off in Glasgow, and then I came to Wrenwick. *That* was for love. Jane was studying in Glasgow when I met her, but Wrenwick was home for her. So I followed her here and then we had Polly and...' He shrugged. 'It seemed as good a place as any to bring Polly up, and when Jane left me I didn't want to move Polly back to Ireland – the one thing she needed was stability and moving her wouldn't give her that.'

Nina's chin rested on a fist as she listened. 'It must have been really hard for you,' she said when he'd finished.

'I guess you might say I had it bad, but I don't see it that way.'

'I've heard people complain a lot more about a lot less,' Nina said.

'It's all relative – that's how I look at it. If your world has never collapsed then a crack looks bad enough, doesn't it?'

Nina smiled, her heart dancing again. This man... this wonderful, optimistic, kind, fun-loving man could be so good for her if only she could put aside her doubts and guilt completely and let him. There was a physical attraction too, as strong and potent as anything she'd felt for Gray, though she found it harder to acknowledge that. The truth was, she liked Colm – she liked him a lot. Maybe one day she could even love him.

Beyond the windows of the pub, strings of yellow bulbs garlanded the beer garden, reflecting onto the dark waters of the canal like little drops of fire. The night was bitterly cold and yet drinkers still sat outside beneath the warm glow of patio heaters, wrapped in fleece blankets, newly stepped off their narrowboats to take a cheering beer or two before they continued on their way to the next lock. The boats were painted red and green and gold, gleaming lacquer reflected in the light from the pub as they gently knocked against their moorings.

'Are you alright?'

Nina shook herself, Colm's warm tones bringing her back to the room.

'I'm sorry,' she said, giving a little self-conscious laugh. 'It's the boats… they look like fun, don't they?'

'I've never given it much thought before but I suppose they do.'

'I think it would be nice to float along without a care in the world. For a couple of weeks at least.'

'I suppose it would. You've never been on one?'

'No. You?'

He shook his head. 'But maybe,' he added with a deliciously mischievous gleam in his sea-blue eyes, 'it's something we could do together some day.'

Nina smiled. There was no doubt in his expression at all, only absolute certainty that they had a future well beyond tonight. She liked his confidence, and it was infectious, because she was beginning to see that future too. One thing she knew with as much certainty was that she didn't want tonight to be the one and only night like this.

Chapter Seventeen

A week before, Nina would have been nervous about the prospect of returning to the studios at Wrenwick Community Radio to have another crack at Sammy's show. But today she was strangely unfazed as she sat with Robyn in his studio for the second time, waiting to go on air. In fact, she suspected Sammy was more nervous than either her or Robyn – though perhaps that was to be expected given what had happened the last time they were here, and that it was his first day back on air, having flouted his doctors' advice and gone back to work weeks earlier than he ought to have done. Perhaps he was already beginning to regret that decision as he was far from his usual relaxed self, going back and forth across the studio space, checking and rechecking equipment and muttering to himself.

'Is it just me who doesn't think he should be here?' Robyn whispered to Nina, watching him carefully. 'He's not right, is he?'

'I know,' Nina whispered back. 'He hasn't even offered us coffee in a dirty mug so you can tell he's not right.'

Robyn gave a quick grin. 'You are, though. Things are going well with that hunk of leprechaun? Haven't you seen him every night this week?'

'Not quite,' Nina said, beaming in spite of Robyn's sarcasm. Besides, she wasn't far wrong really. 'He has a daughter, don't forget. I don't think she'd be happy if he was out every night.'

'Oh, OK, *almost* every night. Every time I phone you to come round for a chat, that's for sure.'

Nina's smile grew. 'You're one to talk anyway. You've been off the radar since Peter's split from his wife was made official.'

'Walking like John Wayne and proud of it.' Robyn winked and Nina muffled a shriek of shocked laughter.

'I *do not* need to know about that!'

'That's OK – I'm not going to tell you.'

Nina laughed. 'Oh, now that's just being a spoilsport. At least give me something so I get the opportunity to tell you how disgusted I am.'

Robyn grinned again.

'It's going well then?' Nina asked.

'I really like him.'

'I guessed that much.'

'I liked him all along; it was just the wife thing… and you – dark horse. I knew there was something about Colm you weren't telling me. You should have said when I asked; I feel awful that I was going after him. Imagine if—'

'Don't,' Nina said softly. 'It wouldn't have been your fault – it would have been mine, and if you'd ended up together I'd have been happy for you.'

Robyn raised her eyebrows. 'Really?'

'Yes,' Nina said firmly. 'Absolutely. Even if it had killed me.'

Robyn smiled at Nina fondly.

'Are you ready, girls?'

They both looked to see Sammy regarding them with a vague look that didn't fill them with confidence. It was clear that he was not as well as he'd reassured them, but then, that was nothing they hadn't already guessed. The fact was, there was no telling him so they'd just have to hope the show went as smoothly and with as little stress as possible.

'Are you sure you're up to this?' Robyn asked anyway. 'Being back at work, I mean. I don't fancy another day at the hospital.'

'Whether I am or not, fame is fickle and you're soon forgotten,' Sammy said in a solemn tone. 'If I don't get back on the horse sooner rather than later, there'll be some youngster ready to take this slot and I'll be out on my ear.'

Nina was quite sure that wasn't true, because the old folk of Wrenwick who made up most of his audience were very fond of Sammy.

She smiled brightly. 'Just take it easy – that's all we're saying.'

He regarded them both warmly, and a little of the old Sammy shone through, the one who hadn't recently been thoroughly rattled by an unwelcome reminder of his own mortality.

'I'm almost sure God has sent me a pair of guardian angels to watch over me,' he said.

Robyn spluttered, her shocked laughter ringing across the studio.

'Bloody hell!' she cried. 'If we're the best He's got to offer then He doesn't like you as much as you think He does!'

Sammy grinned now. 'He must have heard the show then. Still,' he sniffed, 'beggars can't be choosers, can they?'

'Cheeky bugger! I think you've just turned your compliment into an insult!'

There was a knock at the studio window and someone pointed at a clock festooned with threadbare tinsel. Along with a tiny tree on the desk, it was the one and only concession to the approaching festive season as far as Nina could see.

'Shit!' Sammy said, plonking himself down at the desk and punching a button.

'Here we go,' Robyn whispered as the show jingle began to play. Nina glanced at Robyn, who looked as excited as she'd ever seen her. She loved seeing her friend so happy and content with life – goodness knew she deserved it. In fact, when she really thought about it, Nina couldn't remember a time when life had looked quite this rosy for her either. Maybe things were looking up for both of them.

Nina wasn't entirely sure about the choice of venue. After all, she'd come to Roberto's with her mum and dad for many years as a girl and Winston was well aware of that. But for some reason, he'd seized on the rather old-fashioned pizzeria as his new favourite place since he'd been there again with Nina and broken the news of his imminent engagement. In the circumstances, it seemed like an odd venue to introduce her mother's replacement. Perhaps Winston hadn't really seen it in quite the same way as Nina. Maybe it was a man thing.

He sat across from his daughter now, fingers knotted together on the table, legs bouncing beneath it, his gaze flitting back and forth between the street beyond the window and the restaurant interior. He was wearing a shirt and tie. Nina had only ever seen him wear a tie for weddings and funerals, and she didn't want to dwell on the latter because it would bring back too many painful memories that would hardly help her today of all days.

'She'll be here soon, I expect,' he said. He'd said the same thing at least four times since they'd arrived.

'Perhaps the traffic's bad,' Nina offered. 'An accident maybe?'

'I expect that's it. I should have gone to pick her up.'

'Then you'd have both been stuck in traffic.'

'Yes, yes... but she's very independent, you know. Self-sufficient. No bother to anyone at all.'

'Mum used to be like that,' Nina said.

'Yes, yes she did...' Winston gave an uneasy laugh. Nina hadn't meant to send him on a guilt trip but perhaps, inadvertently, she had. 'I suppose I must have a *type*.'

'I suppose you must,' Nina said with a smile that she hoped would put him more at ease.

Winston's eyes went to the window again. 'I'm sure she'll be here at any minute.'

'Maybe you should phone her?'

He shook his head. 'She'd never answer if she's driving; she's good like that. You'll like her,' he added, though he seemed to be convincing himself of that rather than Nina. As far as Nina was concerned, it didn't really matter whether she liked Pam or not in the end, because only her dad got to choose who he might spend his twilight years with. Pam would have to be abominable to provoke a reaction from Nina that might make her question her dad's choice, because she was determined to tolerate a lot from anyone who made her dad happy, no matter how she might personally feel about them.

And, Nina thought vaguely, if things continued the way they were going with Colm, Winston wasn't the only one who was going to have to seek approval for a new partner. He and Winston had met before, of course, and they seemed to like each other, but that was when Nina had introduced him as someone who was simply helping them to repair their community gardens, rather than as a partner.

'Ah!'

Winston almost leapt from his seat as he spotted someone out on the street. Nina followed his gaze to the woman who'd just pulled up and was currently getting a ticket from a parking meter. From this distance it was hard to tell much about her, save that she looked quite short and what Robyn would have called a bit on the cuddly side, though she was wrapped in a thick, padded coat that might well have been adding a few pounds to her frame. As Winston was watching attentively, and as she was the only new arrival on the street, Nina had to assume that this was, indeed, Pam, the woman who'd recently accepted her father's proposal and was now her new stepmother-to-be.

Nina's stomach did a curious and unexpected cartwheel, and so she could only imagine how nervous Pam might be. When she thought about it, perhaps Pam had every reason to be more worried than Nina about whether they'd get along. Nina had a whole lifetime's worth of love and loyalty from her dad to fall back on, whereas Pam was the new woman trying to fit in somewhere. For her dad's sake, Nina was determined to make a good impression regardless, because life would be a lot easier if everyone could get along.

She and Winston watched together in silence as the woman crossed the road to the restaurant. It wasn't until Winston spoke that Nina realised just how silent they'd been.

'I feel sick,' he said faintly. It was almost as if he'd forgotten Nina was there. She looked over and her heart went out to him. She'd been so wrapped up in how she and Pam might get along that she hadn't fully appreciated just how nervous her dad was about this meeting, but now she saw more clearly than ever just how important it was to him. It was testament to how much he cared for Pam and how badly he wanted his daughter and his new fiancée to get along. Nina reached for his hand across the table and gave it a gentle pat.

'She looks lovely, Dad.'

In the next moment, the door to the restaurant opened and Pam bumbled in. Her cheeks and nose were rosy from the cold, the skin of her face soft and plump, her eyes bright and good-natured. She smiled broadly as she hurried over to their table. Winston stood to greet her with a light kiss. Pam returned it and then turned to Nina, who stood up too.

'Hello,' Nina said, extending her hand. 'I'm so pleased to meet you – Dad's told me all about you.'

'Oh, it's so lovely to finally meet you too!' Pam exclaimed, forsaking the hand and pulling Nina into an unexpected hug. 'Oh, and your dad was right – you're absolutely beautiful! What gorgeous hair! You're just lovely!'

Nina threw a bemused smile at her dad.

'Oh yes… he's always talking about you…' Pam shrugged off her coat to reveal an embroidered needlecord dress. She wore her grey hair short while tiny pearls hung from her ears.

'I like your earrings,' Nina said, sitting down again as Pam took her seat next to Winston.

'Thank you. They belonged to my grandmother. I suppose that makes them terribly old by now, doesn't it?'

'They might be but the thing about pearls is they're classic – they never go out of style.'

'Oh, I agree!' Pam beamed, and Nina smiled back, glancing at Winston as she did to see him relax a little. Nina felt more relaxed too – so far, so good. She already liked Pam and perhaps today wouldn't be too much of a test after all.

The waiter came over to their table. 'Would you like your drinks now?' he asked.

'Oh, yes please,' Nina said. 'And do you want a jug of water for the table too, Dad?'

Winston nodded. Nina ordered herself a gin and orange while Pam asked for lemonade. Nina's dad said he'd make do with water.

'It's lovely in here,' Pam said as the waiter left them again. 'I used to come here with my Bruce.'

Nina frowned slightly.

'My ex,' Pam said.

'You're divorced then?'

'Yes. When he told me he wanted to leave me it was a shock, I can tell you. But it was a good few years ago now so I don't think about it all that much any more.'

'That's good,' Nina said, not knowing what else she could say to that.

'It's his loss and my gain,' Winston said, giving Pam a fond look.

Pam laughed. 'I'm sure he wouldn't agree. Anyway, I think it was me who had the lucky escape in the end. You should see how he's let himself go. Not like your dad here who's stayed lovely and trim and handsome.'

Winston batted away the compliment, almost giggling like a teenage girl. He looked so giddy, so happy, that Nina couldn't help but smile. If this was the effect Pam was going to have on her dad, then she loved her almost as much as he did already. The waiter returned with their drinks.

'Are you ready to order your starters?' he asked.

'Oh goodness, we haven't even looked at the menu yet we've been so busy chatting!' Pam said, throwing Nina a broad smile. 'Could you give us another minute?'

'Certainly,' the waiter said.

'Oh dear,' Pam said as he left the table again. She picked up a menu and stuck her face into it. 'We'd better decide what we want before we get told off again.' She looked at Winston. 'What are you having?'

'I'm not sure… perhaps I'll have the little ball things.'

'That sounds lovely; I might have those too.' Pam looked at Nina. 'I don't think I'll have a starter.'

Pam nodded. 'That's why you're so slim, I'll bet. I'll always have the starter. Pudding too. A meal feels lopsided if I don't have the whole set – I can't help it. That's why I'm shaped this way.'

'You're shaped perfectly,' Winston said, and it was Pam's turn to giggle like a schoolgirl now.

'Oh you!' she said.

Nina looked between the two of them and smiled again, though a bit of her was wondering when the pet names were going to come out. If they did, was it something she really wanted to hear? She was all for her dad being happy but there was such a thing as too much information.

Winston raised his glass. 'A toast,' he said. 'To new beginnings.'

Nina raised hers too, touched glasses with the both of them and repeated: 'To new beginnings.'

There seemed to be a lot of those going on right now.

Chapter Eighteen

Nina had wondered whether their regular curry night would become a thing of the past. Robyn had been spending more and more time with Peter over the last couple of weeks, not to mention that she was keeping a closer eye on Toby these days too – and Nina was spending more time with Colm. All this meant that Nina and Robyn had had very little time to see each other. They'd been in regular contact, of course, as the requests and donations for their memory project had started to come in (in part as a result of the radio interview with Sammy that Robyn had managed to make hilarious and entertaining), but that wasn't the same as having proper time to sit and talk about what was going on in their lives, which, when Nina thought about it, was quite a lot these days.

It wasn't just a case of new relationships and the garden project – Nina still had to find a job. The search wasn't going quite as well as she'd hoped. She'd discovered, as she'd suspected, that retail jobs weren't quite as plentiful as they'd once been, that seasonal work had been all but snapped up by the time you got this close to Christmas and that on paper, as capable as she might be in real life, she wasn't qualified for a lot else. The only one very promising lead was the pub where her dad had put in a word, but that was yet to yield anything definite.

However, Robyn had phoned earlier that day to see if Nina was free in the evening and Nina had gladly confirmed that she was, Colm having to go to parents' evening with Polly. Though she was enjoying time with Colm, she'd missed Robyn too. Things were new and strange right now, even though they were a good kind of strange, and Nina couldn't help but reflect that it would be nice to settle back into an old comfortable routine every now and again. It would certainly help to keep her grounded.

'I'm afraid it's sauce from a jar again,' Nina said as Robyn chopped the onions. Robyn always chopped the onions when she was there, because they made Nina cry so much that Robyn said it seemed cruel to make her do it.

'Tastes just as good,' Robyn replied airily.

'Yes, but I did promise myself I was going to start making more things from scratch – I've just been a bit busy lately.' Nina dabbed at her eyes, which were watering from being in close proximity to a particularly potent onion, despite the fact that she wasn't even chopping it.

'So,' Robyn asked as she glanced up with a wry smile. 'Lots to tell me?'

Nina smiled. 'You could say that. I suspect I could ask the same of you too.'

'Hmm, you could. But you first. How's that hunk of Irish beefcake?'

'He's good.' Nina's smile became a broad grin. The merest mention of Colm had the power to warm her from the inside out. Whenever she thought of him, life looked suddenly brighter. 'How's your hunk of council worker?'

Robyn frowned. 'Hunk of council worker? Now, that doesn't have the same sex appeal at all, does it? Remind me I've got the boring one, why don't you?'

'You don't mean that at all.'

It was Robyn's turn to give a soppy, faraway grin. 'No, I don't. He's fantastic. You know how they say the quiet ones are the ones you need to watch? Well, boy, does he need watching!'

'OK – stop right there! If we're going down a mucky path here I don't need to hear it.'

'Isn't that the only path worth going down?'

'I wouldn't know.'

Robyn looked up and paused her chopping. 'But you must be at that stage now? I mean, you and Colm must have…'

'No,' Nina said. 'We've agreed that there's no need to rush it and we're happy as we are right now. We've only been together a couple of weeks and we barely know each other really, so why do we need to think about other things yet?'

Robyn fixed her with a shrewd, piercing look. 'It makes you nervous,' she said. 'Guilty for desiring someone else – and looking at him, there's no way on this earth you wouldn't be thinking about *it*. Even I think about *it* when I look at him, and I'm not going out with him! And let me hazard a guess that there's a bit of you that's scared you'll even like it better with him—'

Nina shook her head. 'It's too soon, that's all. There's time, and Colm's happy to wait. So am I.'

'OK…' Robyn said slowly, her tone announcing that she respected Nina's wish to leave that particular topic, though she hardly bought Nina's excuses. 'So how's the great love affair that is Winston and Pam?'

'Oh, well Pam's lovely…'

'I sense a *but* coming.'

'No, she is. She's just… enthusiastic.'

'That's good, isn't it?'

'Well, yes, of course, but I just feel a bit overwhelmed by her sometimes. Of course, she makes Dad very happy and I'm sure I'll get used to her in time. She's not Mum, I suppose, and perhaps, at the end of the day, that's all it is.'

'He's been on his own a long time too. I'll bet it seemed as if he was going to stay on his own forever.'

'Yes, I suppose that's true too, so maybe a bit of me had got used to the idea and never imagined I'd have to get to know a new person in his life. I mean, this is the first time he's even introduced me to a lady friend, and now it's engagement parties and wedding planning…'

'Engagement party?' Robyn raised her eyebrows. 'I thought you said it was going to be low-key.'

'That's what Dad wanted, but now Pam's got all excited and it's turning into the royal wedding or something. And she wants to do it straight away – she's even talking about before Christmas.'

'Before Christmas! But that's, like, less than three weeks away! So, excited could be an understatement then?'

'Bless her – I suppose I ought to be glad because it means she's as keen as Dad is.'

'But you're not?'

'Yes, yes I am,' Nina said, but the doubt in her voice said otherwise. Though it was out of her power to do anything, no matter how she felt, she couldn't shake a nagging doubt that her dad might be falling into marriage with Pam just a little too quickly. But to say it out loud seemed churlish, so she didn't. 'It's just going to take some getting used to. Which reminds me, Dad said I should invite you to the engagement party. And Peter and Toby too, if they want to come.'

'I doubt Toby would but I can ask Peter. Tell your dad thanks. Where is it?'

'The Old Apple Loft. At least that's where she said she wanted it when I last saw them – I'm not sure if she's actually managed to book it yet.'

Robyn pulled a sympathetic face. 'Ouch.'

'I know,' Nina said. 'Pam's idea, and I can hardly phone her and tell her to change the venue because I used to go there with Gray, can I? Apart from anything else it sounds so maudlin.'

'I'm surprised your dad didn't say something.'

'I doubt he's even remembered there's anything significant about the place.' She shook her head. 'It's silly anyway – I need to be a big girl and get over it. I can't spend the rest of my life avoiding places I used to go with Gray.'

Robyn gave a nod of approval and Nina could tell what she was thinking. Things had changed over the past few weeks: once upon a time, Nina would have taken great care to avoid the places she'd gone to with Gray because of the memories there. It had hurt to think about those times because they'd never be again, and it still hurt, but maybe a little less these days. Nina didn't know how to feel about this. It was progress, of sorts, but she wasn't sure if it was the sort of progress that made her happy. Despite her growing feelings for Colm, there was still a constant war in her heart, the conflict between a love that could be and one that she wasn't quite ready to let go of yet. She was scared that loving Colm would mean she'd forget about Gray, and she could never do that.

'Is Colm going to go to the party?' Robyn asked, her voice cutting into Nina's thoughts.

'Pam said to ask him. She said he could bring Polly too, but that would be the first time I'd be meeting Polly and the first time Pam had met either of them…'

'Hmm, a bit awkward all round. Maybe more for you. Couldn't you meet Polly beforehand? I'm a bit surprised you haven't already considering how much time you're spending with her dad.'

'I think Colm is being a bit cautious, you know. Polly had a tough time getting over Jane – Colm's wife – leaving them and I think he's been a bit wary about introducing her to someone new. He thinks that Polly is still holding out hope that her mum will come back one day and everything will go back to the way it was.'

'That's hardly going to happen,' Robyn huffed as she tipped the chopped onions into the frying pan. 'How long has she been at that commune up in Scotland – five years, did you say?'

Nina nodded.

'Doesn't sound like she's in any rush to come back. Sounds to me like she's made a new life there.'

'Yes, but kids don't see it like that, do they? Life's a lot more black and white for them.'

'I don't know about that,' Robyn said, and Nina wondered whether that was a reference to Toby. If it was, then she was sure she'd hear about it soon enough so she didn't ask.

The pan began to hiss and the smell of frying onions lifted into the air. 'So they want it before Christmas? They don't mess about, do they? Surely they're not going to get the wedding in that quick?'

'Dad said there was no point in waiting around and Pam agreed. They're going to set a date for the wedding early in the new year if they can find a venue that Pam likes and that can fit them in so soon.'

'A shotgun wedding?' Robyn grinned and Nina had to laugh.

'I think they might be a bit past that – at least I hope so! I don't blame them one bit for being impatient really. Dad and I both know that happiness can be fleeting and it can be snatched from under your nose. If they love each other – and they seem to – then why not just get on with it and be together?'

Robyn picked up the jar of curry sauce and yanked off the lid. 'Where are they going to live?'

'I don't actually know,' Nina said thoughtfully. It wasn't something she'd considered, though now she thought about it, it seemed like an obvious question. She couldn't imagine Pam wanting to inhabit the shrine to Nina's mum that Winston called home, and she couldn't imagine Winston letting anyone eradicate those last traces of his late wife, no matter how much he might love them. She could only guess at some heated discussions on the matter, though her dad hadn't said anything about them if they had indeed taken place.

'I expect they'll start somewhere fresh,' Robyn said. 'Most do.'

'Do they?'

'Well, what would you do?'

Nina was silent for a moment. She tipped the washed rice into a pan of water that was now bubbling. What would she do? She could hardly imagine a point where she might have to consider her own home in Sparrow Street and what it would mean to whomever else might come into her life, but perhaps one day she'd have to.

'I don't know,' she said finally. 'It's not something I've thought about.'

'Maybe you'll have to,' Robyn said, echoing Nina's thoughts.

'Not for ages I should think.'

'Who knows?'

Nina looked around her little kitchen. Could she leave this place if she had to, this little house so full of her life with Gray? She might love again, but she could never forget that life and she wouldn't want to. But she could understand that it might be hard for another man to come into a place where every stick of furniture spoke of the man who'd been there before, of the man who would have still been Nina's one true love if life had allowed it. Nina couldn't imagine how hard it might be to make that compromise and she wouldn't wish it on anyone. It seemed like a long way off now, but if things continued to go well with Colm then that day might come soon enough.

The fact was, Nina didn't really know how Colm might feel about this house because he'd never even set foot in it. There seemed to be an innate understanding of boundaries, of respect for the delicacy of her feelings. They'd seen each other almost every day for the past couple of weeks but they'd always spent time somewhere public. Besides Colm not wanting to impose himself on Nina's home life, she'd been cautious about doing the same to him, mindful of the fact that perhaps he wanted to be sure of her before she went to his home and met Polly.

From what Colm had told Nina about Polly, she was still clinging to the hope that one day Jane would come back, and so she might struggle with the idea that Colm had fallen in love with someone new. Nina understood that the situation needed to be handled sensitively and she was fine with that. For now. But like everything else, she and Colm were both aware of the unspoken truth – that things couldn't stay like this forever.

'You want to get the oven on to warm the naans?' Robyn asked.

Nina turned to her. 'Huh?'

Robyn rolled her eyes. 'Dreaming of Mr Right again?'

Nina had to grin at this. She hadn't been – not in the way Robyn had thought, but now she'd been reminded of him she could have happily sat down and dreamt away.

'Honestly,' Robyn said. 'And I thought I was bad.'

Nina was about to reply when she noticed the rice pan boiling over. She rushed to turn the heat down. 'Shit!' she said, noting the sticky water already congealing on the hob.

'That's what you get for daydreaming,' Robyn replied serenely. Nina laughed.

'It is.'

Half an hour later they were ready to eat.

'I'm bloody starving!'

Robyn sat at the table as Nina brought warmed plates over.

'I must admit I'm hungry too,' she said. 'I've been saving myself since breakfast so I'd have plenty of room to stuff my face.'

Robyn smiled as she tore off a strip of naan bread. 'I have missed our curry nights, you know.'

'Me too. We'll have to make a new rule that we never stop doing it, no matter how busy we get with other things.'

'Like fellas?'

Nina laughed. 'Yes.'

'I suppose we could let them eat curry with us.'

'We could, but then we wouldn't be able to talk about them.'

Robyn grinned. 'True.'

The warm tang of spices on the air was making Nina's mouth water as she spooned rice onto her plate. Like she'd told Robyn, she'd been saving herself, but she hadn't realised quite how hungry she was until the smells of cooking had begun to fill the kitchen. Now, she fell on her meal with gusto, the flavours of tomatoes and spiced cream bursting into life in her mouth.

'This is *so* good!' Robyn mumbled through a mouthful of naan bread. 'Whatever did we do without curry?'

Nina laughed. 'No idea!'

'I'll tell you what, though,' Robyn added. 'This needs a beer.'

'There are a couple from last time in the fridge,' Nina said. Robyn got up to look but had barely left her chair when there was a frantic hammering at Nina's front door. They exchanged a look of alarm.

'Not expecting anyone then?' Robyn asked.

'No. I suppose it could be one of the neighbours after something. I'd better go and look.'

Nina went out to the hallway and Robyn followed. The knock that had threatened to batter the door down was hardly the casual knock of a neighbour who perhaps wanted to borrow a cup of sugar and clearly Robyn was as rattled as Nina. She stood behind her as Nina opened the door. But there was nobody outside.

'Weird,' Nina said quietly, more unnerved than she had been a moment before. She glanced at Robyn, who looked just as spooked.

'Probably kids,' she said, sounding unconvinced.

Then they heard shouting and stepped outside to look down the street. Nina frowned. Waddling from door to door, calling everyone out as he knocked at each house was the answer to the riddle – Ron.

'What the hell…?' Robyn shouted.

'Come and see this!' Ron called to nobody in particular, but in a tone of great self-importance. 'Come and see why we've all been wasting our time for all these weeks!'

'Does that man ever stop complaining?' Robyn said to Nina. 'How do you put up with him?'

'Something's bothering him,' Nina said. 'We'd better go and see.'

As they stepped out onto the street, Nasser came out of his house in shirtsleeves and slippers, looking as though he'd been woken from a doze in front of the TV. 'What's going on?' he shouted.

'Broad daylight!' Ron bellowed, still padding from door to door to bring out more neighbours. 'Caught the little bastards red-handed I did!'

The street was in darkness and it wouldn't have escaped anyone's attention, but nobody was about to correct Ron on his spurious broad-daylight claim. Something had riled him and anyone wanting to tangle with an angry Ron probably needed their heads looking at. Some people came out onto the street, as Nina and Robyn had, while some simply rolled their eyes when they saw who was making the fuss and went back inside. But most who'd been involved with the Sparrow Street garden renovations took note, because that's where Ron was now hurrying to, beckoning them to follow. There was a sudden, strange, heavy feeling in Nina's gut as she began to realise what the problem might be. She glanced at Robyn, the two of them now following Ron, and saw that she'd come to the same conclusion too.

And then they found themselves staring at the carnage of upturned benches with obscene messages spray painted onto them, uprooted saplings and trampled flower beds.

'Fat lot of good this fencing was,' Ron said savagely. 'They were straight over the gate – might as well have had a big sign telling them to come on in and do whatever they liked.'

'It's not Colm's fault!' Nina said, so hotly that some of her neighbours stared in mild surprise.

'I didn't say that,' Ron shot back. 'I'm just saying that the stuff he put up did nothing but look pretty.'

Nina opened her mouth to argue, blood rushing to her face, but Nasser cut in.

'How many of them would you say there were, Ron?'

'Three, four… not sure,' Ron replied tersely. 'Enough to make a mess. Does it matter? I chased 'em off anyway.'

'It's lucky you were here,' Nasser said soothingly. 'It was brave of you to act. Did you see them climb the railings?'

'I did when they made their getaway – like rats out of a pipe. Took them seconds to clear the gates and leg it – might as well not have gates at all.'

Nasser was thoughtful as he looked at the fencing. 'It's a pity but we might have to invest in some anti-vandal paint.'

'What good will paint do?' Ron asked with a look of vague outrage and incredulity.

'Well, it might make them think twice about trying to climb the railings if their clothes are going to be ruined,' Robyn put in.

'A bloody good caning is what they want – never mind paint,' Ron huffed. 'That's what these lads need – should never have got rid of caning in schools. I'll volunteer to go round Bluebird Street and find them; I'd enjoy teaching them a lesson!'

'And get done for assault?' Robyn offered Ron a withering look. 'Where have you been? It's the twenty-first century – you can't just go around beating kids no matter what you think they've done!'

'Honestly,' Nasser added. 'They may only be teenagers but seeing the size of some of them I wouldn't want to mess with them anyway. Best to leave it to the police.'

'It looks like someone already ruined their clothes,' Nina said, pointing to a scrap of fabric flapping from a point on the top of the fencing. Robyn stared at where she was pointing.

'Oh! A clue!' a voice squeaked from behind Nina. She turned to see that Ada and Martha had appeared. They both had curlers in their hair and were bundled up in matching candlewick dressing gowns.

'I wonder if the police can do forensics on it,' Ada said.

'Oh, yes!' Martha replied. 'They can do forensics on anything these days; it's on the television.'

'So it is!' Ada said, the pitch of her voice rising with her excitement. 'We saw that programme last week, didn't we? The one where they found fingerprints on a mushroom.'

'That was a marshmallow,' Martha said.

'No,' Ada insisted, 'I'm quite sure it was a mushroom.'

Nina stared at them. Firstly, did it matter? And secondly, what kind of weird crime was being investigated here?

'Well,' Robyn said firmly, 'I very much doubt the police will be interested in running forensic tests on a bit of old coat. Let's face it; this is hardly the crime of the century, is it? We'd be lucky if they sent anyone out at all.'

'Sadly, I have to agree,' Nasser said. 'It's hardly worth reporting really.'

'Are you *serious*?' Ron cried. 'You're going to let these little buggers get away with it?'

'I don't see what else we can do,' Nasser said.

Ron let out a noisy sigh of disapproval, though even he must have been able to see that Nasser had a point. The police had real crimes to solve and they were stretched enough doing that – they hardly needed the extra work of coming out to look at a few overturned ceramic planters. The residents of Sparrow Street might have been upset by the second attack on their garden, but the police had more important things to worry about.

'What about the CCTV?' Nina asked suddenly. 'Will we have anything on there we could possibly show the police? That's why Colm got it for us, after all.'

Nasser looked sheepish. 'There might be a problem there... I'm afraid I haven't quite got around to purchasing a memory card for it...'

'So, essentially there's no film in it?' Robyn asked.

'It doesn't use film,' Nasser said. 'It's digital; it needs—'

'But it's useless?' Robyn demanded, arms folding tight across her chest.

Nasser gave an awkward shrug. 'I'm sorry. I meant to do it but I just haven't had the time.'

'You could have asked one of us to do it.' Nina looked to see that Kelly had just turned up. She could smell the wine on her breath even across the few feet that stood between them. 'At least it would have been sorted.'

'I didn't want to bother anyone when you've all given so much time already,' Nasser said.

'Time that's been wasted again now,' Kelly snapped, and while Nina thought her tone was unnecessarily harsh, she did think that she might have a point.

Ron threw his hands into the air. 'Well, that's just brilliant, isn't it? I risk life and limb to protect this place but you can't be bothered to nip to the camera shop to get some film.'

'It's not like a conventional video camera—' Nasser began, but Ron cut him off.

'Typical! Wants to be the boss of everything but only when it doesn't involve any actual effort!'

'Hey!' Robyn shouted. 'That's out of order! He's worked harder than you on this!'

'What's it got to do with you?' Ron pointed a stubby finger at Robyn. 'You don't even live here so keep your nose out!'

'Don't you talk to me like that, you sweaty gorilla!' Robyn snapped.

'I'll talk how I want! And don't call me a—'

'Please!' Nina cried. 'This is not helping! The fact of the matter is we don't have CCTV and no amount of arguing will change that! We have a bit of coat and maybe we'll have some footprints in the mud or something and that's a start – right?'

'Perfect,' Kelly slurred. 'So what are you going to do with them, Miss Marple?'

Nina turned to stare at her.

'Oh, Kelly!' Ada cried, clutching at her breast.

'That's horrible!' Martha chimed in. 'Nina was only trying to help!'

'Oh, you can shut up, Dumb and Dumber,' Ron hissed.

Nina looked helplessly on, her eyes filling with tears. The garden was supposed to bring the community together, not cause all-out war. This wasn't how it was supposed to be at all. She sniffed hard and straightened herself up. She could still rescue this situation if she could just stay calm.

'I'll phone Colm – he'll come and look.'

Ron eyed her suspiciously 'Why do we need him again? You've got a hotline or something? Does he need to come? If he hasn't got anything better to do then he can't be as good a gardener as he thinks he is.'

'Got any better suggestions?' Robyn rested her hands on her hips and stared hard at Ron.

'Yeah, find someone halfway decent.'

'He's good!' Nina began, but Ron cut her off.

'We don't need him. We didn't need him before – we can do it.'

Nina narrowed her eyes. Ron had no right to be so unreasonable about this and he had no right to dismiss all Colm's previous efforts.

'He offers professional knowledge,' she said, trying to keep her voice level.

Ron let out a scathing guffaw. '*Professional knowledge*? How hard can it be to dig some soil and stick some flowers in the hole?'

'That's not what you said when we were doing it the first time,' Kelly cut in with a drunken laugh, swaying on her feet. 'I've never heard anyone complain as much as you did – I wanted to cut off my ears!'

'I didn't complain!' Ron shot back. 'Why don't you sod off home and finish that bottle, alky?'

'What did you say?' Kelly thundered.

'We've all seen your empties in the recycling,' Ron sniped. 'Everyone knows you've got a drink problem.'

'Ron!' Nina shouted. 'Enough! For once in your life shut up and listen to what others have to say – yours is not always the most important voice in the room!'

'And this is not helping to repair the damage,' Nasser said, glancing from one neighbour to another with the sort of disappointed look a teacher might give a favourite pupil after finding out they'd cheated on an exam. Ron stared him down, but he didn't flinch.

'So…' Nina put in, her head spinning, in the mood to call it a day and admit defeat. Even if they did fix the garden again they'd need to find a way to keep it secure and safe from further damage while still making it accessible to anyone who wanted to use it. That was hardly going to happen if they turned it into a place where the security rivalled the Tower of London. 'Do people want Colm or not?'

'No,' Ron said at the same time that Nasser said, 'Yes.'

'Won't he want paying?' Kelly slurred.

Nina paused. Kelly might just have a point there, a surprisingly astute one considering her inebriated state. Colm had given a lot of his time for free – far more than the hours he would have worked for Sammy and Diana. Perhaps it wasn't fair to keep asking him.

'So we leave it?' she asked.

Nasser nodded, though he looked less convinced. Nina guessed that if he could have had more of Colm's input he'd probably like that. 'Perhaps for the time being,' he said.

There was a brief lull in the debate, and Nina glanced to her side to see that Robyn was walking towards the railings, looking up to where they were topped by iron points. She reached on tiptoes to retrieve the scrap of cloth they'd noticed earlier.

'It looks like a coat – parka or something,' she said, looking pensively at it.

'I suppose it's a pretty common coat,' Nina said. 'Maybe it won't be much of a clue after all – I bet half the youths of Wrenwick own one.'

'Maybe,' Robyn said, and she stuffed the fabric in her pocket. Nobody questioned the action – perhaps they'd all just had enough for one night.

'It's freezing out here,' was all Kelly had to say, before turning on her heel and walking away.

'It might be,' Robyn muttered as she watched her go, 'but you're so pissed I don't know how you can tell. Stupid cow.'

'Leave it,' Nina said quietly. 'She won't remember any of this in the morning so don't take offence to anything she's said tonight.'

'She can say what she likes to me – I was taking offence for you.'

'Thanks, but there's no need.' Nina turned to Nasser. 'There's not a lot we can do tonight, is there?'

'Not really.' He looked around at the small crowd gathered there. 'Everyone might as well go home. I'll call to see you all at some point tomorrow.'

'That'd be lovely,' Ada said.

'We'll make tea,' Martha added.

The sisters linked arms and headed back to their own house so closely in step that they could have been one entity. Ron followed, not a single word of goodbye coming from him. Nina wished she could like him more, because despite his gruff ways and bad temper, he could be a good neighbour. But it was hard to like him when he didn't give anyone any reasons to, and he certainly hadn't done that tonight.

'Goodnight,' Nasser said.

'Goodnight,' Nina replied, while Robyn nodded acknowledgement, and they made their way back to Nina's house and their abandoned meal together.

'I can't believe it's happened again,' Nina said, looking at the table. Their food was cold but she didn't much feel like eating it now that she looked at it, her appetite completely gone. But she supposed Robyn would still want to eat so she collected up their plates to reheat the food in the microwave. 'It makes you wonder whether any of this is worth the bother.'

'I imagine it does,' Robyn agreed. 'What do you think will happen?'

Nina started the microwave and stepped back, arms folded, eyes trained on the plate as it went round and round inside. 'I suppose that depends how much damage we find when we get a good look at it in the daylight,' she said slowly. 'If Ron caught them before they'd had a chance to make too much of a mess then it might not take that much to fix after all.'

'Well, you can moan about the miserable old git, but at least there might be that to be thankful for. A lot of people would have turned a blind eye rather than trying to tackle whoever was in there.'

'Yes. Lucky for us, eh?'

'You hope.'

'Yes, we hope,' Nina said with a nod.

The microwave pinged and she pulled out the first steaming plate, handing it to Robyn before putting the second one in.

'I should probably eat this and head home,' Robyn said, taking it to the table.

Nina looked up at her with a vague frown. 'You're not going to stay a while?'

'Better not – I've got a few things to do.'

'Oh…'

Nina turned to watch the microwave again. She'd assumed that they'd spend the evening together as they always did on curry night, especially as they hadn't been able to do it so much lately. It didn't matter if Robyn had to go – the early night wouldn't hurt Nina – but she couldn't help feeling disappointed and slightly bemused. She also couldn't help but notice that her friend's mood seemed to have changed, and not for the better. It was nothing obvious, just a subtle shift that wasn't hard to detect for someone who knew her as well as Nina did.

She turned back to her, deciding to address it. 'Is everything OK?'

Robyn looked up from her meal. She was eating already, not bothering to wait for Nina to join her, and she never usually did that. In fact, they usually took ages to eat their meal because they were busy talking and it was often cold by the time they'd finished.

'Fine,' she said.

'Just… the going home early… You're sure everything is alright?'

'Job applications… I want to get them off before the deadline and I just remembered them. A couple are due tomorrow.'

'If they're online, you could do them from here.'

'I wouldn't be able to concentrate here. They've got to be good – you know? Things are getting a bit desperate.'

That might have been true, but Nina still wasn't convinced Robyn was telling her everything. For now, she didn't have much choice but to take her excuse at face value, though. And if that was the real reason, then she couldn't really argue. When all was said and done, Nina supposed that she ought to be filling in job applications too.

'Right,' she said.

The microwave pinged a second time and Nina took out her own meal. When she got to the table, Robyn had already eaten half of hers. *She must really want one of those jobs*, Nina thought. *Either that, or there's something I'm missing.*

Chapter Nineteen

Nina was beginning to love this little place by the canal, with its thatched roof and worn bricks, its cosy wooden snug that smelt like fresh beeswax polish and its beer garden, always full of narrowboat travellers taking a well-earned break from a day on the water. The pub was dressed for Christmas now, but in a delightfully old-fashioned way with colourful paper chains draped around the walls and a mighty spruce taking up a whole corner of the bar area, decked in scarlet bows and wooden toys. In the cavernous grate a fire cracked and roared, the lucky customers who'd got there early enough sitting in prime position and looking very sleepy and content in its glow.

Colm returned from the bar with two drinks and put one down on the table in front of Nina. They'd nabbed their favourite table – the one they'd occupied on their first date – and beyond the windows alongside it Nina could see groups of friends laughing as they huddled around the glowing outdoor heaters, perhaps listening to some boating anecdote or other. Who knew, but she loved to see them having such a good time. The moon was high, casting a silvery glow over the canal and the boats and the frosted fields that stretched away beyond them. She looked up at Colm and smiled.

'Thank you.'

'I didn't think it would be this busy here tonight,' he said.

'I don't mind that.'

'The landlord just said it's this full most nights.'

'I can see why – I really like it here.'

'Me too,' Colm said, holding her gaze and making her heart race. 'So the garden doesn't look too bad?'

Nina looked up. 'Nothing we can't fix. Ron did everyone a favour by catching them so soon. I should think a few hours' tidying will do it.'

'And you're sure you don't need me?'

Nina was reminded of Ron's hostility and perhaps that was something she didn't really want to subject Colm to if she didn't have to. 'I'd say we could always do with you, but I think everyone else was worried about taking advantage of your good nature.'

'I wouldn't see it that way. It's no problem at all for me to take a look.'

'You have a living to earn.' Nina smiled. 'And a daughter to provide for. Don't worry about it – use your time to do your own work.'

'Actually…' he said, looking nervous now, 'I wanted to ask you about that.'

Nina gave her head a tiny shake. 'About what?'

'Polly. I wondered… well, I told her about you.'

Nina's mouth was suddenly dry. 'You did? And what did she say?'

'Actually, she took it well – better than I was expecting.' His laugh showed the nerves he was trying hard to hide. Bringing Nina and Polly together had to be as nerve-wracking for him as it would be for either of them. 'She's keen to meet you.'

'Oh, God… Colm, I—'

'I think it's a grand idea.'

'You don't think it's too soon? I mean, we haven't been seeing each other all that long.'

'Do you think it's too soon?' he asked, a note of uncertainty in his voice.

A small part of Nina was encouraged by the fact that Colm wanted this. It meant he wanted Nina in his life for a lot more than just a few casual dates, but even then… 'It's just that… what if she doesn't like me?'

'She'll like you.'

'But what if she doesn't?'

'Then we'd have to work on it. But I'm willing to bet she will. Anyone would find it impossible to dislike you.'

'But Polly… I'm not her mum.'

He laughed softly. 'I had noticed that. I think Polly might too.'

'She might think I'm trying to replace her.'

'No, she won't. She'll think I'm doing what thousands of single men do and finding someone to love. She's old enough to understand it now and she's being very mature about it. She says she's happy for me.'

'So… she's not happy *per se*? She's just happy for you?'

Colm grabbed Nina's hand and lifted it to his lips. 'You worry too much. I kind of like that about you but there's no need in this case. Polly's alright with us, and she'll like you. She's had enough years now to accept that her mam isn't coming back and that I can't spend the rest of my life waiting for her, and she's grown-up enough now that we can discuss how she feels about that.'

'And did you?'

'What?'

'Discuss how she feels?'

'Yes, and she feels comfortable with it. She just wants to meet you; that's all.'

Nina was silent for a moment as she took in what he'd said, her gaze travelling to the windows to look at the boats moored at the canal-side, their dark hulks gleaming in the lights from the patio.

'I suppose that's understandable,' she said finally. Everything Colm had said was right and obvious but it still didn't make her feel any less certain about it. 'Colm... you don't still think... well, you're not still holding out for Jane to come back, are you? I mean, it's been five years and you haven't tried to divorce her yet...'

Colm smoothed back a frown. 'I thought we'd sorted this. I told you I had so much to worry about just bringing Polly up I didn't see the point in giving myself anything else to worry about. It would have happened sooner or later – it just took a while. Don't you believe me?'

'Of course I do, it's just... well, maybe subconsciously you don't realise it yourself.'

'I promise, any feelings I had for Jane are in the past. Perhaps I'm still a little fond of her but that's not the same as being in love. She made her decision when she ran off to Scotland to join some crazy commune rather than stay home with her family. From that moment she forfeited any right to love from me.'

'She might have forfeited it, but that doesn't mean it's not still there. Why did she leave? You never said.'

'If you asked her why she left, I doubt even she could tell you. I certainly can't. I'd known for a while she was getting restless. She's always had that in her but I thought... in my foolish youth I thought perhaps I could tame her. She'd do odd things every now and again – take off somewhere on a whim – but it would never be more than a week or so and she'd be home. Then one day, she said she'd had enough of the sort of life we had – she'd met some woman who was starting this commune and she wanted to go with her. We had some almighty rows, of course, but in the end, I could hardly stop her.'

'Didn't she stop and think once about leaving Polly, if not you?'

'I never understood what went on in her head and I don't think I ever will. I'd like to believe that she missed Polly, that she felt guilty for leaving her, but she's never said so. I don't think she was ever really cut out to be a mother and that's the truth of it.'

'She sounds… well, to be honest, she sounds like a free spirit. Exciting, you know? Like the sort of fascinating woman you read about in stories. Not like me.'

'Nina… where is this going? What do you want me to say?'

Nina sighed. 'I guess I'm nervous. It's going so well between us and I want… I want to be sure that there's a future in it.'

'If there was no future,' he said gently, 'then I wouldn't be asking you to meet Polly, would I? Jane might be fascinating, but she's also unreliable and selfish. There's no future for anyone with a woman like that. Why would I want her when I could have someone like you?'

'OK.' Nina nodded. 'You're right and I'm sorry for doubting you.'

'It doesn't matter.'

'Polly and I ought to meet – of course we should.'

He gave her an encouraging smile. 'It feels like a lot happening at once, doesn't it?'

'You can say that again. First my dad and Pam and now Polly. One way or another, I'm having to be on my best behaviour a lot these days.'

'I'll bet your dad's girlfriend was a lot more nervous than you.'

'I hadn't really thought of it that way, but now I'm in the same position she has my absolute sympathy,' Nina said with a nervous laugh. 'You really think Polly will like me?'

'Polly will love you; I know she will.'

'I wish I could feel that confident.' Nina turned to her drink and took a gulp.

'There's something else…' he said slowly.

She looked up. He seemed even more apprehensive than he had been about the idea of introducing her and Polly to each other.

'Polly's staying at her friend's house tonight,' he said. 'And going straight to school from there in the morning. I thought maybe… as I have the place to myself… that you might want to spend the night. I mean, say no if you don't want to, and even if you do it doesn't mean we have to… but it might be nice to have somewhere private to spend time together. We're always out at this pub or that restaurant… which is great, of course, but…'

His sentence tailed off, and as he'd made his case it seemed he'd forgotten to breathe. But he looked at Nina now earnestly as she looked at him in silence, caught off guard. She'd thought about their first night together – of course she had; she'd even discussed it with Robyn not so long ago. But right now, she was still getting used to the fact that she even had another man in her life. This was still too soon, wasn't it?

'It doesn't matter,' he said, quickly backtracking.

Nina drew in a breath. 'No, it does matter. You're right – we're always out in public places and we've never really had a chance to spend some time together… intimately. I'd love to come over tonight.'

Colm's face lit in a broad smile. 'There's no rush, obviously. We'll eat here as we planned, get a few drinks…'

Nina nodded. Her heart was thudding and she could barely control her breath. This was a huge moment for her, and she wondered if he could ever understand just how massive it was. She hadn't been intimate with anyone since Gray, of course, but more than that she hadn't wanted to. But she realised now as she gazed at Colm and his impossibly blue eyes gazed back at her, that she wanted him. She wanted this gentle giant of a man with his musical accent and striking dark hair so much her whole being ached for him. She was scared and excited all at the same time, and while she always wanted to make the evening last when she was with him, she also wanted it to be over so they could be driving back to his place. For the next few hours, she was sure she would be able to think of little else.

'You're happy?' he asked. And she knew he was referring to a specific decision that they'd both just taken. They were moving their relationship forward, making it a real, solid thing and Colm was doing what he always did – caring enough to check it was what she really wanted.

'Yes,' she said. 'Completely.'

That warm smile spread across his face again and she wasn't sure how much more her heart could take. He held her gaze for a moment longer, and then seemed to rouse himself from a dreamy moment of longing.

'I suppose we should eat,' he said in a husky voice. 'What are you having?'

'I don't know,' Nina said, reaching for the menu. She stared at it but couldn't seem to read the words. She didn't really care about food now. 'Maybe something light – I'm not all that hungry.'

'I thought you said you wanted to eat when we were driving up?'

'I did. It's funny, it seems to have gone off now. Maybe I'm excited,' she said, smiling up at him. Then they moved as one, meeting across the table, and he took her face in his hands and kissed her.

'We don't have to eat right now,' he said, pulling free, but his eyes still locked onto hers. 'I mean, we could eat later… at home… at my place…'

'That sounds nice,' Nina said softly, her stomach seemingly full of tiny butterflies that wouldn't have let her eat even if she wanted to.

He stood and held out his hand. 'Come on then,' he said. 'Let's go.'

❁

They raced to Colm's car like a couple of excited kids bunking off school. Colm clicked to unlock it from a few feet away and they hurried to get in. He looked at Nina and grinned as he fastened his seatbelt, and her stomach did an Olympic-standard somersault.

'Still OK?' he asked.

'Yes.'

He turned the key and the throb of the engine sent a roar of anticipation through her. This was really going to happen and she couldn't quite believe it, but now that they'd reached this point, she could hardly wait.

It was as they pulled out of the car park that Nina's phone began to ring and she looked to see that it was Robyn. For a moment she thought about letting it ring, afraid it might be something that would distract her from this moment, something that would take her away from their plans. Colm glanced at her as she watched Robyn's name flash up, the ringtone seeming more urgent with every second Nina failed to respond to it.

She caught his eye, her face lit by the screen. 'It's Robyn,' she said by way of a reply to his silent question.

'Right.'

Colm turned back to the road, his non-committal reply giving no clue of whether he approved or not of Nina's actions, and in the end, she could stand it no longer. She did what she'd always do, no matter what else was happening. She couldn't leave Robyn hanging. Her friend knew she was out with Colm tonight so it stood to reason that if Robyn was calling now, she must have really needed to.

'Hey…' Nina said. And then she frowned as Robyn began to talk. 'Oh,' she said finally, a weary resignation to her tone. 'We're probably about half an hour away… no, no, it's fine, we weren't doing anything in particular. We'll be over as quick as we can.' Nina ended the call and looked across at Colm. 'I'm sorry – could we detour to Robyn's house? I promise to try and keep it short.'

'What's wrong?' he asked, and if he was irritated by the change of plan he didn't show it.

'You know I told you we found what looked like a piece of coat at the garden last time it was vandalised? Well, Robyn's figured out where it came from, and let's just say if we don't go over and stop her, she might just kill her son when he gets home.'

Chapter Twenty

When Nina and Colm arrived at Robyn's house, Nina turned to him as the car came to a stop at the kerbside.

'You don't need to wait for me if you'd rather go straight home. I'm sure Robyn can give me a lift once we've worked this out.'

'You want me to go home? But what about—'

'No.' Nina smiled ruefully. 'I don't want you to go home at all, but this is hardly your problem and it's not fair to ask you to stay while we work it out. I don't really know how long it might take.'

'That doesn't matter – I can wait.'

Nina raised her eyebrows. 'I know you would, but I feel it's a lot to ask.'

'You never know – I might be able to help.'

Nina didn't see how Colm could help with this situation. He didn't know Robyn that well and he didn't know Toby at all. Apart from his connection to the garden it really wasn't his problem. But maybe it was his subtle way of saying he wanted to stick around because he thought their night might not be completely lost just yet. Nina couldn't tell but secretly she hoped so too. And maybe he wanted to stick around to show Nina that what mattered to her mattered to him.

'It might be useful to have a man around,' he added. Nina looked at him with a silent question. 'All I mean is that I was once a teenage boy. It was a long time ago, granted, but I still kind of know how they think.'

'I'll bet you were never this much trouble.'

'Ah, well, you'd have to ask my mam that but I've a feeling she'd tell you otherwise.'

Nina gave a vague smile as she looked towards the house. The front downstairs window was lit but the curtains were closed so she couldn't see if anyone was in there.

'Poor Robyn,' she said quietly, undoing her seatbelt. 'She doesn't have it easy.'

'I know something of that, to be sure,' Colm said, unclipping his own seatbelt and following her out of the car. They walked the path to Robyn's front door together and Nina rang the bell. She shivered; she wasn't really dressed to be out and the night air was colder than she'd anticipated. Colm instinctively reached to put an arm around her, and she found herself wishing for so much more as they waited for Robyn to let them in.

A moment later, Robyn opened the door. She looked slightly taken aback to see Colm, and Nina wondered whether she'd imagined he would have dropped her off and left. On any other night, perhaps he would have.

'You don't mind me being here?' he asked. 'I thought perhaps... well, I didn't want to...'

'Of course not.' Robyn forced a stiff smile as she ushered them in. 'Any help is greatly appreciated.'

'Where is he?' Nina asked.

'Still out with his stupid, no-good mates.' Robyn looked as if she'd been crying. It wasn't what Nina had expected to see – Robyn had been raising Toby alone for a long time now and she always seemed to take it in her stride, no matter how much of a handful he was. It looked as if she'd finally reached the end of a very long tether, though.

She flopped onto the sofa with a heavy sigh. 'I'm just so ashamed of him right now. I don't know that I'll be able to look him in the face without slapping him.'

'When's he coming back?'

'I phoned him just before I called you and he said he'd come back straight away, but…' She lifted a hand to indicate the distinct lack of Toby. 'I could tell he was with his little gang so I wouldn't be surprised if he doesn't turn up anytime soon. He'll be showing off somewhere, telling them he doesn't give a shit about my phone call. That's if they're not wrecking someone else's property.'

'Did you tell him why he had to come home?'

'No, because if I did he wouldn't come. He knew I wasn't happy, though, and he knew it was something serious.'

'And you're sure it was him?' Nina asked. 'I mean, that bit of cloth…'

Robyn pushed herself up from the sofa and retrieved a mud-stained coat from a hook behind the kitchen door. She returned a second later and laid it out so that a tear could plainly be seen at the hem, and then she slotted the scrap they'd pulled from the railings on Sparrow Street into the gap. It fitted perfectly, but even if it hadn't, the coincidence would have been too great to ignore.

'Oh,' Nina said. She glanced at Colm, who simply looked on with a grim expression.

'Maybe he ripped it somewhere else and the scrap just happens to look like it belongs?' Nina suggested helplessly. 'Or maybe he was messing around on the railings at Sparrow Street but it wasn't him who did the damage in the garden?'

Robyn raised her eyebrows and Nina had to admit it was a long shot. She'd just hoped there was another explanation because she knew how much this was hurting her friend and how hard this was going to be for Robyn to address.

'He could be a good boy,' Robyn said as she sat down again. 'That's what's so frustrating about all this. Give him the right company and he could be brilliant. He doesn't have bad bones; he's just a bad judge of character and so bloody easily led.'

Nina sat beside her and patted her hand. 'I know. He's always been lovely whenever I've spent time with him. I've never thought he has bad bones, and I doubt anyone else does either.'

Robyn looked at her. 'What the hell am I going to tell your neighbours? They'll hate us.'

'No, they won't. Besides, I'm not going to tell them.'

'Won't you have to?'

'What good will it do? It'll cause a lot of upset and make things twenty times more drawn out and difficult. As things are now, they'll forget in no time once the garden is fixed, and, presumably, when you've spoken to Toby about it he won't do it again.'

'But he has to learn that I can't cover for him. He has to understand that his actions have consequences. If we gloss this over and he thinks he's got away with it he won't learn that.'

'There may be other ways of teaching him that lesson without the likes of Ron getting involved,' Nina said firmly.

Colm spoke now. For the last few minutes he'd been listening closely, still and silent, taking it all in.

'I'd say that's a good call. Nobody has any proof anyway so why stir up this hornets' nest?'

'Toby will quickly realise there's no proof too,' Robyn said. 'Especially if we're not telling anyone – he'll think that's because we can't prove it.'

'Unless we make some proof up,' Colm said.

Both Robyn and Nina frowned at him.

'For instance,' he continued, 'how's your wee man to know there was no memory card in the CCTV camera?'

Robyn was thoughtful for a moment. 'Good point,' she said finally.

'Give him a choice,' Colm said. 'Tell him you have CCTV footage. Tell him he either stops seeing the boys who are getting him into trouble or you'll take the video to the police and have every one of the gang identified and slapped in a young offenders' centre. I guarantee he'll play ball because he won't want to get them all dropped in it.'

Robyn nodded slowly. 'You know, that could work. Of course, the big problem is that Toby could promise whatever I ask but I can't keep an eye on where he is twenty-four-seven and he knows that. He could easily slip off and spend time with them and I'd never know.'

'Then limit the time he has to spare,' Nina said. 'I'm sure the offer my dad made would still stand. Make it part of the deal that he has to go and work for my dad for so many hours a week. That way, he stays out of trouble, learns some valuable skills and makes a little pocket money into the bargain. If we can make him see that's all a good proposition then it might just tip the balance in our favour and help him start to turn things around for the better.'

Robyn was thoughtful, taking in everything that Nina and Colm had said, but there was no time to discuss it further because the sound of a key turning in the lock of the front door reached them and a moment later Toby appeared. He looked at Nina and Colm in some surprise and confusion.

'Hey,' he said, greeting Nina uncertainly. Then he turned to his mum. 'What did you want me for?'

'I see you've got your old coat on tonight,' Robyn said in a deceptively even tone. 'I thought you didn't like that one any more.'

'I changed my mind,' Toby said evasively, his gaze travelling to the damaged coat still sitting on the sofa where Robyn had left it. It was obvious that he was already working things out, guessing what might come next.

Robyn held up the coat, the ripped hem clearly on display. 'Care to explain how this happened?'

Toby licked his lips. He glanced at Nina and Colm, and then turned back to his mother. Perhaps he was wondering what Nina and Colm had to do with it, but there could be no doubting that he knew his mum was onto something.

'Must have done it on a nail or something at college,' he said. 'Didn't even realise I'd done it.'

Robyn folded it up again with very deliberate care. 'So you didn't… I don't know, maybe catch it on some railings when you escaped from a garden you'd just trashed…?'

Toby coloured, and in that moment Nina couldn't help but feel a little sorry for him. His face told the truth, even if his words didn't, and to his credit, showed a little shame too.

'No,' he said despite this, the lie coming with little conviction. He was going through the motions, like there was a system to this, one where he got caught but he lied anyway, because that was how these things worked. He didn't look like a boy who thought for a minute the lie would be believed.

'Don't, Toby,' Robyn said with a calmness that must have been taking superhuman strength. 'Don't take the piss. I know what happened. In fact, it was me who pulled the bit of coat from the railings. As soon as I saw it I had a feeling I might know where it had come from, but I didn't want to believe it. Not him, not my Toby – he wouldn't do something this shitty. Imagine how I felt then when I saw this…'

Robyn held up the coat again for a second before letting it drop back to the sofa.

'It wasn't me...' Toby began, red blotches climbing his neck. 'I was on lookout; I didn't do it!'

Robyn narrowed her eyes. 'You think that makes it better? You think that's OK?'

'Well, no, but I didn't do any of the bad stuff—'

'You let the bad stuff happen! You *helped* the bad stuff happen! And I'll bet you had a good laugh about it afterwards! Why should anyone have anything nice, anything that matters to them? Why shouldn't we ruin it? And it's not the first time, is it? Tell me, Tobe, were you on lookout the first time too? Or did you get stuck in that time because nobody caught you?'

Toby's gaze went to the floor but he said nothing.

'Even after I told you how upset everyone had been,' Robyn continued, her voice simmering dangerously to breaking point now, 'even after I told you that, you went back to have another go? You disgust me. I thought I'd brought you up better than that. Right now, I don't even know how I can call you my son without feeling sick.'

'It's just a garden,' Toby muttered savagely. 'Nobody got hurt.'

Nina glanced at Colm, half-expecting him to say something, but he didn't.

Robyn shot to her feet.

'*Just a garden?* How dare you! I worked hard on that garden! Nina and Colm worked on that garden! That garden meant a lot of things to a lot of people and they all gave their time and money to make it nice. Doesn't that mean anything to you?'

Toby dared to raise his eyes, but at the sight of his mother's fury, he quickly dropped his gaze to the floor again. He was sorry – Nina could see it, but Robyn wasn't finished with him yet.

'I'm ashamed to call you my son,' she said. 'Your dad would have been too. We can only be thankful that he's not here to see this now because it would break his heart.'

Toby looked up again, and this time there were tears of defiance and rage and hurt in his eyes. When all was said and done, he was a seventeen-year-old boy, still finding his way in the world, still figuring out how to get by without his father. Nina's heart went out to him, and a small part of her had to question if perhaps Robyn had gone too far. She glanced briefly at Colm and wondered if he was thinking the same thing. She also felt that this was more than they needed to see, despite Robyn having asked Nina to be there. This was something for Robyn and Toby to sort out in private as mother and son, and she thought that she and Colm ought to say their goodbyes and leave them to it. The problem was, there didn't seem to be an appropriate moment to jump in and say so.

'I'm glad Dad isn't here to see you messing around with that dickhead from the council,' Toby fired back, and it was all Nina could do not to suck in a sharp breath of shock.

'Peter has nothing to do with this!' Robyn yelled.

'Yeah? Well why do you think I have to be out all the time? You think I want to sit around here and watch him try and get into your knickers?'

Robyn stepped forward, her hand flying. Before anyone could stop her, she'd slapped Toby across the face. Toby recoiled in shock, hand clamped to his cheek.

'You were making trouble long before Peter started to come over,' Robyn said, struggling to control her rage. 'How dare you blame this on him!'

Toby stared at her. He looked again at Nina and Colm, and then he turned back to Robyn. 'I hate you!' he hissed. 'I wish you'd died instead of Dad!'

Robyn opened her mouth to reply, but before she could, he stormed out of the room. A second later they heard the front door slam.

'Shit…' Robyn started after him, but Colm pulled her back.

'You're too close to this – let me try. Man to man, you know? He might talk to me.'

'Colm's right,' Nina said. 'You're too close and too emotional right now. Let Colm go and fetch him back.'

Robyn looked uncertain, but she was close to tears again, and maybe she felt she'd run out of options, because she finally nodded agreement. Colm strode out without another word. Nina put her arm around Robyn and the tears she'd been holding back began to fall.

'Why does it have to be so hard?'

Nina rubbed her back. 'I can't imagine how tough it must be but you do a brilliant job. God knows how useless I'd have been if Gray had left me with a child to raise alone.'

'If I'm doing such a brilliant job then explain the spawn of Satan out there.'

Nina couldn't help a little laugh. Things would have to be dark indeed for Robyn's spirit to desert her completely.

'He'll come good in the end – you said it yourself; he just needs the right guidance.'

'I don't know who the hell can give that, but it's not me.'

'One day,' Nina said softly, 'he'll realise just how amazing you are and how lucky he is to have you. It's just that he hasn't quite got to that day yet.'

Robyn shook her head. 'Maybe I ought to get the police involved after all. Maybe the short, sharp shock method is the only way – terrify him into taking the right path.'

'Maybe, but wouldn't that point the finger of blame at the other boys too?'

'I expect it would eventually, but it would put a stop to their association.'

'And it might also make Toby some nasty enemies in the process. Do you know much about these other boys – who else they know, what they're capable of, how they might react to being implicated?'

Robyn nodded. 'You could be right.'

'Though,' Nina added slowly, 'there's no reason why we can't use it as leverage.'

'Go on…'

'Just like Colm said before – tell Toby that if he doesn't cut ties then we'll send the video of them all vandalising the garden to the police.'

'You mean the video we don't have?'

Nina nodded. 'As we also established before, Toby doesn't know that.'

Robyn gave her a watery smile. 'You're a bloody genius.'

'Well, it wasn't really my suggestion, was it?' Nina's phone bleeped and she pulled it out to see a text from Colm.

We're going for a burger and a chat. Don't worry; be back soon.

Nina turned her phone to show Robyn the message; she blew out a long breath.

'Wow; he's got hidden depths, that one. I don't know anyone else who could have got around Toby like that so quickly.'

'It must be that legendary Irish charm,' Nina said. 'Works on everyone.'

'It certainly worked on you.'

Nina gave a rueful smile as she recalled the plans that now looked well and truly thwarted. Even if Colm wasn't out long with Toby, Robyn would probably need a little extra support. And even if Robyn didn't need Nina to stay, the night's events were hardly conducive to further romance. Still, she couldn't help but feel proud of Colm for the way he'd stepped in so selflessly.

'It did,' she said quietly, looking towards the door through which he'd just left. 'He really is one in a million.'

Nina and Robyn waited for two hours. Nina found herself desperate to phone Colm for news, but she realised that to disturb them might interrupt some deep and meaningful conversation and that no news was probably good news. If they'd been out together this long then it had to mean they were getting along, and perhaps that Toby was opening up to Colm. Which was weird when Nina really thought about it, because Colm was a complete stranger to Toby. According to Robyn, her son never opened up to her or anyone else in the family, so why a man he'd only just met? But Colm had this soothing, warm way about him, something that just seemed to invite trust, and Nina somehow knew that if anyone could get through to Toby then he could. Strangely, Robyn agreed when Nina said this to her, and she told Nina that she was grateful for his efforts.

It was close to 11 p.m. when Colm and Toby finally returned. As they walked in, Robyn ran to grab her son in a desperate hug.

'Sorry, Mum…' he mumbled into her shoulder. 'I don't know why I did it.'

'It doesn't matter now,' Robyn said. 'I'm sorry I wasn't there for you. If you went off the rails then it's my fault for not being the mother you needed.'

'No…' Toby shook his head, and then his gaze went down, and Nina saw a lone tear fall onto the carpet. He sniffed hard as Robyn drew him close again and held him tight.

Nina shot a grateful smile at Colm. He looked tired as he returned it, but whatever he'd said or done with Toby, it looked as though he'd achieved a minor miracle from where she was standing.

'We'll leave you two to talk,' she said, looking over at where Robyn still held Toby. Robyn glanced up at the sound of Nina's voice, and Toby extricated himself from her arms, looking anywhere but at her or Colm. It was clear that he was deeply ashamed and mortified and that it would take him some time to come to terms with those uncomfortable feelings.

'Thank you,' Robyn said.

'I'll call you tomorrow,' Nina said.

Robyn nodded and, without another word, Nina and Colm let themselves out of the house.

'They'll be OK,' Colm said as they walked to his car.

'What on earth did you say to bring him round?'

'Nothing much. I mostly let him have as much milkshake as he wanted and time to get things off his chest.'

'Well, it's more than anyone else has been able to get out of him for a long time.'

Colm shrugged. 'The wee man just needed someone to listen. Sometimes it's easier to see that when you're viewing it from a distance. He seems like a good lad on the whole – reminds me a lot of how I was growing up.'

'If he turns out half the man you are, I think Robyn will be a lucky mum.' Nina climbed into the car beside him. In the next moment, he reached for her, pulling her into a kiss that was impossibly desperate and tender, chaste and yet passionate, so full of heat that she could hardly bear it.

'Oh God…' she murmured as he pulled away. It took a second for her eyes to open, and somehow it was like the world hadn't quite returned. There was just him, filling her senses.

'Do you still want to stay over?' he asked. 'I mean, it's late and you've had a tough night… I understand if you want to go home—'

Nina reached to kiss him again. She wanted to spend the night with this incredible man – she wanted it so badly she felt the passion might explode from within her. In this moment, everything else was forgotten, and nothing else would matter until the morning brought real life back again like a cold slap. Now, she only wanted to be close to him, to be wrapped in his arms, to feel his skin against hers, to be as one.

'No,' she said. 'I don't want to go home – not at all.'

Colm gave a slow smile and she thought her heart might burst. With every minute she spent in his company she felt more and more convinced that she might just have found her second chance of happiness, and for once, she didn't feel a bit guilty about it.

Chapter Twenty-One

Sometime in the early hours, Nina began to drift off in Colm's arms and she began to dream. Later, as a hazy memory returned to her, she'd decided that it must have been a dream, because it had been such a strange thing for him to say. But her eyes had been closing and his heartbeat had been lulling her to sleep, and she couldn't quite decide if she'd been awake or whether she'd finally gone under when she'd heard it.

Don't disappear, Nina.

It was puzzling, but something about it still made her happy and she clung to the words the next day as she went about the business of checking her emails and phone messages. The donations and dedication requests for their memory tree were coming in at a healthy rate now and there was plenty to do with the inauguration event speeding ever closer. It was hard to concentrate when her mind kept drifting back to a night that had been all she'd hoped for and so much more, where not once had she felt anything less than cared for and worshipped, and yet she really had to.

Robyn called at her house just before lunch. Nina opened the front door to see that her friend looked exhausted but much calmer than when they'd left her the night before.

'I was just about to phone you,' Nina said. 'I'd got up late, though, and there were things I had to get done first.'

'I'm not disturbing you now, am I?'

'No, of course not…' Nina ushered her inside. 'I was just saying I hadn't forgotten about you.'

'I hope you don't mind me coming over like this – I just needed to get out of the house for a while. I went for a walk and I sort of ended up on your street.' Robyn shook out a wet umbrella before she stepped inside and left it in the antique umbrella stand that Nina kept by the door.

'How did you get on after we'd left?' Nina asked. Robyn followed her to the kitchen, where she filled the kettle and switched it on. There was no need to ask if Robyn wanted tea – she always wanted tea and never more than on a day like today.

'Well,' Robyn said as she took off her coat and hung it on the back of a chair, 'I don't know what Colm said or did but he made more headway than I have in years.'

'You got on after we'd left?'

'He was willing to listen, at least, which is more than I've had from him in a long time. He totally bought the CCTV thing. I told him we wouldn't take the video to the police if he promised to cut ties with the other boys – made it sound a bit noble, like he was saving them from prison or something by distancing himself. Though I suspect he was also thinking about saving himself from a battering, which is probably what he thinks would happen if they discovered one of their own had squealed on them. I don't know if these boys are all that tough, but I don't care either way because that seemed to do the job and Toby agreed.'

'You're not worried about them getting nasty, are you?'

'I'd be lying if I said I wasn't, but I'm as sure as I can be that things will settle peacefully soon enough.' She gave a rueful half-smile. 'It's not like we live in the Bronx, is it? Although,' she added, 'Toby does seem a bit friendless now, and I feel a bit sorry for him for that much.'

'I'm sure he'll find new friends.' Nina busied herself making the tea while Robyn took a seat at the table.

'Not at college. It seems things were worse than I thought, and it all came out last night when we finally had a proper conversation. Right now, he's not even sure he wants to continue on his course at all, though I think that's more to do with him feeling at sea over his friends than what he's being taught. Since his old friends are now off limits he doesn't really know who he can hang around with; besides which – and I can see his point – he doesn't know how he can avoid them while they're all in the same classes.'

'What did you say to that?'

'I told him he'd better find a way to avoid them because they'd all end up in a juvenile detention centre if he didn't. I must admit I don't like the lie, but I've got to get him straight by whatever means necessary, haven't I? One day, hopefully, he'll thank me for this.'

'When he's old enough to see things for what they are, he will,' Nina agreed. 'So, he needs something to fill his time now that he's going to be home a lot more? You definitely want my dad to help this time?'

'Definitely! I think you were right all along – it's something that would do Toby good. Did you manage to talk to him about it?'

'This morning. He's more than happy to give Toby another chance to go and help with the cars.'

'It'd certainly be a welcome distraction. At least for a while until he finds some new friends and other things to fill his time.'

'You never know; he might even like it,' Nina said with a wry smile. 'When my dad got interested, I don't think he was that much older than Toby, and he's been a classic car enthusiast ever since.' She brought two mugs to the table. 'Do you think Toby will go this time?'

'If he doesn't I'll kill him – and he knows it.'

'I'll ask my dad about dates and we'll fix up a day for Toby to visit for an hour or so.'

'This time I'll drive him there myself and escort him through the front door and I won't let him persuade me that he'll do it himself.'

Nina sat across from Robyn and curled her fingers around her mug. 'It'll be alright, you know,' she said. 'I'm sure it's just a wobble.'

Robyn looked pensive but she offered no reply. Perhaps it was too easy for Nina to say those things and not really know what she was talking about. It had occurred to her before that not having the experience of raising children of her own put her at a disadvantage in so many situations, and she wondered whether Robyn might feel she had overstepped the mark commenting on things she didn't really understand. Perhaps if she'd had children of her own she'd see things very differently. She at least understood that it might not look as black and white to Robyn as it did to her. All she could do in that regard was try to appear positive and hope that helped Robyn to feel more positive too.

After a few silent moments, Robyn looked up. Whatever had been running through her brain, she seemed to have worked it out, because she looked brighter now.

'I'm sorry I kept you so late last night,' she said. 'What time did you get back here?'

'About nine,' Nina said airily.

Robyn frowned. 'Nine? But you left me at… *Nine this morning?*'

Nina gave a sheepish smile. She was opening herself to a merciless ribbing, and Robyn would want details, but she was too happy to care. She hadn't felt like this in such a long time that she didn't think anything could spoil it – certainly not a little embarrassment. She waited for Robyn to start teasing, but it didn't come. When Robyn spoke again it was with an absolute sincerity that threw Nina.

'I'm happy for you,' she said. 'I don't know much about him but he seems like a decent man. And you... well, you're an angel sent to earth; you know I think that even if I don't say it. I'm glad you've found someone because nobody deserves it more than you.'

Nina's gaze dropped to her tea. It wasn't often that sort of honesty came from Robyn without at least a little banter attached, and Nina didn't quite know what to do with it.

'He's a lucky bloke,' Robyn said.

Nina looked up and acknowledged her with a smile.

'Really,' Robyn said. 'I mean it.'

'I know. I think I might be lucky too.'

'I hope so. I hope he's the one to bring the smile back to your face again.'

'You're saying I don't smile?'

Robyn grinned. 'Not as much as I'd like to see; and I know I'm hilarious but there's only so much I can do about it.'

'Thank you,' Nina said.

Robyn sipped at her tea. 'For what?' she asked, putting her cup down again.

'Just for being there when I needed you.'

'You were there for me too. Let's call it a draw, shall we?'

'OK,' Nina said, and then paused, not knowing what else to say.

'So,' Robyn cut in, her breezy tone signalling that all the deep sincerity was now out of the way. 'You're keeping track of the donations OK?'

'I could do with some help if you've got time.'

'For you I've always got time. Plus, we all know you can't count.'

'Says who?'

'I've seen you trying to split a restaurant bill.'

It was Nina's turn to grin now. This was the Robyn she knew and loved, and although she liked the other one well enough, this was the one who made sense to her.

'I could really do with some help if you can give it.'

Robyn nodded, slurping at her tea. 'You want to get the notebook out and we can go through it together?'

'It's right here,' Nina said, going to a drawer and pulling it out. She placed it in front of Robyn, who put down her mug and opened it up.

'Yep,' she said, looking up with a grin. 'An angel sent to earth who can't count for toffee!'

Nina couldn't argue with the fact that since her relationship with Colm had moved into a whole new phase, it made perfect sense that she should meet his daughter. Not just perfect sense, but really it was imperative and best done sooner rather than later. So if it made this much sense, why was Nina so nervous now?

The only comfort in this whole situation was that Polly seemed as anxious as Nina to make a good impression. It was a promising start, because it meant that at least she was open to the idea that her dad would want to date and that she was willing to be friends with the lucky woman. Nina had been dreading what kind of reception might be waiting for her at Colm's house, despite his reassurances that his daughter was happy to meet her. She'd half-expected a stroppy, judgemental and uncommunicative teen, but Polly couldn't have been further from that.

The most striking thing as Nina sat in his living room, looking across at her now, was how little of Colm there was to see in his daughter's features. Where he was dark she was fair – somewhere between honey and strawberry blonde – and her eyes were a gentle hazel while his were that dazzling, unforgettable blue. Polly didn't even have a trace of the Dublin accent that was so prominent when Colm spoke. She'd been brought up in Wrenwick, of course, but still it seemed mildly surprising to Nina that she hadn't even picked up the faintest twang from years of listening to her father. Maybe there was something of him around the mouth, and in a certain tilt of her head or a sideways glance, but if Nina hadn't been told that she was Colm's daughter she would never have guessed it.

Polly wore jeans and a hooded sweatshirt of soft grey, her hair in a long plait over one shoulder. If she'd inherited her looks from her mother, then Nina thought that her mother must be very pretty indeed. The idea was still vaguely unnerving to Nina, though she tried not to let it be. She didn't imagine for a moment that Colm would ever knowingly compare Nina to his estranged wife, but perhaps unconsciously it was inevitable. She couldn't help but wonder how she stacked up compared to the absent Jane, who had become something of a perfect specimen in Nina's mind now that she'd seen Polly.

'So…' Nina asked, hands clasped together in her lap as if superglued together. 'How's school?'

Inwardly, she cringed. Even her limited experience with teenagers told her that she'd probably asked the single most boring question anyone could ask a teenager, but it had come out as if of its own volition – something, anything to fill the empty space of the air between them. Colm had gone to the kitchen to get drinks, and while the conversation was stilted with newness when he was there, with him gone it had almost died a horrible death. They were both trying, of course, but they hardly knew each other and Nina had never been good at small talk anyway.

'It's fine,' Polly said politely. 'I don't tend to think about it much when I'm not there.'

'That's good. I used to worry all the time about my school work.'

'I don't. Dad always says, "*Que será.*" It means everything will be OK in the end... or something like that.'

'Yes, it's an old song.'

'I know that song,' Polly said, brightening a little now. 'I think it's sometimes on the radio.'

'What music are you into?'

Polly shrugged. 'Just the usual.'

Nina had no idea what that meant but there wasn't a reply to it either.

'Nina's a nice name,' Polly added.

'Oh... thank you. I think Polly's a nicer name.'

'Nah, it's silly. Yours sounds like Russian or something. Is it?'

'I've no idea.'

'Did your mum choose it or your dad?'

'I don't really know that either. I think maybe I already had it when they got me.' Polly frowned and Nina gave a hesitant smile. 'I'm adopted, you see,' she said.

'Are you?' Polly sat forward now, looking interested beyond politeness for the first time. 'Do you remember your real parents?'

'Actually, I consider the people who brought me up to be my real parents. The other ones are just the people who made me. And no, I don't remember them.'

'Don't you want to know about them?'

'Not especially. My mum and dad are so lovely that I never really missed the biological ones. They gave me the happiest childhood a girl could have.'

'So you've never tried to look for them?'

'No.'

'But what if you meet someone – like a boyfriend – and you're related to them and you don't even know?'

'I don't know… I suppose there are a lot of adopted people out there in that boat. I think if we all worried about that all the time we'd go mad and never go out with anyone.'

'But if you married someone…' Polly insisted.

Nina paused. She wasn't sure where this conversation was going but it felt awkward now. Was she somehow hinting at physical relationships? Like she guessed Nina might have with Colm? What was she supposed to say to this?

'Umm, I suppose if I was really worried I'd have to get a DNA test or something.'

'Oh, yes, you could do that,' Polly agreed. 'My geography teacher told us they do that in Iceland.'

'They do?' Nina raised her eyebrows.

Polly nodded. 'Because the population is so small. They have a DNA database and everything so if you want to marry someone you can check you're not related to them first. That's mad, isn't it?'

'Wow, your geography teacher knows a lot about it.'

'Iceland's his favourite place – he's always going on about it. I expect it's because they've got all those volcanoes.'

'Hmm,' Nina said uncertainly. She looked up to see Colm return, and she didn't think she'd ever been gladder to see someone.

'Lemonades,' he said, handing them out. 'One with ice and one without for my little fusspot.'

'That's no way to talk about Nina,' Polly said, and they both began to laugh. Nina smiled. OK, so maybe Polly didn't look much like Colm but it seemed she'd inherited his humour. Nina relaxed a little too. If

Polly could find something to laugh about then perhaps Nina was really worrying too much about the impression she was making. Perhaps she didn't need to try quite as hard as she'd told herself she did.

She took her lemonade with a grateful smile and Colm sat next to Polly on the sofa, across from Nina, who was on a soft armchair. It was a very deliberate move and Nina couldn't help but reflect on how clever it was that he'd chosen to do that. He was sending a message to Polly that would reassure her; he was telling his daughter that no matter who else came into his life, she would always be the most important person in it, and though Nina wished she could feel his reassuring presence close to her, she understood his action perfectly.

'So,' he said, looking between the two of them, 'what did I miss?'

'We were talking about you, Dad,' Polly said. 'Which means we can't tell you what we were saying.' She grinned at Nina, who smiled in return.

'Oh, I see,' Colm said, playing along. 'So who will I have to torture to get the information? Let's see... who's most likely to crack?'

'Well, that's obviously going to be me,' Nina said.

'I do believe you could be right,' Colm said. 'Believe me, after many years of interrogating Polly, I can tell you that she never cracks.'

'I have to keep my secrets, Dad,' Polly said with an angelic look as she sipped at her lemonade. 'If you knew the half of what goes on when you're not there your hair would turn white.'

'Better not tell me then,' he said.

Nina looked between the two of them and saw that despite their banter, there was absolute trust. Even at this point, where she hardly knew what the dynamic was, she could tell that they were different to Robyn and Toby. Colm trusted Polly to be sensible and Polly trusted that she could bring anything to her dad and that he would react with patience and love. Not that Robyn didn't love Toby, of course, but at times it felt like a private war raged between the two of them, and that Robyn couldn't always trust Toby and that Toby didn't feel he could bring anything to her. The last few weeks had shown that, though Nina didn't doubt for a moment that Robyn never did anything less than her best for her son.

'Actually,' Polly said, 'Nina was telling me about being adopted.'

'Ah,' Colm replied hesitantly. He knew the story by now, of course, but perhaps he didn't know how Nina liked to tell it to people other than him and didn't know what to add.

'I was saying how it doesn't really bother me and how I think of my parents as my real parents,' Nina said.

'Right.' Colm took a sip of his own drink. 'He's a grand fella is your da.'

'I think so too,' Nina said.

Polly smiled at her. Then she turned to Colm. 'Can we have pizza?'

'Tonight?'

'Nina's here – why not?' She looked at Nina. 'You are staying for a while, aren't you?'

'I think so… if I'm OK to do that?'

'Of course you are,' Colm said warmly. 'Stay for as long as you want.'

'But she'll have to go home at some point,' Polly reminded him. Nina had to wonder if she'd meant it in quite the way it sounded. Because it sounded very much as if there were going to be ground rules from the start, which included no staying over. Perhaps it was to be expected, and perhaps Nina ought to be happy enough with their progress so far. They were all getting along brilliantly, and she couldn't expect total acceptance straight away.

'Pizza sounds lovely,' Nina said.

'Good,' Polly said, giving Colm an emphatic look that expected no argument. They might have had a trusting, understanding relationship, but at that moment there was no doubting that Polly had got used to getting her own way more often than not too.

'Right,' Colm said. 'Pizza it is.'

Chapter Twenty-Two

Nina arranged the holly wreath against the headstone and stepped back with a critical gaze. The scarlet berries were rich against the waxy leaves and perfectly Christmassy. December, and Christmas especially, had been hard over the last few years but this one felt different. It was still hard, of course – not a Christmas would ever go by when she didn't reflect on her loss of Gray – but the sorrow she always felt had been softened this time by the undeniable murmurings of hope. If things went well with Colm, if he was here to stay, perhaps the hope would soon become louder than the sorrow, until one day she'd be able to hear the sorrow only if she listened hard for it. Drowning it out wouldn't mean that she'd forgotten about Gray, or that he would disappear from her thoughts, only that perhaps his loss wouldn't constantly consume them.

But laying a wreath wasn't the only reason she was here today. Here seemed as good a place as any to meet with Gray's mother. Nina was filled with apprehension when she thought about the reason she'd asked Connie to meet her, but it had to be better to be open than let her mother-in-law find out through the town's gossip network. Not that she thought for a minute Connie would have any issues, but still, Nina would rest easier having received her explicit blessing. She scanned the churchyard now, looking for the familiar figure painfully shuffling down the path on her crutches, but as yet, Nina was still alone amongst the graves, the only sounds that of birdcalls echoing through the still air.

Drawing in an icy breath, she looked down at the stone again.

'So,' she began, wrapping her arms around herself. 'I expect you know why I'm here but I'll say it anyway. I've met someone. I really like him, Gray, and I really feel like it could go somewhere and I just hope you understand. I think if you could tell me you'd say you do, and I think you'd be happy for me.'

She let out a sigh, breath escaping in a plume that rose into the blue skies, and took a moment to collect her thoughts.

'I wish I could ask you,' she continued, 'but then I suppose we wouldn't need to have this conversation because you'd still be here and you know that would have always been enough for me. I would never have looked at another man if not for... You know how lonely I've been without you and now... well, I don't feel so lonely any more. I can see a future where things look better and brighter again, and it makes me so happy. I've met his daughter and she's lovely and I think she approves of me and so there doesn't seem to be any reason for us to be apart when we make so much sense together. He's been lonely too, you see, and so I think... I think we've just been waiting to find each other, you know? And... I don't know... if there's some miraculous way you're hearing this, then a miraculous sign would really be appreciated at this point, just to know that it's OK, otherwise...'

Otherwise what? Was she going to give Colm up? Live the rest of her life alone? She refused to believe for a single second that Gray would want that life for her, sign or not. This had to be it – this moment, right here right now. This, finally, had to be closure. It was time to let go. Never forget, never for a second, but to let go and look to the future regardless, and Nina couldn't allow herself to dwell on any feelings of guilt for that or she would be alone forever. All she wanted now was one more blessing.

As she lifted her eyes to survey again the path that wound through the churchyard, dusted in the snow that had fallen during the early hours and not yet melted, she saw the figure she'd waited for, making her painstaking way over. Nina could have gone to meet her, but there was no point. She was already waiting at Connie's ultimate destination, because for both of them when they came here, it always was. So Nina waited, watching Connie's slow progress, until she was finally standing beside her looking down at Gray's stone too.

'How are you?' Nina asked.

'Oh, not too bad. I'm glad you phoned me because I'd been meaning to call you anyway. I had such a lovely time when we last went to that little café I'd been wondering if you wanted to go again. I don't get a chance to go out much these days.'

Nina smiled. 'Of course. You only had to ask. You only ever have to ask, you know that.'

'Well…' Connie coughed into a gloved hand. 'You're busy – I didn't want to pester.'

'It's not pestering and I'd always make time for you no matter how busy. I can't say I'm all that busy anyway. I still don't have a job for a start.'

'I expect you'll get one soon enough.' Connie turned back to the grave. 'Did you bring the wreath?'

'Yes. I thought… well, it's nearly Christmas after all.'

'It's lovely. I've ordered one from the florist but mine was holly too. I might change it to something else so we don't have two the same.'

'Maybe ivy? Something a bit complementary?'

'Maybe.' Connie coughed again. 'So, did you want to see me about something in particular or did you just want a chat?'

'A bit of both really,' Nina said, hugging herself a little tighter as a chilled gust lifted the hair from her neck. 'I wanted to chat to you, but there was a certain thing I wanted to talk about. *Ask* about, really, I suppose… Ask *for*. I mean, from you.'

Connie looked up at her with an expression of vague bemusement, and it was no wonder, Nina reflected ruefully. She wasn't exactly making herself clear.

'How about we go somewhere warm?' she added. 'The café?'

Connie nodded agreement. She kissed her gloved fingers and laid them on the name engraved onto the headstone and murmured a few words. Nina said her goodbyes too, and then they began to walk at a pace slow enough to accommodate the difficult progress Connie was always forced to make wherever she went these days. The café wasn't far at all – just outside the church grounds – and it would only take a minute or two to get there for most people. It would be more like ten for Nina and Connie today, the wait only adding to Nina's growing anxiety.

Just as she was as sure as she could be about what Gray's reaction would have been, she was as certain as she could be that Connie would understand too, but knowing that didn't make the conversation any easier, and if Connie didn't approve… what then? Nina didn't want to hurt her feelings and she didn't want to upset her, but there was a risk here that she might just do either or both of those things. She valued Connie's friendship and she cared deeply for her – not least because this was Gray's mother – but even if she didn't want them to, things were going to change between the two women once Nina's news was out. It was inevitable and Connie would see that too.

Finally they reached the café. It was housed in a little white cottage with a slate roof and leaded windows that had once belonged to the nearby church. Inside, the walls were rough and whitewashed and the scrubbed wooden floor was dotted with painted tables topped with delicate white vases and simple menus. Iron Victorian radiators gently heated the room.

Nina and Connie went in and took a seat at an empty table. The café was quiet and the only other customers were a trio of elderly ladies chatting animatedly and tucking into large slices of cake. The small talk Nina and Connie had made on the walk here was not like that at all. It had been almost painful when all Nina had wanted to do was say what she'd come to say, but she'd recognised that she'd have to be patient. This had to be done properly, and they had to be settled somewhere warm and comfortable because it was a conversation that might take a while. So they'd talked instead about her job hunting, her dad, Robyn's latest news and the garden on Sparrow Street.

It wasn't until they had a warming pot of tea on the table between them that Nina began. Connie fell silent at once, her pleasant smile now a sombre look of attention, as if she'd been able to tell by Nina's expression that they were about to get down to the real business and that, maybe, she wasn't going to like it.

'Connie… I've met someone.'

The older woman nodded slowly. She didn't miss a beat in her reply. 'I thought as much.'

Nina stared at her.

'It was only a matter of time,' Connie continued. 'You're still a young woman, after all.'

'So… you don't mind?'

'Whether I mind doesn't matter.'

'It matters to me.'

'Why should it?'

'I don't know… because it changes things.'

'I suppose it does,' Connie agreed. 'I suppose I'll see less of you from now on for a start.'

'That's not my intention at all!'

'So that's not why you called me here? You weren't laying the ground for that to happen?'

'Oh, no!' Nina's tone was earnest. 'That would never happen! You're still a dear friend to me!'

Connie gave a slight smile. 'It had already started to happen. It's alright – I never expected anything else. We had Gray to bind us together and now we don't.'

'We still have him; we'll always have him!'

'Well, yes, of course, in a way we do. But let's face it, whenever we meet we meet to remember him, to reflect on how much we miss him. But that's not something you're going to want for much longer if you've met someone else.'

'I would never want to stop meeting up with you.'

Connie carefully poured a cup of tea for herself. 'I'd want to continue meeting up with you too, but it's going to get harder as time goes on if you stay with this new man. For a start, I can't imagine he's going to be happy if you're always thinking of someone else.'

'He's not like that; he understands.'

Connie shook her head. 'He says he does. It's not only that...'

'Because you won't want to hear things about him from me?' Nina asked. 'Is that it? You think I might tell you things about him?'

'To be blunt, yes. I wish you all the best, but I can't deny it will be painful for me to hear how happy you are with a man who's not Gray and I can't pretend otherwise. And even if you don't tell me, I'll be able to see it.'

'It would have always been Gray,' Nina said quietly. 'You know that.'

'I do, but it wasn't to be. It's not your fault, it's not Gray's, and it's not your new man's; it's just the way of things, but none of that makes it any easier to bear.'

Nina stared at the teapot. It was fat, with blue and white stripes like the old Cornish pattern, something homely and comforting about it. The tea here was always good too, but she didn't really want any today. She just wanted this afternoon to be over. Connie had said only what Nina had already thought herself. Of course she'd try to be happy for Nina and she'd never bear her any ill will, but how could she forget that at the root of all this unasked-for change in her life was her dead son?

Connie stirred sugar into her tea. 'Where did you meet him?'

'He's the gardener who worked on our plot on Sparrow Street.'

Connie nodded, silent for a moment. She stirred her tea again. 'And he's nice? He makes you happy?'

'He's kind. Patient and understanding. Yes, he makes me happy.'

'Sounds as if he'd be good for you.'

'He will be. I mean, it's early days yet but…'

'You must like him a lot for us to be having this conversation. I know what Gray meant to you, how hard it's been…'

'I do and I know he feels the same. At least, I believe he does.'

'Then' – Connie smiled sadly as an unsteady hand lifted her teacup from the saucer – 'I couldn't be happier for you.'

'I have your blessing?' Nina asked. That was all she wanted, to hear those words, and she'd know that it was meant to be.

'Yes,' Connie said. 'I don't have a lot to offer, but that I can give. Of course you have my blessing.'

Chapter Twenty-Three

'We're going to need all hands on deck,' Robyn said as she surveyed the boxes of lanterns that had been delivered a couple of days previously. The sounds of cheap swing versions of well-known Christmas songs filled Nina's kitchen, coming from the CD player Robyn had brought over for the occasion. She'd told Nina that there was far too little Christmas spirit at her house and while Nina couldn't think of anything that would make her feel less Christmassy than a CD full of knock-off Christmas classics, she couldn't really argue with that. 'Do you think you can recruit some help?'

'I shouldn't think it will be all that hard,' Nina said with a smile.

'Hmm. Well, Colm's little girl will want to be in your good books for a start so you could ask her,' Robyn said. 'And Toby definitely needs to stay in mine so he's helping whether he wants to or not.'

Nina laughed. 'That's two unwilling volunteers then!'

'Anyone else?'

'We should manage on that, shouldn't we?'

Robyn shrugged. 'Doesn't hurt to have as many bodies as possible. We're up against it now – the tree ceremony is in just under two weeks and we've got a lot to do before then. Not just organising this, but Christmas as well.'

'Christmas can wait as far as I'm concerned.'

Robyn threw her a sideways look. 'No plans with Mr Perfect then?'

'We haven't really talked about it, but I don't suppose so. I mean, we're sort of a bit in between, aren't we? We haven't really been going out long enough so that spending Christmas together is a given, and yet I'd like to.'

'Why don't you just tell him that?'

'Because his priority will be Polly. He told me that she always struggles with Christmas because that's around the time Jane walked out on them, and he said Polly spent every Christmas of her childhood wishing Jane back. I'm sure she's not doing that now, but I still don't feel I can intrude on that time. Polly needs her dad more than ever and I'd be a distraction, wouldn't I?'

'It might be a welcome distraction, though.'

'I don't know. I'm just waiting for Colm to say something, one way or another, but he hasn't yet.'

'Polly's mum doesn't even come to visit at Christmas?' Robyn asked with a look of scathing disbelief. 'What kind of woman is she?'

'Mad, so Colm says.'

'Must be. No matter what, I'd want to see Toby at Christmas. Any parent would want that. This hippy commune she's living in must be something special if she can't even bring herself to leave it for a week or so every year.'

Nina shrugged. 'I don't really know much about it. I think it's on one of the islands off Scotland and it's a long journey to get back down here. I think it's one of those sorts of places where nobody has their own money – you know, you see them on the television where everyone just lives off the land and barters for the things they need from the outside world and they all share everything they have…'

'That wouldn't stop me. Hell or high water wouldn't stop me getting home for Toby. In fact, I wouldn't have left him in the first place.'

'I know, me neither. It probably sounds horrible and selfish but I'm quite happy about her not coming back, whatever the reason. I don't want her coming back now and messing things up between me and Colm – or between me and Polly while I'm getting to know her. From what I've heard she can be unpredictable and that can't be good, can it?'

'I can't blame you for that. But Colm wouldn't take her back now, surely, even if she did show up?'

'He says he wouldn't and I have to believe him, don't I?'

Robyn nodded, and there was a pause. 'So for now it's turkey at Winston's again, then?'

'Probably, but even that might not happen this year. What if Dad wants to go to Pam's and daren't tell me? I'd hate to stop him doing what he really wants to do.'

'He wouldn't go without you.'

'I don't suppose he would but that in itself worries me. I'd feel responsible for him being miserable without her.'

Robyn rolled her eyes. 'It's only one day – I'm sure he can manage.'

'Yes, but he shouldn't have to.'

'Ugh, you're so bloody saintly it's sickening. Why can't you be selfish for once and get what you want instead of worrying about what everyone else wants?'

Nina gave a rueful smile. 'That does sound lovely.'

'Well, you can always come to mine. Obviously, I'll have a houseful of hideous relatives but there's always room for one more.'

'No Peter then?'

'Not for Christmas lunch. I'm sure I'll grab an hour with him Christmas night, though…'

Nina's small smile turned into a broad grin. 'It's still going well, then?'

'I really like him. I mean, *really*.'

'I can tell. I'm glad you two sorted things out because everyone could see you were perfect for each other.'

'I think his wife might beg to differ.'

'Well, she might, but it doesn't sound as if it's any of her business now. She's staying out of the way?'

'Moved in with her sister, so Peter says. He's going to put the house on the market in the new year so it seems like a definite end to their previous cohabiting arrangement.'

Nina nodded. 'That's good. So the way is clear.'

'I suppose it is, at long last.'

'I could do with moving these boxes out of the way until we're ready to start,' Nina said, looking at the fruits of their internet shopping.

'We could get some of them done today.'

'I don't want to do them too soon because then they'll have to lie around my house fully assembled for ages and I might break one. Better if they stay packaged for now and we can put them together and tag them up just before the ceremony. Did you phone Sammy for that?'

'I spoke to Diana – she says he'd fly to the moon for us.'

'So he still thinks we're a pair of angels?'

'Dodgy ones at best but, yeah, basically. I think he might have noticed some of the feathers falling off my wings, though.'

Nina laughed. 'You know what, I was so stressed about this whole memory-tree business but I'm actually quite excited now that the ceremony is getting closer.'

'That also means that Christmas Eve is getting closer too, and I hate to tell you but I am not looking forward to that.'

'Your in-laws?'

'Yep, every Christmas Eve come rain or shine they turn up. Which has been fine for most years – even though they drive me mad – but this year I just know Toby is going to say something about Peter to embarrass me.'

'I thought he was behaving now?'

'He's better – and I think I have your dad to thank for that – but I can't expect miracles straight away.'

'Well Dad thinks he's great – loves having him around. He says he's clever, polite and respectful.'

'He *is* letting the right boy into his home, isn't he?'

Nina laughed. 'Yes! I think so.'

'Well I'd check because that doesn't sound like Toby at all.'

'Dad has a way of bringing out the best in people.'

'He must be doing something right. It still doesn't change the fact that my son is a liability at home, especially where the in-laws are concerned, and especially if he can see a way to get Peter out of the equation.'

Nina gave Robyn a more sympathetic look now. Toby was proving to be a little stubborn when it came to accepting Robyn's new boyfriend, and the situation wasn't a million miles from the one she'd feared she'd encounter with Polly when Colm had come clean with her about his relationship with Nina. She counted her blessings every day that so far Polly had been tolerant and accepting of them, despite the Christmas tradition of wishing for her mum back.

'He doesn't seriously think that he can split you two up by telling Eric's parents about you?'

'He's not that stupid. In fact, he's way cleverer than that – at least he likes to think he is. He's just looking to put pressure on the relationship in any way he can, thinking that will end it by one means or another in a way that doesn't make it look his fault.' Robyn plonked her hands on her hips and looked at Nina. 'He's got a lot to learn about life has that boy of mine. He might think he's got all this influence but he's going to find out he's very wrong. Things rarely go the way you want them to and there's bugger all you can do about it most of the time.'

'You can say that again.'

'So what are you going to do Christmas Day?'

Nina shrugged. 'I don't really know. Connie invited me to go with her to her cousin's house but… well, I have to admit that it feels a bit weird now that she knows about Colm. Like I have no right to her family any more.'

'But they're Gray's family too, so by default that makes them yours.'

'I know; that sort of makes it worse. I can't explain it.'

'You don't need to – I get what you mean. I suppose I might feel the same if I gave a shit.'

Nina chuckled. 'I wish I could be like you.'

'No, you don't.' Robyn sniffed. 'Be like you – it's far nicer.'

'Far more boring.'

'I don't think so. I wouldn't be friends with you if I thought that.'

'Well,' Nina said, colouring at the compliment, 'thank you for being my friend and not finding me boring.'

'I'm pretty sure Colm doesn't find you boring either.'

'Sometimes I wonder why. I'm sure he could have had his choice of women.'

'Yes, and he chose you.'

Nina gave a slow, dreamy smile. 'He did, didn't he?'

'Bloody hell!' Robyn grinned as she looked back at the pile of boxes. 'We'd better get this sorted before I lose you to the fairies. So when do you want to get cracking?'

'This weekend?' Nina asked, trying her best to shake thoughts of Colm so she could concentrate on the task in hand. 'We can't do next weekend because it's my dad's engagement party and the memory-tree ceremony is only few days after that anyway.'

'Next weekend. Book me in then; I'll come over to help. Toby as well.'

'And I'll make some calls to see who else wants to come.'

'What about all these neighbours of yours? There's a whole street of people here you can tap for help.'

'I don't know... I feel like we asked too much of them with the garden and everyone started to fall out, didn't they? I think I'd rather just keep it between us from now on. After all, this tree project is really just ours anyway.'

'Lazy buggers,' Robyn said.

'It's not that. Most of them work so it must be hard enough to fit everything in, let alone extra. I don't work so I don't really have an excuse.'

'You still have a life even if you don't have a job. It's alright – they'd probably just annoy me anyway. If you want to keep it between us that's fine with me.'

'Well, maybe Nasser and Yasmin will help. Kelly might too.'

'Don't ask those sisters – they might force us to eat their cake.'

Nina frowned. 'Oh, we can't leave Ada and Martha out if we're asking others. Out of everyone they'd want to come.'

'Alright then, but they can leave their Victoria sponge at home.'

'I can't promise that, I'm afraid.'

'Bugger. In that case let them make some and we'll use it to threaten people into working faster.'

'That's not actually a bad idea.'

'Honestly, I don't know how you can get cake so wrong. And it's not like they have to make it – there are plenty of shops that sell perfectly good cakes.'

'Everyone's been too polite to say anything to them for so many years it's sort of too late to say anything else now, isn't it? We'll all have to keep pretending until they decide to stop baking.'

'Please, God, let it be soon.'

Nina giggled. 'I'm sure Ron will eat it if nobody else does.'

'He's not coming, is he?'

'I doubt it, but I suppose he won't like being left out of being asked.'

'He's got to be the most infuriating man I've ever met.'

'He can't help the way he is,' Nina said. 'I honestly think he misses Yvette.'

Robyn raised her eyebrows. 'So he wasn't miserable before they went to Spain?'

'Well, I suppose a little bit…'

'There you go then.' Robyn folded her arms. 'Once a git, always a git. Honestly, if I was his wife I'd stay in Spain too.'

'I don't know what happened in Spain but I definitely think he still cares for her.'

'I believe you,' Robyn said, 'though I'll admit to struggling with it.'

Nina smiled. Then she turned to the boxes. 'I think we should go through and quickly open each one to check none of the lanterns have been damaged in transit. At least that way we'll have time to order replacements if any have been broken. What do you think?'

'Sounds like a good idea, boss. Let's get on with it then so we can have a cuppa. I've been standing in your kitchen for at least half an hour and you haven't so much as looked at the kettle yet. It's very poor service, you know.'

'OK,' Nina said, throwing her a brief grin. 'Work then tea. Sounds like a plan.'

Until now, Nina had been reluctant to let Colm into her home. After all, it had been the home she'd shared with Gray, but since her talk with Connie, it didn't seem like such a big deal any more. Perhaps this way was the best way to introduce it too, having him here for the first time along with Polly, Robyn and Toby, and her dad. Ostensibly they were all here to help with the decorations for the memory tree, but though they had lanterns to wire up, strings to tag and candle wicks to trim, they weren't making much progress because there had been far too much chat and laughter.

Robyn had certainly been instrumental in that – her icebreaking skills could free a ship from an Antarctic sheet. While Nina was always more hesitant, worrying about everyone getting along (while simultaneously realising that if they were going to get along they'd have to be in the same room together sooner or later and then worrying about that too), Robyn was straight in there, cracking jokes and generally ribbing everyone in the most merciless way. She was quite fond of sharing embarrassing anecdotes too, where she had them, and this afternoon found Toby on the receiving end of quite a lot of them. As far as Robyn was concerned, it was heartily deserved, because not long after Toby and Polly had been introduced, he'd embarked on a sustained and earnest campaign of trying to impress the young girl.

'You know, Polly,' Robyn began as her son did his best to look disinterested in the proceedings while also trying very hard to get Polly to notice how disinterested he was, 'he might seem cool now but he wasn't always. Like when he was three, he was obsessed with his fireman's uniform. God, did he wear it everywhere – in bed, to the shops, to nursery. We even had to bathe him in it, which was lucky because we wouldn't have been able to get it off him to wash it anyway. If you tried to take it off he'd burst into tears and threaten to call the fire brigade to take you away!'

Toby turned an impressive shade of red and Polly gave a polite but uncertain little laugh. Winston, on the other hand, found it all too funny.

'Oh, and there was me giving you boring old overalls!' He chuckled. 'I'll see if I can pick you a little fire officer uniform up for next week!'

Toby looked like he didn't know whether to punch someone or run away, but Robyn winked at Nina. If she was being honest, Nina did feel sorry for Toby and wondered if Robyn wasn't being a little unfair. But then, after the weeks of turmoil they'd had and in light of how hard Robyn was trying to set Toby on a straighter path than he'd been on of late, she realised that perhaps this was her friend's way of keeping his feet firmly on the ground when she felt he was getting too cocky for his own good.

As afternoon turned into evening, Winston announced that he quite fancied a takeaway and so now, along with the candles and wire and lanterns, there was also an assortment of Chinese dishes in foil trays on Nina's kitchen table. Colm insisted on paying, but then Winston decided he was paying for it, followed by Robyn and Nina's offers to contribute, and a good-natured argument ensued, culminating in Winston and Colm splitting the bill between them. They went to collect it together too, and although Nina had been anxious watching them go, when they returned all smiles and banter, she felt a huge weight – one of many – lift from her shoulders. They liked each other and another important hurdle had been leapt over with apparent ease. But then, to meet either of these men was perhaps to wonder who on earth wouldn't like them.

They took a break to eat and it was a chatty, informal affair, with everyone picking from this tray and that, the food having been left in the takeaway cartons for ease, and, if they were honest, for laziness. But it was nicer that way, encouraging everyone to interact and let their guard down. In fact, everyone was getting on so well it was more than Nina could have hoped for. She couldn't remember when her little house had last been filled with such life and fun.

One by one, people abandoned the food and began to pick up odds and ends to work on again. When Nina was certain everyone had finished, she and Colm began to collect the leftovers to wrap up and put in the fridge. Polly's offer of help raised a broad smile from Nina, who was only too happy to let her. When they were done, everyone sat back down to start on the lanterns again.

They'd been working for twenty minutes when Polly frowned at the list of dedications. 'What's this one?' She turned to Colm. 'Dad, is this one for…?'

Colm nodded as she showed him. Nina guessed she'd seen the dedication for her twin brother Billy, who'd died as a baby. Polly smiled up at Colm. There was no sadness in it – perhaps it was hard to be sad for someone she'd never really met – but there was a significant appreciation of the gesture, and there was affection and support too, a recognition of the pain that the loss must always cause her dad, even after fifteen years.

They were snapped from the moment by a knock at the front door.

'I expect that will be Ada and Martha,' Nina said, getting up. 'They had something on at the church this afternoon but said they'd come afterwards.'

She opened the front door to find the sisters on the step, smiling up at her.

'Who's here?' Ada asked.

'We never expected there to be so many cars outside your house,' Martha added.

'Hello,' Nina said, not a bit flustered by their blunt question. 'We've got a little chain gang working on the lanterns.'

'Oh, there's still some for us to do?' Ada asked, looking worried.

'We so wanted to help,' Martha said.

'Oh, don't worry, there's plenty to do,' Nina said with a smile.

'Because we saw your father's car,' Ada said. 'At least we thought it was one of his lovely old cars.'

'And your friend's car,' Martha put in.

'And one that would be your gentleman friend's?' Ada asked coyly.

'The handsome gardener,' Martha said, as if it needed clarifying for Nina, and they both broke into giggles as if they'd said something very naughty.

'Yes, he's here,' Nina said.

'Oooh, lovely,' Ada said, clasping Martha's hand in hers and almost dragging her over the threshold. 'I said he'd be here – didn't I say so, Martha?'

'You said he'd be here,' Martha said, as if Ada hadn't just told her as much. With them safely in, Nina closed the door again and ushered them down the hall into the kitchen.

'Oh!' Martha exclaimed.

'So many of you?' Ada squeaked.

'Oh, hello!' Martha added, her gaze settling on Polly.

'We've never seen you before,' Ada said, now looking at Polly too.

'This is my daughter, Polly,' Colm said.

Polly looked suddenly shy and a little uncomfortable. It was hardly surprising really with Ada and Martha scrutinising her so carefully. 'Hello.'

'She's kindly agreed to help us,' Nina said. 'All hands on deck and all that.'

'All hands on deck,' Ada repeated. 'I said that, didn't I, Martha?'

'You said it would be the reason for all the cars,' Martha replied.

'There certainly are a lot of cars.' Ada nodded in fervent agreement, and Nina smiled again because there were only three cars parked outside her house, which was hardly a lot in anyone's estimation.

Ada and Martha hovered uncertainly, smiling at everyone, and Nina suddenly realised she hadn't thought about how many chairs she'd need to seat everyone. She'd managed to source what she'd needed for her current guests, but now she was two short. Robyn guessed what was on her mind as she looked around.

'I could drive to my house and pick up some camping chairs,' she said.

'It seems a bit far just for that,' Nina replied. 'I might have something in the loft if I go and look.'

'Want me to go and look?' Colm asked.

'We have chairs!' Ada said brightly.

'Yes,' Martha said. 'Borrow ours – it's no trouble at all!'

'They are for us, after all,' Ada said.

'We don't mind who sits on them, of course,' Martha finished, though it hardly needed saying.

'Come and get them from our house,' Ada said.

'Why don't I take you to get them?' Martha beckoned Colm.

'I'll take him,' Ada said.

'We can *both* take him then,' Martha said, and Nina wondered for a moment whether she was about to witness them have an argument. She'd never seen them fall out before and, as far as she knew, neither had anyone else on Sparrow Street. She was quite certain that it must happen on occasion, of course, but they'd always seemed to speak as one whenever she'd been around them.

'Colm and I can manage if I can have the keys to your house,' Nina said, hoping to head off any potential disagreement. 'I imagine they'll be quite a weight to carry that far.'

'Oh, it's not locked,' Ada said with a laugh, quite forgetting that she'd almost been annoyed only a moment before.

'Nobody wants to rob us,' Martha added.

'Would you like us to lock up for you when we've got the chairs?' Colm asked. If he thought they were foolish for leaving their home unlocked then he didn't show it.

'Oh, no thank you,' Ada said.

'That's alright,' Martha agreed.

Colm narrowly avoided a frown. 'I really think we ought to.'

Ada threw a hesitant look at her sister. 'Well…' she began uncertainly.

'If you really think so,' Martha finished for her.

'If the key's under the mat like usual there's no need to come with us,' Nina said.

Both sisters nodded and Nina took that to mean that it was.

'Why don't you take our seats and get settled here,' she continued. 'We'll be back before you know it and we'll bring the key with us so you can stay as long as you want without having to worry about your own house.'

At the offer of an extended stay, both sisters brightened.

'We could, couldn't we, Ada?'

'What a lovely idea,' Ada agreed.

Colm turned to the door, Nina following.

'Need any help?' Nina turned back to see Robyn grinning lazily at her. 'Of course you don't,' she added wryly.

Polly looked up, perhaps mildly perplexed by the statement – if she'd noticed it at all – but said nothing. Only Winston looked vaguely uncomfortable, and Nina made a note to give Robyn a good slapping the next time they were alone. She'd plan some sort of revenge but it was pointless, because nothing ever seemed to embarrass Robyn.

'Have fun!' Robyn called as they left the room. Colm gave a low chuckle.

'Honestly,' Nina hissed.

'Let her have her fun,' Colm said, still laughing. 'We'll pay her back somehow.'

'I've just been thinking that, but if the thing that makes Robyn blush exists, I haven't found it yet. I honestly don't think it does.'

'I'll bet I can think of something.'

'Good luck with that,' Nina said, reaching for his hand with barely a conscious thought about it. She felt it close over hers, warm and reassuring, and they headed out into the evening.

As Nina and Colm let themselves into Ada and Martha's darkened house, Colm was still chuckling softly. Nina was glad he could see the funny side of things, because sometimes Robyn could be an acquired taste and life might have been very difficult indeed if he and her best friend couldn't get along. Colm felt along the wall for a second before the hallway was flooded with yellow light.

'Jesus, Mary and Joseph!' he exclaimed, almost choking on his words as he stared around at the walls.

'Oh!' Nina laughed. 'I should have warned you about the puppy posters.'

'I wish you had. I like a cute dog as much as the next man but I feel like I've seen something from a Stephen King novel here. I'll be having nightmares later.'

'Will you need me to come and keep you safe while you sleep?'

'Maybe I will…' he said, giving her a flirty look. 'Or at least give me something to take my mind off what I've seen in here today.'

Nina laughed again as they went through to the dining room.

'They don't have their heating on much, do they?' Colm said, sniffing the air.

'I don't think they have much money to spare,' Nina said. 'I suppose if you can save on the heating you will.'

He shook his head. 'It's not right, is it? People going without the most basic comforts. Someone ought to be looking out for them.'

'I agree, but even if you tried to help them with it they wouldn't accept it. They may seem a little silly if you don't know them but they're actually very proud and independent. We do try to look out for them as best we can.'

'You mean *you* do?'

'Everyone in the street does.'

Colm raised his eyebrows.

'Well,' Nina said, laughing, 'some of us more than others.' She crossed the room and picked up a high-backed wooden chair, but then looked up to see Colm walk towards her and take it from her hands.

'I can manage—' she began, thinking he was going to try and carry both the chairs they'd come to fetch, but he put it down before grabbing her and planting a passionate kiss on her lips.

After a few moments, Nina pulled away and smiled up at him. 'I wasn't expecting that.'

'I didn't see the point in wasting a perfectly good opportunity,' he said. 'The truth is, Robyn wasn't that far off the mark. I've been dying to do that all afternoon and here we are... alone. How could I not?'

'It's perhaps just as well you managed to wait. It might have turned a few heads if you'd done it in my dining room – it was rather... Hot.'

'I'm glad you thought so. I do my best.'

'Your best isn't too bad.'

'You know,' he said, holding her in a smouldering gaze, 'I ought to go and shake wee Toby by the hand.'

'Why's that?'

'Well, if he hadn't made such a pig's ear of your garden I never would have met you.'

'That's true,' Nina said. 'I hadn't really thought of it before.'

'I have. A lot. And I don't mind saying it's changed my life...' He stroked a dark curl away from her face. '*You've* changed my life.'

'Me?'

He kissed her again. 'What do you think? I wouldn't say it if it wasn't true.'

'It's just...' Nina shook her head.

'You don't feel the same?' he asked, his tone now tinged with uncertainty.

'Oh God, of course I do! You've made everything so much better! I feel so lucky to have met you!'

He threaded his fingers into hers and gazed at her in perfect silence and time stopped. 'If you'll let me,' he said finally in a low, husky voice, 'there's something I want to say.'

Nina gave a small nod, her heart beating faster than ought to be possible.

But then a reedy voice rang down the hall.

'Coooeeee!'

Nina couldn't help but laugh, the tension of the moment suddenly popping like a soap bubble.

'Ada,' she breathed.

'You locked the door after us?' Colm asked.

'Yes.'

He cocked his head with a grin. 'So we could make them wait.'

Nina slapped his arm, laughing. 'Wait to be let into their own house? Don't be mean!'

'Could you let us in?' Martha called through the letterbox.

'We have cake in the pantry,' Ada shouted.

'Everyone at your house wants some,' Martha added.

'I'll bet they don't,' Colm said.

'Shhh!' Nina giggled. 'They'll hear you!'

Colm let her out of his embrace, but he seemed reluctant to. Whatever he'd been about to say, it looked as if it would have to wait. Nina couldn't tell how significant it might have been and part of her was perhaps a little relieved that she wouldn't have to deal with it just yet. She liked Colm a lot and loved where this might be going, but it was moving so fast that at times she felt a little outpaced by it. Maybe it wouldn't hurt for circumstances to put the brakes on things from time to time, just to let her catch up.

'We'd better let them in,' she said, straightening her top. 'Apart from anything else they're the biggest gossips; let them get the wrong idea and half the street will think we had sex on their dining table by tomorrow morning.'

Colm laughed. 'Now there's an opportunity I didn't see.'

Nina tried not to, but her cheeks burned as the very graphic image suddenly presented itself. She was slightly ashamed of herself, despite this, but she still had to wonder that if he'd suggested it, how hard might she have found it to say no?

'Perhaps you're right,' he said, making his way to the door, the grin he was wearing making it obvious he was aware of the effect he was having on her and was fairly pleased about it too. 'We wouldn't want that kind of gossip, would we?'

Colm got the front door and Ada and Martha tumbled into their own hallway like a couple of comic-strip kids caught eavesdropping at the headmaster's door.

'Oh!' Ada cried, righting herself.

'You found the chairs?' Martha asked.

'They weren't too difficult to locate,' Colm said with an air of amusement. Nina waited for him to add something about how chair-shaped and obvious they were but he didn't.

'We thought you might struggle,' Ada said.

Colm looked from one to the other, his amusement growing by the second. 'You did, eh?'

'Because it's a strange house,' Martha said.

Ada nodded eagerly. 'It's not easy to find things in a strange house.'

'Well, no,' Colm replied. 'Although chairs tend to take up a lot of room, and they tend to be in rooms where chairs are required, so…'

Nina was now standing next to him and she dug her elbow into his side, but he didn't flinch. Nor did he show any intentions of dropping his gentle ribbing.

'We'd have had more trouble with the cake, though,' Nina said. 'It's lucky you came round to get that.'

'Oh yes,' Martha said with a vigorous nod.

'Polly said she wanted a slice,' Ada put in.

Colm looked at Nina and she could tell he was dying to laugh but, to his credit, he held it in.

'She's never tried your cake before so I expect she does,' was all he said, and Nina could just imagine the silent addition in his head. *But she won't be quite so keen next time…*

Chapter Twenty-Four

To Pam's bitter disappointment, the pretty Old Apple Loft pub and bistro had been fully booked after all and so she and Winston weren't able to have their engagement party there. Nina had suspected that might be the case and, if she was honest, was a little relieved about it. She'd told Robyn that she wanted to stop connecting every Wrenwick landmark to things she'd once done with Gray, but old habits died hard.

In the end, the only venue Winston and Pam had been able to book at such short notice was the damp and leaky community centre. Still, as Pam was determined that they wouldn't postpone the event, Nina, Robyn and a sizeable army of Pam's relatives had pitched in to dress it with bunting, streamers and various banners bearing messages of congratulations and wishes of good luck and it looked pretty good. Pam had also hired a fantastic caterer and a decent DJ, and on the night there were so many guests packed in you could hardly tell it was damp at all.

The usual neat rows of meeting chairs had been moved to stand against the walls around the room and the DJ played old party classics while the hall pulsed with coloured lights that bounced from a glitter ball. It was all a bit school disco, especially the ball, but it didn't matter because Nina was having so much fun she didn't really care. Anywhere Colm was she was happy to be too these days, no matter where it was. Polly had been invited but had decided she'd rather stay at home, and

Nina could understand this perfectly well. She'd suspected that her dad had only invited Polly out of courtesy to Colm and nobody really thought she'd want to attend. The same had happened in Toby's case, so Robyn and Peter had come without a teenager in tow and were misbehaving quite enough to make up for his absence anyway.

Things had started slowly because the four of them – Nina and Colm and Robyn and Peter – had got to the venue early to help set up, but during the last hour everything had really livened up, more and more as more guests arrived. Nina never danced, and yet Colm had persuaded her easily to get up with him and take to the floor where they'd danced to 'Stayin' Alive', Colm doing his best John Travolta impression, which had made Nina laugh so hard she had almost stopped breathing.

Following that, the DJ ran through a catalogue of hits from Michael Jackson, Wham! and Take That, and then Colm had really shown his dancing feet when the Motown classics came on. Nina had felt self-conscious at first, but it hadn't taken long for him to have her whirling around the room, laughing and not caring how she looked. Occasionally she looked to see that Robyn and Peter were dancing too, and that poor Pam was doing her best to persuade a reluctant-looking Winston that he ought to be gracing the floor with everyone else. Nina smiled at that. Give him any car and he could strip it bare inside an hour and put everything back in place just as easily, but when it came to dancing, he was the proud owner of two firmly left feet and he knew it. He loved music but headbanging to Black Sabbath was about his limit when it came to moving to it.

When she could dance no more, Nina went to take a break. She sat, smiling to herself at a table while Colm went to get drinks, realising that she probably looked silly sitting and smiling at nothing, though she couldn't deny that she found herself doing it a lot these days, regardless. Gradually, she became aware of someone else and looked up to see Pam at the table.

'Are you having a nice time?'

'Lovely,' Nina said. 'It's a great party. Are you and Dad enjoying it?'

'Oh yes, but I expect we'll pay for it tomorrow morning.' Pam laughed. 'My old legs aren't what they used to be. Mind if I join you for a minute or two?'

Nina patted an empty chair beside her. 'Of course not.'

Pam sat down and gave her a fond look. 'I'm so glad we can be friends. I wanted to thank you for that. I was so worried you wouldn't like me; I know… well, I've heard about how wonderful your mother was and how much she meant to you and Winston.'

'Yes, she was, but nobody expected him to be lonely just because she was gone. Honestly, if I could have chosen for him I wouldn't have done much better than you.' Nina smiled. 'As for nerves, I can understand exactly how you feel. I'm sort of in the same boat with Polly, after all.'

'Colm's daughter?'

Nina nodded.

'It's hard, isn't it?' Pam said. 'I expect it's harder still with a teenager.'

'I don't know about that, but I do worry I'm being compared to her mum and I hope she doesn't think I'm trying to replace her because I'd never want to do that. All I want is to be a new part of her life, someone she feels she can spend time with and come to if she ever needs help or advice. If she'll have me, that is.'

'I'm sure you'll be just that.'

'I wish I was so sure,' Nina said.

Pam patted her hand. 'Love has a way of working out in the end. It's not worth having if it doesn't take a bit of effort.'

'You could be right there,' Nina said pensively. Her expression brightened as she looked at Pam. 'For the record, Dad looks happier than I've seen him in ages. Thank you for that.'

'So am I,' Pam said. 'And I have you and your dad to thank for that. It's funny,' she added, 'he says the same about you.'

'What does he say?'

'That he hasn't seen you looking this happy in a long time.'

'Does he? I hadn't realised it was that noticeable.'

'Well, I don't have anything to compare it to but I'd say you look very happy to me too. Radiant, in fact.'

'Thank you.' Nina laughed, not quite sure what else to say. Was her new happiness so obvious to everyone?

'Oh, here he comes now,' Pam said, pushing herself from her chair as Colm returned with the drinks.

'Don't leave on my account,' he said, putting them down on the table. 'In fact, I could get another for you if you want to sit with us for a while. What'll you have?'

Pam shook her head. 'That's kind of you but I really need to find my sister. She has a tendency to get naked when she's drunk and she was looking a bit too close to it last time I saw her.'

Nina's eyes widened and Pam laughed at her look of shock.

'Don't worry,' Pam said. 'It doesn't last long. About ten minutes after she hits the naked stage she hits the fall-asleep stage. If I can keep her covered up for a while until the urge to strip passes, she'll be out cold soon after and we won't need to worry.'

Colm burst out laughing. 'We'd better let you find her then.'

Pam smiled. 'Hopefully I'll catch up with you later.'

Nina nodded and a second later Pam wandered off, disappearing into the crowd. Colm took the seat she'd just vacated.

'You two looked as if you were getting along well,' he said.

'We were. That's what we were talking about actually – about how nerve-wracking it is to be introduced to the children of a new partner.'

'And you were telling her how anxious you've been about Polly?'

'How do you know that?'

'Because I'm learning what makes you tick very quickly. You worry about everyone else – whether they're happy – even if it makes you unhappy in the process. Maybe it's not such a good thing for you but it's still a beautiful trait.' He picked up his beer and took a quick gulp before setting it down again and holding her in a suddenly earnest gaze. 'It's one of the many reasons I love you…'

Nina stared at him.

'Yes,' he said, 'there's nothing like a few drinks to bring out the truth. I've said it now – you can do what you like with it.'

He looked as if he was afraid he might be rejected, that his admission of love might be rejected too. He suddenly looked as if he wished he hadn't said it. Nina simply smiled.

'I love you too,' she said, the words coming so easily and naturally that it almost took her by surprise.

'Right,' he said, breaking into a relieved smile of his own now, 'that could have been awkward.'

Nina leant in to kiss him. 'I love you,' she repeated. 'I don't think there's anything awkward about that, is there?'

'No,' he said. He paused. 'I want to…' he began, but then stopped, a slight shake of his head. 'One thing at a time,' he said, and it seemed to Nina that wasn't what he'd originally meant to say.

'What?' she asked. 'What did you want to do?'

'I…' He gazed at her and she waited, knowing somehow that what she was supposed to have heard would have changed everything again, but she wasn't scared; she could tell it was something good, something that might finally make her complete after so long feeling lost and alone.

'You can say it,' she urged.

'Nina, there's something—'

Just then, a shout went up from the dance floor and everyone looked to see a woman – perhaps in her late fifties – stripped to her bra and flinging her blouse around with gay abandon.

'What the…' Colm stared.

Nina laughed. 'It must be Pam's sister. She wasn't exaggerating when she told us about this then.'

'Jesus, Mary and Joseph…' Colm gulped as he looked again. 'Do you think we ought to do something?'

A horrified Pam rushed across the dance floor with a jacket and wrapped it around her sister while a spontaneous round of applause spread through the room.

'Looks like Pam's got it under control,' Nina said.

'I have to say I'm slightly relieved about that,' Colm replied. 'I didn't fancy rugby-tackling her to the ground to try and get her covered up.'

'Especially as she was likely to get more naked before she fell asleep,' Nina said with a grin.

'This is one party we won't forget in a hurry,' he said.

'It is,' Nina agreed, though she wasn't thinking about Pam's sister now.

Colm reached for his beer and took another swift gulp. The music was loud, the room hot and cramped, and neither of them heard Colm's phone ringing as it sat on the table between them. But then Nina noticed it was flashing an incoming call. It was out so he could keep an eye on it in case Polly needed him as she was currently home alone. Nina saw that it was her name showing on the screen now.

'Maybe you should see what she wants?' she said, angling her head at it.

'Probably wants batteries for the game controller or something,' he said, picking it up. 'Give me a minute?' he added, leaving the table.

'Of course.' Nina watched as he took the phone somewhere quieter.

He was gone for a good ten minutes, which wasn't long, but clearly what Polly had needed to say had turned out to be more than a quick question about batteries. Still, Nina wasn't worried as she watched Pam lead her giggling sister away from the dance floor to more cheers from knowing friends and relatives. How could she be anything other than happy and relaxed when the evening was about as perfect as she could have hoped for?

She was still happy and relaxed when Colm returned, but it didn't last long as she noted the look on his face. In fact, his whole demeanour had changed. Gone was the warm, contented smile he'd worn all evening, replaced by tense anxiety.

'I'm really sorry about this but I have to go.' He gathered his jacket as Nina stared at him. 'Shit...' he added, 'too much to drink... I knew I should have stayed sober.' He looked up at Nina. 'Know any numbers for a cab?'

'What's the matter? What's happened?'

'It's nothing, don't worry,' he said, opening the browser on his phone and searching for a local taxi company. 'Apologise to your dad for me. Will you be able to get home OK?'

'Of course – I expect Robyn and Peter will be able to give me a lift.'

'Peter...' Colm looked up from his phone and scanned the room. 'Quicker than a cab,' he murmured. 'I wonder if he'd mind...'

'Colm! Please tell me what's happened! Is Polly alright?'

'She's…' Colm looked at her now, an internal struggle clear on his face. 'Something's happened at home.'

'What?'

'I don't know if I can…'

'You can tell me; I want to help!'

His expression was sad now and he shook his head slowly. 'Not this time, Nina.'

'Why not?'

'Because it's Jane. She's come home.'

Chapter Twenty-Five

Colm had charged off in such a blind panic that Nina had barely been able to get more than that from him. It wasn't about him seeing Jane, he'd reassured her – it was about being there so that Polly wouldn't have to deal with her return alone, and Nina couldn't really argue with that. She was sure, faced with the same situation, she'd rush home too. Still, it hadn't stopped her going to the toilets for a self-pitying cry once he'd gone. She'd made some excuse for him having to leave early to her dad and anyone else who'd asked, not knowing how much of the truth he'd want her to reveal to others at this stage. She hadn't been able to ask him about that either – the only thing he'd managed to say before he left was that he'd call her the following day. Even with this promise, she couldn't help but feel she'd lost him already.

Nina didn't text Colm the following morning. She didn't call him either; she gave him space. He'd need time with Jane and Polly, time to talk and think and maybe even plan, and Nina recognised this, even though it broke her to think about it. Worse than knowing those discussions were happening was not knowing the outcome. Was Jane planning to stay? Why had she come home now after all this time? Had she turned up out of the blue or had Colm had warnings that he hadn't told Nina about? Had she turned up with an agenda or simply to remind them she was still alive? What was her current state of mind and would that change things? Did Colm want her? He'd told Nina he didn't but realistically he wouldn't have said anything else, would he? Would he have recognised that he wanted her, even if he did? Would seeing her standing in front of him change his feelings, bring love rushing back? And how much influence would Polly have over the outcome?

Nina couldn't know any of the answers to these and so many more questions that plagued her and so she waited, wondering and hoping against hope, wishing, selfishly, that Jane had stayed away. She was slowly coming to the conclusion that somehow life or fate or destiny, or whatever you wanted to call it, meant for Nina to be alone.

It was with mixed feelings that, sometime after midday, Nina opened the front door to find Colm on the doorstep. Her heart beat madly as their eyes met and she saw his pain clearly. Snow was struggling to break free from heavy skies, falling in irregular and sparse bursts. Winston would have said it was too cold to snow, which had never made any sense to Nina, even though he'd often been right. The odd flake settled in Colm's hair now as he waited for Nina to respond to his arrival.

'Can I come in?' he asked.

Nina stepped back from the threshold to admit him and he stepped in, dragging his boots on the doormat to clear the wet from them.

'I'll put the kettle on—' she began, turning to lead the way through to the kitchen, but Colm laid a gentle hand on her arm.

'I can't stay long – I'm sorry. I just thought you deserved an explanation for what happened last night in person rather than on the phone.'

'An explanation,' Nina repeated dully. 'OK.'

'It's knowing where to start…'

'Jane wants to come back for good?' Nina asked. Of course she did – why would it be anything else? When did things ever work out in Nina's interest; when did she ever get what she wanted?

Colm nodded. Nina had a feeling she knew what else was coming. The only way to deal with it was to meet it head-on.

'She wants you to be a family again?' she said.

'Yes.'

'She says she needed time away but she's all better now and she won't do it again?'

'Yes. At least, sort of. The commune has disbanded. Apparently someone stole something from someone else and it all got a bit nasty.'

'So she couldn't go back up there even if she wanted to.'

'She says she was thinking of coming home anyway. She says she's been thinking about us a lot.'

'Do you believe her?'

'I don't know what to believe. Whatever, she's still Polly's ma so I can hardly stop them from being together if that's what they both want.'

Nina caught him squarely in the eye. This was not the time to shrink from the truth and it wouldn't help anyone in the end.

'Is that what you want? She's still your wife too. Do you want to be with her now she's home? Do you want your family together again as much as Polly does?'

'No...' he began, but then rubbed a hand across his chin, looking helpless. 'I don't know.'

'Do you still love her?'

He sighed. 'I don't even know her any more.'

You said you loved me, Nina thought, but she didn't say it. Had she only ever been a substitute after all? Had her position in his life always promised to be tenuous, dependent on the return of his wife? Or had he really meant what he'd said before it all went so wrong?

'How does Polly feel about it?' Nina asked.

'She's thrilled to have her ma back,' he said. Nina sensed a but. She raised her eyebrows in a silent question. 'I don't think she can really see the bigger picture yet,' he admitted.

'Which is?'

Colm dragged a hand through his hair and let out a long breath. 'Jane's been missing for five years. You don't just walk back into a family after five years and pick up like you've never been away. Our family has changed because of her absence. Polly and I have both changed. We can't just go back to being the people she left behind.'

'Polly doesn't see it like that?'

'Neither does Jane.'

'Doesn't that seem insensitive? And a little bit inconsiderate?' Nina asked.

Colm let out another heavy breath. 'God knows what goes on in that woman's mind. I didn't know five years ago and I don't know now.'

Nina was silent for a moment, trying to read him, trying to get a fix on where Jane's sudden return left them. He looked pained, regretful, but his eyes told her nothing more.

'Nina,' he said, breaking the silence. 'You have to believe that I had no idea this might happen. If I had I never would have—'

'I know,' Nina cut in. She didn't want him to say it. Whatever happened now, she wouldn't want to undo those precious, wonderful weeks they'd shared as a couple, even if it never amounted to anything more. And if she'd been able to look into the future, to see where this was going, she would still have chosen to follow that path, even knowing it would end like this.

'I think, perhaps…' she began slowly, 'that I'm a complication right now.'

'What? No!'

'Hear me out,' she said. 'I think you need time, and I think if you were being honest, you know it too.'

'I don't need—'

'If not for Jane or for you then for Polly. There's too much unfinished business there that needs addressing.'

'Nina, please…'

She shook her head with a sad smile. 'I've had the most wonderful time with you and you've given me gifts you couldn't even begin to understand. You can never imagine what you've done for me, how you've helped me to change. Know that I'll always care for you and I'll always think of our time fondly but we can't carry on as we did before – not in the face of this.'

'But last night you said—'

'I did and I meant it. I know you meant it too, but then Jane came home.'

'That doesn't matter.'

'It does. You've said yourself this is the one thing Polly longed for year after year, the one wish she made every Christmas. You told me how damaged you were for a long time after Jane left. I believe that when you said you loved me last night you meant it, but I don't believe I can have the whole of your heart while Jane is in your life.'

'What are you saying?'

'I'm saying that I'm not what you need right now. I'm saying this is me, taking a step back to let you decide what's important and what you really want.'

'But I—'

'Don't. Don't make this harder than it already is.'

'Hard for you! How do you think this is for me?'

Nina gave him a sad smile. 'I know; that's why I'm doing this. I can't be sure that you don't still love Jane a little, and I know for sure that you love Polly most of all. If you thought for a minute that taking this opportunity from her without even trying to make it work would hurt her, you wouldn't think twice about me. And that's OK,' she added, putting a hand up to his protestation, 'it really is. I suppose if I had a son or daughter I'd do the same.'

Colm hesitated. Nina could see the battle raging within clearly on his face, the struggle between duty and family and the promise of something new, something that might make him far happier. She felt safe in the knowledge that when he'd said he loved her it was true, but things had changed and even he couldn't deny that the return of his estranged wife complicated things in a way that neither of them could have foreseen. Nina, however, knew better than anyone the importance of family and she was not about to stand in the way of one that could be whole again if that was what they wanted.

Finally, he bowed his head in a brief nod. 'I'll call when I know more.'

'It might be best if you don't.'

'Please…'

'This is a big deal and I'm sure you need time. Take it – take what you need to sort out what you and Polly want.' She gave him a tight smile. 'I'm not going anywhere.'

She meant that too; if he was destined to come back to her she'd be waiting. But something told her that he wasn't. Once he'd got to grips with a life that had Jane in it again, it would be the end for him and Nina.

He moved towards her and, for a moment, she thought he would kiss her. But then he fell back again looking hopelessly defeated.

'If it's what you want,' he said.

'It's not what I want but it's what I think is needed.'

'I'm sorry, you know, truly. I never meant for any of this to happen.'

'Nobody ever means these things to happen but they do.'

He was silent again, looking at her, waiting, perhaps, for a prompt, for her to tell him what came next.

'I'm sure you need to get back,' she said.

'Right.' He nodded. 'Goodbye then.'

'Goodbye, Colm.'

He didn't leave, even then, but stared forlornly at her for a moment longer. Perhaps he recognised as well as she did that once he walked out of the door there was a good chance it was over between them. But how could Nina ask him to do anything else?

Eventually he left, quietly and without fuss. No grand gesture, no begging, no promises. He simply went, and Nina closed the door, closing out the daylight so it was just her, standing in her gloomy hallway. Then she went to sit at the kitchen table and opened her laptop. She had things to do and they wouldn't wait, not even for a broken heart to mend.

Chapter Twenty-Six

Robyn looked at Nina over the rim of her cup. On the table in front of them was an unfinished pot of tea and the last of the lanterns that needed putting together and labelling, while stacked against a wall were crates containing those they'd completed, waiting to be attached to the tree.

'You know you're an idiot, don't you?' Robyn said. 'The man was crazy about you – not to mention bloody fit – and you just send him packing? Are you mad?'

'What else could I do?'

'You could have put up a fight instead of getting all ridiculous and noble about it. This is real life, not some stupid romance novel.'

'They're a family—' Nina began, but Robyn cut across her.

'Who gives a shit? His wife certainly didn't when she buggered off and left him to cope! She didn't care that they were a family and she should be the one left out in the cold now, not you.'

'I don't think Polly would agree with you.'

'She's fifteen – what does she know?'

Nina frowned but Robyn put her drink down with a shrug and reached for a fresh card to write on.

'I'm just saying… she thinks she wants her mum now but all the grown-ups in the room know that it's only a matter of time before the flaky wench runs off again. And when she does it'll be ten times worse picking up the pieces than it was the first time.'

Nina couldn't help but wonder if there wasn't some wisdom in what Robyn was saying. Had she done the wrong thing after all? What if giving Colm up wasn't what he'd needed?

'I had to let him go,' she said wearily. 'I had to be sure this wasn't going to come between us sometime down the line.'

'I don't see how it would have done. She chose to leave, and she ought to be the one knocking at the window to get back in. All you've done is open it wide and leave her to get everything back without a bit of a fight.'

'What else could I do?'

Robyn gave an impatient sigh. 'There's no helping you so I'm not even going to try.'

'Come on,' Nina said. 'What would you have done?'

'I wouldn't have handed him over on a plate, that's for sure.'

'You left Peter when you found out his wife was still living there.'

'That's different and you know it. I left Peter because she'd never left their home – I hadn't just let her back in after she'd been missing for years because she fancied another go. This woman has no right to Colm or to Polly for that matter. She left them.'

'As far as I can tell it might not have been that straightforward. Maybe she had mental-health problems.'

'I'm sure she did – it's not rational behaviour – but does that mean you have to pay for that? Her mental health isn't your fault so why should you suffer?'

'I just thought that the last thing Colm needed was to be pressured into a choice.'

'And so…' Robyn looked up from the card she was attaching to a lantern and fixed Nina with a firm gaze. 'What if he chooses her now that you've left him free to do whatever he likes?'

'Then he was never mine at all,' Nina said with more conviction than she felt.

'Bullshit,' Robyn said, sighing as she returned to her task. 'What are you, a bloody Sting song? You love him, right?'

'I don't…'

'Of course you do – I have eyes. You should have fought for him, tooth and nail. I would have done.'

Nina stared into the depths of her mug and pondered Robyn's words. She wanted to believe that what she'd done was right, but what if it wasn't? What if Robyn was right? What if she should have fought for Colm instead of stepping back? What if she'd lost him forever now because of that mistake? Maybe Jane didn't deserve a second chance; maybe Nina had opened the door simply for Jane to hurt him and Polly all over again?

She shook away her doubts and looked up at Robyn. 'This *is* fighting for him. I have to make this sacrifice. If he comes back to me we'll be stronger, more certain for it.'

'And if he doesn't?'

Nina reached for a card and began to attach it to a lantern. Maybe she'd already lost him. Maybe she'd always been destined to lose him, even before they'd begun.

Chapter Twenty-Seven

It was the eve of Christmas Eve and the day they were due to unveil the memory tree. It had been trying to snow for a week now, the days cold and the nights biting, but the most they'd seen was a faint dusting, despite it being forecast. Nina wished that the high pressure would break and the snow would come, if only to warm the air a little. Even with the heating on her house was draughty, and as she still had no job, it seemed prudent to try to save some money and not to run it constantly. This meant that when it was off she was bundled in layer upon layer of fleece and knitwear. In some ways it was a good thing that Colm hadn't been to see her since she'd sent him away to sort things with Jane, because it was hardly a sexy look.

She couldn't deny, though, that his absence weighed heavily on her. It seemed to leach the colour from everything, even though she stood by her decision. He'd phoned once to try and talk to her again about what she'd said and about what might happen, but she'd told him it was pointless because she'd made up her mind and she was convinced that it was the only sensible way forward. Perhaps he'd seen it as some kind of rejection, or perhaps things really were as complicated as she'd feared after all. Perhaps even now, despite what he'd told her, he was trying to rebuild his life with Jane.

She'd been tempted to call him many times since that last phone conversation but she'd decided against it every time. Phoning him would only confuse things for all of them, she was sure of that, but she still had to admit that she missed him terribly. At least she had the memory tree to keep her occupied and she'd thrown herself into the planning and preparation with new vigour, determined that everything would be perfect. Thus, the garden was now immaculate, with neat borders, spotless paths, weed-free beds and a new stone birdbath that had been gifted to them by the local rotary club. The bird feeders and boxes and the insect hotel were in place again, and the rope swing had been restored. A little water feature gurgled in a quiet corner mimicking a mountain stream, with a set of benches close enough to sit and listen on a warm day. It had been Colm's suggestion and it remained one of Nina's favourite features of the garden, despite everything that had happened since. And then there was their special tree, tall and strong and thick with pine needles.

Sammy Star had been booked to help the celebrations along and the local vicar had agreed to attend to make the opening official. The church choir and freelance caterers were on hand, while Ada, Martha and Kelly were all making mince pies and mulled wine. Nina could only hope that Kelly's influence on the twins would be enough to turn out some decent baking this time, although she was slightly concerned that Kelly might also drink all the wine before they'd even got it to the garden. Nina and Robyn had been busy dressing the tree and directing operations while all this had been going on. Come hell or high water, everything was going to be perfect – they'd worked too long and too hard to let anything happen to ruin that.

It was hard to predict how many people would attend, but Nina had asked around during the previous days and, from what people had told her, she'd guessed at a few hundred. What they might spend on additional fundraising events like the tombola, raffle and collection tins would be added to the money they'd already raised from donations for the tree dedications and would make a nice pot of cash for the charities everyone had agreed would benefit. If nothing else made Nina happy right now, at least that did.

The preparations had not been without hiccups, though. The candles they'd planned to use inside the lanterns had proved to be impractical and unreliable, forcing Nina to make a last-minute dash to the wholesalers to purchase a whole mound of battery-powered lights that looked like candles. As she hadn't wanted to take the funds from the money they'd raised for charity so far, she'd ended up footing the bill herself. At least they'd been cheap, sold to her at cost by a friend of Sammy, who was proving to be very useful when it came to friends and acquaintances – although some introductions, she reflected with more than a little irony, had given her more than she'd bargained for.

And then there had been the small matter of Nina's aversion to the limelight. The last thing she wanted to do was get up to make a speech about the tree, to announce it in any way, to tell the story of how it came to be, or anything that involved the crowd looking directly at her. Sammy, who loved all of this, came to her rescue once again and agreed to host the evening in its entirety. He'd offer a brief nod to Nina and Robyn, who'd happily lurk in the shadows ensuring everything was running smoothly and mingling in the crowd to offer personal thanks to people for their support. In fact, there'd been plenty of that already and there were a lot of people to thank. Many of Nina's neighbours had been in the garden with Nina and Robyn since the early morning helping with the preparations, not to mention the people who were making contributions from their homes. No matter Nina's emotions, she only had to think of that to feel lucky to be part of such a caring community.

It was mid-afternoon now, and the light was already beginning to fail. They'd done much of what they needed to do, however, and though they were tired already, the gathering dusk turning the skies saffron and peach over the rooftops was pretty enough to lift the lowest of spirits.

Nasser flicked a switch and the fairy lights he'd strung beneath the eaves of the potting shed burst into life. It was amazing how something as simple as a string of lights could transform the dullest construction into something magical.

'OK?' he asked Robyn, who was standing with her hands on her hips, looking on.

'Perfect,' she replied.

'You want some anywhere else? I've got three sets going spare.'

Nina had been attaching the winning raffle numbers to some prizes on an old decorating table Ron had put together for her. Having just finished, she wandered over to see what else still needed to be done, catching the tail end of the exchange. 'How about those crab apple trees?'

'Yes, they'll look nice there,' Robyn agreed.

'No problem.' Nasser picked up the box containing the remaining sets of lights and strode over to the trees at the far side of the garden.

'Ron's got the ladder if you need it!' Nina called after him.

'It's looking pretty good, isn't it?' Robyn said, turning to Nina. 'It's a shame the man who did most of the landscaping work won't be here to see it tonight.'

'Don't…' Nina warned her.

'So… no word from him?'

Nina shook her head.

'Looks like the ex got her man back then—'

'Please,' Nina said. 'I don't want to talk about it – especially not now. I've got too much else going on.'

Robyn looked like she was itching to say something more on the matter, but then she reached into her pocket and pulled out a roll of sticky tape.

'This was left over from setting up the pin the tail on the donkey,' she said. 'Need it?'

Nina took it from her and stashed it into a cloth bag full of odds and ends she was wearing on her shoulder.

'At least Ron looks happy today,' Robyn said airily.

'I must admit he does seem surprisingly cheery today. Didn't need to be asked twice about helping here and didn't complain at all…'

She looked at Ron now, whistling tunelessly as he held the ladder for Nasser, and it was hard to deny that he had a spring in his step. She wondered what it could be. Whatever it was, even the street's biggest gossips Ada and Martha didn't seem to know, though everyone had noticed a change.

Robyn clicked her fingers in front of Nina's face. 'Wakey wakey. We've still got plenty to do.'

'Sorry,' Nina said, shaking herself.

'Seriously, though,' Robyn asked. 'You're alright? I know it's been a tough few days…'

'I'm fine.' Nina forced a smile. 'It's not like I was with him for years, was it?'

'New love is sometimes the worst to get over,' Robyn said. 'That's when it's all fresh and potent, when you absolutely can't breathe without them.'

'Yeah, well…' Nina hitched her bag onto her shoulder. 'I'll just have to get air tanks, won't I, because it doesn't look like he's coming back anytime soon.'

❀

An hour before the tree ceremony was due to begin the garden was filling up nicely. Nina was happy to see people crowding at the stalls, trying their luck at the tombola and raffles, having a whack at the piñata, buying mulled wine and mince pies. (Knowing who'd baked them, Nina had been forced to sample one, just to ensure that they were fit for human consumption, and they'd actually turned out to be surprisingly good.) She was busy helping set up the stage for Sammy when she heard a greeting and looked up to see her dad, hand in hand with Pam. She couldn't remember the last time she'd seen him hand in hand with anyone – not even her mum, who'd never really been one for public displays of affection – and he looked as happy as he always did whenever Pam was with him. At least that thought was enough to lift her own depressed spirits. While she'd been busy, she'd been able to pull her focus from the ache of missing Colm, but it had still been there in the background.

'Want some help with that?' Winston asked.

'Oh, you could just plug that in for me over there,' she said with a broad smile.

'Lucky the weather's holding for you,' he said, taking the plug from her. 'I don't think rain or snow would have done much for your electrics here.'

'I'm keeping my fingers crossed; a couple of hours is all I need. The forecast says it won't snow until tomorrow but you can never trust it. I'm trying not to think about the electrics exploding.'

'I'm sure Sammy's holding his breath too.'

'Probably,' Nina said with a quick grin.

'So, how have you been, love?' he asked. 'Since… you know.'

'Oh, not too bad.' Nina tried to keep her tone light. She'd had to tell her dad about Colm and Jane in the end but she didn't want him to worry. 'Honestly, I've been too busy to give it more than a second of thought.'

'You've certainly done a wonderful job here,' Pam said, sending an admiring glance around the fairy-lit garden. Nina looked too. She'd been so busy concentrating on one task or another that she hadn't really seen the whole picture, but now that she stopped to look, she couldn't help but agree. There were shining, glittering baubles hanging from bare trees, reflecting the lights that were dotted like fireflies all around; bells that swayed from branches and rang to sound like sleigh bells when the wind took them; covered stalls dressed in rich reds and velvet greens, the cinnamon-spiced aromas of festive treats drifting from them. And in the middle of it all was the lush fir, their memory tree, decked in satin bows and tagged lanterns, every one a beautiful reminder of a soul gone but never forgotten.

'I had plenty of help,' Nina said, pride swelling in her. 'It wasn't that bad in the end. Thanks for all that you and Dad did too, by the way. It was good of you to help.'

Pam waved away the comment. 'It was nothing; happy to help for such a good cause.'

Nina looked up as she saw Robyn making her way over to join them.

'Alright there, Winston… Pam?' she asked. 'How's it going? How's Toby been this week? I'd ask him myself but I barely get a grunt from him these days.'

'Oh, he's a lovely boy,' Pam cut in. 'Always so polite. You've done a good job there.'

Robyn laughed. 'Are you sure that's Toby?'

'Oh, he's as good as gold,' Winston said. 'And he picks things up so fast. I show him once and he's got it, just like that. He'll make a cracking mechanic if that's what he fancies doing in the future.'

Nina's attention was drawn away by Ron, who was sauntering over, hands in his pockets and looking casual, but very deliberately heading their way. As usual, he was alone, preferring to keep a distance from everyone on Sparrow Street, but – also as usual – it didn't seem to bother him.

'I've finished up,' he said. 'Unless there's anything else you need me to do?'

Nina shook her head. 'I don't think so. Feel free to enjoy the festivities. There's mince pies and mulled wine over by the crab apple trees.'

'I've already had a few,' Ron said, and Nina – knowing him well enough – guessed that his few would be more like twenty or so. The threat of Ada and Martha's baking did nothing to put him off and he seemed quite impervious to its effects. He scratched at the bristles on his head and looked suddenly awkward. 'I heard about that gardener fella,' he said. 'His wife came back… Is that right?'

'Yes,' Nina said stiffly. 'She did.'

'So you and him…?'

'Not for the moment, no.'

'Right…' Ron's hands dug into his pockets. 'Sorry to hear that.'

'It's OK; these things happen.'

'They do,' Ron said. 'If you need anything… well, I don't know much about it but I can listen as well as anyone else. And for the record, I think he's made a mistake. He's let a good woman go leaving you for her—'

'He didn't leave me for her,' Nina said. 'It wasn't quite like that…'

She let out a sigh. What was the point of trying to explain how it had happened? What did it matter what people thought? None of that changed the facts.

'I saw him, you know,' he said. 'Out with his daughter and her. Didn't know who she was at the time, of course. Thought it was a bit fishy, though.'

'When was this?' Nina asked, unable to help herself. Had Colm looked happy, she wanted to know – had they looked like a family? But how could she ask these things when she wasn't sure what the answer would do to her? Now, with all this going on around her, was most certainly not the time.

'Couple of days ago at the supermarket. I said hello. If I'd known about this business between you and him I would have given them a piece of my mind. You can't mess people around like that.'

'It doesn't matter,' Nina said. 'I appreciate the sentiment, though.'

Ron puffed out his chest. 'I would have done it for anyone, you know. What's right is right and what's not is not. It's a matter of decency.'

'I know,' Nina said, wishing she could explain to him that things weren't always as simple as right and wrong. There was no point with someone like Ron, though – things *were* that simple to him. She reflected for a moment on how nice that must be, to see the world in such straightforward terms.

'It's funny, though,' he said.

'What is?'

'The coincidence.'

'Coincidence? I don't follow.'

'His wife coming home. Must be something in the water.' He broke into a broad grin, but Nina could only frown, the conversation now completely losing her. Was there something she was supposed to know? 'My Yvette!' he prompted.

Nina's eyes widened. 'Yvette? You mean…'

'She phoned me yesterday – thought someone might have told you. She's had enough of Spain and wants to come home. Of course,' he sniffed, 'I could have told you she'd get there sooner or later – it's too hot there to suit my Yvette and you've got to pay a fortune for English biscuits.'

Nina smiled. At least this explained Ron's unusually cheery mood. Everyone knew he loved his wife to bits. 'That's brilliant, Ron. I'm so pleased for you.'

'It's not a bad Christmas present as they go,' he said.

'Not bad at all.' Nina reached to give him a peck on the cheek. He put a hand to it; if it hadn't been dark, Nina might have seen him blush. 'Good luck,' she said. 'I'm sure it will work out this time.'

'It will if I have anything to do with it,' he said with a grin.

'Will she be back in time for Christmas?'

'Oh yes – she's flying in tonight. She'll have to go back to Spain at some point to sort out the house there but she'll be staying with me until New Year. That's really what I came to tell you – I'll have to leave for the airport to collect her before you do the tree announcement so I'm sorry but I won't be here.'

Nina smiled. 'Don't even give it a second thought. Why ever didn't you say something earlier today?'

'I thought you knew. And with your news I thought… well, I didn't like to rub it in.'

'You wouldn't have done that,' Nina said, wishing that everyone would stop treating her like she was made of china. Colm was gone – she didn't know if it was for forever, but she had to get on with things regardless. She couldn't just mope around and she didn't think anyone ought to give her licence to. 'You should have told me. I bet you had things to get ready at home for her arrival and instead you've been stuck here all day.'

'It wasn't too bad. I got some extra food in last night and cleaned around a bit. You don't make much of a mess when it's just you.

And I'd already got her a Christmas present... just in case... you know...'

Nina nodded, thinking of the gifts she'd bought for Colm and Polly, now tucked in a drawer at home and unlikely to reach them. At least, not by Christmas Day anyway.

'So, I'd best be off then,' he added. 'If it's all the same to you and you don't need me for anything else.'

'Of course!' Nina smiled. 'Thanks for everything – I really do appreciate it.'

He turned to go but Nina called him back. 'And if I don't see you before, Happy Christmas.'

'You too.' He gave her a last smile and wandered away, keys jangling in his pockets as he went.

'What was all that about?' Winston asked, coming to join Nina now as she watched Ron disappear into the crowd. He'd been chatting to Pam and Robyn, but Nina guessed he might have been keeping a close eye on the proceedings here despite that.

'Ron's wife's coming back from Spain.'

'For Christmas?'

'For good – or so he seems to think. I do hope so.'

'Ah,' Winston said. 'So all's well that ends well.'

'Looks like it.'

Nina thought back to Ron's news that he'd seen Colm, Polly and Jane out together. Only food shopping, she told herself, and if Jane was there at the house then of course they'd need extra food. But did they need to shop for it together? Had they looked happy? If Jane was staying at the house they'd once shared as a family – and it was fair to assume she was – whose bed was she sleeping in?

'Are you alright?' Winston asked gently.

'Of course,' Nina said, forcing a bright smile. 'I was just thinking I ought to find Sammy to see if he has everything he needs. I'm pretty sure I saw him loitering at the hot-dog stand.'

'Diana will love that,' Robyn said dryly. 'It'll do wonders for his cholesterol if he's stuffing sausages down his neck.'

'That's true,' Nina said with a light laugh. 'I should probably go and save him from himself.'

Winston didn't look convinced by Nina's performance but he nodded. 'If you're sure you're alright…'

'I'm sure. Honestly, Dad, there's no need to worry. Why don't you go and get Pam a glass of mulled wine? It's so cold tonight I wouldn't be surprised if it doesn't sell out before too long.'

'Don't think trying to get rid of me is going to put me off the scent,' he said.

'I'm not,' Nina said, really laughing now, despite herself. 'Go. I'll come and find you later.'

With a last frown, Winston relented. Catching hold of Pam's hand, they disappeared into the crowd together.

At 8 p.m., almost everyone was gathered around the tree in anticipation of Sammy's speech. He was currently standing at the mic, about to begin. He looked to Nina, who nodded, and then he addressed the crowd. Diana was standing next to Nina with Robyn at the other side. Diana had come to the event even though she'd been under no pressure to, partly to support Nina and Robyn and the work they were doing for a good cause, but partly, Nina suspected, to keep a hawk-like watch on Sammy to make sure he didn't overdo things. She'd complained bitterly to Nina and Robyn earlier that evening, saying that it hadn't taken him long to fall back into the bad habits that had helped bring on his heart attack and that he kept telling her not to worry. How could she not worry, she said, when she'd been so close to losing her soul mate once before? She'd asked for Nina and Robyn's advice, but neither of them felt particularly well equipped to give it, and so they'd made vague offerings that hadn't really amounted to anything useful at all.

'Before I declare the memory tree officially...' Sammy paused. 'Open? You can't really declare a tree open, can you? It's just sort of there.'

The crowd laughed.

'Well,' he continued, 'I'll have to work with what I have here. So before I declare the tree... there... I'd like to give a special mention to the two fabulous ladies who had the vision to make this happen. I know they're both too shy to come up and speak to you themselves but I'm sure they'd want me to express how grateful they are for your support tonight. And I think it's only fair that we thank them for all their hard work, so I'd like to ask you all to raise glasses, mince pies, burgers, pork baps... whatever you have in your hands... To Nina and Robyn!'

'To Nina and Robyn,' the crowd repeated, before bursting into spontaneous cheers and applause. Most of them probably didn't have a clue who they were cheering for but a few looked Nina and Robyn's way and smiled, lifting whatever refreshments they had in their hand in a toast. Nina would rather not have had the attention but she could tell Robyn was loving it.

'We want everyone to have fun tonight,' Sammy continued as the noise died down again. 'But I want to be serious too for just one second. When you look at the tree, see the names and messages on the lanterns. Take a moment to reflect that they were someone very much loved, someone who is very much missed. But above all, remember them with happiness for what they brought to our lives, not what their passing took away.'

There was another round of applause. Nina wiped away a tear, and she saw many others do the same. She'd been determined not to cry but it looked as if she'd failed. She felt a hand cover hers and turned to see her dad now at her side where Robyn had been, smiling down at her.

'Your mum would have been so proud,' he said. 'Gray too.'

Nina nodded, but she couldn't speak because she was too busy fighting the torrent of tears that threatened to fall now. All she could do was smile through them and hope that her dad would understand.

She looked around at the garden and the crowds. She was proud of what she'd done – though she'd never say it out loud – and she was proud of the community who had helped her. There was so much love here, lifting into the night air in waves as the crowd clapped. It shone in the faces of the people who were gazing up at the tree, many of them knowing their message to their loved one was there and remembering all that they had lost, celebrating all that they had once had. It was in the faces of Winston and Pam as they gazed at one another and it was in the face of Peter, who had just arrived to surprise Robyn, sneaking behind her with hands over her eyes and a kiss as she turned around with a squeal of joy to see him revealed. It was with Ada and Martha, sitting at their mince-pie stall, and it was with Nasser as he looked on with pride at Yasmin and his children, and it was with Diana, who watched with a huge smile on her face as her husband spoke.

If not for the glaring omission, the one important person who was missing, this might have been one of the happiest nights of Nina's life. And when all was said and done, he had a card on the tree too, one that he'd written for Polly's lost twin. Nina had wondered whether that, at least, might have brought him here.

She wondered what he was doing now. Was he thinking about the garden and the special ceremony that Nina had put so much work into, knowing that it was taking place right now? Was he even thinking about Nina at all?

Chapter Twenty-Eight

She didn't want to think of it this way, but being at Gray's grave on Christmas Eve, alone, as she'd been every Christmas Eve since his death, almost felt like she'd gone back to the start. Back to when she'd first lost him and an empty future had stretched before her. The excitement and purpose of getting ready for the memory-tree event had abated now, and today felt like a huge anticlimax after the high of the evening before. It was like the bustle had been keeping her afloat and she wasn't quite sure what the point of her was now it was over.

Her dad and Pam had offered to come to the churchyard with her today but Nina had told them not to. It was hardly somewhere Pam wanted to be on a day like today – her first Christmas Eve with the man she planned to spend the rest of her life with. Nina felt that ought to be happy and joyous, something Pam would look back on with fondness – her dad too for that matter. The churchyard where Gray was buried hardly screamed joyous. Winston had been reluctant, but eventually he'd relented. Nina knew he'd already made a private visit to her mum's grave and he'd made his peace with his dead wife as she'd once done with Gray, ready to move on with the next phase of his life.

Robyn had initially said she'd come too, but she'd called that morning to say she wouldn't be able to make it after all, though would find time to visit on Christmas morning with Toby to lay a wreath for Eric. It was probably better for them to be here without Nina anyway – for Robyn and Toby it was a family thing and Nina understood that. She had wondered if she might bump into Connie, though, despite the fact that she hadn't told Gray's mother that she was coming. On her walk along the iced paths she'd nodded acknowledgement to a few others that she often saw on her visits there, though she had no idea whose graves they visited. She hadn't brought anything to lay at Gray's this time, trusting that the holly she'd set down only recently would still be fresh. She arrived at the grave to see that it was, and that another wreath had now joined it – most likely Connie's, which probably meant that her mother-in-law had already been.

'Hey,' she said, bending to dust a layer of powdery overnight snow from the stone. 'So, I thought I'd come and see you before Christmas. It's going to be a bit hectic tomorrow I expect – Dad's fiancée has invited me for dinner. I thought maybe she'd want it to be just her and Dad for their first Christmas but it seems like she really wants me there so...'

Nina shuffled on the path, toes numbing from the cold that seeped through the soles of her boots.

'Robyn's happy. I think things are going well with her and Peter now and since Toby started to spend time working with Dad on the cars he's like a different kid. They get on so well – we all hoped they would but you can never tell. You know Dad, though, so easy-going I can't imagine anyone not getting along with him. Who knows, maybe Dad will even give Toby the business one day.'

She laughed lightly. 'Well, it's not really a business, is it? You always said it's like no business you'd ever seen and it's a miracle he makes any money. You never know, maybe one day Toby will turn it into a proper one with account books and offices and all that. It'd have to be him because it certainly won't be Dad and I wouldn't know where to start.

Which reminds me, I have an interview for a job. Weirdly, it's at the café not far from here. I saw the card in the window on my way here this morning and popped in… They know me so I'm hopeful that will swing it my way. I think I'd like working there too, so I hope I get it. I'd be able to come and talk to you during my breaks too. That would be good, wouldn't it?'

Nina closed her eyes against her tears. It wouldn't be good, not really. This wasn't where she was supposed to end up again. Life was supposed to have taken her somewhere else entirely.

'It didn't work out with Colm,' she said, opening her eyes again. 'I don't know, his wife came back and I just thought… I was scared, I suppose. Scared that I'd be rejected so I sort of pre-empted that by letting him go. I know it was a stupid thing to do but it's done now and I haven't heard from him so I suppose… well, I suppose in the end I was proved right. This is how it would have ended anyway, even if I hadn't pushed it. All I did was make everything happen quicker. You don't need to worry about me, though – I'll be just fine. I've got my little house and lovely neighbours and maybe I'll have a nice job with good colleagues and that's all I need really, isn't it?' She pulled her coat tight as a cold wind blasted across the grounds, lifting litter from a nearby bin.

'I'm not staying long,' she said. 'Sorry – I hope you don't mind. It's just that… well, I've got things to do.'

There was nothing she needed to do, but to say it would make her feel more than useless.

'I just wanted to say Merry Christmas now, as I won't be coming tomorrow.'

Nina looked down at the stone, cold and silent, as it always had been, as it always would be. She shook her head sadly. Why was she still doing this?

Instead of going home, Nina went to Sparrow Street's garden. It was still decorated from the night before, the remains of stalls still standing where it had been too late to clear away. Seeing it empty now made it seem sad. Ada and Martha had volunteered to come with Kelly to clear up, insisting that Nina have a day off, but it looked as if no one had been as yet. She was here now, so Nina decided to start cleaning by herself anyway. She didn't have much else to do and it would save them a job later.

Before she started, she went to look at the tree. She looked briefly at Colm's card for his baby son before moving on to some of the others. She'd thought she might have been upset to see it again, to be reminded of what she herself had lost, but found herself curiously numb about the whole thing. Colm had not contacted her and so it seemed that chapter of her life had now closed. Maybe she'd meet someone else. It didn't seem likely that they'd be like Colm – there couldn't be two such men – but she was hopeful at least that they might make her happy. She'd felt that way after losing Gray too, she reminded herself, rallying now, that there couldn't be another man like that in the world, and then she'd met Colm. There was plenty to be optimistic about and she was finally ready to admit that she was tired of being lonely. Everyone around her was getting their happy ending, even Ron, whose curtains had been closed as she'd passed his house, even though it was now late morning. But if there was a happy ending for everyone, then where was hers?

She was still gazing up at the tree when she heard a slight cough from behind her. She turned, expecting Ada and Martha or perhaps Kelly, but she was unable to hide her surprise when she saw who it was.

'Hello,' Polly said. 'I went to your house but you weren't there so then I thought I'd try here because I know you had the tree thing last night and I guessed you might be tidying up.' She looked up at the tree. 'Did it go OK? Sorry we didn't come but... well, it's just that... Dad said... I know he wants to come and look at Billy's card though...'

Polly's sentence tailed off. Nina stared at her, heart thumping, fully expecting Colm to appear next.

'Are you... how's your dad?' Nina asked.

Polly shrugged. 'Is there somewhere we can go?'

Nina's forehead creased into a slight frown; she was feeling more puzzled by the second. If Colm wasn't here, why had Polly come?

'Your dad isn't with you?'

'No, I came on my own. He doesn't know I'm here.'

'Why not?'

'Because it's him I need to talk to you about.'

Because Nina had been out for most of the day the house was cold. She rushed to flick on the central heating, bursting to know what it was that Polly had come to talk about. They'd barely spoken on the short walk along Sparrow Street, though it was clear Polly was agitated and anxious about something. Were they in some sort of trouble? Did Colm need help? If he did, what sort of help could it be that only Nina could give? Or perhaps, she mused, quickly pushing away the hope, Jane had gone again.

'I bet you're freezing,' Nina said as she returned to the sitting room where she'd left Polly to get comfortable. Colm's daughter was still in her coat, and Nina didn't blame her for that because she had no intention of taking hers off either, not until the house was a decent temperature. 'Do you want something to warm you up? Hot chocolate or something?'

'No thanks,' Polly said.

'Did you walk all the way here?'

'It's not that far.'

'Far enough – it must have taken ages. Won't your dad miss you? Should we phone him and tell him where you are?'

'Maybe, but I need to talk to you first.'

Nina took the seat across from Polly. 'OK,' she said, hands in her lap.

'Mum's gone.'

Nina stared at her. 'Gone? Left you again?'

'She's moved in with Gran this time.'

'OK,' Nina said, not particularly worried when it came to Jane's whereabouts and wondering vaguely where this was going. If Colm was free and he wanted to try again with Nina, why hadn't he come himself?

'We thought we'd all be able to live together again but...' Polly hesitated, as if wondering how much she could tell Nina. 'I was so excited to have her back; it was like all my wishes had come true and I was so happy. But it didn't stay like that. It was weird. It was like living with a stranger. We don't know her any more and all those things I thought I remembered about her weren't true. I'd made them up in my head, turned her into this amazing person because I missed having my mum around and the truth is... well, the truth is she's not very nice. Especially to Dad and he's tried so hard for her. Now I think he only did it for me and I feel just horrible about it.'

'Right,' Nina said, at a loss for anything else. What was she supposed to do with this information? What did Polly want from her? 'You're sure about all this? I mean, she's only been back a few days really; perhaps it's just going to take time for everyone to adjust.'

Polly shook her head. 'I just know it's not right. I knew the first day and it wouldn't matter how many days she stayed, I'd still feel the same. I don't think they…' Polly gave an awkward shrug. 'Dad slept in the spare room. He gave Mum the big bed.'

'When did your mum move out?'

'A couple of days ago.'

Nina did a quick calculation. Ron had seen them at the supermarket almost that recently too. Jane must have left shortly after that. 'What made her go?'

'Dad. He told her we could be a family but they'd never be a couple again. She was angry and she tried to get me to take her side but… well, I didn't want to. She makes Dad miserable and the truth is I didn't remember what she was really like. I mean, I spoke to her on the phone and stuff while she was away, but it's not the same, is it? You can hide the person you are in a half-hour phone call every now and again. She's selfish and she only thinks about what she wants. The truth is she makes me miserable too… Nina, do you think I'm a bad person because I don't like my own mum?'

'Of course not!' Nina dug into her pocket for a pack of fresh tissues and handed one to Polly to dry her eyes. 'You can love someone dearly and still not like them very much. They say you can't choose your family and if you could, a lot of us would choose differently.'

'Not you – your dad's really nice.'

Nina smiled. 'I just got lucky, I suppose.'

'I liked it better when it was just me and Dad.'

Nina's smile became sad. 'I'm sure you did.'

'But it was OK when you were with him too,' Polly added quickly, perhaps sensing that her simple statement had hurt Nina. 'I know it wasn't for long but I think it would have been good. Dad was always happy when you were there with him. He said you broke up with him.'

'Well, yes, but that was because your mum had come home and I thought that was what he wanted.'

'You thought he would want to get back with her?'

'Yes, and if I'm being honest, I thought that was what you wanted too.'

'I suppose I did a bit. I said it to Dad, but that was before I knew what she'd be like, before I realised that I'd got it all wrong.'

'Do you think you might change your mind? That your dad might change his mind?'

Polly shook her head. 'He's so miserable. He tries to pretend he's OK but I know. I thought it might be about Mum but it's not – it's about you.'

'He said that to you?'

Polly nodded.

'Why didn't he come and see me then?'

'He thought you didn't want to hear it. And when Mum moved out he said he couldn't ask you to keep going back and forth for him. I don't even know what that means but he wouldn't say anything else about it.'

'I think I do,' Nina said.

'So you'll go out with him again?'

'I don't know if I should.'

'Why not?'

'Because I don't know if that's how he truly feels. Going to him and saying I want us to be together again might just complicate things. How do I know that's what he wants if he doesn't tell me?'

'I know it!' Polly said. 'I can see how sad he is! Even if he doesn't come to you and say that's what he wants, I know it is. You have to come and see him!'

'I can't just walk in and—'

'Call him then! Tell him you love him!'

Nina stared at Polly, lost for words once again.

'You love him, don't you?' Polly asked.

'Yes,' Nina said quietly, not sure why she was opening up so readily to Polly like this.

'He loves you too.'

'He said that to you?'

'No, but I know it.'

'Polly, I'm sorry but—'

'Don't tell me I don't know what I'm talking about! Don't tell me that I'm too young to understand, that I don't know anything about it!' Polly cried. 'I do understand! It's you who doesn't understand!'

'OK,' Nina said, her mind racing. 'Then what do you think I should do?'

'Come and talk to him. All you have to do is tell him you love him.'

'But…'

Polly's phone started to ring and she took the call.

'Dad, I'm fine; I'm at Nina's. You should come over,' she added, throwing a meaningful glance at Nina that dared her to intervene. 'She's got something very important she needs to say to you.'

Chapter Twenty-Nine

There had been so much food at Christmas lunch that nobody had been able to move afterwards. Winston had always been a decent cook but living alone he could rarely be bothered. Often it was only at Christmas that he made anything from scratch. Nina had barely got over her mountain of turkey with the trimmings when it was time for tea and the feeding frenzy started all over again. It was lovely having lunch with her dad and Pam, but Nina had found it hard to settle, her nerves fizzing about who was due to arrive later in the day.

Almost as soon as Colm had arrived at her house the previous day – at Polly's instruction – she'd known what a huge mistake letting him go had been. She'd seen his face and she'd realised instantly the truth of what Polly had told her. Barely had a word been exchanged and they were back in each other's arms. There had been a lot to discuss, of course, and the discussions did come. They lasted well into the evening, until Polly had reminded them both that it was Christmas Eve and as they all had places to be on Christmas Day, it was probably a good idea for her and Colm to go home. Nina hadn't wanted him to go but she'd reluctantly let him. That hadn't stopped the long phone call an hour after he'd left, and the constant exchange of texts all Christmas morning while Nina struggled to concentrate on lunch at her dad's. Her head was filled only with the thought of seeing Colm's face again when he arrived later that evening, as he'd promised to do.

They'd been treated to a tea of salmon, various salads and finger foods, pastries, cheeses and fruit. The food definitely bore the hallmark of an influence other than Winston, who would have been content enough to make sandwiches with the leftover turkey, and she suspected that Pam had planned and cooked most of it. They'd messed around playing charades and Guess Who? afterwards, drinking and still nibbling, even though nobody had any space left to put away more than the odd peanut. Really, though, Nina could have been handed an old box to eat and she would have been happy. She was more than happy, her joy far too big to be encompassed by a single word.

She could hear Polly now, laughing in the living room at something Winston had said, though she hadn't quite caught what it was. As she reached into the fridge for a new bottle of tonic water, she felt hands settle delicately on her waist and warm breath on her neck. She closed her eyes for a moment, savouring his scent, before she turned with a smile to see Colm there.

'Need any help?' he asked with an impish look.

'With my bottle of tonic water? I think I can manage.'

'Well, you say that but they can be tricky…'

'In what way?'

'OK, you got me bang to rights. I just wanted an excuse to do this…'

He pulled her into a passionate kiss. After a moment, Nina broke away, struggling to open her eyes, her limbs molten.

'I think we need to step away from the fridge,' she said in a dreamy voice. 'I'm worried all that heat might thaw the freezer out.'

'You think that's hot?' he asked. 'I'll show you what hot is when we're alone…'

He reached to kiss her once more and this time she lost herself completely to him, certain that she might never emerge again. He didn't stop, and she didn't want him to.

'We'll have to go back in the other room,' she said finally, not wanting to at all. She wanted to stay here in Colm's arms forever. 'They'll be wondering where we are.'

'Let them,' he said.

'Hmm. What would Polly say?'

He smiled. 'She can hardly complain as this is technically all her doing.'

'Maybe she'd have thought twice about coming to get me if she'd known this would happen.'

'Maybe, but I'm glad she did.'

'Me too…'

Nina frowned slightly. She'd tried to keep anything but happy thoughts from her mind but one kept creeping in, no matter how hard she tried to ignore it.

'About Jane…' she began.

'I told you yesterday you don't need to worry about that and nothing has changed. I have no feelings for her now. I've told her I want a divorce as soon as possible.'

'She's not going anywhere, though. You said the commune is all packed up.'

'I can't do much about that. She's not coming back into my home – that's one thing I can do something about.'

'It's her home too.'

'*Was* her home. When she helps to pay the bills she can argue that point with me. Until then it's mine and Polly's and maybe sometimes yours… when you want it to be.'

'I'd like that,' Nina said.

'So,' he said. 'Are you happy?'

'What do you think?'

'I don't know; I wouldn't want to presume anything… I'll leave that sort of thing up to you.'

Nina slapped his arm playfully. 'I thought it was the right thing to do. Now I know it was stupid.'

'Only a wee bit,' he said. 'And I was a wee bit stupid too. It's lucky that Polly had enough sense for both of us.'

'It is,' Nina agreed.

'So… you still haven't answered my question. Are you happy?'

'Maybe this will answer it,' Nina said, moving in for yet another breathless kiss.

From the kitchen doorway there was a shocked squeak. Nina and Colm broke apart to see Polly rush back out of the room.

'Oh,' Nina said, blushing, but Colm roared with laughter.

'I should probably go and smooth things over,' he said, though he didn't make a move and he didn't seem all that keen to go anywhere at all.

'You don't think she's upset, do you?' Nina asked.

'I doubt it would last for long even if she was. She's just not used to seeing her old da engaged in such…'

'Filth?' Nina suggested and Colm laughed again. 'I suppose it's not something you want to think about at fifteen, is it – your parents kissing like that?'

'When it comes to it, parents don't want to think about their fifteen-year-olds kissing like that either,' Colm said with a chuckle. 'We may have some awkward years ahead of us.'

'Perhaps we ought to save our kissing for later,' Nina said, 'when we're alone.'

'I don't know if I can wait that long.'

'Me neither, but for the sake of everyone else we should probably try.'

'OK, I'll try, but I can't promise anything.' He moved closer, pulling her into him, his voice husky. 'Just your wee face there makes me want to grab you and—'

'That's not helping,' Nina said, putting on a stern voice.

'Then you'll just have to stop looking at me with those eyes of yours…'

Nina giggled. 'What am I supposed to look at you with?'

'Just… I don't know. Wear a bag over your head or something until we get back to my place.'

Nina cast around the kitchen. She couldn't see a bag but her dad did have an old tea towel hanging from a hook by the sink. She grabbed it and draped it over her face.

'Better?'

'Idiot!' Colm laughed, and then his face appeared beneath the towel, so close to hers that…

They were kissing again. Nina could feel that fire build, that need. She wanted him so, so badly that she could barely think of anything else, but she knew she would have to wait and she wasn't sure how she was going to manage.

'My beautiful idiot,' he said as he pulled away. 'Promise you'll never leave me.'

'You'll have to promise me first.'

'I promise.'

Nina pulled the tea towel from their heads and smiled, lost in the sea of his eyes again. She could see a future of happiness stretched out ahead, but there would always be a little sadness with it. Colm couldn't make promises like that, just as Gray hadn't been able to in the end.

Nobody could say what life would bring and Nina had never felt that more keenly than she did right now. Perhaps it didn't matter. Perhaps what mattered was that they grabbed love, greeted every day they got to spend together with joy and gratitude, nurtured and cherished it all the more for its unpredictability. Perhaps, in the end, that was the only way anyone could love. And wasn't just one day of love like this better than a lifetime of emptiness? Even if losing it caused so much pain that it felt like your heart would burst into a thousand pieces, wasn't it better than letting your heart wither and harden from feeling nothing at all?

She let her gaze trace the features of his face and decided that yes, it was. She'd take just one day of love like this over a lifetime of nothing any day, and she wouldn't waste another second being scared of losing it.

A Letter from Tilly

I want to say a huge thank you for choosing to read *The Garden on Sparrow Street*. If you did enjoy it and want to keep up to date with all my latest releases just sign up at the following link. Your email address will never be shared and you can unsubscribe at any time.

www.bookouture.com/tilly-tennant

I'm so excited to share *The Garden on Sparrow Street* with you. It's my twelfth novel for Bookouture and I loved every minute of writing it, especially getting to know Nina and Robyn. I truly have the best job in the world and I've been so proud to share every new book with my lovely readers.

I hope you loved *The Garden on Sparrow Street* and if you did I would be very grateful if you could write a review. I'd love to hear what you think, and it makes such a difference helping new readers to discover one of my books for the first time.

I love hearing from my readers – you can get in touch on my Facebook page, through Twitter, Goodreads or my website.

Thanks,
Tilly

 tillytennant

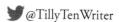 @TillyTenWriter

 www.tillytennant.com

Acknowledgements

The list of people who have offered help and encouragement on my writing journey so far must be truly endless, and it would take a novel in itself to mention them all. However, my heartfelt gratitude goes out to each and every one of you, whose involvement, whether small or large, has been invaluable and appreciated more than I can say.

There are a few people that I must mention. Obviously, my family – the people who put up with my whining and self-doubt on a daily basis – have to be top of the list. My ex-colleagues at the Royal Stoke University Hospital, who let me lead a double life for far longer than is acceptable and have given me so many ideas for future books! The lecturers at Staffordshire University English and Creative Writing Department, who saw a talent worth nurturing in me and continue to support me still, long after they finished getting paid for it. They are not only tutors but friends as well. I have to thank the team at Bookouture for their continued support, patience and amazing publishing flair, particularly Lydia Vassar-Smith – my incredible and patient editor – Kim Nash, Noelle Holten, Peta Nightingale, Leodora Darlington and Jessie Botterill. Their belief, able assistance and encouragement mean the world to me. I truly believe I have the best team an author could ask for.

My friend, Kath Hickton, always gets a shout-out for putting up with me since primary school. Louise Coquio also gets an honourable mention for getting me through university and suffering me ever since, likewise her lovely family. And thanks go to Storm Constantine for giving me my first break in publishing. I also have to thank Mel Sherratt and Holly Martin, fellow writers and amazing friends who have both been incredibly supportive over the years and have been my shoulders to cry on in the darker moments. Thanks to Tracy Bloom, Emma

Davies, Jack Croxall, Clare Davidson, Angie Marsons, Sue Watson and Jaimie Admans: not only brilliant authors in their own right but hugely supportive of others. My Bookouture colleagues are all incredible, of course, unfailing and generous in their support of fellow authors – life would be a lot duller without the gang! I have to thank all the brilliant and dedicated book bloggers (there are so many of you but you know who you are!) and readers, and anyone else who has championed my work, reviewed it, shared it, or simply told me that they liked it. Every one of those actions is priceless and you are all very special people. Some of you I am even proud to call friends now – and I'm looking at you in particular, Kerry Ann Parsons and Steph Lawrence!

Last but not least, I'd like to give a special mention to Georgia McVeigh and my lovely agent, Madeleine Milburn, who both keep me organised!

Printed in Great Britain
by Amazon